THE ASSASSINATION OF BILLY JEELING

Brian Herbert

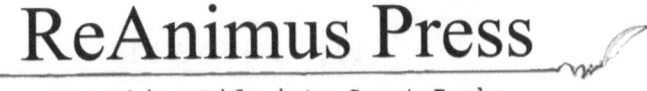

ReAnimus Press
Breathing Life into Great Books

ReAnimus Press
1100 Johnson Road #16-143
Golden, CO 80402
www.ReAnimus.com

Cover Art by Clay Hagebusch

ISBN-13: 978-0-9672984-7-4

First edition: November, 2018

10 9 8 7 6 5 4 3 2 1

This book is for Jan, the most complex and interesting woman I have ever met.
I have loved you since the summer I met you in California, when you were 16, and I was 17.

CHAPTER 1

He's the most famous man in history, and the most misunderstood.

—B. Villison, *The Sky Monarch* (unauthorized biography)

High above AmEarth, an immense gold and silver craft flew on one of its regular rounds, as it had been doing for years. Skyship was legendary. The air-cleansing and restoration station—in the shape of an oblate spheroid—was almost fifteen kilometers long, and rose four thousand meters from its main level to the glittering domes on top, and the pinnacle that rose above them. It formed the nucleus of the largest geoengineering project in the history of mankind.

The solar-powered ship was also a flying city, with a human population of more than 100,000, and even more robots—mechanical sentients who performed a wide range of duties, including most of the police and security work, and the piloting of small onboard aircraft.

On the command bridge, beneath the forward dome, a crippled black man sat on his custom maglev chair. He gazed out on mists of purple gas emitted by onboard generators, and at a steady stream of small orbs that exited the enormous vessel, a fleet of skyminers assigned to vacuum pollutants, gases, and specific compounds from various grids of the atmosphere and accumulate them in inflatable tank-trailers, to be loaded aboard the massive mother ship when full.

More than seventy years old now, Billy Jeeling was the heroic, celebrated figure who had saved hundreds of millions of lives with his incredible technology—keeping people from dying of melanoma, emphysema, lung cancer, and a whole host of other ailments—all caused by UV damage to their skin and by inhaling polluted, carcinogenic air. He had dramatically reduced the acid rain that had caused so much damage to classic buildings and sculptures, and had improved the climate by controlling CO_2, thus slowing the rise of oceans and climate change caused by higher global temperatures. Through his many efforts he had made the atmosphere cleaner all over the world, allowing humans and other life forms to breathe easier, and to see more clearly through the air, without harmful smog and other airborne particulates.

This afternoon Billy had a lot on his mind, more than the slight vibration he felt in the deck or the faint odor of ozone gas that he detected—matters that only required minor adjustments by the vessel's technicians—alterations that were underway at this moment, according to the instrument readings on the console in front of him. Ozone was only one of the ingredients in the secret gas mixture emitted by the great craft, and was the key to one of his most widely heralded accomplishments. With Skyship's hidden technology, Billy Jeeling had repaired ozone holes all over the world, including the largest one over Antarctica.

The gigantic vessel was more than an air-cleansing and restoration station, and much more than even Billy himself could ascertain— many of its operations were mysterious even to him. He was constantly discovering new things about its ability to purify the atmosphere, surprising and impressive features. If anyone ever learned how limited his knowledge really was, they would ask how this could possibly be the case, when he had directed the construction of the great ship and was supposed to know everything about it. But during the long years of fabrication and testing he had only followed the secret, detailed instructions of the late genius, Branson Tobek.

A highly unusual man, Tobek had worshiped Jesus Christ in his own way, without most of the trappings of organized religion—he never attended church services or adhered to any formal Christian belief. Yet he professed to be a follower of the peaceful ways of the Messiah, and had even designed a huge symbol to honor Jesus into the construction of Skyship—a high walkway and maglev track in the shape of a Christian cross, beneath clear domes arranged in the same shape. When the lights of the cross were activated and illumination was cast into the domes, anyone above the great ship—presumably including God himself—could see the glowing emblem in the heavens.

Brilliant and reclusive, the great scientist had not sought any credit for his fantastic invention. Above all else, Tobek had wanted Skyship to clean the air efficiently, for the benefit of AmEarth and its billions of inhabitants—and he'd insisted that Billy receive all of the recognition for this. So, the old man had remained in his hidden laboratories—first on AmEarth and later on Skyship itself—passing technical instructions on to Billy for implementation with workmen and the crew, and having Billy sign all government contracts.

Then came Tobek's strange and disturbing death—a tragic loss that Billy concealed, never revealing it to anyone but his most trusted robots. Nor had he ever mentioned the name of the great man to any living person; it was as if he had never existed. And that was the exactly the way Tobek had wanted it.

Hearing a voice behind him, Billy turned his chair and watched a slender woman approaching, carrying an envelope in one hand. Appearing to be around thirty, Lainey Forster was a light-skinned Caucasian woman, with short auburn hair and a graceful way of moving, like a ballet dancer. Her neck was long and swanlike—which fit her movements. She wore a dark gray uniform with silver buttons; the clear-blue-sky insignia of Skyship adorned her lapel. She had large hazel eyes, very pretty and inquisitive.

Lainey was the Employment Manager of Skyship, and Billy had also made her his Director of Public Relations, assigned to deal with problems that had surfaced in recent months, huge public demonstrations against him on AmEarth. Some people down there were inciting the population by spreading false information about him, attempting to ruin his reputation, though he'd tried to put it out of his mind, and let her handle it.

She leaned down and kissed him on the mouth. Her lips were warm and pleasantly moist. "How are you feeling today?" she asked. "Any pain in the stumps of your legs?"

"No discomfort, I'm doing much better. Dr. Ginsberg adjusted my med implant."

She smiled warmly. "Good."

Billy cared deeply for Lainey, but there were things even she did not know, and he could never tell her.

Despite the fact that Billy was a paraplegic without legs, he and Lainey made love often. He had been injured during one of the construction phases of Skyship, in an explosion of the secret gas formula—an event that caused only limited damage to the ship (due to containment procedures), but had a much more serious, disastrous effect on his legs, which had to be amputated. Nonetheless, Billy was a persistent man, and had resumed work in only a few weeks—aided by a high-speed maglev chair that carried him around the interior of Skyship. He preferred it to wearing prosthetics, which he found uncomfortable.

Before the accident, Tobek had already designed a high-speed maglev system into the ship—using technology that was usually reserved for long-distance train travel on AmEarth. Its customized Skyship version proved to be highly efficient—and accommodated Billy's maglev chair without the necessity of a passenger pod, because the chair had built-in features that provided him with the necessary protection against g-forces. Billy had designed the chair himself, customizing it to fit into Tobek's onboard transportation system.

Now Lainey took on a serious expression, and her eyes narrowed. She handed him the envelope.

"I printed this without reading the contents," she said. "It's marked urgent, and for your eyes only."

He opened the envelope and read the confidential letter, which was from Renaldo Yhatt, the Prime Minister of AmEarth's one-world government. At one time Billy and Yhatt's maternal uncle—Princeton Kelly—had been close, when Kelly was Prime Minister himself, serving for two terms. The men had reached agreement about the operation of Skyship and the payment to Billy Jeeling of billions of amdollars each year—they'd even gone on vacation together to Europaea. The old man was still alive, but in recent months their relationship had been strained, ever since the bizarre and unfounded public demonstrations began. And lately, Billy had been feeling increasingly estranged, from not only the Kellys and the Yhatts, but from many other wealthy and influential people he'd known in the past.

Balling up the letter, he tossed it into a trash recycler, heard the brief whir of machinery as it dissolved the paper.

"What is it?" she asked.

"Now the bastard wants me to resign, 'for the good of the AmEarth Empire.' He says I've been up here too long, that I've out-lived my welcome and should allow others to take my place, that the care of the atmosphere shouldn't be anyone's private reserve. He wants me to turn over all operating instructions for Skyship to a gov-ernment agency, so it can take over."

"I was afraid of that. The demonstrations are spreading to every major city, and are becoming more raucous. We tried to counter them with the public relations materials you authorized—but as I told you earlier, a more aggressive counter-attack program is needed. Much more aggressive."

"After all I've done for AmEarth, they want me to resign?"

"Your detractors are saying your fleet of skyminers is sucking bil-lions of ambucks worth of elements out of the sky, and you're selling them for huge profits."

"What a lie! Many of those elements are ingredients in my secret gas formula, while other ingredients are segregated and sold to pri-vate businesses, admittedly—but we use all the profits solely for *Sky-ship operation*, not to dress me in silks and gold, not to pamper me with lavish banquets and dancing girls. They criticize me for being a good businessman? It's character assassination, pure and simple."

"It's outrageous, no question about it."

"I wish I'd never become famous."

For years, Billy had enjoyed the adulation he'd received, and he had deserved some of it, for contributing his efforts to the construc-tion, and for designing most of the robots and computer systems on the station—features that were beneficial to the operations of Skyship, and to its security. But Billy didn't deserve all of the accolades—and this wore on his conscience. Still, he had given his word to Tobek that the truth would never come out.

And now, in view of the mounting criticisms against Billy, he could never admit anything. If he did, the furor would only increase.

Secrets. They were double-edged, depending upon who knew them and who did not. In the case of Billy Jeeling's monopoly on worldwide atmospheric repairs and the mining of the air, his technologies and chemical formulas were extremely valuable. The gas emitted by Skyship was a complex mixture containing ozone as well as cleansing agents to scrub CO_2, methane, industrial gases, and other harmful ingredients from the atmosphere. The formula even had bonding and disintegration agents, and scramblers to keep any outsider from unraveling it—a formula that Billy knew, but only to a limited extent. He knew what Tobek had called "the initial stage" of the formula, and that initial stage, in its gaseous form, had to be loaded into Skyship's distribution machinery, to be further refined through arcane, automatic processes, and then fired into the atmosphere through large nozzles on the hull of the craft.

There were other Skyship secrets that Billy didn't know, too—kept from him intentionally by Tobek—and they were proving to be troubling, and potentially embarrassing.

Problems on top of problems.

For one thing the huge craft, ostensibly under his control, had a way of mysteriously going onto automatic navigation programs. Much of the time Billy had control over where to go in the sky and in low planetary orbit, but if he forgot an area of the atmosphere that needed to be processed (or didn't know about it), the ship would make up for this—and later would return the controls to him when the task was completed. All the time, Billy, like a lip-syncher trying to give the impression that he was singing a song, attempted to act as if he were fully in charge.

"What would happen," Billy now asked Lainey, "if I decided to disband the operations of Skyship and dismantle the whole thing, or mothball it? Sure, ozone-destroying CFC... chlorofluorocarbon... gas releases are down substantially in advanced provinces like AmEastica, and that helps the ozone layer. There are new industrial and vehicle emissions standards that are helping CO_2 levels, too. But the underdeveloped provinces don't understand clean-air technology. They're way out of control, misusing industrial solvents, synthetic foams, cooling fluids, insulation, and halocarbons, flooding the atmosphere with inert chemicals. In the ozonosphere, those discharges break down in sunlight, creating chlorine atoms and other elements harmful to O_3 molecules. And that's just the ozone portion of the problem—I could go on and on about the rest of it—the burning of fossil fuels, causing air that is still so thick in some part of the world that you could chew it."

"Right, Billy."

He knew she had heard this before. Lainey probably thought he was addicted to repeating it, not seeming to recall the last time he'd said it, or to whom. She had made comments suggesting his short-term memory might be failing with advancing age, and one of the companion symptoms was that he could still recall details from decades ago with remarkable clarity, but not recent events. As if she were a clinical expert! Sometimes, she could be quite irritating.

"If I bail out of this operation, the damned atmosphere is going to hell in a hand-cart. That's worse than a hand-basket, much faster." He smiled, but didn't intend to be funny. It was more of a rueful smile, tinged with anger.

"Right, Billy." By her subdued tone and words, it was obvious to him that she was trying to calm him down. But he didn't *want* to calm down. This was upsetting to him, *damned* upsetting.

He glanced at his smart watch, depressed the crystal, illuminating its small screen. "Forty-five point seven-eight kilometers above AmEarth at this moment," he said. "You know, there's important work to be done here, and we don't have time to lobby for popularity. Let 'em stew. I do as I please, and it's for the good of the people, whether they know it or not."

He heard loud alarm klaxons and saw a small flying wing outside the window, a flash of silver emerging from the mists of purple gas. The wing looped and went back into the proprietary gas, scooping samples from high concentrations in an effort to collect the formula before it dissipated into the atmosphere, and then take it somewhere for analysis. He didn't see a pilot, assumed it must be remote-operated.

This had been attempted before, with a variety of intruding craft—and it didn't really matter if they took samples, because the formula had scrambling safeguards to prevent it from being identified and recreated by any outsider. The ingredients could not even be penetrated by spectral analysis, nor by any other known method. This was one of the scientific matters that Tobek *had* explained to him, and Billy understood some of it, enough to reassure him, to a degree. But Billy didn't like intruders coming this close and bothering him—and besides, some smart scientist might figure out how to get around the safeguards if he ever got ahold of a more concentrated sample.

"Ready to fire in seven seconds unless you countermand," a voice said over the onboard tele-speakers. It was one of his men at the defensive guns that bristled all over the hull of Skyship.

Billy didn't respond.

A white-hot laser light reached out from Skyship, like a living appendage of the immense craft, and placed the touch of death on the flying wing. Seconds later, the intruder craft exploded with only a little noise reaching Billy's ears, scattering debris harmlessly in the stratosphere.

"Just a typical day," Billy said, nodding to Lainey. "See you at dinner this evening."

He touched a button on the control console of his high-tech chair, causing a wall to iris open on his left. The chair whirled around to face the opening, and a clearplaz protective cocoon surrounded Billy. He moved a control toggle, and the chair zipped on a cushion of air through the opening, onto a sidetrack that led to a high-speed maglev guideway that connected his work stations, apartment, and other locations around the vast interior of the ship.

This time he was going for a speedy ride around the tubular guideways, which he enjoyed. He liked to do this on occasion, to soothe him and clear the troubles out of his thoughts. Afterward, an hour from now, he was scheduled to meet with his son Devv, who was the Security Commander on Skyship—in charge of safety, police, and defense operations.

CHAPTER 2

Negative information about a public figure spreads like a virus, and when that happens the virus can never be killed. The targeted person's reputation is permanently sullied, even if lies, half truths, and distortions are being told about him—and damage lingers even if the fabrications come to light.

—Bengal Tate, reporter for Imperial City News, a defender of Billy Jeeling

Fog enveloped the sprawling industrial facility, except for seven bright red stacks that poked through the soup into the cerulean sky, each bearing the golden imperial emblem of the AmEarth Empire. It was just before the morning shift, and Yürgen Zayeddi trudged across the parking lot with other workers. A big, burly man with eyeglasses, he scuffled his feet as he gazed up at yellow, pollutant-free smoke that belched intermittently from the stacks. A sour, metallic odor wrinkled his nostrils, a smell he had never gotten used to.

Some of the fog was beginning to clear, and to the east a ghostly moon hung just above the horizon, a fading remnant of night.

This humbaby factory, on the outskirts of Jefferson Township in the Atlandia Province, performed all stages of production, from the harvesting of raw materials to the design and assembly of the insect-shaped aircraft that were so prevalent in large cities, and also flew around the cavernous interior of Billy Jeeling's Skyship, high over AmEarth.

Reportedly this factory was responsible for a high percentage of all humbabies that were used by the one-world government of the planet, aircraft that were constructed entirely of high-strength plastics. Zayeddi wondered what percentage his own efforts at the facility contributed. Incalculably low, he presumed, and he envisioned a huge analog calculator with a fat decimal point on its screen and trillions of zeros to the right of the point. Somewhere on the infinite right would be the numerals indicating the nano-percentage of his own contribution.

He knew how to fly all of the humbaby models in manual mode, having learned from one of the quality-control technicians, an older woman who was a friend of his. He thought the aircraft were simple to operate for specialty work outside of autopilot mode, but he'd heard others say they couldn't get the hang of the controls. They were tricky for some folks, he supposed, with a console operated via a thought-command headset worn by the pilot, but he'd had no trouble at all. His friend said he could be a quality-control technician himself someday, and she arranged to put Yürgen on a waiting list for one of those plum jobs. He hoped to be selected one day, so that he could escape the drudgery of his present position.

Now he heard the argumentative voices of men and women, and saw a man in a rumpled gray suit addressing the workers from a grazzeen knoll.

Yürgen pushed his glasses onto the bridge of his nose, hurried around other workers to see what was going on. Two associates of the man on the knoll, identically attired in frumpy suits, were distributing leaflets.

Some of the factory workers discarded the leaflets and stalked away in disgust, while others listened impassively or read the literature. The name Billy Jeeling was in the air, on the lips of the rumpled orator.

"We need to get rid of Jeeling," the man shouted. "He's outlived any usefulness he ever had, and is way overpaid for what he does."

"We'd better get back to work," one of the onlookers said, a gruff little oriental woman. "Where's Plant Security?" Tama Suzuki was one of the supervisors in Zayeddi's department. She marched off, followed by a number of her co-workers, heading toward a high rollup door that was partially visible in the fog.

"Jeeling is the biggest crook in history!" the man on the knoll bellowed. "He's had the Empire mesmerized... he pulls in billions of am-bucks a year from his Skyship monopoly, paid out of *your* atmospheric gas taxes. Can you imagine money like that? How do you suppose he's managed to garner all that cash? He's got powerful political and business leaders in his pocket, that's how! He's paying them off!"

"Filthy liar!" a woman shouted.

"Skyship is Billy's money pump!" the man retorted. And the insolent man kept talking... despicable, heretical utterances that Yürgen couldn't bear to hear. As far as he was concerned, Billy Jeeling was a god, and could do nothing wrong. But this detractor's lips kept going, and he droned on and on.

The fellow's suit was bargain-basement, with the sheen and double creases of poor ironing. He was young, with a prominent nose, and spoke with an artificial passion... as if he didn't believe his own words. White, lying spittle frothed around his mouth.

"Shut up about Billy!" Yürgen shouted.

The man shot back: "Our atmospheric gas taxes give us the right to know what kind of a man Jeeling is!"

"You're insulting our greatest hero!" Yürgen screamed. "The man who designed and built Skyship!"

"Almost forty years ago. Big damned deal."

"It's still functioning well, still doing its job. Show some respect for Billy."

"He costs us too damned much!"

Yürgen Zayeddi knew this wasn't true. He'd read everything he could find about the great man. "Are you kidding? His Skyship restored atmospheric gases to healthy, balanced levels, including the ozone layer — going into operation when millions of people were dying each year from skin cancer, and going blind, when UV-rads were pouring in and most of the air on the planet was unhealthy to breathe. Billy saved us all, you damned ignorant fool!"

"You've obviously been brainwashed, and we're here to tell the truth about him."

"Bull, that's all you're slinging! You don't know what you're talking about. Key life forms in the food chain were dying off before Billy rescued AmEarth, and the crisis was especially acute in the oceans — the essential food chain of organisms we need to keep the fish we eat healthy. Ocean acidification was preventing crustaceans from growing shells. Global warming was altering ocean currents, while other human-caused factors were killing coral reefs and depleting oxygen levels in the seas, creating huge dead zones where fish could no longer live, and only jellyfish could survive. It was the beginning of the end for all of us, a fast track to the complete extinction of humanity. Billy deserves whatever the hell he's paid!"

Without being fully aware of it, Yürgen had moved onto the grazzeen knoll, very near to the man, closer than anyone else. The infidel kept blabbering against Billy Jeeling. Nonsensical, inflammatory stuff. The wildest of lies. Behind him, in the distant sky just above the horizon, the spheroid shape of Skyship appeared, casting a golden day-glow, as if it were a second sun in the heavens — a trick of onboard projection mechanisms, Zayeddi had heard. It was a bit of showmanship that he liked.

He felt an infusion of righteous rage, could hardly keep himself from tearing the bastard apart. He saw the unholy mouth that wouldn't stop moving, and felt violently ill to his stomach, with a burning, bubbling bile coming up.

"Get out of here!" Yürgen shouted, leveling a death-stare at the defamer.

Looking suddenly frightened, the man ceased his chatter and inched backward.

No one on God's green AmEarth, not even the High Deity Himself, stood above Billy Jeeling in the estimation of Zayeddi. As far as he was concerned, Jeeling always spoke the truth, the purest, most virtuous flow of words in all of creation.

I love Billy Jeeling, he thought, his emotions having welled to the surface. He couldn't see Skyship anymore, perhaps because the projection mechanism had been turned off.

He lunged at the young man, who stumbled backward, only saving himself from falling at the last possible moment. "Do you know you're going to die today?" Yürgen asked, reaching into a jacket pocket, as if to bring out a gun.

"All right!" the man said, backing up even more. "I'm leaving, OK?" He waved his hands to his associates. "Let's clear out!" he yelled.

They packed their remaining leaflets and hastened across the parking lot. Zayeddi was so angry that he felt as if his blood pressure was rising to a dangerous level, and his entire body seemed about to explode. He tried hard to slow his racing pulse, heard dim voices around him, people hurrying away to work.

Before he could recover, he decided to chase after the proselytizers. When they saw the large, angry man coming, they quickened their pace.

"Why did you come here?" Yürgen screamed. "Who are you?"

They didn't respond. Leaflets fell from the grasp of one of them, and a gust of wind lifted the papers, scattering them over parked vehicles.

Yürgen was gaining on them. He could almost smell their fear, the reeking terror discharged by lying, crawling things, and he wanted to tear out their lying tongues. No one spoke against his idol Billy Jeeling!

The men hurried out of sight around a high metal fence, and Zayeddi heard several small jet engines start, one after another.

Three rocket-cycles shot out in a line and lifted into the air in flashes of golden color, a helmeted man leaning forward on each, his baggy suit flowing in the wind. Over the parking lot, a packet whooshed high in the air from the rear of each cycle, followed by three little midair bursts. Thousands of leaflets rained down on the lot and the parked vehicles.

Moments later, he saw activity on a hillside above the mill, where two roads intersected. He wiped his eyeglasses, and spun a tiny dial on the edge of the frame, zooming the intersection into a clearer view. The zoom didn't hold at first, and he had to tweak the dial until the image finally held.

At least a dozen cycle riders were in rendezvous there, all dressed in rumpled suits like missionaries, and riding gleaming, golden-hued cycles. Presently they raced away together into the morning sun that was just rising over the hilltop.

Unable to settle himself down, Yürgen Zayeddi headed for the factory. He would be late, but it was unavoidable. Maybe he should bring a weapon to work from now on, to deal more effectively with any heretics who might come back. They'd be sorry if they did.

He grabbed one of the leaflets and read it as he hurried to work, going through the rollup door. It was headed, "JEELING LOOTS PUBLIC COFFERS!" The text rambled with wild allegations, including charges that Jeeling overbilled the AmEarth Empire for expenses, and carried on illicit sexual activities with the young men and women in his employ, members of his intensely loyal corps of JeeJees. Fuming, Zayeddi spent a few minutes cleaning up more of the leaflets and throwing them in trash receptacles.

He was almost an hour late when he finally made it to the long assembly line on the main floor, where he faced his scowling supervisor, Nelson Badger. The supervisor was small and stocky, at least a head shorter than Yürgen. The line was in motion, and beside it Yürgen saw someone else working at his station.

"Didn't anyone call Security?" Yürgen demanded, raising his voice to be heard over the machinery and voices in the factory. "I expected help out there, didn't get any. You heard what happened in the parking lot?"

"I did, and you were observed in argumentative, vociferous behavior... on company property." Badger's thick black brows were knitted in displeasure as he looked up at the much larger man.

"They were spouting lies about Billy!"

"Ah yes, our Great Benefactor, Mr. Billy McVie Jeeling. And you, I am told, are the most ardent of his supporters."

Yürgen studied the supervisor for a moment, noting that Badger's mouth was framed with deep furrows across the sides and bottom. The thin lips were turned up sardonically at each end, showing that he was poised to criticize whatever Yürgen said.

Just say one thing against Billy, Yürgen thought, *and I'll ruin your day.* He felt his gaze narrow dangerously. His skin felt hot.

"You're late for work," Badger said. "We can't have that."

"But I was chasing them off and cleaning up the mess they left."

Badger shook his head. "Uh, uh, uh," he said. "Not in your job description. You are an assembly-line technician, second class, nothing more. You are assigned to connect parts on the landing gear of the humbaby and pass them on down the line, all according to procedure, according to government regulation. You are not a guard dog."

Yürgen hadn't been in a fist fight since high school more than fifteen years ago, but if Badger pushed him only a little more...

"Well, off to work with you," Badger said, almost matter-of-factly. His expression went blank. "We have a schedule to run."

"Is Security going to keep guys like that from coming back?" Yürgen pressed.

"Stay within your job description, Mr. Zayeddi. We don't need Billy-Boy fanatics wasting our time around here!"

"You'd better stop talking that way."

"Or what?"

This guy deserved a split lip, as a minimum.

Yürgen took a wild roundhouse swing, but missed when Badger saw it coming and stepped back nimbly, while shouting for help. Four uniformed security men rushed over, gripped Yürgen with strong arms and escorted him toward the open rollup door. In the background he heard Badger shouting that he was fired, and he was shoved outside into the parking lot.

The fog had cleared, and the morning sun was well over the top of the hill now, brightening the intersection where the cyclists had rendezvoused. Soon Zayeddi would pass that intersection, going home from this place for the last time. He lingered outside the factory building for several moments. The finality of it hit him hard. He'd worked here for seven years, had gotten used to it.

"Beat it fella," one of the security guards said, from behind, "before we have to bring in real cops."

Feeling despondent, Yürgen walked away slowly. When he was outside the gates, a tall, thin man with a neatly-cropped beard approached him. He wore a dark suit, was accompanied by an unusual robot that was much shorter. The machine had a protrusion on top resembling a head, but without a face—except for what looked like a speaker patch in front where a face might have been. On the front of the torso, a vertical light tube pulsed soft orange. The light washed over Zayeddi for a moment, then withdrew. He didn't like that. It gave him a brief tingling sensation, which he found disturbing.

"I'm Vernon Tracy," the man said. He extended a hand, but Yürgen didn't shake it.

"I saw the whole thing," Tracy said, withdrawing his hand, "the way you courageously stopped those men from spreading their lies and chased them off. Most impressive on your part, I must say."

"Thank you, but my employer does not agree. I've been fired."

The man nodded, as if he already knew this. "You must be very upset," he said.

"What did that robot just do to me?" Yürgen asked. "The orange light that touched me for a moment?"

"He was just testing your veracity and sincerity. Mmmm, one of the more basic forms of lie detection that we use." He looked at a screen on the robot's side, then turned to Zayeddi and asked, "How would you like to go up to Skyship?"

"Are you kidding? What do you mean?"

"We're on the lookout for dedicated Billy Jeeling loyalists like you. We have a growing public relations program that you might be interested in, organizing people to spread the truth. You would be trained on Skyship, and then assigned to duties back here on AmEarth. Up until now, this has only been a small program, but our manager, Lainey Forster, wants to enlarge it."

It sounded terribly exciting to Yürgen, but he wanted more information before accepting. He'd never heard of such a program.

He noticed that small white bubbles had begun to move up inside the robot's orange light tube, didn't know what this meant.

Yürgen narrowed his gaze, studied the man and his peculiar companion. He had never heard of the PR program, was trying to determine if it was real or some ruse by Billy's enemies, to get him off the street, maybe even to harm him. What was that robot doing?

"Well, does this sound interesting to you, or not?"

"Are you offering me a job? I'd be paid?" The man did look sincere, and Yürgen wanted so *much* to believe. He had no job or other source of income, and would like to do something significant to help Billy, even if it involved taking a chance.

"Yes to both," the man said. He named a salary that sounded good, then extended his hand once more. "Now, shall we try this again?"

The offer was a little more than Yürgen had been earning in the factory.

Finally, he nodded and shook the man's hand, noting a firm grip. They talked for a few more minutes, in which the new recruit obtained details of what he needed to do next, and where he was supposed to report to a shuttle the next morning, to be taken up to Skyship.

He could hardly contain his excitement.

CHAPTER 3

Skyship is the greatest technological wonder in history, and the most mysterious.

—Rolf Joseph, AmEarth News Service

Lainey stood just inside the high-arched doorway of Billy's office, looking at him. He sat at his gleaming white desk, on that remarkable maglev chair. He smiled at her, then grunted as he lifted himself onto a platform beside the chair, and then slid back down onto the seat of the chair again—one of the exercise regimes he followed every day. Back and forth he went. The paraplegic wore a black and tan Sky-Corps uniform, with the blue-sky emblem of Skyship on his lapel. He had powerful arms and shoulders, compensating for the loss of his amputated legs.

Despite this, and despite the fact that Billy was getting old now, Lainey Forster thought he was the most handsome man she'd ever met, and the most magnificent representative of the black race she'd ever seen, even in the movies. His skin had very few lines and was quite dark, as if there had not been much interbreeding in his lineage with lighter-skinned races, such as her own. The explosion on Skyship had destroyed his legs, but it had not changed his good looks or gentle personality, and had not prevented him from making love with her. She only wished Billy would fight back more against the ongoing smear attacks against his character, the rapidly mounting campaign of innuendos and lies.

He was one of many people who refused to use the internet, or the implanted mindwave technologies. To keep up with current events, Billy only read printed newspapers and reports from his staff—all delivered to him daily. She saw the morning editions stacked neatly on a side table, looking very old-fashioned in the midst of all of the technology in his office and on Skyship. She couldn't tell if he had looked at these periodicals yet, but noted that the issue on top was turned face-down. The daily staff report sat beside it.

Through the window behind him, Lainey saw the glistening spires of the unique onboard city, and fat, insect-like humbabies flying back and forth, carrying passengers. Many of the buildings were connected by elevated, clearplaz-enclosed walkways, and she saw people and robots scurrying back and forth on them, going about their assignments. There were countless tasks to perform on Skyship, and most were important, designed to keep the ship operating at peak efficiency.

She struggled to frame the words she wanted to say to this great man, the important advice she needed to give him now. She took a deep, apprehensive breath, anticipating the usual resistance from him to her ideas about the need for more effective and widespread public relations efforts. His oversized desk was almost completely bare, and high-polished. The only item on it was a glassplaz cube, containing an opaque purple liquid... he'd told her it was the initial stage of the secret atmospheric-gas mix, in liquid form.

"Have you seen the newspapers today?" she asked.

He didn't reply and kept exercising, going back and forth from chair to platform, sweating and breathing harder. His black, curly hair was uncombed and longer than normal, with graying locks dropping across his eyes, making it difficult at times to determine the direction of his gaze. His long-sleeved uniform had plain epaulets on the shoulders—nothing to distinguish rank. She noted dark marks of perspiration around his armpits.

He completed the exercises, returned to his high-tech chair, and looked at her importunately. His dark eyes were clear and alert, despite his age. "Well?" he said. "What is it you want to say to me this time?"

He seemed to already know, was acting edgy. She moved closer and stood in front of the desk. "You've seen the papers?"

"Just the headlines, the increasing demonstrations against me in the major cities. The details don't interest me. I don't really care that much what people think of me."

"But of course you do."

He didn't reply, but from his hurt expression she could see that he did care. He cared a great deal.

"There's a new story in several papers," she said, "that you lied about your family history, that your ancestors were never slaves at all, and instead they were nobility, AmAfrican chieftains who kidnapped men and women from enemy villages and sold them to slavers, to be taken far away in forced servitude, on other continents. That's not true, is it Billy?"

He hesitated for a long moment, then looked pained when he said, "I'm afraid it is. More ignobility than nobility, I'm afraid."

"But why, Billy? Why did you lie about such a thing?"

He stared hard at her. "It was a fiction my grandparents came up with decades ago, to survive in the black community, to keep people from turning against them. It was just a harmless family story, carried from generation to generation. In turn, I carried it on, as my father and mother did before me."

"The newspapers are also saying you lied about your entire personal history, Billy, that you enhanced it by claiming you received a degree in science from a black university and then went to work in the aeronautics industry. They said you never specified the school in any interviews or press releases because you didn't even graduate high school, and you never named the aeronautics companies because you never actually worked for them."

He sat there looking sad, hanging his head a little and not commenting.

Lainey didn't like this conversation, as if she were a prosecutor or an interrogator digging deep into the lies of a witness. But she pressed on. As the Director of Public Relations she *had* to know the truth. "Apparently there *is* a record of you entering a robotics contest when you were in high school, but you never submitted anything for judging. You were living with an aunt at the time, but you seemed to vanish afterward, and no one knows where she went."

"She was my great aunt, actually, and she was quite old. She died not long after I moved out of her house." He paused, shook his head in dismay. "Everything you just said about my background is correct. It's all true, but I don't want to admit it in public."

"And who is Devv's mother? People are asking about that, too."

His gaze narrowed. "*People* are asking, Lainey, or are *you* the one asking?"

The comment stung. "They're asking, believe me. Look, I'm here to help you, not attack you."

"His mother's name is my business. It's very personal, okay?"

"Why don't you just tell the truth about everything, Billy? You've still accomplished great things with Skyship. Where were you in those early years of your life, after you dropped out of high school? What were you really doing, and how did that cause you to design and build Skyship? Who is your son's mother, and how did you meet her? Where is she now?"

"I won't answer any of that. I'm sorry, but I have my reasons, and they are good reasons."

"Your enemies are making a field day out of this, Billy. They're saying, 'where there's smoke, there's fire.' Meaning, you must be concealing much more. And that, it seems, is true."

"I'm tired of talking about this crap. I don't have time for ridiculous discussions. It's a waste of my valuable time."

"I understand what you're saying, Billy, I'm with you. But the reality is that there are opposition groups popping up all over the AmEarth Empire and even in the off-world colonies... and the numbers are growing at an alarming rate. We need more PR efforts. Your enemies are increasing their attacks against you, coordinating them cleverly with the various groups. These people are highly organized, Billy, and it's getting worse because of your lackluster responses. We need to put far more effort into this than we have in the past. You need to tell the complete truth about your early history, and about your family. Get it all out, admit to whatever lies and half-truths you've been telling. People will forgive you because of all you've accomplished."

"All of them won't forgive me."

"No, but many will. I'm pleading with you, let me do more counter-propaganda. So far you haven't allowed my people to do much; you wouldn't approve the 'details' of what I wanted to do—except for allowing us to distribute old press releases about you... flattering stuff. We sent them to media people in the larger cities, asking them to run favorable pieces on you. Some did, and some didn't. But it's horribly obvious that we need to do a *lot* more. The ugliness is increasing too quickly, and I'm afraid—"

Billy Jeeling raised a hand to quiet her, shook his head stubbornly. Obviously he wasn't interested in hearing any more of this. Nonetheless, she pressed on.

"As much as you hate to hear this, we need to use the internet," she said, "as well as the mindwave systems that are implanted in billions of people—I'm sure your enemies are using these technologies against you, so you need to do the same against them. We can send audiovisual broadcasts from here that will be received instantaneously by a variety of technologies all over the Empire, including on the remote colonies. We can broadcast your voice, your face, your words."

Billy smiled ruefully. "When people wake up in the morning, it will be to me in their brains telling them what a great guy I am?"

"Could be, if they're tuned to receive our broadcasts. And I think they will be. Anything you say is interesting, Billy, it's big news. Whether the messages appear in their brains or not—that's up to the users. As part of a stepped-up print-media campaign, candid interviews with you would be good, and a documentary on your fascinating life—including the construction of Skyship. We can feature scientific reports too, about the horror of skin cancer, eye problems, breathing diseases, and a variety of deadly afflictions people suffered, before your wonderful, miraculous discoveries were implemented. This is urgent, Billy. We need to do something, really *do* something. And we need to do it right away."

"Needed it yesterday, right?"

She nodded.

He gestured for her to sit down, and she slipped into one of the white hover chairs in front of his desk, supported by a barely discernible platform of air. The chair felt a little loose when she sat on it, so perhaps it needed to be adjusted. It was something she'd mentioned to Billy in the past, because he liked to tinker with mechanical things and electronics. But this was not a good time to mention that. She was already after him about much more important matters.

He didn't say anything for several long moments, so perhaps he was at least considering what she'd been saying.

As she waited, a ringing filled her ears... along with other noises... the faint whirring of precision machinery? She couldn't quite identify the sounds, had heard them around Skyship on numerous occasions; they came and went. She'd asked Billy about them, but had received only vague replies... something about the atmospheric-stationing mechanism on the ship, he usually said, while suggesting that she was probably sensitive to particular frequencies. Right now, the irritating sounds seemed to come from beyond a wall, or beneath her feet. At times they seemed to almost be inside her head.

Lainey chewed on her lower lip, stared at Billy. She didn't want to say anything about the whirring now, but found it so deeply disturbing that she couldn't help herself. "I'm hearing those machine noises again," she said. "They're very strange. I've never been able to figure out exactly where they come from, and you haven't clarified—"

"Don't worry about them. They're simply part of Skyship. As I told you before, you needn't concern yourself with them."

"All right, Billy. Whatever you say. But they are irritating."

He grabbed the pile of newspapers, along with summary sheets that were secured to each. While she waited, he read the summaries, one after another, and scanned some of the actual articles and editorials, commenting on a couple of them to her. Then he studied the latest report from his staff.

Finally he stopped reading, and leaned back in his maglev chair, which made a curiously antique squeaking noise. Lainey followed the direction of his gaze, toward a large viewing port on one wall. Skyship was tilted slightly in its atmospheric-stationing, so that AmEarth was visible clearly below them, one of the attitudes that the vessel's automatic systems took on a regular basis, while maintaining the onboard gravitonic system; the passengers did not feel anything unusual, despite the off-kilter views. The planet was a blue-green giant swirling in angry white clouds. She identified the vortex and eye of a hurricane kilometers below, so far away that it wouldn't affect them.

Billy Jeeling's dark eyes grew moist momentarily, and he pushed the newspapers and summaries toward her on top of the desk.

"Other than my personal and family history, the stories about me are garbage," he said. "A complete crock. I'm not making huge profits for myself or 'my cronies,' or living like a king. You know that yourself, Lainey. Facts are being blown out of proportion, or manufactured out of thin air. Much of it is innuendo, with no proof whatsoever."

"Proof doesn't matter, Billy, once your enemies say what they want to say about you, it finds its way onto social media and goes viral. When we don't respond to many of the allegations, or have only weak responses, some portion of the public thinks it's all true. And the numbers of people who oppose you increase."

"The sleaziest reporters are coming out of the woodwork, writing about me."

"Yes, they are." Lainey didn't hear the machinery sounds anymore. That was something good, anyway.

He fell silent.

"Billions of people still love you, Billy. Before you came to the rescue, the atmosphere was peppered with ozone holes, letting in ultraviolet and cosmic radiation. The air in major cities was unfit to breathe, and that's where most of the protests are occurring? It makes no sense! But this can be part of our counter-attack. Those people are breathing easier because of you, their kids are healthy because of you, so they should be grateful, not critical." She nodded. "Yes, we can do something with that."

"It's completely bizarre, Lainey."

She slid the papers to one side of his desktop. "We can call the stepped-up PR effort the Truth and Fairness Campaign, or something like that."

"All right, I'm listening."

Finally, she thought.

He activated his chair, and it traveled smoothly on air to a magnascope by the window. The scope had a hooded overhang, and he went under it. A screen in the hooded area flashed on, throwing pale gray light past him into the office. The scope moved, made a series of computer tones.

"What are you looking at, Billy?" she asked, walking over and standing behind him.

"Sunbathers on a beach. I'm zoom-focusing. Young couple lying on their backs in Southern AmCal; their bodies are perfect, Lainey. Skin just right, not too tan. They aren't afraid of the sun, are too young to ever have been. It's completely safe to go to almost any beach on the planet now, because of my Skyship!"

"Those young people are the fruits of your work," she said, "the healthy, breathing future of mankind."

He motioned for her to step further under the hood, and when she was fully inside he adjusted the magnascope. It beeped and moved, and a beautiful desert scene appeared, with a camel caravan proceeding past sand dunes that were sculpted like waves. Billy touched more controls, and brought up the view of a wide river flowing through a verdant green valley, dotted with picturesque farms. While she watched silently, he showed cities with gleaming buildings that reached for the sky, as well as a range of jagged mountain peaks, and a pristine alpine lake surrounded by tall pines. Finally, he showed her the ocean and a large pod of humpback whales that was not going anywhere; the marine animals just appeared to be having a good time with one another.

"I love AmEarth," he said, as he switched off the scope and they moved out from under the hood. He looked at her, wiped a tear from his eye. "Don't people understand that? Don't they understand that I want the whole planet to be vibrant, and all of its inhabitants to enjoy healthy, productive lives? I love the forests, the lakes, the mountains, the oceans, and all living creatures. I even love my enemies, and only want the best for them, as I do for everyone else. I don't have a personal bank account, and all of the money I earn goes toward keeping Skyship operational. I don't live opulently, just in a small, cramped apartment. The Prime Minister of the AmEarth Empire lives in a palace, not me."

"Your enemies—including the Prime Minister, I'm afraid—are clever, and are casting you in an unfavorable light, while touting their own achievements with parades and other pageantry. Sometimes I think the Empire is more illusion than reality, more spectacle than substance."

Billy said bitterly, "The people love their imperial leader in his ceremonial uniform, his pretty wife, and their attractive family."

"Yes, they do—and many people are living well because of the military conquests of the Empire, and the front seats they've had in the big, plundering show. But lots of people also know about your altruism, your environmental activism. I don't know how you'll feel about this, Billy, but I'm going to admit to you that I've taken the liberty of recruiting loyalists for a new public relations campaign, hoping you will allow me to send them out on important assignments, more than you've permitted in the past. A shuttle of volunteers will be arriving soon."

"Yes, use the recruits as you see fit. But keep this in mind. I'm not going to talk about my family, my education, or my early work history. And nothing about the identity of Devv's mother. No mention of these things in our responses, either, Lainey. They are not open for discussion."

She could tell he meant it, by his emphatic words and the intensity in his dark face, so she just said, "We'll have to work around those things, then. We'll target other matters. I'll take care of it, exactly as you wish."

He went back to the gleaming white desk, but positioned his chair on one side now. She waited for him to say whether he wanted to talk more, or whether she should leave and go about her duties. She stood a few meters away, noticed stains on his tan slacks. He needed tending all of the time, mothering, almost—although she didn't feel like a mother toward him. She loved him in a different way, and wanted only the best for him. This was a truly great man, a magnificent person in all ways.

"Now it's time for us to strike back hard," she said. "You and I both know that some high-level leaders are targeting you, trying to bring you down. Prime Minister Yhatt, and that rude, outspoken officer in the Imperial Army, General Moore. There are others, too. Maybe we should go after *them* in the court of public opinion."

"No, I only want to focus on defending my record, because it's a good one, and we have a lot of facts to prove it. I will not sink to their level."

"All right."

"Without the gas mixture I pump into the air, it would have taken centuries to restore the atmosphere naturally, assuming that human-kind could have made any substantial headway against the industrial and other sources of pollution. I provided a shortcut to salvation. In your new PR campaign, I want you to emphasize the condition of the atmosphere before Skyship, and what we've done to improve it."

"What *you've* done to improve it, Billy."

He nodded somberly.

Her heart went out to him, and she wanted to just hold him and comfort him. But he was obviously not in any mood for that sort of thing.

"We'll go head-to-head against the unfounded criticisms, Billy. We can bring in some psych-war specialists to mount a strong counter-attack. Barrage the AmEarth Empire with *our* propaganda."

"Don't go too far. I want to spread the truth, not the distortions that typically come with propaganda. I want to take the high road in everything we do."

"I understand, but to strike back effectively, you may need to fight the way they do, putting a spin on things. You say you don't want to make personal attacks against your leading critics, okay. But we have to tell a story, your story, and we need to make it compelling."

He shook his head, causing his graying, curly locks to flip farther back, off his forehead. "Keep it clean, Lainey. Tell my story with dirt free, provable facts, but don't spin anything, don't twist anything. We'll fight this my way. I want you to run the details past me for ap-proval."

"That will slow things down."

He glowered. "It's the way I want it."

"All right. How about dispatching a team of rebuttal robots with standard messages and standard responses? Just a few hundred of them that we spread around the planet. You could design and build them yourself."

"I'm not sure about that idea, but we'll talk more about it. I agree that we need to do more."

She sighed. "We're making some progress in this discussion, anyway."

"Remember, we're not going to sling mud at their level. We're above them, in more ways than one." He glanced at his wrist watch, depressed the crystal and forced a smile. "Forty-nine point five-six kilometers above them at this moment."

He patted the cube of inky formula on his desk, what he called the "initial stage" ingredients, part of a much more complex formula that was processed by Skyship and emitted into the atmosphere. "This is just one example. Set up an interview of me in this office, and I'll talk about this cube and its significance. I think about the importance of the proprietary gas formula every day. People need to understand better who I am, what I've done for AmEarth, and what I'm continuing to do. I have *not* outlived my usefulness."

She saw him staring at a headline on one of the newspapers, accusing him of shanghaiing young people into the SkyCorps that operated many of the services on the great ship, and into the JeeJees who supported him with almost fanatical devotion.

"Billy, maybe you shouldn't look at the details so much, maybe you should—"

"Aw, to hell with it!" Jeeling snapped. He swung a forearm, sent the stack of newspapers flying. Only the purple cube remained on his desk.

"I should be leaving," Lainey said. She bowed in her graceful manner, with a sweep of one arm and then up, a dancer's motion. She liked to move this way, and in privacy she practiced her many dance moves. It was relaxing for her, a natural talent she'd always had, back to her earliest memories as a little girl on AmEarth when she used to perform for her family.

"I have things to do myself." Billy guided his maglev chair on its cushion of air to the wall, where the opening to the guideway slid open smoothly, with a small click. Moments later he was inside, and she heard smooth machinery sounds as he sped away into the honeycomb of tunnels, passages, and chambers on the great ship.

CHAPTER 4

The list of what I know is much shorter than anyone realizes.

—Billy Jeeling

Billy Jeeling awoke before dawn to the jarring sound of an explosion that he felt and heard. It was not a good way to start the day.

He slid his crippled body onto a dressing platform, waited impatiently while robotic arms helped him into a black uniform shirt and tan slacks. This took only a few minutes, but seemed like longer. Then, sliding off the other side of the platform, he dropped onto his maglev chair, and rode it into the corridor outside his apartment. His son Devv was already there, hurrying toward the maglev tube, to catch a high-speed passenger capsule. The two Jeelings lived next door to one another, each with small, humble living arrangements.

"Something blew up!" Billy said.

Devv nodded but didn't reply. A younger version of his father, he had AmAfrican features and a strong bone structure. He stood there for a moment, listening to the mindwave communication system that was linked to his brain—messages that were called "mindcoms." If he wanted to, he could switch to audiovisual that both of them could see who was talking on the other end, in a two-way VR bubble, but he didn't activate that option.

The mindwave units that people had installed voluntarily in their brains were manufactured by a variety of competitive private companies, and had to meet certain criterion. Because they were implanted devices, they met strict medical standards for quality and safety. They also had to be compatible with one another, so that all brands featured virtual-reality bubbles, and all could communicate clearly with one another in both sound and picture.

Billy didn't use the system, didn't want one of the mindwave implants himself. He wasn't a Luddite, just didn't like certain technologies, such as the internet and mindwave. He considered both to be intrusive, and had a long list of reasons why he loathed them.

In his mid thirties, with curly black hair that was shorter and neater than his father's, Devv wore a blue Security Commander's uniform, with white trim; it was wrinkled, with no cap or tie. He had a classically handsome face like his father's, but not as broad, and his skin was a little lighter. The effect was just different enough from Billy that the ghost of Devv's mysterious mother seemed to be just beneath Devv's skin. In particular, the eyes were not remotely Billy Jeeling's. They were pale blue, delicate and penetrating, fragile and aware. Highly unusual for a black man, and quite striking in appearance.

"I got a mindwave report a few minutes ago," the young Security Commander said. "Something blew in Sector H-577. Damage has been contained, but the sooner we get there to inspect, the better. Luckily, Skyship is compartmentalized—smart design on your part, Father—so we can isolate the trouble, keeping it in a small area. That explosion was close."

"Anything about whether it was an accident, or sabotage?" Billy asked.

"No."

Billy flipped down the sidecar of his maglev chair, and the second seat folded open, allowing his son to climb aboard. A clearplaz protective cocoon went up to protect the passengers. Glancing to his right, Billy saw Devv secure his safety harness, then clip on a headset so that the two of them could converse more easily, over the droning noise that would soon fill the capsule. The enclosed chair whooshed on a cushion of air to the maglev tube. A door slid open, and they accelerated into the guideway, a long, curving tunnel that sloped slightly upward.

The tunnel was clearplaz, affording them a view of the onboard city with its high-rise office buildings and habitation units. Small, top-rotor aircraft flew around the spacious interior of the metropolis, which reminded Billy of a huge, hollowed out eggshell. The small aircraft, humbabies, looked like bees or other insects, and some of them—the ones with multiple rotors on top—were large enough to accommodate as many as eight passengers. In this tunnel he couldn't hear them over the drone of the maglev system, yet out in the city they produced a constant background hum.

Billy wore a headset, but in his customary fashion, no safety harness, and pressed the control bar to open the chair all the way up, to top speed. He enjoyed going fast, and if he could make the device go any faster, he would. Already the chair and its guideway system were fitted with superchargers, and he was forever tinkering with the technology, giving his engineering and construction robots detailed instructions for them to make subtle improvements.

The clearplaz tunnel enclosing the guideway provided some feeling of security, along with the knowledge that when Billy's chair was in the system, all other vehicles were shoved onto sidings, to await the moment when he disembarked. At least he and Devv couldn't get in a collision with another vehicle. But if they ever de-tracked accidentally, the decking alongside the guideway was hard to fall against, and so was the clearplaz. There were no walls at the end of any section—everything was continuous loop—and some of the turns were very sharp.

Once, Lainey Forster had asked Billy if he needed speed to compensate for the loss of his legs, and he'd responded with a laugh. "Not at all, I've always been a little nuts."

"More information coming in," Devv said, listening to the mindwave unit in his skull. Glancing to the side, Billy saw the energy of the transmission dancing in front of Devv's eyes. "They're collecting evidence," he said, "analyzing it to see what happened."

The maglev capsule reached top speed, and Billy saw Devv holding onto a bar in front of him with white knuckles, as if he were a small child on a carnival ride. Devv was not normally worried about his personal safety. In fact, in running the Skyship Security Force, he had shown great courage in going after saboteurs, and once had even engaged in a shootout against an intruding commando team, killing all four of them single-handed. But something about this maglev system terrified him.

"We're almost there," Billy announced, in a reassuring, paternal voice. He saw Devv nod, but the younger man's muscles did not start to relax until the maglev chair decelerated and came to an abrupt stop.

"We're not at the station," Billy said, feeling his pulse quicken. "That was almost an emergency stop." He peered ahead, and in the low illumination of the guideway he saw flickering lights and shadowy shapes.

"Those are my officers," Devv said. "They're mindcomming me. They say the explosion tore apart a section of the guideway track."

Billy knew that most members of the Skyship Security Force were robots, and all could transmit to humans over the mindwave system. He had designed them himself, and had supervised much of their design and assembly. Now he opened the plaz shell, and used a manual override to move the maglev chair forward slowly.

A robot officer appeared beside the chair, and motioned Billy forward for a ways, then put up a metal hand to stop. "We're not finished with the security sweep ahead, sir. The protocol is for you to stay back." Billy knew this was true; Devv had explained the reason for it, saying Billy was the one irreplaceable person on Skyship.

"What the hell happened here?" Billy demanded. He smelled dust from the explosion, and odd odors that he couldn't identify. Chemicals that were used in a sabotage?

Devv stepped out of the sidecar, said, "I'll see what I can find out." He walked ahead a ways.

Billy lifted himself onto a ledge between his cushioned seat and the sidecar, for a better view. His leg stumps hung uselessly; he reached down to scratch one of them, a nervous thing he sometimes did. He saw a gaping hole in the side of Skyship, heard the loud sounds of onboard atmospherics, and saw the breach being sealed over automatically by built-in systems. The replacement wall-section was pale, translucent green, contrasting with the original gray.

Human and robotic officers collected fragments of evidence, pieces of Skyship, and perhaps fragments of an explosive device if one had been used—Billy couldn't tell. The robots cast a yellow glow around their gleaming bodies as they scanned all of the items on the spot.

Devv stood in their midst, watching and waiting. They told him something and he nodded, then walked back to Billy.

"Sabotage for damn sure," Devv reported. "No evidence of plaz-teke explosives or unstable chemicals, but the surveillance system for this section was disabled, although my robotic guard force has no recollection of anyone getting in. Curiously, the explosive they used left no trace evidence behind."

"Could there have been a memory wipe on the robots? I could check that."

The younger man shook his head. "That's already been checked, using your own procedural instructions. No wipes were done. Unfortunately, we have one dead officer—Naklos Averon—a trusted human I stationed on the guard force for this section. Sorry to lose him; he had potential to rise in the ranks. He died horribly, his body torn apart."

"I didn't know him. He's not a suspect."

"No, he was a good man—I'm sure he could not possibly have been involved in the explosion; the lie-detection robots went over him thoroughly before he was hired and regularly afterward, along with every other human on my force. He wasn't a suicide bomber or anything crazy like that."

Billy chewed nervously on the inside of his mouth. This was the third instance of sabotage in the past year, and he had no idea who was doing it. All the human workers on Skyship—no matter their jobs—had been carefully checked by the specialty robots with their infallible lie-detection methods; none of the people were telling anything but the truth. That meant the saboteur—or saboteurs—had gained entry to the vessel surreptitiously, and might still be hiding somewhere on board. Billy had suggested this possibility to his son before, concerning the other sabotages, and the police had searched everywhere they could think of, without finding anything.

"I can't believe any fool would want to harm Skyship," Billy said, "not with all the horrendous consequences that could ensue."

Devv nodded. Both of them knew what he was referring to, a dire warning Billy had delivered to Prime Minister Yhatt and the people of AmEarth, that if the great vessel were ever destroyed, it would set off huge atmospheric explosions that would exterminate virtually all life on the planet.

The Imperial government had accused Billy of either lying or gross exaggeration, and had demanded a detailed, scientific explanation. He had not been able to provide that, however, because Tobek was the only one who knew, and he'd died strangely and horribly, taking the secret information with him. The old inventor's tone when he'd spoken to Billy of the danger had been ominous, unwavering, and convincing. Billy had believed him, and had waited for the promised explanation that never came, because of Tobek's unexpected and untimely death.

Billy had responded to the government that he was not going to provide details, because it was part of the proprietary information he was keeping to himself about the operation of Skyship. This had been convincing to some, it turned out, but not to everyone.

Billy didn't know much about the exact nature of the danger, and what little he did know he'd only revealed to a few of his most trusted robots. As for Devv, he only knew what Billy had said publicly, and though the younger man had pressed him for information, Billy had deferred, saying he couldn't talk about it yet. This was highly ironic, considering the position Billy had been in earlier, trying to find out more than he was being told.

"It would take time to rebuild Skyship, but you could do it," Devv said now. "You're the designer, know all the architectural and scientific details."

Scowling, Billy said, "It would not be so easy."

"Maybe not, but you could do it. I assume you've placed full blueprints and other documents in safe storage away from here, down on the planet?"

Billy looked away, didn't respond. The answer was no, because he had nothing meaningful to store. He had part of the secret gas mix formula, of course, and maybe he could place a copy of what he knew somewhere on AmEarth—if he could figure out how to do it without risking its premature discovery. But Skyship's destruction would be an irreparable loss, because his knowledge of the vessel's secrets was minimal and superficial. Its impenetrable technology could never be replaced, not even if Billy survived the ongoing sabotage attempts—

and that technology was essential to the processing of the initial stage ingredients of the gaseous atmospheric-repair mixture, and essential to the method by which it was released into the atmosphere.

Billy knew quite a bit about the robots, because they had been his specialty, and he had some other information, but it was not enough. And there were even things about the robots that Billy didn't know, despite his own expertise. Tobek had taught him robotics in the first place, and eventually had said that Billy's skills exceeded his own. But Billy had never believed that was really true, and Tobek had designed and built his own laboratory robots.

And even if Billy knew everything that was important about the robots, Skyship was a lot more than these sentient, mobile machines — and Tobek had died with the lion's share of his secrets.

Devv didn't know about Tobek or his strange and disturbing death, or a lot of other things. He didn't need to know.

"Maybe a robot or robots did this," Devv said. "I don't think it's a human hiding somewhere, because we've searched every nook and cranny on Skyship. By process of elimination, that means it's probably a robot, one that's had its operating systems compromised. Maybe there really was a memory wipe, and you need to check the 'bots yourself, delving even more into their program histories."

"It doesn't seem possible," Billy said, "but you're right. I'll arrange for my specialists to make the deepest probes possible, and compile a report on the results. We need to check every possibility."

CHAPTER 5

You aren't really human until you take big chances.

—Anonymous

"You did *what*?" The young woman's voice was shrill as she looked up from her window seat, where she'd been reading a book. The volume slipped from her grasp, closed itself on her lap.

It was hot in the rental bungalow Yürgen Zayeddi shared with her. She always kept it that way; it was just one of their many disagreements. He waved a hand at the thermostat, tapped the smaller dial on his smart watch, and heard the furnace go off. He'd been telling her what had happened at the plant that day, the disturbing events.

Suzanne Lansbury had stringy brown hair secured at the back and a puffiness to her face. A black collar peeked around the neck of her dowdy sweater, and the cuffs of a yellow shirt could be seen at the wrists. She was forever cold and complaining, and layered on clothing in such eclectic abundance that it made her appear heavier than she really was. Only in her mid-twenties, she'd been pretty a couple of years ago, and had taken care of her personal hygiene better, but she'd gotten lax and let herself go. Yürgen didn't blame her entirely; the two of them had lost their enthusiasm for one another. They'd been quarreling incessantly, and each had been threatening to move out on the other.

This was going to be a bad fight over the job. He could tell by the furious look on her face. Her eyes were wild.

"How could you be so stupid?" she shrilled. "You lost your job at the factory? How idiotic is that? An argument over Billy Jeeling? That

43

old fool in the sky?" She thrust herself out of the window seat, letting the book tumble away, then brushed past him, leaving a stench of body odor in her wake as she headed toward the kitchen.

"It was unavoidable. I couldn't stand the things they were saying about Billy."

Yürgen removed his eyeglasses, tossed them on a side table. He was about to tell her about the exciting job offer on Skyship, but was having second thoughts, in view of her attitude toward the renowned Hero of the Sky.

"I think I'd better move out," he said, "and get this relationship over with. For your sake, Suzanne, and for mine—before one of us kills the other."

She was focused on something else. "Billy, Billy! This place is overflowing with Billy Jeeling memorabilia. Honestly, I wish you'd grow up. I should clean it out and throw it all in the garbage."

Yürgen glowered at her, then rummaged through a drawer in the side table. "Do you know where my spare eyeglasses are?" he asked. "The zoom isn't working very well on those."

"How should I know where your junk is? You've got so much crap around here that's it's a wonder you can ever find anything."

"I bought two extra pair and both were in this drawer. Are you sure you didn't move them?"

"I didn't touch them!"

"Did you hear me? I'm moving out."

"So hurry up and go. Don't stand around talking about it."

Zayeddi located a package of contact lenses, pulled out a set and spread his eyelids open one at a time to insert the lenses. He didn't care much for contacts, as they didn't have the zoom-vision feature. But at least they were the liquid-suspension type that he could leave in for months and forget about.

"Don't expect me to pay your half of the rent now," she said, thrusting open the refrigerator door. "You signed the lease along with me, so you're on the hook, too. You'd better hustle right out and get your job back."

"What do you know about getting a job, Suzanne, living off your divorce settlement? That's how you've been paying your share of expenses."

Increased anger moved across her face. "I read books, keep up on current events. And I manage my investments... that's my job, and I do it very well, thank you."

"You're a loser," he said, "a parasite looking for the next person to leech onto."

She said something in response, but he didn't hear it.

The next few minutes became a blur to Yürgen, as he packed hurriedly, not bothering to find everything he owned. Just priorities. Later he recalled seeing Suzanne banging around the kitchen, stuffing food in her mouth, with her shrill voice going constantly, never stopping. She was worse than ever.

At one point, following a shrieking cacophony of senseless noise from her, Yürgen hurried out the door and made good his escape, without bothering to say good-bye. It was too bad. At one time, they'd been quite close, but things had gone in the wrong direction for both of them.

Maybe they could become friends again, once they were not living together. But he doubted it. Both of them had said things that could not be taken back — things that hurt and would never be forgotten.

CHAPTER 6

How did Billy Jeeling get away with using government funds to construct that huge Christian cross on
top of Skyship? And we pay for the incredible amount
of power required to illuminate the cross, too, so that it
can seen from space and AmEarth. It's a gross misuse
of public funds, and a violation of the separation of
church and state doctrine.

—Excerpt, anti-Jeeling propaganda broadcast

Billy's apartment was small and austere, overflowing with piles of
documents and books, all in printed form because it was the way he
preferred to read them. As Lainey Forster sat naked on the bed waiting for Billy to return, she recognized the printout of an e-message she
had sent to him three years ago—it was on top of a pile, as if it were
current. She found this troubling. After pulling a sheet and blanket
over her chest, she sipped a glass of expensive pinot noir. It had a fine
bouquet and a beautiful red color, as well as a subtle, fruity flavor.
Billy only rarely enjoyed fine things such as this, but he had saved
some of the modest salary he allotted to himself, enough to buy this
nice wine for her, because he knew she liked it. He was so thoughtful
at times, and always insisted on paying for "extras" such as this that
he used.

Lainey heard him outside the bedroom, talking on a radiocom with
his son the Security Commander, about a deep-probe of robots Billy
had ordered—investigating to see if their operating systems had been
compromised by a saboteur. A written report had arrived by courier,
just when she and Billy were heading for the bedroom carrying

47

glasses of wine, feeling tipsy because both of them had a low toler-
ance for alcohol.

Before that they had shared a romantic private dinner in Billy's
quarters, albeit at a small dining table, next to an electronic wall that
projected the image of a full moon. His apartment didn't have a real
view—just this projected one, but it was live. The moon really was
out. All evening long, she had been in the mood for lovemaking. Billy
had been feeling that way, too, until he was interrupted by the courier, and the radiocom system—Devv suddenly talking loudly
through speakers in the small apartment, asking questions about a
copy of the report he had received. So far there was no evidence of
interference with the robotic operating systems. And Devv had other
matters to discuss, which he considered important.

Feeling annoyed, she sighed while waiting in the bedroom. A
mindwave transceiver in Billy's brain would be much more efficient
than couriers or radiocom calls. He was a robotics expert who picked
and chose which technologies he used—as if he were selecting from a
smorgasbord table. She didn't always understand the choices he
made.

Lainey had her own mindwave implant, and so did Billy's son. So
did almost every other person she'd ever met. Except for Billy, she'd
only heard of exceptions for medical reasons. But he was stubborn
about many things, and his wishes were treated by his underlings like
edicts from God-on-High. They jumped to complete whatever he
wanted—and not only the humans. The robots who attended to him
were also sycophants—programmed to be that way, she'd heard.
Some robots were middle managers (even supervising low-level humans), but mostly the automatons performed the most rudimentary,
repetitive tasks.

Lainey was not a yes-person, and neither was Devv. Curiously,
neither were any of Billy's top management team on Skyship—every
one of them human. All spoke their own minds to the master of the
vessel.

He stopped talking now, and poked his head in the doorway of the
bedroom. Billy wore a white robe with an emblem on one lapel, a styl-
ized version of Skyship surrounded by much smaller skyminers, as if

a hive were spewing forth little bumblebees with bulbous tanks trailing behind them.

"Sorry about the interruption," he said to her, "but things have been coming up, more than usual, and important stuff I can't ignore. I'm on the radiocom with my son—I'll only be a few more minutes."

"I've been listening in. The robotics investigation, and Devv wants you to beef up security around the ship. I think that's a good idea, in view of the danger of sabotage. Did I hear him say he wants more human officers?"

"Right. He feels there are a disproportionate number of police and security 'bots. I don't agree with him. I can make the robots do anything he needs, but he's insistent."

"Just do whatever he wants and come to bed," she said.

He smiled. "Maybe that's a good idea. It will get both of you off my back."

She took a sip of red wine, watched as he went back to the radiocom and continued the conversation. It took him longer than promised, so she drank his glass of wine as well as hers.

When he still had not returned, she glared at the empty doorway. Lainey noticed his black and tan uniform jacket on a chair, a jacket he'd worn earlier in the day. It had a lump in one pocket, making her curious about what it might be.

She slid out of bed, walked naked and unsteadily to the chair, then reached a hand into the pocket and brought out a round, black object, the size of a tennis ball. It was cool to her touch, and had small indented places on it. She turned it over, wondered what the indentations were. Buttons? Was this an electronic device of some sort?

She was about to stick a finger into one of the indentations when Billy burst into the room and snatched the object away from her. "What are you doing?" he asked. "Snooping in my pockets? I didn't think you would stoop to anything like that."

He slipped the object into a pocket of his robe.

"What is that thing?" she asked.

"Nothing." His eyes were steely.

"Nothing? Then why are you so upset about it?"

"How would *you* feel if you found someone going through your pockets?"

"But Billy, you and I are so close, it shouldn't matter. It doesn't *really* matter, does it?"

His expression softened, and he smiled slightly. "No, I guess it doesn't. Sorry, I'm just irritated by the interruptions—it isn't the first time for us, is it?"

"No, it isn't."

"There never seems to be enough quality time for us, Lainey. Sometimes I wish I could just retire and stop worrying about everything it takes to keep Skyship running. That would make my enemies happy, wouldn't it?"

She nodded somberly, didn't want to irritate him more by asking him what the strange, round object was. Maybe another time, when he was in a better mood.

"I'm sorry I took so long with Devv," he said.

Billy removed his robe and slid naked into bed with her. Lainey felt her anger fade as he massaged her back gently. She warmed to his touch, and shivered as she felt herself being carried on a wave of passion, drawing her closer and closer to him. "I love you, Billy," she whispered.

"And I love you, my darling."

It was not first occasion on which he'd said these words to her, but this time she thought she heard a note of deep sincerity that had been missing before. It gave her hope that they might get even closer. Sometimes their personal relationship seemed superficial, that they had little more than a professional association on Skyship, with intermittent moments of intimacy.

Now the great man seemed ready to say something more, but Lainey pressed her lips to his, and held a long, tender kiss. When she finally withdrew, she said, "Billy, I want to have your baby."

His eyes opened wide, and he pulled away from her.

"I've told you this before," she said. "You know I've been trying to get pregnant."

"Yes, Lainey, I know. But I'm afraid we can't have children, and I think you need to face the cold, hard facts. It's been almost five years, with no results."

"It's still possible for us to conceive," she insisted. "I know it is!" And she really believed this, with all of her heart and all of her being.

CHAPTER 7

To kill him, or not to kill him. That is the question.

—General Rivington Moore VIII

"Billy Jeeling will never leave gracefully," said the little man at the head of the dining room table. "I know the stubborn son of a *puta*-whore, and there's only one good way to bring him down. Public opinion!"

Jonathan Racker cleared his throat, adjusted his bifocals. He was an old man, a Latino who was one of the most famous industrialists in the AmEarth Empire. His words were sharply delivered and concise, with a slight Spanish accent. He wore a tuxedo with an open-collar shirt and no tie—Racker could get away with this in posh surroundings, because he was so rich.

Maureen Stuart was one of the invited guests for lunch in an elegant private dining room, in Imperial City's vine-covered Tomaah Club, a haven for good old boys where women were hardly ever invited. She felt out of place here. They were in the midst of the luncheon, with clinking silverware, glittering crystal wine glasses, and the murmur of conversation.

She had her left wrist in a medical wrap, from falling in Founders' Park while jogging two nights ago. It had been late in the evening, not a safe thing to do at that hour, but she was a fast runner and decided to risk it anyway, needing to wind down after a long day at the law firm where she worked. But on one of the dimly-lit garden paths she'd heard something rustling in the bushes, and had increased her speed. Looking back, she saw a man running after her, and shouting crazy things, accusing her of trespassing. It was impossible, of course, because it was a public park, but this guy had staked out at least part of it as his personal turf. At the top of a rise Maureen fell and sprained the wrist, but got up quickly and ran on, managing to outdistance him.

As she glanced around the table now, she noticed two elegantly-dressed men staring at her... one an aged crony of Racker's with a disapproving gaze, and the other a handsome young Army officer in dress-military uniform, General Rivington Moore VIII—who smiled at her. Each had different things in mind, she thought, because Moore was a well-known womanizer. From a patrician family, he was one of society's most eligible bachelors, and had used his family connections to rise mercurially through the ranks. He was a five-star general now at the age of 36, and a swaggering, charismatic leader of men. It was said that they would do anything for him. There were stories of a cult of personality forming around him, a fanatically loyal officer corps. She thought he could be dangerous with such charisma, but she'd never spoken out against him. That would be a dangerous thing to do.

His great grandfather, Rivington Moore V, had been one of the most famous and decorated generals in the Final Sweep, a huge military operation that brought every country on the planet, even the most stubborn holdouts, under one world government—the AmEarth Empire. It had involved a series of brutal, multi-pronged onslaughts, but necessary, or so the Imperial leaders claimed, to improve the efficiency of business and political operations on the planet. There was even proof that the subjugated peoples were doing better economically under the unified government than they'd done previously under the control of their own people, because of all the graft and corruption that had been occurring in those individual regimes.

In the days before the Empire, there had also been wave after wave of genocide, of tribes killing each other for the most petty of reasons. Such crimes against humanity had ended with the inauguration of the new unified government, and Maureen had to admit that people she knew seemed happy now, and she was, too, though she did not have any point of comparison with the way it used to be here in the pre-Empire days. That was too long ago, generations past.

For the most part, Maureen believed in the Imperial government and lifestyle, though she was intelligent enough to recognize the fault in this line of reasoning, noticing the way the Prime Minister and other top politicians justified the favored position their privileged caste held, lording over the other peoples of the world. She hoped that what she'd heard was true, that the natives were being treated with more respect now and doing better than they might have otherwise, and were really allowed to follow any religion they chose, as long as they did it peacefully. Even the most radical wings of Islam had been destroyed, and this was the case with the radical fringes of the other major religions as well—Judaism, Buddhism, Hinduism, Sikhism, and even Christianity—as almost all of the violent fundamentalists had either been eradicated or re-educated into the mainstream and more moderate, tolerant views.

A muscular man, the youthful General Moore had dark brown eyes, a small moustache, and a square jaw. She found his eyes hypnotic, and held gaze with him momentarily, before he winked and she looked away quickly. Lady-killer eyes.

Damned sexist! she thought, as she cut a piece of her prime rib with some difficulty, favoring her sore wrist, and took a bite. *I've got to push back against him, but carefully, without blowing up. Strictly business between us, and at the end of the day I go home and forget about it. They're paying me well for my legal advice.*

"How did you hurt yourself?" Moore asked.

"Punching one of your junior officers who got fresh," she said, with a wry smile. "His jaw was harder than I thought."

"Is that so? Maybe I could teach you some martial arts, and you'd do better next time."

"I already have those fighting skills," she said, and that part was true. But she added, "I took a crash course right after meeting you, knowing I might need to defend myself against *you* someday." She smiled prettily.

His eyes burned a little before he smiled in return. "Is that so?" he said.

"I am married, you know." She held a cool gaze on him, made him look away first this time.

"I hate like hell going against Billy," a silver-haired man on Maureen's left said, rubbing his forehead with an age-spotted hand. "We used to be close, and I remember a lot of good things about him." Paul Paulo was quite slender, and dressed extravagantly in a white and silver suit, with a tufted white shirt, a diamond watch and glittering rings on his fingers. A stock trader extraordinaire, he was CEO of the world's largest stock and commodities brokerage, Paulo Hoon & Benedict. He also had a vast real estate empire in the territories, and had been involved with companies that built many of the largest buildings in the capital of the Empire—Imperial City—including the tall and imposing Racker Building.

This magnificent capital city—built from scratch and designed with regal splendor in mind—had been constructed in the Pacific Northwest region of the former United States of America, on the site of what had once been the City of Seattle. The old metropolis had been razed and completely rebuilt in a style more befitting of empire, with broad boulevards, heroic statues, blazing torches, fluttering banners, and buildings in the classic tradition of ancient Greece and Rome. Most of the hills had been flattened so that the planners could lay out the streets and structures in the most dramatic, awe-inspiring fashion.

Beside Paulo sat a man with blond hair and a short blond moustache, Harrison Jennings. A stuffy, erudite man, he was Prime Minister Yhatt's top assistant, and was known to wear subtle electronic devices to record meetings and transmit them to his boss. She saw a small banner of the AmEarth Empire on his lapel glowing slightly, suggesting to her that it might be electronic.

Paulo cleared his throat. "I remember Billy the way he used to be when Jonathan and I knew him in our younger years, when Billy was making deals with politicians for the operation of Skyship. We were friends with him then, or it seemed that way, and I don't turn against a friend easily, but he turned his back on us first. Billy Jeeling betrayed everyone on this planet when he placed his own interests above the common good."

"Here, here!" Racker said, thumping the table. "I'm afraid we're all sick of dear old Billy, sick of his never-ending monopoly and massive profits. He's not the way he used to be. His ego got the better of him, and greed."

"It's not that we aren't grateful," Paulo said. "He did save the biosphere, managing to put the proverbial genie back in the bottle, so to speak. It's just that he's gone too far—he's no longer an environmental savior; he's an eco-despot."

A waiterbot stood beside two high, chateau-style entrance doors of the private dining room, scanning the table with its Cyclopean eye for service needs. The 'bot wore a black tuxedo, had a white towel draped over one forearm. Two other waiterbots refilled water and wine glasses.

Stuart was a top attorney, having made her reputation on Prime Minister Yhatt's legal team, and in more than twenty years of specializing in political law. Now she ran her own law firm, having left Yhatt's employment a couple of years ago, but the two of them remained close personally, and often had dinner together in the Imperial Palace, with their spouses. Her husband, Paddy Stuart, was a well-known artist, working overseas now on an important commission for one of the territorial governors. He often gave advice to the First Lady of the Empire, Lorissa Yhatt, who was developing her own skills as a painter. Maureen's marriage had its ups and downs; they'd quarreled the day before Paddy left, but made up that evening, with lovemaking. He had his ways of melting her heart, and her resistance.

Maureen made a quick perusal of the table, noted a number of business, military and political leaders. Old Racker himself, though barely a meter and a half tall, more than compensated for his "infirmity" (as he called his height) by fighting his way to the top of Imperial society. He was a mailroom to riches story with his fingers in everything, from transportation to computers. He even wrote bestselling books and produced documentaries.

The old industrialist had his fingers in everything, it seemed, with the exception of Billy Jeeling's monopoly on regeneration and maintenance of the atmosphere, including full ownership of all elements in the air, which only he was allowed to mine and use for a profit. Jeeling held the most closely-guarded secrets in the solar system, so arcane that they weren't even patented.

"Billy has a signed legal contract," Stuart said after wiping her mouth with a napkin, "an agreement reached with one of Yhatt's predecessors, Prime Minister Kelly. The contract is perpetual. I was not on the legal team that set it up—it was before my time, you know—but Prime Minister Yhatt asked me to analyze it later to see if it had loopholes, and I couldn't find any. Not even a pinhole."

"And Billy's son is in line for succession," Moore said, in a resonant voice. "An aristocracy of the atmosphere. Mister Billy Jeeling and Son, the Monarch and Prince of the Sky."

Stuart didn't like Moore's voice. It was too perfect, as if he had practiced to develop it, and he drew some words out like musical notes. Something had never seemed right to her about him. He was overly charming in all things he did, which undoubtedly enabled him to get his way. But he also had the full force of the entire Imperial Army behind him.

"Mmmm, Mr. Renaldo Yhatt will soon be out of office," Paulo said. "He's helped us somewhat, but in only a few months his term is up. What then? Will his successor agree with us, or take Billy's side?" He looked at Stuart.

"I know you would like to see the contract broken quickly," she said, "but Jeeling has a legal team that is more than equal to anything we or the current administration can throw at him in an attempt to break the contract. Take my word for it, this is a dead-end. All we can do is what we've already been doing—the propaganda campaign to bring Billy down."

Mutterings of concurrence passed around the table. Waiterbots began clearing some of the plates, while others poured tea and coffee.

Moore: "We've tried everything to get details on the gas Billy pumps from Skyship into the atmosphere, even shooting spectrals at it, but he's got a helluva shielding mechanism up. Our people suspect the gas contains ozone, because his skyminer fleet seeks and absorbs the ozone-eating elements, and restores the ozone layer. He's also scrubbing CO_2 from most of the atmosphere to make it healthier, but he could also be injecting CO_2 into the ozonosphere to cool it, thus decreasing the rate of O_3 destruction."

"Temperature in the ozone layer is down two degrees since Skyship went into operation," a thin Army officer said, on General

Moore's right. "And he's cleaned up the rest of the atmosphere, too." Flight General Tilson Bishop was at least twenty years older than Moore, and was his adjutant. In a dress uniform that glittered even more than his superior, Bishop had a chest full of military medals and ribbons.

"We've even vacuumed the air after Skyship passed through," Bishop continued, "at different altitudes. What little we can retrieve of his gas seems to indicate that it's a complex formula we can't break down. It seems to be inert in all circumstances, even in intense sunlight. We can't even get it to react to ozone."

"I think nitrogen is in there," General Moore said.

"We've tried our own experiments with a variety of formulas," the thin officer added. "Nothing we try works very well."

"Some of Billy's actions could be decoys," Racker suggested. "Showmanship. He's all over the troposphere, the stratosphere, and the mesosphere. It's baffling what he's doing up there."

"Maybe we can blame him for screwing up the weather," suggested a small black woman on Stuart's side of the table. A career government appointee under the past three prime ministers, Elvira Johnson was the Chancellor of the Exchequer now, with the authority to make large financial decisions—such as how to pay for military ventures. This gave her de facto veto power over General Moore, who was always coming up with big, expensive military plans. But she never seemed to wield that power against him.

Uneasy laughter carried through the room, but none came from Moore. "Hmm," he said, "couldn't we use damage to the weather as a battering ram to break through the walls of the contract?"

"Not a chance," Stuart said. "I've already considered that angle and looked into it in depth. It's weak, not worth the expenditure of our time or assets. Technically he hasn't violated the agreement. He's doing a good job on the atmosphere, as evidenced by infinitesimally low levels of skin cancer and respiratory diseases all over the globe. And believe it or not, he's doing it all within prescribed cost guidelines."

"Within cost guidelines?" General Moore exclaimed, his voice booming forth, as if he were using a loudspeaker. "What a joke! He receives two hundred billion tax-free ambucks a year, and that's just for starters, for the *use* of his secrets. We also pay hundreds of billions to operate Skyship, including salaries for everyone aboard including Billy, unlimited transportation for all who work on the vessel, enabling them to get to the Moon, the Asteroid Colonies, and AmEarth, and every other ridiculous expense you can think of. They even receive cost-of-living adjustments."

"I'd hate to calculate the total cost of that operation," Jonathan Racker said.

His gaze wandered and he squinted, as if looking for something in the far distance. It turned out to be a memory. "Decades ago, I was one of the lucky ones with enough money to afford one of those funny-looking UV-suits," he said. "I hated the face masks the most. And Paul, do you remember complaining that they never came up with a comfortable, decent-looking design?"

Paul Paulo nodded.

Continuing, Racker said, "I hated walking around in that getup looking at people who couldn't afford to protect themselves properly. They were the walking dead, a lot of them. Especially the fair-skinned ones."

Maureen nodded. "I was only a child, but I especially hated seeing young people exposed. I lost several classmates, and a five-year old cousin. The sweetest little boy in the world."

"Yeah. There were skin creams, oral treatments, injections and other treatments for most everyone... but only the UV-suits — radsuits, they called them — were really effective."

Moore shook his head. "Despite any good Jeeling did in the past, we've been spending bi-i-i-g bucks on him. Really big, useless, bucks, because we don't need the bastard any more. Everyone at this table knows Skyship should be run by the Imperial government, but he doesn't want that, of course. It would cut off his flow of cash — actually drastically *reduce* it, if we pay him a pension."

"And if we do manage to take over," Chancellor Johnson said, "we're bound to find financial irregularities, money he spent lavishly on himself. He's turned Skyship into the biggest squander-mill in history."

"A huge personal piggy bank," Moore said, "that he can dip into for anything he wants, without the requirement of any expense reports or audits."

"We're looking into the historical matter," Maureen Stuart said, "the possibility that our Prime Minister at the time—Princeton Kelly—sold the world out on more than one matter, including this big one. We might be able to target his legacy as a way of getting at Billy—pressure from that direction. For one thing, we learned that Kelly's former business partners were heavily involved in the Antarctic platinum rush that upset so many environmentalists. So Kelly wasn't the great supporter of the environment that he claimed to be, and if we crack him on that front, maybe it'll be easier to get to his buddy, Billy Jeeling. Guilt by association. Tar both of them with the same brush. But that's not going to be an easy process. Kelly is fabulously wealthy, and so is Jeeling. They can throw monkey wrenches at us from all directions."

"Billy isn't cozy with Kelly anymore, or with our current Prime Minister, either," Paulo said. "Yhatt told him to resign."

"Yhatt was just going through the motions," Moore said, shaking his head. He waved a waiterbot away, not wanting anything more, and added, "Our eminent leader should have been more emphatic, should have spoken out more against Billy."

"I don't like your tone," Harrison Jennings said.

"Nor do I," said Chancellor Johnson.

"Your objections are duly noted," Moore said, his tone and expression condescending. "And anticipated, since you are both political appointees in the current administration, sycophantic followers of the Prime Minister, bending to his every whim and desire."

They glared at him, and exchanged uneasy glances between themselves.

"Getting rid of Billy Jeeling could require a full-scale military assault on Skyship," General Moore said.

"Not advisable," Paulo said. "That would risk the destruction of everything. Ozone holes could reappear, along with dangerous ultraviolet radiation—UV-a, b, and c—high pollution would come back, too, and we'd find ourselves praying for another Billy Jeeling. It's not possible to move everyone to the Moon or the Asteroid Colonies."

"I'd still like to call Mister Jeeling's bluff," General Moore said. "See who blinks first when we line up our nukes, photon beams and—"

"Out of the question," Paulo said. "Billy has warned us that the destruction of Skyship would set off a series of massive detonations in the air, damaging the atmosphere so severely that it could destroy virtually all life on AmEarth. And I don't think it's an idle threat."

"The downside of Jeeling's great plan," Racker said.

"A clever bluff," Moore said. "He's lying."

"My experts are not so sure," Paulo said. "With all the ozone and other chemicals aboard Skyship, it could very well be a bomb. You know how touchy that stuff is, and our scientists are afraid it's even more volatile with the secret ingredients in Jeeling's mix. Some of the scientists speculate that this could be the secret of the danger—if Skyship blows in the heart of the ozone layer it could set off a chain of horrendous events, ripping through the entire ozonosphere, giving everyone on AmEarth a final, lethal dosage of DUV—damaging ultraviolet. With the exception of a few of us, that is. We still have some rather expensive, cumbersome suits to put on that will protect us. Maybe that's what Billy's threat means—a huge absorption of lethal DUV."

"There won't be any disaster," Moore said. "I've seen other studies; I've even had my people calculate the odds, and the risk is infinitesimally low."

"I've seen studies that say otherwise," Paulo said, "and with the stakes this high, we must assume the worst... and take extreme care. We don't want to bumble into anything."

General Moore glared at him.

"I wonder if Billy ever revealed the danger of atmospheric destruction to anyone before the contract was signed," Racker said. He turned to Stuart. "Couldn't that be misrepresentation?"

"No. For one thing, Billy claims it's a danger that only turned up after Skyship went into operation. We'd have to prove he knew something about it beforehand—not a simple task. And we'd have to know details of what the danger is. But even if we could prove he knew about the danger in the beginning, it doesn't matter what happened before the contract was signed. He has the most complete hold harmless and indemnity clauses I've ever seen. The people of AmEarth and the Empire hold him completely harmless for anything he does in his attempt to restore the atmosphere, including anything unforeseen, and including anything he might have known about all along but didn't reveal.

"He's not only protected fully, but he has a complete indemnity agreement that goes the other way—the people of AmEarth and the Empire agree to pay him for damages if anyone harms his operation. I'm surprised that indemnity clause hasn't been mentioned by Billy or his supporters, because he could make a strong legal claim against all of us, and maybe even against the citizens of the planet—at least the ones marching in the streets and writing against him—for the harm being done to his reputation. Libel and slander, pure and simple."

"Balderdash!" Moore said. "He's harmed his own reputation by being a stubborn old fool who doesn't know when it's time to quit."

She shrugged. "Who can say? The matter could be argued endlessly in court, far beyond the lifetimes of anyone here today."

"Remind me, what sort of military defenses does Jeeling have?" Racker asked. "I've forgotten some of the details, the things that have been turned up by spies we've sent in, and through other methods." He took a sip of water, looked at General Moore.

"Stiff," General Moore said. "Reagan shielding, with kinetic kill missiles, KK480 cannons, Nuke-Packs, one and two-man assault ships—along with a large fleet of armed skyminers—the works. He even has something we don't—super-cop robots that are nearly invincible, supposedly invented by Jeeling himself."

"All that's under the control of Devv Jeeling," Racker said. "His title is Security Commander, a deceptive commission. He's as much a military officer as you are, General Moore."

The young officer grunted in affirmation. "So all we can do is to attack him through public opinion, the way we've already been doing? I'd like to do more, a lot more."

"We just need to be patient," Paul Paulo said. "We're gaining important momentum, turning the public against him in increasing numbers."

"That's right," Racker said. "Patience is our byword."

"If only we could somehow get the Skyship contract declared invalid," Harrison Jennings said, "it would start the thing snowballing, turning people against Billy even more quickly."

Stuart had already been over this so she didn't comment again, except to shake her head at the impossibility of attacking the matter legally.

"Jeeling once referred to the people of AmEarth as his family," Racker said. "I found it in the transcript of a speech he gave years ago... and if that's the case, he would feel crushed if most of the public turned against him, which hasn't happened yet. Right now he's hated by large numbers of people in the biggest cities, but if the protests grow more widespread and almost everyone turns against him, he'll be emotionally crushed. I know the man, remember. And so does Paul. Billy has always been sensitive, with manic depressive tendencies, and now he might even be suicidal."

Paul Paulo nodded somberly. "That speech reveals his Achilles heel. He won't be able to take the heat if most of his 'family' turns against him. It'll eat up his insides."

"I must advise you to use the utmost caution," Stuart said, as everyone rose from their chairs, preparing to leave. "Remember what I said about Jeeling potentially accusing us of libel and slander, and besides that, we don't want to provide him with any justification for destroying his secrets. It's a delicate balance, and we need to be *extremely* careful."

"We sure as hell can't sit back and let his little game continue," General Moore said. Then he muttered something to himself. Stuart saw that he had an odd look on his face, with a very strange, cruel smile. And there was something in his eyes that she'd discerned before, something not right. Though manly and physically attractive, he did not look entirely sane to her, but no one else seemed to notice.

CHAPTER 8

For all sentient life, data passes through mental fil-
ters, so that the life-form sees only what it wants to
see, and ignores everything contrary to this world view.
This results in a distortion of reality, but it is also a key
aspect of staying sane, of filtering out anything that can
lead to madness.

—Billy Jeeling, journal entry

Billy was peering through the magnascope in his office, looking at
the nighttime surface of AmEarth, and beyond that, all the way to the
inky depths of starlit space. This was a powerful instrument, and
among the mysteries of Skyship that Branson Tobek had left for him.
The scope had the most incredibly clear resolution that Billy had ever
seen, enabling him to see even small objects on the moon. Tobek had
warned him to never open the scope up, because the internal workings were highly sensitive, and virtually impossible to repair. So far
the remarkable device had not failed, so Billy had seen no reason to
risk destroying it by trying to analyze it.

He'd received the same admonition from Tobek about Skyship itself—don't disturb the internal workings. And the warning that harm
to the great vessel would set off catastrophic, planet-wide destruction.
Not *could* set it off, but *would* set it off. A certainty. And a troubling
lack of explanation.

Some of the operations of the huge ship were automatic, while
others were not. It was the non-automatic systems that Billy understood the best, and in his office he had control panels for some of the
features—most of them camouflaged by panels and other methods,

for a more relaxed appearance. But there were other systems on Sky-ship, intriguing and frustrating to him at the same time. Still, he didn't want to tamper, didn't want to go against the wishes of the brilliant old inventor. It was a matter of common sense, because things were functioning with precision, and had been for years, even after Tobek's disturbing death in his own laboratory, while he was constructing something—something he wouldn't tell Billy about.

Now Billy vowed again, as he often did, not to disturb the sealed laboratory or anything else. It was a matter of duty for him, and of keeping his word.

He had been admonished to never go inside the laboratory com-plex where the old inventor had died. But answers were in there; Billy knew it. They could be on the pages of journals that Tobek kept, which the robots had sealed inside the tiny apartment where Tobek had lived, within Skyship's original laboratory section. On numerous occasions, Billy had seen the inventor making entries in the journals, and they comprised three thick volumes, with deep red, leather-bound covers. It would be interesting to read them, *fascinating*, Billy thought. But he was honor-bound to stay out of there.

Skyship was so large that some of its human inhabitants never left it. These were the ones who didn't feel confined on board, or any urge to visit AmEarth, the ones who loved Billy Jeeling so much that they would rather be near him than anywhere else in the Empire.

The immense craft contained office towers, apartment buildings, stores, restaurants, parks and other recreational areas, as well as en-tertainment facilities, some of which were actually utilized by the more advanced sentient robots that worked on Skyship. For human employees, room and board and clothing were provided at no charge, along with entertainment and other expenses—and generous salaries were paid. Some people placed orders for products through the inter-net, and had items delivered to them (subject to weight restrictions and safety rules), while others took shuttles down to AmEarth, and shopped personally. Whenever they returned to Skyship, they were subjected to tight security inspections, including rigorous lie-detection tests conducted by annoying robots that specialized in such things.

Dr. Rachel Ginsberg was one of the most dedicated humans on staff. She had not been on the surface of AmEarth for more than three years, and insisted she was content to never go there again—not even to visit family members or once-close friends. In her early forties, she was a scholarly, silver-haired woman with small eyes and an intelligent, thoughtful manner.

Billy watched her enter the office and take a chair in front of his gleaming desk. He met her brown-eyed gaze and smiled. Dr. Ginsberg was one of his most trusted confidantes, even more than Lainey, although Billy slept with Lainey and actually loved her.

He opened a desk drawer and brought out the round, black device that Lainey had found in his apartment. He'd dodged her questions about it, had not told her anything meaningful.

"You know what this is," he said to the doctor, knowing she'd seen it before. He placed it on the desk. "Lainey almost pressed one of the buttons. That could have caused problems, as you know, making her act erratically."

"Maybe you should just tell her the truth and get it over with. You've been hiding a pretty big secret from her for a long time. She's smart, and because you care about her, it would be best for you to volunteer the information, instead of having her find it out some other way." Dr. Ginsberg smiled gently. "I'm talking as if she were a real live flesh-and-blood woman with normal emotions, but she's not human, is she? And she can never get pregnant."

He nodded stiffly. "It's too bad about that, because she really wants a baby, but it's not possible. Lainey is my crowning achievement, one of the Lazarus-series robots who look and act so human that they are almost undetectable." There were eleven others on board Skyship, androids performing a variety of jobs, and more backup units in storage, with no imprinted human traits.

He rolled the device back and forth on the desktop, let it roll bumpily on its own until it come to a stop, just before tumbling off the edge. It wasn't perfectly round, had small flat areas around the eight recessed buttons. When in range of Lainey, he could modify her moods with the transmitter whenever she became overly emotive or argumentative—but such modifications only had a limited effect, and he had to use the device near her without letting her see what he was doing. He did the same with the other Lazarus units.

For Lainey, sometimes he used the transmitter while she was reading a technical e-file, or watching a work-related film, or doing something else that distracted her from him. If she ever became really upset, as she did on occasion, he insisted that she see Dr. Ginsberg, because it went beyond programming, and Lainey was that close to being human. For such occasions the doctor had psychological treatments that she used on the Lazarus series, along with certain medicines, some of which actually seemed to work on robots... experimental medications. As advanced as these automatons were, Lainey and the others like her were still prototypes, and Rachel and Billy were compiling files on each of them, to see what worked and what did not. Curiously, what worked on one robot did not always work on another in the same series, and that was intriguing, because Billy had designed and built each of them with the same internal workings — except some were male and others were female, and each of them had different personality and appearance imprints.

"I've tried using the transmitter on Lainey for something that has been troubling me," he said, "but she needs more treatment this time, so I want you to handle it. Her next regular physical is a couple of weeks from now, so that would be a good opportunity for you."

Dr. Ginsberg nodded. "It always seems peculiar, calling an examination of a robot a 'physical.'"

"Technically, it's more of a tune-up, isn't it?" he said.

"Yes. What exactly is troubling you about her?"

"Her intense loyalty has gone too far. I mean, she loves me too much. It's one of the things about her that I find most endearing, but—I need you to mute it a bit. She tends to be a bit... clingy at times."

"That's a new one. I thought you liked her devotion to you."

"I do, but I need some space from her, a little breathing room. Especially now, when I'm under so much pressure, facing so many problems."

"I'll see what I can do."

"Of course, I could shut Lainey down and take her back into the shop for deep work. But as you know, I used very special cellular material for her human imprinting, and I don't want to damage those cells. Besides, Lainey is an important, highly useful employee, and I do care deeply for her. I don't want to do anything too radical to her, don't want her to change too much. Just a little, OK? Maybe you can figure out what's going on in her mind and dial it back a bit."

Dr. Ginsberg nodded. "Sometimes I feel like we're playing God."

"And perhaps we are, my good and true friend. If I ever built thousands of Lazarus models—using automated factories to exponentially increase the output—we could have what looks like a new race of human beings on our hands, except they'd be androids—or maybe something in between. In any event, it could be a dangerous and unpredictable course to take. I prefer keeping the experimental group small and manageable."

"Maybe the problem with Lainey is too much for either of us to fix," Rachel said, "but I'll do my best, keeping in mind that the unique cellular material you just referred to has to receive special treatment; you took loving care to build Lainey in the image of your lost human love, Reanne, and Lainey is a remarkable likeness. She not only looks like your late wife, according to what you've shown me; she acts like her, thinks like her, has the same personality. She even has the advanced skills of a professional dancer, as Reanne did."

Billy nodded sadly, admitted, "The lovemaking is virtually the same, too. Yet she's not quite the same in other ways. Despite all the work I've done to create an exact replica of my beloved Reanne, I'm constantly noticing little differences in behavior, things no one else would ever notice, yet they don't diminish her overall personality, or her strength of character and dedication to me, which I adore. But I see the differences. Reanne was devoted to me, but not in a clinging, needy sense, not the way Lainey acts at times."

"You even gave Lainey the childhood memories of Reanne, didn't you?"

He nodded. "At least what I knew of them, including her young adult years before I met her, how she loved to dance as a child... things like that. But I wasn't actually there during Reanne's formative years, only knew what she told me about them afterward. And apparently the background of her that I implanted in the Lainey robot is lacking something significant, resulting in a slightly different person — or machine person, I should say."

"I'm terribly sorry your Reanne died," Rachel said. "Knowing Lainey, I can see that Reanne was an incredible person. I wish I could have known her."

"You do in a way, through the robot I built in her likeness. Reanne could have been a professional dancer, and I think she would have become one, too, if she hadn't met me. I was overly demanding of her time, didn't leave her enough space for her to be herself. It's something I can never make up for."

Rachel fell silent. From the caring look in her eyes, she seemed to notice that he was slipping into silent melancholy. She let him reflect for a few moments.

Billy's eyes misted over as he thought back. His wife — they'd only been married a year — died in a tragic accident thirty-seven years ago, when an earthquake destroyed an apartment building and took her life, along with dozens of others. At the time, Billy had been working on Skyship with Branson Tobek, going over a list of instructions the old inventor had for Billy to pass on to the robotic contractors. They were just getting the great vessel finished at the time of the tragedy, and had been working intensely on it for years. If Billy hadn't been spending so much time with the old man he might have been killed with Reanne, because they had been living together. She'd been barely thirty, filled with love for him and hopes for their life together. Reanne would have done anything for him, and in the brief time they'd had together, she had done exactly that.

With all the pain Billy had been feeling since her loss, he often wished he had died with her. It was a recurring thought, and he'd been having it with more frequency lately as he endured the pressures being put on him by his enemies, and the mounting public outcry against him. The unrelenting campaign of character assassination.

Life was so unfair — to Reanne, and to him.

CHAPTER 9

Bad taste is one of the principle characteristics of empire.

—Branson Tobek, historical observation

At midday, Yürgen Zayeddi disembarked from the shuttle with other recruits. He was tired from all the last-minute preparations for the trip, but thrilled to be invited to Skyship. He was anxious to meet Billy Jeeling personally, but realized that might never be possible. From what he'd heard, he would be lucky to get a glimpse of the legendary figure, perhaps when he gave one of his speeches on board the vessel.

The seventeen recruits had been talking during the flight, wondering what it would be like to actually be on the giant air-cleansing and mining facility, working on behalf of the great man. Yürgen had been conversing the most with Sim Robie, a young man who had obtained his training assignment through family connections, but whose zeal for Billy Jeeling matched Yürgen's.

"We're extremely lucky to be included," Robie had said. "This is the opportunity of a lifetime." He had a round, jowly face with large, dark eyes.

"The opportunity of a *lifetime*? Why do you say that?" a woman had asked, from across the aisle. The oldest of the trainees, LaBecca Moscone appeared to be at least forty, with a stocky build and spiky, auburn hair.

"Because this is our chance to serve Billy Jeeling, of course," Robie had said. "It is a great honor, and a rare privilege." He'd looked annoyed that she would even ask such a question, and Yürgen shared his feelings.

Some of the recruits had speculated about what the public relations training would be like, but no one seemed to know. They only knew that they would learn how to spread the truth about Billy Jeeling throughout the Empire, and would be called JeeJees, a special force of Billy Jeeling loyalists.

Now they all walked down a metal rampway, each of them carrying a matching shoulder bag that had been provided for the few personal effects they were allowed to bring with them. At the bottom, an attractive young blonde waited, looking at them closely, disapprovingly, absorbing all details. Her dress was black with tan trim, tight across her full bosom and cut high on the thighs. She was tall and leggy, with skin of the palest, most delicate hue. A blue crescent of stars adorned her left shoulder, the famous emblem of the JeeJees who dedicated their lives to serving Billy Jeeling. Yürgen envied her for that, hoped he would earn his own crescent soon.

"Welcome to Skyship," the young woman said, with a curt smile. "I am Sandra Orr, one of the proctors. This way, please."

She showed the way to a highlift that took them up several floors. When they stepped off, Orr led them toward a high-arched doorway that was framed by Doric columns, through which Zayeddi could see a busy sidewalk and people on it, bustling back and forth. Just beyond them he saw a coffee shop and a toy store, both with illuminated signs. It had never occurred to him that there might be children on Skyship, but there must be families working here, so the toy retailer made sense. He even saw one woman with a small terrier on a leash, so there were pets here, too. The dog yapped at a passerby, but she pulled it away.

At the doorway, a towering robot stepped in front of the recruits. At least twice as tall as the smaller one Yürgen had seen on AmEarth, it also had a vertical light tube on the front—except instead of pulsing soft orange, this one throbbed an array of colors, the entire spectrum of visible light.

"A truthbot," Orr said. "It will probe more deeply into your minds than you already experienced on AmEarth. This advanced model has several methods of truth detection, one of which is to ask you questions. If that is the method employed, you must take extreme care to answer honestly, concealing nothing—because hiding information is the same as lying."

"And what if we do lie?" one of the recruits asked, in a smart-aleck tone. "Do we get killed on the spot?" Small and thin, he had baby-soft features and long, dishwater blond hair.

Orr glared at him. "This is a very serious matter, and the sooner you understand that, the better off you'll be. There have been sabotage attempts against this ship, and our security force—mostly robots—must be on constant alert. If you even hint at being disloyal, it will not go well for you."

She smiled, with a cruel edge. "You might wish you were killed on the spot when you find out what is in store for you."

The recruit reddened, stammered something Yürgen could not hear. Yürgen's thoughts raced. What had she meant by that remark? Torture? It seemed impossible, but for such an important cause—for the essential task Billy had taken on—perhaps there were no limits when it came to maintaining security, to keep Skyship going. He didn't have to worry personally, because he felt only dedication to Billy, and a desire to do everything he could to advance the glorious mission of Skyship.

As it turned out, this truthbot did not ask questions. Its entire body glowed the spectrum of colors, and its variegated light washed over each of the recruits, one at a time. Yürgen watched Sim Robie stand erect, straight and true, without flinching or wavering, followed by the smart-aleck recruit, who stood there shaking during the process, his face a mask of fear. He grimaced, as if in pain. But he passed, like Robie. Or they both seemed to, as the robot kept moving on.

When Yürgen's turn came, he understood the grimace. As moments passed with the light still on him, his head ached and he felt brief, sharp lances of pain, little needle pricks, as if something was piercing the cells of his brain, probing and traveling into them. He must have made a face, and almost cried out, but didn't. Fortunately, the process did not take long, and the pain went away quickly.

As soon as all of the recruits had been inspected without incident, the truthbot stepped back, and its scary spectrum of light melted back into its body. Sonya Orr touched a plate on the robot's torso, then read a small screen there, lit up in the middle. "All of you are in the good to excellent range," she announced as she turned to face them, "you all did well."

Zayeddi wondered what the difference was between good and excellent, but didn't ask. Wasn't the truth an inflexible thing? At least the way she'd described it, where nothing could be concealed? Though curious, he did not want to ask a question that might single him out, saying something that could put him — he almost chuckled at the unintentional witticism — in a bad light.

Sandra Orr said, "I see that some of you have interesting skills, which can be useful here on Skyship. While public relations will be your primary assignments, a couple of you will be assigned to backup duties. LaBecca Moscone, I see that you worked as a sous-chef for a top restaurant. I want you to serve periodically on a food-inspection team, when needed. That is of great importance on this vessel, where food-borne illnesses can be so harmful. If you do well at that, you might be assigned to a team that checks food, preventing Billy Jeeling from being poisoned. And Yürgen Zayeddi, you apparently know how to operate humbabies. What is your skill level?"

"Fairly good. I learned how to fly from a co-worker at the hum-baby plant where I worked. She said I was proficient at it, but I got fired before being able to work in the department I wanted, where I could have flown humbabies regularly for quality control."

"Sounds like brave work, being a test-pilot."

He laughed. "Oh, humbabies are quite safe. Even with defective mechanisms, the cabins are built of high-strength plastics, with high-tech interior cushioning, restraints, and puff-bags. Humbabies have been known to fall out of the sky and just bounce. Pilots walk away from accidents all the time."

"Is that so? Can you operate the morph-babies, too? The ones that change shape and are capable of connecting to other craft of their kind?"

"Yeah, those, too. No problem at all. In fact, they're the most fun of all."

"We have them here on Skyship," she said. "The cops use them."

"I know. The company where I used to work is one of your major suppliers."

"Well, you are to report to security headquarters and demonstrate your flying skills, with the idea that you might become a reserve pilot, called to duty in case of emergency."

He nodded.

Sandra Orr picked out a couple of others for comment, then went on to say that she was pleased to have so many truthful recruits. She narrowed her gaze. "I'd hate to have to order punishments for people when they have barely set foot on Skyship."

He couldn't tell if she was kidding or not. Maybe not. She didn't appear to be unkind, but looked very serious, and that robot with her looked deadly, with its no-nonsense demeanor and panels on its body that undoubtedly concealed weapons.

Yürgen hefted his shoulder bag into place and adjusted the strap, as he and his companions followed the attractive woman through the high doorway, to the sidewalk beyond. As he passed the Doric columns he noticed they were cracked and chipped, and the surface beneath Zayeddi's feet was of a marble-like material, with swirls of black and white. It was badly scratched and worn. The group emerged into the middle of the cavernous interior of Skyship City, a disorienting sensation to him, as he'd thought they would be on one edge of the airborne metropolis, because of where they docked. Buildings around him had unsightly gray or brown patches on their sides, and streaks of black. He found all of this surprising, even startling.

The scale of the flying city was staggering, as he found himself in the midst of a dense conglomeration of high-rise buildings, with hovercars and hoverbuses flying among them, and the odd little helicopter-like humbabies—faster than hovercars—speeding about in large numbers, most of them carrying only one passenger. There were numerous businesses on the street... a restaurant, a clothing store, a pharmacy, a movie theater, and more. He didn't see any children, but they might be in school.

A group of JeeJees passed by on the sidewalk, wearing black and tan shirts and pants, and he noticed other people milling about nearby, looking around and up at the tall buildings—they were members of various races who were dressed in the colorful provincial costumes of the Empire, yet these were obviously expensive outfits made of fine fabrics with the best tailoring, gold embroidery, and tiers of jewelry. This group looked quite wealthy, and conducted themselves with the perfect posture and demeanor of the high-bred. Confirming this to him, Sonya said they were members of elite native families around the world who were financial supporters of Billy Jeeling, and had made large donations to Skyship. To get on board, they had undergone the usual security checks, including examination by truthbots.

He heard them speaking different dialects. Zayeddi had a good ear, and had worked with various nationalities in his former job. To him they sounded Slavic, AmAnglo, Oriental, Spanish, French, AmAfrican, and perhaps even Latin. Other people, and robots, hurried along a sidewalk that ran parallel to the first one he'd seen—with each sidewalk handling only one-way traffic, going in opposite directions. He saw no motorized vehicles, no place for them, with the exception of a handful of morph-babies at street level, moving carefully through the crowds with uniformed police officers inside, apparently making their customary security rounds.

"I'll show you to your living quarters," Orr said. "The building is within walking distance." Getting close to her, Yürgen noticed that she smelled of an exotic perfume, an unknown (but pleasing) scent to him.

She motioned for the trainees to follow, and led the way at a brisk pace along the sidewalk beneath tall buildings. Yürgen hurried to keep up, moving to her side ahead of the other recruits, and going around other people ahead of them who were not walking as rapidly.

Whenever possible he craned his neck to look upward. The towering buildings were in a variety of architectural styles, many with store-fronts on the street level. Beyond the tops of the buildings he saw what looked like a blue sky, with wisps of clouds—but he knew it had to be artificial. At this altitude, the thin atmosphere wouldn't look like that, and would be darker, with the twinkling vastness of space showing—as he'd seen from the shuttle before it went into its docking clamps.

Now Zayeddi detected a slight odor in the air, a chlorine-like pungency that he presumed was Billy Jeeling's secret air-restoration mixture, or something from the skyminers that worked in the skies over AmEarth.

"As you may know," Orr said, "we're in the mesosphere at the moment, but will be dropping lower in the atmosphere tomorrow. A lot of thrust is required to move this immense vessel around. We're roughly the shape of a blimp—a huge one—but we are not a lighter-than-air craft. There are two hundred thousand solar-powered rocket-thrusters on Skyship, with many of them firing constantly to maintain altitude and attitude. If all the systems fail, we drop like a rock." She chuckled. "But don't worry. There are so many backup systems that the chances of falling out of the sky are infinitesimal—short of some major, unforeseen disaster, of course."

"I've read about the thruster system," Yürgen said. "A secret rocket fuel is used, I believe. There are many secret mixtures around here, from what I hear, more than just the formula Billy Jeeling uses to recondition the atmosphere."

"I wouldn't know about that," the young woman responded, with an edge to her tone.

Appearing to be a little put off by his comment, she stopped and waited for the other recruits to catch up, who were being delayed by throngs of children emerging from a school building. They made happy, boisterous sounds. More children were coming from other directions, threading their way through the crowd, entering the building.

His gaze caught hers for a lingering moment. Orr's eyes were almond-shaped, and forest green. She called out to the others, who were finally catching up with them.

"It's the end of one school shift," she explained, "and the beginning of another one. Work shifts are that way, too. All the buildings on Skyship are in operation twenty-four / seven. Even here, where the interior of the great ship looks so large, space is at a premium."

She led them around a corner, and in another two blocks she climbed the steps to enter the ground floor of a high-rise building that had enclosed balconies on the front, as did other structures in this block. She stopped in the lobby.

"You've each been issued a small studio apartment," Orr said. "Prepare yourselves for this mentally, because the units are *very* small. Nothing fancy here... and mine isn't much larger. How much space does a person need, anyway?"

No one answered the rhetorical question.

They took a highlift to the sixty-eighth floor, and Sonya Orr led them along a narrow, disturbingly dingy corridor. A gray mouse scurried by underfoot, but no one said anything. Orr opened a door, revealing a small, utilitarian room. "Mr. Zayeddi, you're here."

His eyebrows raised. "Is this my apartment?"

She smiled. "I know, it looks like no more than an inelegant little room, but it is efficiently laid out, so we like to call it an apartment."

Grinning, he said, "As long as I can get through the doorway and find a place to lie down and sleep, it's big enough for me."

"That's the attitude I want to see!" At least she wasn't upset with him anymore, so she seemed to have forgotten about his earlier comments—or at least she was willing to overlook them.

She slid a key-transmitter ring onto the forefinger of his right hand, and in a moment it tightened to fit snugly. These devices were so common that she didn't ask if he knew how to use it. He noted a round blue spot on top, where he would need to press to open the door, and lock it when he was inside.

He stepped inside while she paused in the doorway. The small room had no windows and was quite dark, even when the ceiling lights went on automatically as he stepped inside. He intended to make the best of it, though, and smiled to himself. For sure, this wasn't really an apartment, and was barely a room.

"Any questions?" she asked.

"No, this will do just fine."

She nodded. "I know it's a sacrifice to live so frugally, but you're going to be given an important job after you complete training—an infinitely more important position than you've ever had before. You can take a break for this evening, but meet me in the lobby tomorrow morning for breakfast, with the other recruits. A buzzer will ring in your room at 5:15 when it's time to wake up. You will then have forty-five minutes to get ready and show up downstairs."

She moved on with the others, leaving him alone in his bleak surroundings. Yürgen closed and locked the door, then removed his backpack and unloaded the clothing and other personal articles into a compartment under the bed. The room was efficiently laid out, he had to admit, with a small closet and high shelves. It had no bathroom, but a sign and diagram on the inside of the door described where it was, a shared facility down the corridor. There was no kitchen, either, but he did see an electric tea pot and a container of wrapped teas. He lifted the pot, saw no place to fill it with water. Must have to take it to the bathroom. He sighed.

Yürgen removed his clothing, climbed wearily into bed. Even though the mattress was stiff and uncomfortable, he was deeply fatigued, and didn't think it would take long for him to fall asleep. But he was so excited at actually being on Billy Jeeling's great ship that he laid awake for more than an hour.

CHAPTER 10

The stars are a marvelous symphony of light.

—Billy Jeeling, to his son Devv

Lainey appreciated everything Billy did for her. This private dance studio, for one thing. It wasn't large, because space was limited on Skyship. But it had a nice hardwood floor, sturdy bars for stretching, and even mirrored walls, so that she could watch her moves and perfect them. Paintings of dancers adorned the walls, including one that was her favorite of all, a reproduction of *The Rehearsal*, by Edgar Degas.

Dancing had always seemed so natural to Lainey, as if she had been born with the ability. She had never taken lessons, but recalled performing in her home as a small child, with her parents, brothers, and cousins for an audience, and their enthusiastic applause. They had always encouraged her, and so had Billy.

Now she wore a white skirt and black leotard, as she went through a series of jazz dance exercises that she liked to do each day for conditioning—energetic moves that included acrobatic leaps in the air, tumbles, and jazz splits. It pleased her that she could perform some of the most difficult routines without professional training, but today she felt a little out of breath. Yet, overall, her conditioning program had a positive effect on her. When she completed these exercises, she often performed a series of graceful *pas seul* ballet routines.

Billy Jeeling seemed to care deeply for her, but at times she had the uneasy sense that she was not enough for him. Other women flirted with the famous man all the time, but as far as she knew he didn't return their attentions. Even the relationship he had with Dr. Rachel Ginsberg seemed platonic — Lainey was more confident about that now, though she had once harbored doubts, and fears, about what was going on between them. But recently she and Rachel had engaged in a long, heart to heart conversation, and Lainey went away with the strong impression that the scholarly woman was not her competitor, at least not directly. Rachel was devoted to Billy; that much was quite apparent. Yet she insisted that she didn't expect more than a professional relationship with him. Then she'd qualified that statement by adding, "Not as long as he cares about you as much as he does."

Assuming that was true, it put Rachel in a backup position to Lainey — one woman waiting for another to make a mistake. Lainey didn't like that tenuous arrangement, but at least Rachel had seemed truthful, and honorable in her actions, and didn't impress her as the type who would do things behind Lainey's back. If the roles were reversed, Lainey might have acted the same way. Even at Billy's advanced age, he was an extremely attractive man, and she held no delusions that other women would not line up at his proverbial doorstep, seeking his affections. Rachel seemed to be at the head of that line, and keeping this in mind, Lainey always took great care not to make mistakes, while showing Billy how much she cared about him all the time, constantly telling him how much she loved him.

Lainey took a short break, used one of the stretching bars for her calves and hamstrings. In the stillness of the moment, she heard those irritating machine sounds again. Faint and barely perceptible, like a person with mild tinnitus of the ears who heard ringing whenever focusing upon it, yet trying not to think about it most of the time.

Her thoughts returned to Billy, as they did so often. Was she showing him too much affection? Was she smothering him with her attentions, leaving him no room to breathe? At times he did seem mildly irritated with her, or perhaps it was his natural impatience to get back to his important work. The truth be told, Lainey realized, his work came first, and both Lainey and Rachel were in line for whatever he had left after devoting his energies to his critical environmental restoration work. It was because of his tremendous success in that endeavor that he was the most famous man in the world, and probably the most famous man who would ever live.

Sensing movement on her left, she saw Devv Jeeling enter the studio and stand just inside the doorway, waiting for her. He wore his blue Security Commander's uniform, neatly pressed. The young black man carried his silver-braided officer's cap, and his curly hair glistened, as if he had just showered.

Lainey and Billy's son were good friends, and professionally they often discussed police and other security matters that Devv handled for the great ship, and how they coordinated with Lainey's public relations efforts. Sometimes she even relaxed her guard and told him how she felt about his father, and the young man was kind enough to give her useful advice.

Now she completed her dance routine, finishing with a double somersault and landing perfectly on her feet, facing him.

"Not bad," he said, reaching out to touch her forehead. "A little more perspiration than the last time I saw you, though. You need to maintain your conditioning better."

She smiled stiffly. "I am not one of your departmental recruits." By that, she meant the human ones. "Is there a problem?" she inquired, while leading him to a tiny alcove where she kept a dispenser machine for coffee, tea, and other beverages.

They ordered cups of steaming aromatic coffee, and stood while sipping them, instead of sitting on chairs that could be folded open from the wall.

"I want to talk to you about Sonya," he said. "I asked her to marry me, but she said she has too much work to do on Skyship for that, too much responsibility with her job. Her *job*? She's a proctor, working for you, Lainey. That's not such a huge job, not like mine; you have several other proctors like her. From what I hear, their workload isn't so big. In contrast, I run an entire police-and-security force, more than four thousand machine and human officers. I'm the one with all the responsibilities and concerns, but Sonya makes a comment about *her* job? I'm deeply afraid that it's just an excuse, that she's slipping away from me."

"Maybe she really means that your job is in the way, not hers."

"Then why doesn't she just come out and say that? Why be indirect?"

Lainey smiled. "Women can be like that at times. But you might be on the right track. Maybe it is something else, and not her work at all. I've watched you two together, and talked with you enough to think that maybe you need to back off a little, Devv. Maybe you put too much pressure on Sonya. She could feel smothered by your constant attentions."

"Did she tell you that?"

"No, but I bring this up because I've been wondering the same thing about my own behavior toward Billy, if I've been pushing him too hard, not giving him enough space. It could be, so I'm wondering if you and I are both making the same mistake." She paused. "I can't say for sure if that's what either of us are doing wrong, if anything, but it's just a thought."

He shook his head. "No, I think she has other reasons. I've been getting reports on Sonya from my officers, so I know she's flirtatious with some of the men on the ship, including her own students. Perhaps it is all innocent, but she is playing with fire, especially with her physical beauty."

"I've never seen her doing anything like that."

"Actually, I have confirming videos taken by robots on my force. Her flirtations are mild, at least in public, but they do exist. I'm not making it up."

"I see. It sounds rather, uh, French? Or Italian? Innocent flirtations are a way of life in some societies, and Sonya's father was French, wasn't he?"

"Yes, you could be right. Maybe I'm reading too much into it. But I always think of the old adage, 'where there's smoke there's fire,' so I'm going to keep my eye on her. Both eyes, in fact."

"You are a policeman, after all, among your duties for the security of Skyship."

Devv nodded.

"She is awfully pretty," Lainey said, "so other men naturally take notice of her. Tall and blonde with blue eyes. You have your hands full."

"You and I are both suffering from unrequited love," Devv said, ruefully. "Maybe we should get involved with each other and forget those other two."

"We're good friends, Devv. You know that. Just good friends."

He sipped his coffee as he stood there, made a face as if it didn't taste good and slipped it into a waste processor chute, generating a brief noise of machinery.

"Yeah," he said. "I know that. Anyway, thanks for the talk. Now I gotta get back to work." He turned and walked away, crossing the practice floor.

It seemed to Lainey that something was not quite right about Devv Jeeling; she'd been thinking this way for some time now, without knowing exactly what it was that bothered her. She had no evidence that anything was wrong with him, not in the slightest, except for a nagging tickle in her brain that wouldn't go away, a sense that something was slightly off about him, something he wasn't revealing to her.

He could not possibly be a danger to Billy, because he was the great man's son and heir apparent, and Billy had always treated him extremely well. Devv had never complained to her about Billy, and had always challenged anyone who dared to make even the slightest negative comment about his father.

She knew, as well, that Devv had saved his father two years ago from an attempt on his life, when a pair of assassins managed to get past several levels of security, and were apprehended when Devv saw the scan reports on them, and noticed their suspicious behavior. He later said he only sensed something about them, that they were not really the legitimate businessmen they had been portraying themselves to be, and were not actually there to discuss making a large financial donation to Billy's pet project.

Devv had sensed something then, just as Lainey was sensing something about him now. She felt absolutely certain that he posed no danger to Billy. So, it had to be something else. But what?

CHAPTER 11

Skyship is a money-making machine for Billy Jeeling.
The only question is, where is he hiding all of his ill-gotten treasure?

—Connor Luxor, formerly a trusted Jeeling adviser, now considered a traitor by the JeeJees

It was a clear, sunny day, with the sky the prettiest shade of blue that Maureen Stuart had ever seen. Wearing a black helmet with a golden emblem, she stood by a rocket cycle outside Imperial City, waiting to board it as a passenger, while its pilot went through a safety check. They were at one of Jonathan Racker's many industrial sites, a private landing field for company executives. Her sprained wrist was feeling better, but she had not removed the wrap from it yet.

The rocket cycle was long, bright blue and sleek, with black, swept-back wings, tight by the frame, and two seats, one in front of the other. It was one of the larger models. Each seat had a storage compartment underneath, containing capsules filled with anti-Jeeling leaflets. The cycle's canopy was swung open now, and the pilot—a young Asian man in a rumpled gray suit and blue helmet—was examining it closely, checking the locking devices. She'd been wanting to go up in the air on one of these machines for some time now, because she liked to experience all aspects of the campaign against Billy Jeeling, so that she could offer more reasoned opinions on everything to her superiors.

Maureen did not particularly enjoy working against the man who had created Skyship. In her mid-forties now, she recalled being a child and admiring him and his exploits, and she had family members who had been saved by his amazing environmental actions. At least that was what her Uncle Eddie had told her, based upon having lost two brothers and his mother to environmentally-caused cancers, in the time before Billy restored the ozone layer, removed pollutants, and made other atmospheric improvements. Her family, with roots tracing back to Ireland and Scotland, were all fair-skinned, with red-dish hair—traits that were said to make them more susceptible to sunburns and serious skin conditions. Maureen had lost her favorite little cousin, Sandy, to melanoma.

In her teens Maureen had even fantasized about marrying Billy one day, just one of millions of girls and women who'd felt that way. He was so handsome, and such a gallant, heroic figure. But all that changed when Maureen was hired by Jonathan Racker and Paul Paulo to analyze the contracts Jeeling had entered into with the AmEarth government, granting him a monopoly on all skymining and atmospheric restoration work. It was then, upon digging into the legalese and into other details about Billy's business dealings, that she began to share the same feelings as his detractors. Any good the man had ever done in his life was not worth the monopoly he held, a dynasty in effect, as his son Devv was slated to take over after Billy was gone.

Growing up, she'd only been able to see the good in Billy, even though she vaguely remembered criticisms of him, even then. Now it was the exact opposite; she couldn't see much, if anything, good about him—at least not the way he was behaving now—and she was convinced that he had exploited a good cause to advance himself and his family, at the expense of the citizens of AmEarth. He was not the first to hide behind a good cause for personal gain; there had been many historical examples. But he seemed like the worst of all.

"It's safe to board now, ma'am," the pilot said, after introducing himself as Hiroki Iwakuma. He was quite good looking, with light brown skin, alert eyes, and a nice smile. Knowing it was her first time on a rocket cycle, he helped her into the seat behind his own, showed her how the safety restraints worked as he connected them into place. Not that they would do much good if this thing crashed, she thought. But she wasn't in the least bit afraid. He looked attentive and compe-tent, the machine was almost new, and she enjoyed adventure. He closed the visor of her helmet over her face, secured it in place, and smiled confidently.

There were missionaries like Iwakuma all over the world, dispatched on rocket cycles to spread negative information about Billy Jeeling and everything he did, business or personal. Admittedly, some of the material involved distortions and innuendos, even some outright lies — but Maureen had vetted everything legally, and given her blessings. Let him sue the organizers of the campaign, one of her bosses had said to her, Jonathan Racker. The uber-wealthy industrialist actually seemed to welcome legal action, saying it would only increase the amount of bad publicity against Jeeling — because most of what they had been saying about him was true, or based on truth, and Jeeling wouldn't win that battle for his reputation. Even if he recovered monetary damages for libel or slander, he would lose in the end, because so much of the truth would come out, and he would not look good in the bright light being cast on him. Without any doubt, Billy had fabricated his family history, and had probably lied about his education and early work experience as well.

Iwakuma was in his seat ahead of hers now, and he fired up the twin jet engines, producing a smooth, powerful purr. The canopy clicked shut over them.

"Hang on," he said across a speaker inside her helmet. He glanced back over his shoulder, around his high seat back. "You ready for this?"

"Of course," she said. "Don't hold anything back on account of me."

"Knowing you're a lawyer, maybe I should have had you sign a legal release," he quipped. But he didn't wait for her reply, and hit the jets.

Maureen's head jerked back against her seat, and for several seconds she closed her eyes. The sensation of speed was more sudden and extreme than anything she'd ever experienced before.

Feeling invigorated, she shouted into her helmet, "Can't you make this thing go any faster?"

"You're kidding, ma'am. We're at top acceleration now, and from the look on your face that I see on my screen, you're more than a little scared."

She didn't reply, held onto a bar in front of her as the cycle banked right and left, then shot almost straight up and then abruptly down, as the pilot was apparently trying to get her to scream out in fear.

Maureen grinned, hoped he was looking at her on the screen now. She might have felt a little trepidation moments ago, but she didn't feel any at all now, and was confident that her facial expression showed this.

"You've got a lot of guts, ma'am. Have to give that to you." Iwakuma chuckled as the craft settled into steady flight at a more moderate speed, skimming over the rooftops of apartment buildings below. "I wouldn't want to be a passenger if you were at the controls, though. Pardon me for saying so, but you might be a little bit crazy."

"You've got me figured out perfectly," she said. "A thrill seeker, that's what I am." She wasn't really that, at least not to an extreme. But it amused Maureen to say it. She touched a button in front of her, as he'd told her to do when she wanted, and watched one of the canisters shoot out of the side of the craft. Looking down, she saw it open in midair and spread leaflets over the neighborhood below.

The message was yet another demand for Billy Jeeling to turn the operation of Skyship over to the Imperial government—quotes from leading officials saying this, including Prime Minister Renaldo Yhatt. Public opinion against Billy was mounting rapidly, and if it kept going like this, his detractors would soon be in the majority. Now it was still a slim majority in Billy's favor, but not so long ago his approval rating had been more than 90%. That was before the concerted campaign to get him to quit, a campaign that was producing good results.

Admittedly, it was an ugly smear campaign, and might not be totally fair to the man. She'd used that term to her superiors, and they'd said that was exactly what they wanted. Take him from beloved hero to despised goat, from point A to point B as quickly as possible. That's how they projected the end of Billy's career, calling it "an unfortunate necessity." Already his popularity was plummeting, and soon it would crash.

She and Iwakuma released the rest of their canisters. Then the pilot turned around in a sharp u-turn, and headed back to the landing field.

CHAPTER 12

*The process of learning—of really learning about a
thing—is one of the great challenges of life, and for me
the most rewarding.*

—Branson Tobek, opening entry in his laboratory journals

Following the secret instructions of Branson Tobek, Billy Jeeling
had supervised the construction of a high walkway, a sky bridge in
the shape of an immense Cross of Jesus, stretching half the length of
the great ship, laid on the tops of several high-rise buildings, directly
beneath the matching arrangement of clear exterior domes that
looked out into space. When the lights on the cross were activated
and illumination was thrown into the domes, the symbol glowed so
brightly that it could be seen from the heavens—and from AmEarth
when the great ship was geostationary and tilted toward the planet.
The unusual walkway and its central maglev track was a favorite retreat for Billy, and he often spent time meditating there, thinking
about his many challenges.

He had other places to go as well, such as a secret room at the pinnacle of Skyship, a spot that was even more elevated than the
domes—but he only went up there on rare occasions, because his
maglev chair could not get him to the pinnacle, though he still had an
alternate, less comfortable way of getting there.

Billy was the only one who operated a maglev unit on the high
walkway and track—in his case the unique high-speed chair—but he
did allow a small number of managers to utilize the narrow walkways on either side of the track, for getting from one building to another, and for conducting business with him.

It was late night now, and Billy sat alone in his unique custom chair, at the crux of the cross, the heart of the great religious symbol. With the lights of the cross switched off, he gazed upward, into the starlit sky. He identified the constellations he was seeing, having learned them by name from Tobek, and had memorized them. Billy and the old inventor had not taken many breaks, as both of them worked very hard — but on occasion they had taken time off together, and invariably they used such occasions to come up here and gaze out into the majesty and mystery of the universe.

Yet when Billy thought about it after Tobek's death, it occurred to him that constellation names were worthless, since they were merely human reference points, for mortal purposes. God did not need anything like that. The Supreme Being knew where everything was in the cosmos, and could journey to any destination, anytime He chose to do so. Or, perhaps He already occupied each of those places simultaneously — and was not a bearded old man in the sky at all. Yes, Billy rather liked the thought of a deity that was simultaneously everywhere at the same time. It might be the God of Christianity, or an all-inclusive deity that was an amalgamation of the beliefs of all major religious faiths.

Billy had never considered himself to be a Christian. And even Tobek's religious beliefs seemed to be on the fringes of Christianity, in Billy's view, because Branson had never attended church, and had not done the things that Christians customarily did. He just had this Christian symbol, this huge cross, and had never answered questions put to him about it. Billy thought it was spectacular, though, and a perfect setting in which he could seek and find calmness.

To Billy, the giant cross symbolized something far broader than one religious faith, and even more than the combination of all major religions, because such concepts were limited by human perception. It didn't take much of a leap in thinking to realize that there had to be other perceptions out in the galaxy, beyond anything involving AmEarth and its self-serving, plundering Empire. Here at the heart of the great symbol, alone at night and gazing into the heavens, he felt a deep, all-inclusive spirituality.

But this evening, in the smallest portion of himself, his *human* self, he also felt a deep sense of hopelessness, that he was being whipped one way and another by events on the surface of the planet beneath him, and could do little or nothing to influence them. Things were turning against him too quickly for him to keep up.

He had devoted most of his life to the welfare of AmEarth. His eyes misted over in sadness. Despite all he'd done for the benefit of humankind, he had kept no financial benefits for himself, and lived very simply, rather like an austere priest, it seemed to him. Billy had never accepted invitations to appear in parades, had never agreed to receive the numerous medals, honorary degrees and ribbons that had been offered to him. He had sanctioned no ostentatious statues, no plaques, no world holidays in his name, no honoraria of any kind... though all had been offered at one time or another, and a great deal more. Each time he'd ever heard about anything like that, he'd always let it be known that he did not want it, and had taken steps to prevent it.

People seemed to have forgotten that.

He realized now that he might have done better if he'd allowed the monuments to go up, if he'd received all the honoraria. It would have strengthened and enhanced his public image, his legend. Yet, that was not something he'd ever sought, so perhaps it was for the best that he had avoided such trappings.

And he did have great riches after all, earned from Skyship. These riches were of tremendous value, though they were not monetary. Instead, they amounted to his personal fame and the positive feelings this had given him for decades, and to his tacit "ownership" of Skyship, and the ability to pass it on to his son, Devv. To some extent, he understood what riches his enemies were after. Perhaps he had sinned by enjoying his fame too much, and by designating Devv as his successor. But when he named Devv, it was not what anyone thought. Not at all. They would be surprised if they knew the real reason, very surprised.

There were endless secrets surrounding the workings of Billy's inner mind, and his activities, compartmentalized so that one person knew certain things and another did not. He thought of all the secrets Branson Tobek had kept from him, and which perplexed him to this day. Those secrets were vitally important, and Billy wondered why they had been kept from him. He'd always assumed that Tobek had intended to reveal them eventually, but had died too soon.

Why, if Tobek was not a practicing Christian, did he make the statement of placing a giant cross high inside the vaulted interior of Skyship? Billy had asked him that very question several times, and had made other inquiries about his religious and spiritual beliefs, and always Branson had said that his beliefs were his own, and not easily explained in words. It had almost sounded Zen to Billy, like a wordless truth. But the old inventor had wanted the huge Christian cross, and gone to great pains to make certain it was built according to his exact specifications.

There had been clues about Tobek's spirituality, though. Billy knew that he had essentially been a pacifist, because he had railed against the endless succession of wars caused by male aggression and imperialism, and had said that there should be more female energy in the star system to balance the violent, destructive tendencies of men. So, in putting up the great symbol, Tobek might have been harkening back to the remarkable Sermon on the Mount of Jesus, and to other peaceful things the Christ said, many of which were recounted in the *Bible* and other religious texts. Tobek must not have been honoring the crusades or other terrible wars fought in the name of Christianity, wars that the deeply nonviolent Jesus would never have condoned.

Yet why hadn't Tobek chosen an earlier symbol of Christianity, the fish? The answer came to Billy when he recalled that Tobek once said he admired the brave way that Jesus had died on the cross, and how he'd done that for the sake of humankind, making a great and historic sacrifice. In his own way, Tobek had also died for humanity, though he could not have seen that coming, the disturbing, horrible way he was killed.

And now Billy Jeeling was himself nailed to a symbolic cross, dying from the wounds inflicted on his reputation, the assassination of his good name. After all he'd done for people, it had come to this.

Despite his personal suffering and the depressions it sent him into, Billy didn't really like Lainey's public relations campaign, even though he had agreed to let her conduct it on a limited basis, and it was for his benefit. He felt that the truth should win out if it deserved to win out.

But life wasn't that way, not at all. For him, it was not following that particular script.

A political leader of centuries past, a beloved American president who was ultimately assassinated, once observed that life was not fair. How prescient and ironic. And true! The thoughts gave Billy some solace; at least he was not the only person to ever have been treated unfairly, far from it. It happened all the time. Not on the scale it was happening to him, perhaps, but all of the time nonetheless. It was part of the human condition, part of the suffering of mankind. It was history, it was the present, it was the future.

He activated his smart watch, saw the green dial light up. Almost 2:00 am.

Just then a person approached on one of the walkways, wearing an illuminated headlamp. Soon Billy recognized the characteristic stride of Devv Jeeling. His son was always punctual. Billy had summoned him here to talk. They did this on the elevated walkway whenever they could, on nights when they could have solitude and gaze into the timeless, serene infinity of the universe.

It wasn't as if Billy had anything really important to say to Devv this time. There were certain things he could not tell him. But in Billy's increasing despondency he liked to talk with his son, and with the others who were close to him, including Lainey Forster and Rachel Ginsberg. Now it was Devv's turn.

The younger man paused on the walkway, next to Billy's high-tech chair, which rested on a raised maglev track, so that the eye levels of the two men were the same. Billy activated a panel of soft lights around his chair, and Devv switched off the headlamp.

"I'm happy to come to you whenever you need me, Father. Even though I've had a long day, and just had a bad argument with Sonya over her flirtations with other men. Before that, it was a day full of police problems, sapping me of energy. I've told you we need more human officers, and again I request your blessing to get more. Sometimes the robots are problematic, not responding well to unusual situations, even though they were programmed to do so. Humans are naturally more adaptable."

"That is true, but I assume your programmers are looking at the robots now?"

"Yes." Devv provided additional details, many of which he had mentioned before, about why he wanted more non-machine officers. Then he asked, "Is it all right if I make arrangements for additional human recruits?"

Billy took a moment to consider this, and finally he nodded. Even though he would prefer an all-robot police and security force, he had too many problems to argue with his son about this. "As for the robots, if your programmers have trouble figuring them out, let me know and I'll see what I can do." He smiled softly, added, "They are my family, almost as much as you are, because I created them."

"I know," Devv said, "but I don't want to add another problem to your already-long list. The glitches with the machines are nothing I can't handle, or at least supervise. You've said yourself, the programmers are doing a fine job, and they've trained replacements for themselves, so you don't need to be involved. Besides, we have plenty of backup 'bots in storage, and can put them on duty while we're having others worked on."

"Sounds like you've got it all under control. Wish I could say the same about my own responsibilities. I just received my daily stack of reports from our operatives on AmEarth, describing the campaign of personal attacks that is increasing against me, in city after city, community after community. It's character assassination, pure and simple. A mountain of lies and distortions. And I have to admit to you, I feel myself dying inside."

Devv placed a hand on his father's shoulder. "I wish I knew what to do for you, Father, to make the pain go away. I wish I could help."

"You're helping by just being here. I admit, I have countless personal flaws; I am not perfect. I am human, I hurt and I weep. The attacks on me are so unjustified that they tear at my very soul!" His voice trailed off.

"The verbal assaults are overwhelming you, Father. You're suffering an injustice that cries out for redemption, for one hell of a good donnybrook to get even. Don't you ever feel like mounting a military attack against the Empire, or at least sending assassins to kill the leaders of the conspiracy against you?"

He shook his head. "That is not my way."

They talked for another hour, about this and other matters, even about their own strong personal relationship. Then Devv climbed into the sidecar of Billy's chair, and they returned together.

CHAPTER 13

People are never what they appear to be. It is only a
matter of degree, of how much is concealed behind the
façade they attempt to maintain.

—"Deception in the Human Animal," a government study

Walking right behind the tall, attractive proctor, Yürgen Zayeddi accompanied thirty-four other students as they made their way toward one of the docking areas on the perimeter of the ship, passing through tunnels and airlocks to get there. Earlier that morning he had reported to security headquarters to demonstrate his skills as a humbaby pilot. Impressing several officers, he had been injected with a special identification implant and assigned to the reserve force, to be activated in case of an emergency. Now he was about to board an entirely different ship—a skyminer, and not as a pilot. He would be a passenger, learning how the robotic operated vessels performed their work in the atmosphere.

On the way to the docking area, Yürgen noted numerous dents, smudges, and scratches on the walls and rampways, as well as places where he had to watch his footing on worn or damaged metal, to keep from tripping—or worse, from falling several floors to one of the hangar levels below that he could see through the grates. The handrails might be strong enough, but rattled in some places when class members used them, so Yürgen thought it was better to avoid them, while staying in the center of each ramp and walking carefully. He was not alone in noticing such things, as he heard some of the muted expressions of concern around him.

He caught up with Sonya Orr, and said to her, "Before coming to Skyship, I never imagined the interior would be anything like this. I expected to find everything in pristine condition, shiny white, silver, and clean, but instead, wherever I go I see evidence of wear."

She nodded. "There've been multitudes of people and robots traversing every square centimeter of this great ship, leaving signs of their passage behind them. You aren't disappointed, are you?"

"Not at all." He grinned. "I couldn't possibly be disappointed, being here with Billy Jeeling. I'm more surprised than anything else. I had preconceived images of perfection, I guess, and I'd never seen photographs of the interior of Skyship."

"For reasons of security, Billy doesn't permit photographs here. The small number of elite tourists who are allowed to visit us are prohibited from documenting anything on board—and there are technological barriers to prevent photography, or video or audio recording. The prohibition goes for Skyship employees, too, and when they visit AmEarth they can't even talk about what they do here, or take any form of information with them to pass on."

Yürgen had no idea what this meant for ex-workers who were now on the surface of the planet—but somehow there was a broad blanket of secrecy about the operation of the great vessel, as if it was being run by one of the worldwide security agencies.

Sonya continued, saying, "Billy even manages to enforce his strict prohibition against any form of recording with respect to the exterior, to the extent that he can. Nevertheless, images of the outside of our great ship make it down to the people of AmEarth, with some photos taken from aircraft."

"I thought they'd be shot down if they came near."

"They take pictures with long-distance lenses, when they're beyond the range of being shot down. Some pictures are also taken from the surface of the planet, using high-powered cameras."

"I saw one of those pictures years ago," Yürgen said, visualizing it in his memory. "A grainy photograph with scores of small skyminers around the mother ship. I'm surprised there are any photos at all, as security-conscious as Billy Jeeling is."

"There are always people trying to get around rules," Sonya said. "As for the somewhat worn conditions you see here, I assure you that

Skyship is perfectly sound, structurally and mechanically. It's a matter of priorities. We don't waste time making our surroundings look unnecessarily perfect. Repairs are made as necessary, and we're always having to repaint. Billy's air-treatment mix is in the interior air, including particles of ozone, nothing for us to worry about breathing it. But the mixture is hard on paint, rubber, and fabrics. The production of Billy's mixture is a critical, time-consuming project, much more important than the cosmetics of the ship."

Zayeddi stared at the tall blonde as he walked beside her, noting the unblemished skin, the proud way she held her head high, and her large blue eyes.

"You're quite beautiful," he said. Then he felt his face flush, in embarrassment. "Forgive me for saying that. I know you're Devv Jeeling's girlfriend. I'm sorry."

After a moment's surprise she smiled, and returned to what they'd been talking about before that. "I've been assured that the atmospheric-repair equipment is all maintained to the hilt, and so are the onboard life-safety systems — which is reassuring, no matter the appearance."

They walked along in silence, ahead of the others.

Earlier, Yürgen had noticed her looking at him, with apparent interest. He'd like to do something about it at the first opportunity, but another man was in her life, and a powerful one — the son of Billy Jeeling. This worried and frustrated him, created a barricade. He didn't want to be fired, and had to keep his priorities straight or he'd be thrown off the ship. But he found himself extremely attracted to her. There was no denying that, and she seemed responsive to his attentions.

Presently Sonya and her class stood in a cavernous area where the air was much cooler and had slightly less oxygen due to the intrusion of the thin atmosphere from outside, despite an elaborate system of re-oxygenation, and a series of airlocks through which the class had passed. Yürgen felt his breathing shift, as he took more breaths to compensate in the thinner air. He saw high metal beams overhead, and streaky, gray-black walls, with no semblance of aesthetics. Everything was utilitarian, built for functionality, not for looks.

Yürgen and his classmates were taken to the edge of the sealed main dock, where they prepared to go through an egress tunnel and board the skyminers. Through a clearplaz screen he saw the robot-operated ships in their docking clamps, each vessel a two-seater with a sealed, oxygenated cabin and a robot already inside, at the controls. Robots didn't need oxygen, but these craft were for taking human passengers out to air-mining sites, often on inspection trips made by Billy or one of his managers. The robots looked humanoid on their upper bodies, and had two arms, but Sonya said they had no lower bodies because they were built-into the aircraft, connected to the machinery.

The students entered the tunnel, and one by one they boarded the small ships, which took off quickly. When Yürgen's turn came, he climbed into the seat behind the robot pilot, and as the hatch closed behind him he felt a change in cabin pressure that made one of his ears click. Looking around, he was relieved and delighted to see that this particular craft appeared to be brand new. Everything was shiny and unused, with arrays of lighted instruments in front of both the pilot and the passenger.

The aircraft accelerated away from the immense mother ship and descended in the atmosphere. The robot explained, in its detached, mechanical voice, "Instruments in front of you show airspeed and other flight characteristics, as well as a constant analysis of the contents of the air we fly through and are about to collect. Since we are in constant motion, these percentages vary from moment to moment, so you are looking at changing averages. My name is Eric, and that is the name of this skymining ship, too."

Acceleration pushed Zayeddi back in his seat, but for only a few moments. He saw the sudden increase in speed register on a small analog screen, until it leveled off at a little over 300 k.p.h., and an altitude of eight kilometers. The craft made a wide turn and decelerated until it was going very slowly. He became aware of other skyminers around him, opening large collector sacks behind them in great puffy forms that were much larger than the craft. He saw that his own ship was doing the same thing.

"We are beginning to mine the air," the robot reported. "We have located an air current that is saturated with industrial pollution and vehicle emissions. Carbon dioxide—CO_2—and other elements are being scrubbed from the air, compressed, and stored for future use."

Yürgen studied a rectangular screen registering the elements in the air that were being pulled into compartments in the container sack, and accumulating: CO_2, as well as sulfur dioxide and the various by-products of smelting and refining plants and other industries that burned fossil fuels (gas, oil, or coal), as well as hydrocarbons and carbon monoxide emitted by motor vehicle engines. Even at this altitude, he saw a "smog" entry, which further described its peroxyacetyl nitrate and other components. In addition, he noted measurements of pollen, dust, and even live bacteria that could live high above the surface of the planet.

Zayeddi had already heard about other benefits of Skyship, such as how the reduction of CO_2 in the atmosphere resulted in the benefit of a slightly cooler climate, reducing the greenhouse effect that had been causing so much damage. Already the polar icecaps were either not melting, or were regenerating, and ocean levels were hardly rising at all any more, and appeared to be about to stop rising completely. On a periodic basis, Skyship even mined water vapors from cloud formations and shipped the water down to technicians on the surface of the planet, who used it to recharge aquifers, and irrigate dry areas. The mining of water vapors had the added benefit of reducing the monsoon deluges that were so destructive in some territories, but this had to be done with utmost care, to avoid creating droughts.

It amazed him not only to be on Skyship, but to go out in the ingenious skymining machines that were so integral to its operations. And he was learning so much!

As soon as he completed his training, Yürgen could return to AmEarth and speak with more authority about the good work Billy Jeeling was doing. Sonya Orr had told the class that they would be assigned to public-relations teams on the planet, traveling to trouble spots and improving the image of the Master of Skyship. When Zayeddi graduated, he would not only have his passionate loyalty toward the great man, but he would have a lot of technical information as well, facts to counter anything the lying detractors might say. Their words were like filthy pollution, and he vowed to clean them up.

CHAPTER 14

.

All evidence points to Jeeling hiding something significant about his past, much more serious than we've ever imagined. He might even have murdered someone to get where he is today. Your task is to turn over rocks and see what scurries out, so that we can expose him.

—Instruction to one of General Moore's operatives

As a child, and later when he grew up and made choices about his education and career path, Rand Baker had never intended to be a saboteur. It had never been a class he took, had not been on any list of possible futures. He'd never dreamed of doing this. Yet now, as he disembarked from the shuttle with twenty-five other PR recruits, he thought back on the series of events that had brought him to this place in the sky over AmEarth, and to this place in his life.

He was a bit taller than average, with a look of nobility to him — in the bone structure and in the way he carried himself. His hair was wavy and sandy-brown, and the eyes hazel. He was so good-looking, in fact, that women often approached him and tried to strike up a conversation. But he wasn't interested in them. He wasn't interested in men, either. Baker was decidedly asexual, and had been that way from an early age. When his friends were growing up and maturing sexually, he hadn't felt any interest in any aspect of that. By the time he was seventeen, he came to the opinion that it was not his purpose in life to breed, or to have any form of sexual activity. He didn't want to waste his time with such pursuits, such shallow and base entertainments. Life was too short for nonsense. Instead, he wanted to do something really important with the time allotted to him, and each decision he made advanced him toward that goal.

As a technician in the Army Flight Corps, Rand had become proficient at working on all sorts of aircraft engines and flight components, including complex weapons systems, and as a result of his excellent work he had been offered promotions. But he had turned all of them down, even though he could have been on a path toward becoming an officer. But Rand didn't want to sit at a desk, or command airmen on one mission or another, didn't want to be an airman at all, for that matter. Rather, he had wanted to be where he could tinker with flight mechanisms and weapons and repair them, making warplanes ready to take off and complete their missions. Let someone else perform the tasks of actually flying and shooting, which he considered inferior to his own, and dependent upon his expertise. He liked to work with his hands, and get them dirty.

Now as Rand made his way down a series of three long ramps with his fellow recruits, he found that the air was cold and a little thin (even though this was a sealed area), and he had to adjust his breathing. He took several deep breaths, finally began to feel more comfortable. He noticed some of his companions going through an adjustment process, too.

Baker knew that he was about to get his hands really dirty here, with the assignment that General Moore had secretly given to him — he was to sabotage all of the defensive weapons of Skyship. This included the large kinetic kill missiles set up like torpedoes to fire out of Skyship in all directions, along with KK480 cannons and Nuke-Packs. Even the large fleet of skyminers could potentially be used for defensive purposes, as all of the craft were armed with conventional cannons, and with sting-melt guns that could inflict a lot of damage.

He was on his own now. He couldn't even make contact with any other agents he'd heard were aboard. He didn't know their names or where they were assigned to work on the huge air station, but if they were only spies gathering information, and not saboteurs, he was a step above them. His expertise required training of a precise nature, and he was highly paid for his ability to complete any assignment that was given to him.

For this mission everything would have to be timed perfectly, so that all of the onboard weapons were rendered inoperable at precisely the right time. He'd been told that they were undoubtedly under a central command system, and that he needed to get to the heart of it and take everything off line. The fleet of skyminers was another matter, as each of the aircraft had its own weapons. The best idea—postulated by the General—seemed to be to shut down the Skyship defensive system when most or all of the fleet was out on their air-scrubbing and mining missions. Baker also needed to shut down the docks, blocking any of the vessels from returning.

Then in a narrow window of time, General Moore would attack with his high-speed strike force, and get inside the great ship through the one access point that Baker would leave open, with the mission of taking over.

Some of the in-flight skyminers might shoot at the attackers, but they didn't have firepower on the scale of what would be coming against them, and eventually all of these defenders would run out of fuel and be forced down. With any luck, every one of the skyminers would become piles of burned, twisted metal on the ground, having crashed on the surface of the planet.

"Welcome to Skyship," a young woman said, at the base of the last ramp. "I am Sandra Orr, one of the proctors."

She was tall and beyond-belief gorgeous, with pale skin and large blue eyes. From intelligence reports, he knew this was Devv Jeeling's girlfriend, and that he was very possessive of her, jealous to the point of being dangerous. There was a report of at least one fistfight between the younger Jeeling and a man who showed interest in her. With his own lack of interest in sex, Baker would have no trouble avoiding any such entanglement. But something about this woman interested him, almost aroused him. She was exceptionally attractive, and was looking directly at him now with those seductive eyes.

Some of the other recruits were shivering from the cold, but Orr told them it would warm up soon, when they went deeper into the ship. Baker heard machinery sounds behind them, saw the docking area and ramps being closed off by mottled gray panels that slid slowly into place.

Sandra Orr turned and led them toward an arched doorway, where a towering robot stepped out to greet them. Baker had heard about these mechanical men, and had prepared for them as much as possible. General Moore's operatives had infiltrated the technology of the police robots, though not truthbots like this one, because of their impenetrable self-destruct systems. However, Moore's military experts had implanted a new mindwave unit into Rand's brain, one that could communicate on military and civilian frequencies, and had the ability to sort thoughts and block the detection of any that were conspiratorial. It was an experimental device, and he'd heard of failures. He only hoped his worked.

Baker tried to relax as a spectrum of light passed over his body, shooting darts of pain into his brain. In his surface thoughts, and in the thoughts comprising his apparent memories, he was another person, totally devoted to Billy Jeeling, worshipping the man in the great ship as if he were a god.

But buried in Rand's consciousness he had a backup plan that Moore had given him—to kill Billy Jeeling if the opportunity arose. He felt the tingling of the scan stop, and he was given the signal to move on. He had passed....

CHAPTER 15

In all the centuries of recorded history, empires have come and gone; they have risen and fallen, burned brightly and gone dark. With the AmEarth Empire, however, the old pattern has ended. Our rule will last for 100,000 years; it is the empire to end all other empires.

—Former Prime Minister Princeton Kelly

Maureen Stuart had been summoned to a meeting by Jonathan Racker, and she was hurrying to get there on time. She'd been delayed by a temporary shutdown of the capital city's transportation system, a mechanical glitch of some sort, and now she was stepping out of the highlift. It was mid-morning, and she walked quickly across the lobby.

Racker's office was on the top floor of his own building, the tallest structure in the AmEarth Empire, with sweeping views of Orca Sound and the craggy, white-capped peaks of the Olympus Mountains to the west. This structure differed from the classic designs that were so prevalent here in Imperial City, something he could get away with because of his fabulous wealth and high-level connections. The radical design of his building made it the target of whispered controversy, and there had been derisive comments made about it and insulting names for it, but always anonymously on social media venues.

The detractors said it resembled an immense mushroom from the northwest woods with a long thick stalk, because the vaulted uppermost level was much wider than the floors below. Or that it looked too much like the old retro-style Space Needle that used to be in this vicinity, one of the structures that had been torn down when the whole city was razed and rebuilt as the glorious new Imperial capital.

Racker's headquarters building had a clear glassplaz exterior, so that the black metal frame and the inner workings of each level—including the highlift elevators—could be seen from outside. Yet, only a select few ever got permission to see that realm from such a vantage, just the approved passengers of tourist aircraft that were permitted to fly nearby. These were all carefully screened people, selected only from the most elite of society throughout the Empire. Rank had its privilege, as the saying went.

Now as Maureen Stuart entered Racker's office, she saw the diminutive old Latino at the window, staring at a passing ornithopter, a white craft with red Department of Tourism markings on the hull. The flying ship hovered in one place for several moments like a hummingbird, its wings flapping in a blur, and then flew off.

His overdressed wife, Carmela, stood beside him. None of the other meeting participants who were supposed to be here had arrived yet.

A full-figured brunette with long hair that tumbled around her shoulders, Carmela was not usually at their meetings. Taller than Racker, she accentuated this with stiletto heels, so that she stood almost a head above him at the window. To Maureen, the woman's pale yellow dress, while expensive and embroidered in small jewels, was gauche, as were the gleaming diamonds on her rings, her necklace, and even her smart watch.

Carmela turned theatrically and narrowed her gaze suspiciously at Maureen, then looked at her watch. She didn't make any comment; Maureen was exactly on time. In any event, Racker didn't seem to be concerned about the time. He appeared to be deep in thought. But it could be something else, a medical issue; he was quite old.

Known to be jealous of other females, Mrs. Racker thought every woman was out to get her husband's money, and she might be right about many of them, but not about Maureen, who only tolerated Racker, and barely put up with his wife.

Carmela had recently gone in for a full-body makeover, getting her face, teeth, hair, tummy, neck, breasts, arms, legs, and everything else tuned up at the same time—reportedly in a five-day marathon of top surgeons and cosmetic technicians from all over the world. She'd tried to be secretive about the procedures she'd gone through, but social media was buzzing about what she'd done, and most of the comments were favorable — except for the anonymous detractors.

She might look fine in photographs and public appearances (to warrant the approvals), but up close and in person, Maureen thought she almost looked frightening, like a horror movie character. She was younger than Racker, but was still over sixty, and the things she'd done to her face this time — having even the tiniest lines removed, as well as reducing the size of her nose, enlarging her lips and implanting rouge in them — gave her a mask-like appearance. And something had changed with her hairline — it was lower on her forehead now, with a new widow's peak. There was something peculiar about her eyes, too. The lids were different, and the corneas around the dark pupils looked too white.

Maureen sympathized with women who worried so much about their looks. Personally, she would rather age gracefully.

Realizing that Carmela was taking too much notice of her, Maureen gazed past her, and out the window. To the west over the city, the sky was hazy, and Maureen saw a squadron of skyminers working above the tall buildings, gathering the bad air into their bulbous bags, as well as separating minerals and other elements for processing by the mother ship, which she saw in the distant sky.

The tycoon's office, and the much smaller offices and cubicles of his staff, were all on one immense circular floor, on a level that was triple the size of each circular floor beneath it — with the vaulted top floor supported by a cantilever system that extended horizontally, reaching out a considerable distance beyond the core of the building.

The top level had a clearplaz floor, providing Maureen with a stunning view straight down past her feet to the tops of office and residential buildings far below. It didn't frighten her at all, didn't make her feel at all queasy, not even when the floor moved a little as Paul Paulo walked past her.

The wiry, silver-haired man had just arrived behind her, carrying a worn-leather case under one arm. The overly handsome General Rivington Moore followed, walking with his characteristic swagger, in full uniform with his cap in place. It amazed her that a man that young had so many medals, and held such a high rank, even with all of his charisma. He gazed around the office, had more than the usual expression of confidence on his face.

Racker turned, motioned for the other three to take seats in soft chairs around a low table, where a serving woman was setting up a silver tea pot and porcelain cups. She looked at him, asked, "Will that be all, sir?"

He nodded.

She bowed crisply and left.

The old industrialist looked at his wife, said with an edge of sarcasm, "Don't you have one of your appointments about now?"

Carmela nodded. Then, gazing coldly at Maureen, she said, "I suppose you think I'm going shopping, but that isn't true at all. Actually, I'm taking classes to improve my mind, learning all sorts of things—math, science, the military history of the Empire, even. And business, of course, with so much money to handle. Does that surprise you?"

"Of course not," Maureen said. "You are a very intelligent woman, and you know what is best for yourself." *So*, Maureen thought, *your brain is also part of the full-body makeover.*

Carmela Racker smiled stiffly, gave her husband a peck on the cheek, and left. She had a sensual manner of walking, Maureen had always noticed, the way she swayed her hips and held herself in a posture that pushed her breasts out to their maximum possible effect. According to anonymous social media comments, Carmela had captured Racker with a sexual hook, and then reeled him in; she caught a really big fish. It had undoubtedly been a seduction, Maureen thought, and despite Carmela's overt sexuality she really was an intelligent woman, with good common sense. She was far more than a body, more than the appearance that she worked so hard to perfect.

Jonathan Racker joined the others, who had been pouring steaming hot tea in their cups while they waited. The old man still seemed to be deep in thought, and had shown a little irritation with his wife. Maureen had seen him shoot a couple of brief glares in her direction as she went out the door.

"I'm pleased to report some progress toward getting rid of Mr. Jeeling," Paulo said, breaking the uneasiness in the air. He opened the leather case, passed documents around the table.

While Maureen examined her copy, Paulo said, "As you can see, Jeeling is increasingly despondent, spending more and more time alone on the high walkway at night, gazing at the stars. He values his reputation very highly, and we're shooting arrows in it."

General Moore set his ornate cap on the table, flipped through the pages. "Jeeling is mounting a more organized response to some of our criticisms, providing purported proof that he's not profiting personally from Skyship or living in regal splendor. Funny, though, he's remaining silent about his educational, work, and family histories—including the charge that he does not descend from slaves, as he always claimed."

"It's a pattern I've noticed in legal matters," Stuart said, nodding. "People comment on areas where they feel strongest, but are silent about areas where they are weak."

"We have evidence of his family history," Moore said. "They were AmAfrican chieftains who sold enemy villagers into slavery. But we have only vague information about Billy's life before he undertook the Skyship project."

"He's weak in those areas," Stuart said, "stronger in others."

General Moore scowled. "The next thing we know, he'll be using the race card, saying we're attacking him because he's black."

"No sign of that yet," Maureen said.

Moore slapped his copy of the document on the table with a disgusted look on his face. "The report doesn't say when that ni—... when he will be gone."

Maureen scowled. The officer had been about to use the verboten "n" word, which she'd heard him do in the past, sometimes receiving criticism from his fellow conspirators for doing it. This time he refrained, but she still considered him to be contemptible.

"That's hard to say," Paulo said, with his own scowl. "Could be weeks, or months."

"Or *years*," Moore said.

Maureen tore her gaze away from the good-looking officer, and asked, "Who provided this report?"

"Last page," Paulo said, pointing at one of the open documents. "Middle paragraph. A metalworker named Sulls Johan. The only agent we've managed to infiltrate onto Skyship. Says he got the information from a robot he was repairing the body on, just working on a limited assignment—repairing a metal body plate. Suddenly the whole machine malfunctioned, and data spewed out of its speaker screen."

"I have *six* agents on Skyship," Moore said. "Three spies and an equal number of saboteurs. My people have already caused some damage, designed to get Jeeling's attention."

"Six agents?" Paulo said, "in addition to ours?"

Moore grinned. "Six to one, my friend. I win."

Stuart stared in disbelief at Moore, and saw shock registering on the faces of Paulo and Racker.

"What the hell are you talking about?" Paulo demanded. "What wild, unauthorized action have you taken?"

"I've grown tired of the waiting game," Moore said, with a hard smile, "and your one weakling agent, who doesn't do much except interrogate broken robots. So I decided to take action to end the stand-off. I've already staged a nice little explosion on board that blew a hole in the hull. It was repaired quickly, as I anticipated—just a little warning to them. My men also broke a few things in recent months, machinery, robots, and they disabled the highlifts that Billy uses the most. Small stuff, to make him know he's no longer welcome on Sky-ship. We've forced his son to do constant security sweeps, having put both of them in a constant state of nervousness."

"Call your saboteurs back!" Paulo said. "We don't want Billy killed or Skyship damaged! We don't know how it operates. The technology has been kept secret from us. And the disaster warning. Have you forgotten? Skyship can't be destroyed or attacked!"

"Rubbish!" General Moore said. "Jeeling fabricated that threat to scare us off. He's bluffing."

"Do you know that for sure?" Racker asked.

"He's bluffing. I can always tell when a man is telling a tall tale, even if no one else here can recognize the signs."

"And what are those signs, exactly?" Maureen asked.

"You wouldn't understand if I explained them to you. No one here would." Glaring, General Moore put on his cap and rose to his feet, then looked at the doorway, indicating that he was about to leave.

Paulo was on his feet, too, and moved with surprising speed for an old man, to stand between Moore and the door. "Call your saboteurs back, General. And do it quick."

"Yes," Racker said. "Do it before something serious happens to Skyship."

"Don't worry," Moore said. "They're not going to blow the thing out of the air. Any sabotage will be limited, and if one of my people can get to Jeeling and kill him, that would be the best of all possible results. As soon as he's out of the way, we can send in experts to tear into the workings of Skyship."

"I want the names of all your operatives," Jonathan Racker said. He walked slowly over and stood beside Paulo, glaring up at Moore.

"Sure," the General said, "after one of them becomes a hero." He stepped around both men, strode toward the door. "And don't try to stop me. I have full control of the officer corps, and our entire military force."

"I have another idea," Maureen said. "Let the good General keep his operatives on the ship. General Moore, I have a suggestion that might work for all of us."

The officer hesitated, looked at her suspiciously. His eyes were afire, but he heaved a small sigh and remained where he was.

She continued. "Have your operatives remain in place, General, but tell them to suspend activities. Just for a while, so that we can send a peace delegation up to Skyship, a group of trained negotiators who can get through to Billy and find some way to end this stand-off."

Moore folded his arms across his chest, which she interpreted as negative body language, but the expression on his face softened a bit, as he seemed to be considering the idea.

"We haven't played the negotiation card with him yet, gentlemen," Stuart said. "Instead, we've only sent demands for him to step down, and so has Prime Minister Yhatt. All in the form of electronic communications that Billy's staff prints out for him to read."

"I'd rather *tell* him what to do, instead of asking," General Moore said. "That's my way of doing things." He smiled at Maureen and said, "I am a military man, after all, and that's the way we do it."

She smiled in return, but then looked away quickly. He was using those lady-killer eyes on her again. *Is he trying to seduce me? Is he saying, he'll go along with my idea if I...?*

She dismissed the idea as a figment of her imagination. Her physical side might like to sleep with him, even if she was married, but intellectually and emotionally, she knew it would be a huge mistake. She loved her husband Paddy despite their quarrels, and besides, this was a man who conquered people, and then moved on — as if he were going from one military objective to another.

General Moore looked at Racker, said, "Get ahold of Prime Minister Yhatt and tell him we're sending a negotiation team."

The old industrialist glared, but nodded. All of them knew that Yhatt was little more than a figurehead leader for the AmEarth Empire, propped up by powerful corporate and military interests. He would not argue with this.

"In fact, I like Stuart's idea so much," Moore said, "that I think she should go on the mission. And Paul, too." Looking at the stock and commodities tycoon, he added, "Billy used to like you better than anybody on our side, from what I hear."

"That was a long time ago," Paul Paulo said. He thought for a moment, then said, "All right, I'll go." Then he looked at Maureen.

She nodded. "I think it's a good idea."

Moore grunted something that Maureen couldn't make out, and marched out of the office.

When he was gone, Paulo said, "Now we have another problem. That cocky son-of-a-bitch is on the verge of going renegade on us."

CHAPTER 16

Some of Billy's detractors even question the wisdom of Skyship, because of its intervention in the natural processes of the planet and its atmosphere. They assert that he is playing with science, potentially setting in motion an ecological disaster, brought on by his unwise tampering. They completely ignore the fact that the atmosphere was not ruined by natural processes; it was ruined by the careless actions of human beings.

—From the *JeeJee Training Manual*

Billy Jeeling had his own secrets, places in his mind where only he could venture, and places on Skyship that were similar — where no one was permitted to go except him — not even his most trusted robots. Years ago he had been the only confidante of the brilliant inventor Branson Tobek, and most of the secrets — at least the ones that mattered most to Billy — were not his own. They were Tobek's, and the old man took them with him when he died. Billy had become famous because of Skyship, but the great vessel was largely a mystery to him, the way it kept going on its airborne rounds, mostly on automatic. It was like a perpetual motion machine, which seemed impossible.

Now Billy sat at a viewing window, gazing into a hidden laboratory at the heart of Skyship, part of a large core section around which the great ship had been built. One of his personal security robots stood nearby, alert to dangers, awaiting any command he might give. The sentient machine buzzed softly, while the vertical light tube on its torso pulsed pale green.

This was one of the older models that Billy had designed and constructed himself; they knew sensitive things that he didn't want to get out to the other robots, or to any of their handlers, or other technicians. He had a name for each of this series, to which they responded. In the Starbot series, this was the first Starbot, and went by that name. The other five were Starbot 2 through Starbot 6. Billy housed them in a secret place in the core section of the great ship, where only he and these few robots had access. They reported to no one but him, and if any unauthorized person or machine tried to access their secrets, the 'bots would turn violent in unison, and then self-destruct.

It was in the laboratory beyond this window that Branson Tobek had done his most important thinking and testing, where he developed many of the concepts that went into the construction of the massive vessel. He had come up with virtually all of those wondrous ideas himself, while leaving the tasks of assembling and building to others, with Billy as his go-between, making everyone believe that the ideas were Billy's own.

Years before that, a teenage Billy Jeeling had seen a bearded man walking in his neighborhood in a small township, his shoulders slumped over, looking as if he were lost. The man appeared to be in his late seventies and was quite diminutive, and had been wandering around one sunny summer afternoon, talking to himself, but not speaking loudly enough for others to understand. He was in his own universe, and people were saying he must be crazy. Billy had not been so sure about that, and had brought the fellow back to awareness by talking to him and getting him to provide his name.

At first Branson Tobek had been angry at the interruption, for having been pulled out of his deep thoughts. Then, when he realized that he had been like a sleepwalker in daylight, and might have walked out into traffic, he had been gracious and appreciative.

Billy made sure the odd little man got home, and while walking with him Billy had answered questions that were put to him. The young man said he was a top student at his high school, and was on course to graduate with honors in a few months, shortly after his sixteenth birthday. He hoped to attend to a prestigious university on a full scholarship afterward, where he would study engineering. Billy also said he had entered a national robotics contest, and was in the midst of building a robotic baseball player — a mechanical man that could hit prodigious home runs against any pitch, no matter how fast or slow or complex, or how good the pitcher was. After winning the contest, he hoped to show what the robot could do in a demonstration before a major league game.

"So, you want to be famous one day?" Tobek had asked, with a bemused expression on his face.

"I might succeed in getting my fifteen minutes of fame," Billy said. "But if I ever got more than that, I'd reject people who tried to take over my life, you know, agents and the like. I might have to tell them to leave me alone, that I just want to finish high school and be a normal teenager."

"Why the baseball angle?"

"My Dad and Mom are dead now, from a car accident — so I'm living with my great aunt. But Dad used to be a baseball scout for a big league team, and he knew important people — so I'm hoping to use some of his old contacts to let folks know about my robot in a baseball uniform. Hopefully, they'll want to see what it can do."

"Maybe your mechanical slugger can be elected to the Baseball Hall of Fame someday."

Billy laughed. "That would really be something, wouldn't it? Say, you're just kidding me, aren't you?"

"I suppose I am, but I must say you are an impressive young man."

"Well, I am a hard worker, and my mind is always active. Maybe too active at times, some people tell me."

The two walked in silence for awhile, until reaching the door to Tobek's bungalow-style house, where he thanked Billy. "You've performed a very good deed today, young fellow," he said, in a soft voice.

They shook hands. "Thank you, sir," Billy said.

After opening the door, Tobek turned and said, "Robotics is one of my special interests, something I enjoy doing. I'm something of an inventor myself, having developed a variety of things." He chuckled, adding, "If I took the time to do it, maybe I could build a pitching robot to strike out your batting robot every time."

"I'm sure you could, sir," Billy had said, in the most respectful of tones. Always a polite young man, he'd been taught to be that way by his parents and his Great Aunt Lanaya. He always respected older people, anyway, so this fit his personality. Branson Tobek had seemed ancient to him, the way he was stooped over and spoke in such soft tones, but Billy learned later that he was only in his late forties, but looked much older.

Tobek went inside alone, and closed the door behind him.

The following day, Billy went to the door of his own home when Aunt Lanaya told him a woman was there, asking for him. The woman, who gave her name merely as Millie, said she worked for Tobek, shopping for his groceries, doing his laundry, and cleaning his house. She said Mr. Tobek wanted to see him.

So Billy accompanied her there and went inside, where Tobek awaited him in a small parlor, decorated with old furniture and curtains. For an hour, they sat and spoke of a great concern the man had, that the air, land, and water of the planet were all terribly polluted. In a fervent voice he said something needed to be done on a big scale to help the environment, and especially the polluted, damaged atmosphere, because millions of people were dying of skin cancer, breathing problems, and other conditions.

Having heard about a number of environmental issues before this discussion, young Billy understood why Tobek was saying the air was more important than anything else, and from all of the scientific details he was rattling off, this seemed to be his specialty. He had historical comparisons of air quality from an analysis of ancient ice, cliff faces and other methods, and he droned on and on about such things, hardly taking a breath, it seemed.

Finally Tobek paused, and gazed earnestly at Billy. "Are you following what I'm saying?"

"I'm trying very hard, sir."

Tobek nodded, said, "All over the world, the air looks dirty on too many days, and even when it doesn't *look* dirty, it still is. Rarely do we see the lovely blues that the sky should be; instead it often has a sickly yellow filter of pollution through it, muting the natural hues. If we could just clean up the air all over this world, that would be a good place to start, serving as an inspiration for other ecological repair work that is needed, on the land and in the vast, interconnected oceans."

He had spoken so earnestly, with so much passion, that Billy had hardly said anything, not wanting to interrupt him. Yet, every so often, Tobek would pause again and ask, "Are you sure you're following me? Do you understand what I'm talking about?"

The teenager had kept saying he understood, which was an overstatement. Actually, he was only picking up bits and pieces. And on one occasion he said, "You're talking about matters of immense importance, sir."

"That is right, young Billy Jeeling. And know this: I expect to complete the cleanup of the atmosphere in my lifetime—a huge geoengineering project that will restore AmEarth's air to what it was in ancient times. That should keep me busy for a few years."

Billy had thought he must be kidding because he was so old, but saw no twinkle in his eyes, no hint of a smile. He seemed to really believe that he could accomplish something like that in the few years he had remaining.

"That sounds like a Herculean task," Billy had said. "From what I've heard, the skies over the developing nations are badly polluted and getting worse every day, from industrial and auto emissions. Those nations can't afford to take the remedial measures that more advanced countries have had in place for decades. How would you get them to change their habits? It would be tremendously expensive, would require a lot of diplomacy."

Now the gentleman did smile, softly. "I have the answers for you, but to provide them we would need to work closely together." He paused. "You are highly intelligent; I can tell such things about people, and you exude an intellectual curiosity that is nearly equal to my own. Young man, I am offering you a job as my assistant. If you accept, it means you would need to forego your school studies, at least for a few years."

Without asking what the position would pay, Billy said, "Your work sounds very interesting sir, and of critical importance. I'll work for you, but I can only promise you the two remaining months until I graduate high school. After that—"

"Young man, as soon as you see what I have in mind, when you understand the way I intend to achieve my goal, I think you'll prefer to work for me." He nodded. "All right. I'll take the risk of revealing incredible information to you, Billy Jeeling. And I must ask you not to discuss any of the things I teach you with others. They would never be able to understand. It would take too much energy to explain."

Billy nodded, then followed the man down a narrow wooden staircase into the basement. On the way, Billy thought of horror movies he'd seen, where the protagonist wasn't supposed to go down stairs like that, or into a dark alley, or into the shadowy woods. But he continued on anyway, and entered the basement laboratory behind Tobek. It smelled a little musty.

"Even Millie is not permitted to come down here," Tobek said, as he opened the squeaking door of a room in the basement. "You are the first I have invited."

The room contained an array of intriguing machines, which Tobek said were for generating three-dimensional schematics, used in computer simulations, and for building prototypes for testing and analysis. There were projection screens and illuminated computer screens all around the room, running through sequences, calculating and providing recommendations to the inventor. Some screens showed complex but interesting engineering sketches, of devices that Billy could not comprehend.

"Now we begin," Tobek said. "First I will tell you what my big concept is, how a great airborne ship and its fleet of skyminers will fit into the picture, and then we will discuss how these machines are to be built...."

~~~

So many years had gone by since then, so many events had transpired. The laboratory that Billy gazed into now was a different one from the original lab in Tobek's house. Billy moved his maglev chair on its cushion of air, going in reverse a little, and then forward at an angle, changing his position slightly at the glass, to give him a better vantage of the main laboratory, visible through an open doorway at the rear of the closest room.

This entire laboratory complex was much bigger and more advanced than the one in Tobek's home; this was a network of connected rooms, filled with state-of-the-art scientific, mechanical, and computer apparatus. After obtaining funding and arranging for complete secrecy, the facility had been constructed in modular form on AmEarth and then attached to the first sections of Skyship before it lifted off into the air—so that the core contained the propulsion system and numerous lab and habitation rooms, all enclosed in a hull that Tobek said would ultimately be the nucleus of a much larger vessel.

In and of itself, the core was a craft capable of lifting itself into low-AmEarth orbit, which Tobek promptly caused to happen, aided by a crew of robots. Billy had helped in the design and assembly of those 'bots, and of others used in the construction of Skyship, and in the process he had learned amazing things from Tobek, far more than he could have ever imagined figuring out on his own, or learning in the curriculum of any school. Getting the craft off the ground took many years, far beyond the two months that Billy had originally proposed to work.

When Billy dropped out of high school that spring, he soon forgot about missing classes or any traditional form of education. He was now focused on something else, something far more meaningful to him. His young mind was being filled with fantastic ideas!

Aunt Lanaya had been disappointed at first, but had been impressed when she met Tobek and fell under the sway of the inventor's considerable, soft-spoken charm. He hadn't shown the old woman the basement lab, but had used enough impressive words and said enough to convince her that he and her great nephew were working on something that would have a significant and positive effect on AmEarth. It involved a scientific matter of utmost secrecy, he'd told her, while providing her with scant details, basically that it involved the atmosphere, and the environment of the entire planet.

"It will make Billy Jeeling's name remembered for all time," he promised her—and truer words were never spoken, before or since.

Hearing all he had to say, his lofty goals and promises, Lanaya had finally nodded her head. "I can see that this job is important to Billy," she said, "and because it's important to him, it's important to me, too.

He's very smart, so I had hoped he would go on to the university and graduate — that's especially important for young black men, you know — but I think he's going to get an even better education with you."

Tobek had nodded. "You won't be disappointed, ma'am. He's going to be famous and successful. Mark my words."

"Billy is really older than I am, you know," his great aunt had said with a twinkle in her eyes. "He's an old soul in a young body. He's the one who really runs our household."

The kindly old woman had died of natural causes three years later, never learning much about the project.

Four years after her death, when Tobek had the embryonic Skyship in orbit, he began the task of connecting additional modules and components to the core of the craft, making it much larger — on a scale that astounded Billy. Even with all of the discussions he'd had with Tobek beforehand, the unfolding reality around him was more than Billy could have ever envisioned. Module after module were fitted into place in a massive, intricate assembly, and then covered with a sturdy, comparatively lightweight hull. This took almost five more years.

Now as Billy sat at the viewing window, thinking back, he glanced at the robot standing sentinel on his right, emitting its characteristic low sounds, and casting pale green light against the thick glass. Without his having told it to do so, it illuminated a screen around its front and back torso, encircling the robot's metal body with light.

This was not supposed to happen without Billy's command.

Abruptly the robot began to glow yellow all over its body, a sickly hue that meant it had a malfunction, and was trying to correct it automatically. But the robot still operated, barely.

A weak image on the screen rotated slowly around the torso of Starbot, as if it were a camera panning across a view. Billy recognized the images as a live practice session of Lainey Forster's public relations teams, being conducted on the grazzeen central commons of Skyship. In commando-size units they moved in coordination against a throng of raucous people who had been staged to look as if they were demonstrating against Billy Jeeling. He heard angry voices, crowd noises, epithets and threats. At first the volume was low but it grew louder, so that Billy could hear bullhorns and speaker systems—people feigning insults against him. It was all a mock display, but the words hurt.

The robot was bright yellow now, with gangrenous black streaks running vertically up and down its body. The images on the screen grew hazy, too faint to identify, and went quiet, then completely black, as did the robot's body. It had shut itself down. At least that automatic function worked.

With a sigh, Billy turned back to the window. He recalled many discussions he'd had with Tobek inside the laboratory complex the old man loved so much. The two of them had developed a routine in which they met each morning for a couple of hours to go over engineering drawings that Tobek had prepared, drawings that Billy would always take credit for—following Tobek's wishes. The older man had insisted on this, wouldn't allow his presence or identity to be revealed—and only a small number of security robots knew he was involved. Gradually—as Billy's skills with robots were developed—he took over the management of all robotic operations, freeing Tobek for other creative tasks.

Tobek never left the core section where his laboratory rooms and a small apartment were located. It was an area that was accessible through a series of code-activated doors, each of which only permitted Billy or Tobek to pass through, and any special robots that were with them. During construction, it was through these doors that Billy had gone every day to get his instructions from the great man.

Now a tear ran down Billy's cheek as he thought of Tobek's tragic death in his main laboratory—right where Billy was looking now, in the large room visible through the rear doorway. He had witnessed the terrible event, from this very spot. Eleven years ago to this day, he remembered looking through this window and seeing Tobek at a laboratory table, deep in concentration as he worked, assembling something there, something small and elaborate, with small illuminated tubes inside, and other complex internal workings.

Suddenly there had been a silver flash around Tobek, and blood began to pour from his ears, eyes, nose, and mouth, blood that turned from red to silver as it flowed. Somehow he managed to gather the strength necessary to make his way into the smaller laboratory room closest to where Billy had been standing, screaming out instructions to his assistant, his words choked with metallic blood.

"Heed my words, Billy!" he shrieked as he died, his gurgling words blasting across the speaker system, from the inside of the laboratory. "This is my final command to you! Never open the laboratory doors! Leave them sealed!" Then another burst of silver struck him, and he slumped to the floor, in silvery, pooling blood. In a horrific aftermath, his brain exploded in a bright burst of silver, and then smaller explosions erupted from his torso. Quickly, Billy had commanded one of the inside robots to tend to the great man, but it was obviously hopeless. No one could survive such grievous injuries. Tobek was dead.

Whatever the inventor had been building remained on the laboratory table, where Billy could see it now through the rear doorway—small and rectangular in shape, with its internal workings open, showing an elaborate array of electronics and tubes, in an arrangement that Billy had never been able to figure out from just looking at it, not even when he used a magnifying scope from this distance. Billy had also photographed it, and run the details through computer programs in an attempt to unravel the secrets, but to no avail. The device—whatever it was—remained where Tobek had left it on the work table, unfinished and mysterious, of unknown purpose.

Ever since then, Billy had followed his mentor's dying command, and had used the laboratory communication system to arrange for lab 'bots — already inside the sealed complex of rooms—to build a casket out of furniture and place the great man's body inside it. Billy saw one corner of the sealed casket now, not far from where Tobek died.

A replacement robot approached Billy from the side, glowing green on its vertical light tube. He recognized it as Starbot 4. It had received an emergency signal that its companion was out of order, and had come to replace it.

Starbot 4 moved close to him. The green glow became brighter, and the sentient machine said, "Is there anything I can do, Master?" This robot model had been programmed to be sensitive to his moods and needs, an aspect that came in handy sometimes. Now, however, Billy shook his head. He just wanted to be alone with his memories, and feelings.

Billy had been curious for years—he had a haunting desire to know what had killed the great man. None of the lab-access doors had been opened since his death, but could there be another way to find out?

He touched his useless leg stumps, constant reminders of that explosion of Skyship's atmospheric-restoration gas, during the construction of the vessel. After the death of his mentor, Billy had been too upset to pay attention to safety measures, and had paid the price. But Tobek had paid an even greater price for Skyship before that, and for the people of AmEarth.

~~~

That evening, Billy received a communication from two men who had been his friends in Imperial City long ago, but who had been at odds with him in the past few years.

Starbot 4 stood in front of him, with the brief message on a screen across the front of his torso:

> Billy:
> It is time for us to set aside our differences and talk this over like gentlemen, instead of railing at each other in public, which has only pushed us farther and farther apart. The AmEarth Empire would like to send a diplomatic delegation to speak with you, and see if an end can be brought to these unnecessary hostilities.
> Respectfully,
> Paul Paulo and Jonathan Racker

Billy re-read the message. He agreed that the arguing had been going on for too long, beginning with high-level demands that he leave Skyship and turn it over to government control, then building up to the mass public demonstrations against him that were occurring now. He only wanted to be left alone to do his important work, and all of the uproar had been deeply upsetting to him. Maybe the delegation would deliver an apology, or at least agree to stop the demonstrations against him. But if they repeated the demand that he step down, it would be a non-starter, and the meeting would end quickly.

CHAPTER 17

"Trying to defeat the campaign of lies is like trying to stuff the proverbial genie back in the bottle. I fear it cannot be done."

—Lainey Forster, private comment

Yürgen Zayeddi had been assigned to one of the many public-relations teams that were being dispatched to major cities around the world, all hotspots of activity against Billy Jeeling. Because of the urgency of the situation, the PR Manager Lainey Forster had sped up the schedule. Early that morning she had seen off fifteen teams at the main dock on Skyship, telling them, "I wish we had more time for your training, but there is an urgent need for action. You are all dedicated people, and have impressed me with your zeal. I know you will do well."

Sonya Orr had been there, too, as the proctor of Yürgen's team. The tall blonde stood silently near Forster and other proctors, stealing glances at Yürgen every once in a while, and giving him flirtatious little smiles. He didn't know how he felt about this. Should he risk getting fired by trying to get closer to her? She certainly was encouraging him. There was no denying that. He'd never seen a more beautiful woman, and felt a powerful attraction toward her.

Yürgen and his classmates had only undergone five weeks of training, but the simulations had been especially useful. In the neighborhoods of Skyship, the PR teams had practiced dealing with different types of mass demonstrations and anti-Billy speeches, learning methods of diffusing mob rage and getting the truth out....

Now he and two other members of his team disembarked from a groundjet on the surface of the planet, stepping out onto a conveyor walkway that carried them smoothly toward the terminal building. They wore small day packs. Most of their luggage was being sent ahead to the hotel where they would be staying for a week.

It was mid-morning and unseasonably cool for the Southern Europaea Territory. Yürgen shivered, looked past the jetport to the sprawling metropolis beyond. Thorian City was an industrial center that sprawled across a two-kilometer-high plateau, and had once been among the most polluted cities on AmEarth. And yet today (as on all days according to reports) the sky was a lovely shade of cerulean blue, without a hint of pollution. Even though the evidence of Billy's good work was all around the Thorians, and they now breathed clean, pure air, they were still demonstrating against him in increasing numbers. To Yürgen, it didn't make any sense. They were ingrates!

The handsome Rand Baker stood beside him on the moving walkway, and their team leader Nanette Kingston trailed along behind them. She was the tallest of the three, with large green eyes and auburn hair, and a stuffy, condescending manner about her. She didn't seem to like very many people, so Yürgen and Rand had worried privately about her effect on team morale. Still, she was passionately pro-Billy Jeeling, and had expressed her anxiousness to get to work. Yürgen and Rand had agreed to overlook her irritating personality, or at least make the attempt, and just focus on what they had to do.

A big demonstration against Billy was scheduled at midday, in the town plaza. Yürgen's team would barely have time for breakfast, before going on front-line duty for the first time.

After they stepped off the walkway inside the terminal, Nanette stood in front of them and said, "We're going to skip breakfast, so we can check the demonstration site. The energy kits in our packs will have to be sufficient until dinner."

Yürgen and Rand exchanged looks of displeasure. She turned abruptly and walked ahead of them at a brisk pace, leaving no room for discussion. They hurried to keep up.

~~~

By the time they arrived at the town center, it was two hours before the scheduled start of the demonstration, but it was already underway early. Signs and banners hung on buildings around the plaza, and were being set up by demonstrators, proclaiming, "JEELING IS STEALING!" and "KILL YOURSELF, BILLY, BEFORE WE DO IT!" and "BILLY JEELING: THE ANTI-CHRIST." Others made crude sexual jokes based on his initials.

Yürgen thought the comments were unkind and in bad taste, and they infuriated him. Billy didn't deserve to be the brunt of off-color jokes. He wasn't a thief, either, and had never put himself forth as a religious figure, or as satanic. He had the giant cross atop Skyship, that was true, but he allowed complete freedom of religious expression on board the vessel, and had never claimed to be any sort of a messianic figure—so he couldn't be called the Anti-Christ. It made no sense. None of it made any sense.

On side streets, people were bringing in parade floats, each with a hateful message on it, including one that showed Billy in a SkyCorps uniform, being hung in effigy. Another showed his severed head on a pike. The mob was dangerously angry, in a frenzy of hatred.

Yürgen felt acid boiling up from his stomach. The small energy-meal he'd eaten had been too spicy, and besides, he was upset at seeing stupid, ungrateful people protesting against the man he considered to be the greatest, most heroic figure in human history. Yürgen was also hungry, wanted to find something nourishing and soothing to eat.

The three of them spread out and moved into the crowd, tapping control sticks on their belts as they did so. This sent signals to short-circuit bullhorns and loudspeakers all around them, causing them to go silent. People began to mutter and question what was happening, and then even the protestors' individual voices, and the noises of the crowd were reduced to only a few decibels collectively by a blanket of selective noise suppressors, so that Zayeddi—and everyone else—only heard muted sounds.

Now by prearrangement, each of the team members climbed onto places above the throng—any high spot they could find on which to stand. From his perch on top of a jet truck, Zayeddi heard the blaring voices of Nanette Kingston and Rand Baker across the plaza—voices that rang out over the crowd in clarion calls, even as the masses were effectively silenced. Alternating as if they were having a conversation over the heads of the stunned people, these two spewed forth facts about all the good Billy Jeeling had been doing for years, all of the lives he had saved with his planet-wide project to cleanse and restore the atmosphere. Some people tried to shout out in objection, but were unable to do so, as if they were dogs wearing bark collars.

Yürgen Zayeddi was the last to speak of the trio, after his companions were finished and signaled for him to begin. Knowing in advance that many of the people in the crowd would be members of minority races, he had selected a speech that was tailor-made for this occasion.

"Billy Jeeling is the greatest man who ever lived," he said, "and the zenith of anyone who ever will live. He's a black man, of AmAfrican heritage, but to him that is not his defining characteristic, as he considers himself to be merely a human being. Yet to many of his detractors, his race is an undercurrent of their criticisms. There is a simmering rage that he is not only a successful black man, but a proud and outspoken one as well—and refuses to step down in the face of criticism.

"Try to understand the scale of this injustice. The accomplishments of Billy's lifetime are so immense in comparison with anyone else that he cannot step down under criticism. He would only step down of his own free will, without pressure. He would only retire when he considers it is time to do so, when he can do no more to help the people of AmEarth.

"But now is not the time for him to go! The atmosphere is much cleaner than it once was, but there are still pockets of dirty skies over the planet that must be cleaned—regions where multinational corporations secretly paid off someone in the Empire to obtain permits to run factories that burn fossil fuels, spewing black smoke into the atmosphere. These greedy corporations want Billy out of the way, because he has embarrassed them by exposing their bribery and pollution crimes. Don't listen to them!"

A number of people paid attention to what Yürgen Zayeddi was saying, and he saw some of them nodding. But not enough. Others—the majority—had at first been mesmerized, but now were showing increasing anger. He saw a brown-uniformed security force moving toward him, pushing its way through the thick clogs of people.

Yürgen turned and climbed down the other side of the truck, then melded into the throng and disappeared. Half an hour later, he and his companions met on the street outside a restaurant, having sent mindcoms back and forth to settle on a rendezvous point.

"We'll take a few minutes break and then go back," Nanette said.

"Isn't it dangerous to go back?" Rand Baker asked. His eyes were open wide. He looked as if he wished he hadn't volunteered to work on a Jeeling PR team.

"We're armed," Nanette said, touching an array of small camouflaged weapons on her belt.

"I know, but against so many? We're risking our lives out there."

"What the hell did you expect when you volunteered for this work?" she asked. "Roses and candy from people who hate Billy?"

"No, but—"

Nanette interrupted him with a stream of scolding comments, and he fell silent under her tirade.

Yürgen looked past her and Rand, to the restaurant. His stomach growled with hunger. He could see people inside, eating real food and enjoying themselves. He wished he were with them.

But Nanette wasn't interested in that place, even though they had met in front of it. She had only one thing on her mind, getting back into the fray as soon as possible. She finished her rant, then checked her weapons—a poison shooter, a needle gun, and a packet of small throwing knives.

Yürgen understood her passion better than Rand seemed to. A strange fellow, he behaved in a detached way most of the time, not as fervent as he should be about protecting the public image of Billy Jeeling. He almost seemed to be going along with the PR effort just for the ride.

But Rand Baker's instructors had not seemed to notice this, and his grades had been almost as good as Yürgen's. Even so, there were things Baker did—tones of voice, facial expressions—that made him seem to be something other than the way he was presenting himself. It was as if someone had forced him into this duty, a parent, perhaps.

Maybe his family gave him the choice of working for Billy, or service in the military.

Yürgen sighed in exasperation, but realized everyone could not be as passionate about Billy Jeeling as he and Nanette were.

CHAPTER 18

Jeeling is proselytizing on Skyship. Even though he denies it, he uses insidious tricks to pressure everyone on board to convert to Christianity. Why else would he install a huge Christian cross on top of the ship? And what's next after that? Will he attack your own community? He burns non-Christian holy books in incinerators!

—From a pamphlet full of lies, distributed in Cairo City and in the Mumbai Municipality

"I'm sorry to report that you are still not pregnant," Dr. Ginsberg said. The silver-haired woman stood in front of Lainey, who sat on an examination table in a small, pristine room where everything was white and clean.

Lainey felt sadness welling up inside her. She so wanted to have Billy's child. Was it ever going to happen? With each passing day, her hopes waned. But she tried to continue to believe it was possible.

"What do you think our children would look like if I could have a baby?" Lainey asked. "Would they be light-skinned like me, dark like Billy, or something in between—perhaps a beautiful golden brown? I would like that, showing a combination of our races, demonstrating that great beauty can come from mixing the genetics of two very different-looking people."

"I'm sure they would be beautiful," Dr. Ginsberg said, but she had an odd look on her face. Lainey couldn't quite figure it out.

The doctor wore a VR headset, and turned it on. A three-dimensional display popped up in front of her eyes—a blank medical form that she filled in with black lettering that appeared when she spoke into the receiver. She was entering details about this session into the data base for Skyship Hospital.

It was weird to Lainey, with the virtual-reality display floating between them, something that was there, but not there at the same time, because she could pass her hand completely through it, if she wanted to do so. She was seeing it from the backside now, could read some of the words backwards. But this report was not her primary concern.

She felt an infusion of deep sadness. "Billy worries that we can't conceive. He's been saying that more and more, and he's genuinely sad about it. Maybe his worrying is getting in the way, preventing us from having a child. Could you please talk with him, and get him to relax about this? I've heard that tension can prevent conception. That's not an old wives' tale, is it?"

"I've heard the same thing, but have never seen any scientific evidence to support it. Even so, it sounds possible. Of course, I would be happy to talk with Billy about it."

Lainey nodded. There had been rumors that Billy and the doctor were romantically involved. She had asked both of them about it, and received firm denials. They seemed sincere and convincing, and she genuinely liked both of them. She loved Billy, but she also *liked* him. He had a genuine quality about him, an intense focus on his critically important environmental work. And Dr. Ginsberg was similar in a sense, with a passion for her medical work, helping people to get well. A rumor held that she was a spinster, and was going to stay that way for the rest of her life.

I'm a spinster, too, Lainey thought. *But I want to change that.*

Rumors. Lainey shook her head sadly. The terrible things that people on AmEarth said about Billy, depicting him as a monster, and not the savior of humankind he really was. How could they say such awful, unproven things about him?

She peered through the virtual-reality display, studied the doctor's hazel eyes. If she didn't wear those round eyeglasses, and if she did something with her graying hair, she would be quite pretty. Was her appearance a disguise, to prevent Lainey from being jealous? Actually, from being *more* jealous than she already was?

On an intellectual level Lainey understood the nonphysical relationship Billy apparently had with this woman; it made sense. But on an emotional level, on a gut-instinct level, she sensed that the two of them were keeping something from her. She'd seen that inexplicably odd expression on the doctor's face a few moments ago.

What was wrong here? Could it be a genetic trait that Lainey had, or a dread disease, something in her body that prevented her from becoming the loving mother she wanted to be? Or was the problem with Billy? Was he all right physically? He was old, but men could still be fathers at his age. Many were. Maybe it was something else about him physically, something he hadn't revealed to her. Lainey worried more about him than she did about herself.

Dr. Ginsberg noticed Lainey looking at her, and shut off the VR display. "Are you feeling all right, dear?"

Lainey looked away, didn't reply. She didn't want to say what was on her mind. It would make her sound crazy. And a new thought was working its way into her awareness, wriggling in like a venomous snake. Was the doctor doing something to her to *prevent* a pregnancy?

If she ever found that to be true, Lainey felt capable of killing the woman.

Stop taking medications from her, she thought. *And no more shots.*

Dr. Ginsberg turned and went to a cabinet, where she kept such things. She opened a drawer, began preparing a syringe by filling it from a vial.

Lainey leaped off the examination table and ran out of the room. Behind her, the doctor called her name, asking what was wrong. But Lainey didn't answer. She just kept going, as fast as she could.

CHAPTER 19

Every human has a secret life.

—Ancient saying

Billy was up earlier than usual this morning, and used the extra time to take a highlift to the walkway where he sometimes went to think about important matters, and to gaze out into the universe of stars. Except this time he used his security code to go through a wide doorway into a windowless corridor. He passed a glassplaz door, through which he could see one of his private library-reading rooms, and then paused his chair at a second glassplaz door, to look in at a number of Lazarus-series robots he had stored inside, along with mood-modification transmitters, other accessories, and spare parts.

These robots were only skeletons now, with no identifiable features except for the internal workings and exterior characteristics that identified them as male or female—twenty of each gender. These units did not have human imprints on them yet, which would give them customized personalities and appearances, such as the imprint he gave to Lainey. She was one of a dozen operating robots of this model, "men" and "women" who worked on board. There had been problems with some of the units, including Lainey, but nothing so serious that it warranted shutting any of the machines down and replacing them with backups. He could customize the appearances of robots easier than their personalities, so conceivably he could send a robot to replace Lainey that looked exactly like her, but with a completely different (or slightly different) personality.

There were numerous options, and because this model was still experimental, he maintained detailed written records of the experiments he conducted, somewhat like Tobek's leather-bound journals — except Billy's were large dark blue volumes, while Tobek's were red. Billy's completed laboratory journals were stacked neatly on a shelf inside the room, while Tobek's remained inside the sealed laboratory complex where he died. Billy also had audiovisual records.

On his maglev chair he continued down the corridor, to the last glassplaz door on the right, and looked through it into a small specialized laboratory that he maintained, where he kept the genetic samples that were used to imprint human traits onto the Lazarus-series robots. The samples were inside several wide refrigerated cabinets at the back of the room. He could see the small sealed packets through the clear doors of the cabinets, arranged neatly on shelves, with each sample marked as to its source.

Each of the sample packets contained a variety of genetic samples, in sealed packet sleeves — such as blood, hair, saliva, skin scrapings and other cellular material, toenails and fingernails, semen, amniotic fluid, earwax, brain tissue, organ parts, and more — depending upon what was available from a deceased human being (such as Reanne), or a living person whose samples he sometimes collected. One of the packets even had his own name on it, and contained a variety of his genetic materials. The variety of samples from each donor came in handy in the customization of a Lazarus-series robot — because the more different parts of the original body he had on hand, the closer he could make the robotic version match the real human. It was best to grow the various body parts separately from real genetic material (and combined later), but whatever could not be grown that way could be synthesized. Through careful study and experimentation, he had developed methods of generating human parts out of artificial materials, but the more he had to make this way, the less the robot was likely to resemble the original human.

He didn't come up to this level as often as when he was first developing the Lazarus androids, but whenever he had spare time he still liked to tinker around in one of his laboratories, which he had both here and in the secret core of the ship. It reminded him of the time that Branson Tobek had spent in his own laboratories, first on

AmEarth and later on Skyship. They were places to be creative, where new ideas could be developed.

Today, he wrote an entry in an open journal, details he'd been noticing about two of the working Lazarus models that were operating on the ship, little variations from what he had anticipated, and thoughts about what he might do to prevent this from recurring on future activations.

~~~

At midday, a government vessel from the AmEarth Empire hovered just outside Skyship's docking port for visitors, waiting for permission to connect, and for its passengers to come aboard. They identified themselves as emissaries from the government of Prime Minister Yhatt. Skyship was in the upper troposphere, where it would remain for the next couple of days.

Without responding to them yet, Billy Jeeling ordered his son and a squadron of police security robots to meet him in the terminal lobby, a sealed enclosure with a large viewing window.

Devv took a seat in a chair at the viewing window, beside Billy, who was already there in his maglev chair. Billy leaned forward and gazed at the visiting craft. It was long and slim, with retractable wings and an adjustable stem-to-stern arch... the sort of passenger conveyance that had not been popular for decades. In its heyday the designers attributed great aerodynamic and cosmic properties to it. Wind and planetary forces were taken into account, Jeeling recalled them saying, and the ship's configuration could be adjusted to such an arch that it resembled a flying banana, except it was silver, not yellow.

"I know that ship," he said. He straightened.

"Kanaba class passenger ship," Devv Jeeling said. "An old one. High AmEarth range, fully loaded with luxuries. Old style fuel pellets. What's that say on the side?" Devv asked, squinting. "Over the hatch?"

"Top Banana," the elder Jeeling said, without humor. "It's the Prime Minister's personal ship, but apparently he's not aboard."

"Permission to come aboard," a voice said, crackling across the parabolic speakers in the lobby.

Billy let out his breath slowly, glanced up at Devv.

"Put scanners on that ship," Devv shouted to one of the security 'bots. "So we can see this guy."

On the robot's torso, a vertical light tube pulsed blue. The sentient machine rolled to one of the instrument panels, made several settings, and an intense white light bathed the passenger ship. Billy Jeeling and his son moved close to a multi-dimensional screen that went on, casting fuzzy gray light. An image clarified and focused in color, and the picture wandered as scanners moved over the ship, searching for the man who had spoken. There were perhaps two hundred men and women aboard, in their comfortable seats or standing about, talking. Among them were security officers wearing the bright red uniforms of the Imperial Guard. Jeeling estimated twenty-five or thirty of these officers in the main passenger cabin.

The scanner moved to a private cabin at the rear of the ship, and focused on two people there, whom he recognized as his former friend Paul Paulo in a black silk suit, and a woman whom he did not know. The cabin was lavishly decorated, with paintings and sculptures that looked as if they might be originals.

"That's him," Billy said. "Open com."

The robot flipped a lever, opening the lobby's transmitting parabolics, and Billy Jeeling spoke tersely: "Paul, get your wrinkled old ass out of here. I don't want to talk to you or anyone else."

"Ah, Billy!" Paul Paulo responded. His words were a little out of synch with his image, and the 'bot made adjustments to correct this. "And how are you today, my old friend?"

"I've been better."

"That's why I'm here, to see what I can do to improve that. Flip something on so I can see you." The elegant old man toyed nervously with golden buttons on his sleeves.

"I like it better this way. What sort of scheme are you up to now, Paul?"

"I'm not your enemy. I've done nothing against you, Billy, so help me God. Are you looking at me?"

"Yeah. You and your young girlfriend."

"I'm not his girlfriend!" the woman exclaimed. She was not really that young but was quite pretty nonetheless, a brunette with large green eyes.

"This is Maureen Stuart," Paul Paulo said. "She's happily married, and is the legal adviser to a group of your adversaries. I've brought her with a delegation of experts who understand your point of view and the opposite, to see if some progress can be made to end our present difficulties."

"Contrary to some of the rumors on your planet, I remain loyal to the Empire. I always have been. It's just that I don't intend to be forced out of my life's work. I should be appreciated for what I've done, not criticized, burned in effigy, or ridiculed."

"There's truth in what you say, my old friend. It's why I was sent here, to bring the parties together." Paulo nodded somberly, placed one hand in a large pocket of his magnificent black silk suit, and then motioned expansively with the other hand, like a politician delivering a speech. "Billy, I've never said anything against you in public. I'd like to help sort all this out."

"Too late for that. Tangents are spinning off of tangents. Wild rumors are breeding like flies in the dark, in festering, moist crap. Very little of it bears any resemblance to the truth."

"You tell 'em, Billy!" Devv exclaimed.

He didn't look at the Security Commander or show that he'd heard.

"Grant us permission to come aboard," Paulo said. "We'll talk about it." He paused. "For the good and close friends we once were. I ask you as a personal favor. Will you do this for me, Billy?"

He felt his resistance fading, a moment in which fond memories of this man surfaced in his memory. "All right, Paul, but for only an hour. I haven't had my lunch yet. Have you eaten? Would you like to join me?"

"Haven't eaten yet. That would be nice. Thank you."

"Leave your guardsmen on Yhatt's ship. You won't be needing them."

"Of course. Is it all right if Mrs. Stuart joins us? She is quite a rational, balanced person, and good at coming up with solutions to problems. You will like her. Later, with your permission, I could bring more people to negotiate the details with your... specialists."

"I'm not leaving Skyship, so get that out of your head. If that's what you're here about, you might as well turn around and go back."

"All right, Billy, the subject won't even come up. Just me and Mrs. Stuart for a pleasant lunch. All right?"

"OK, then. I will be with my son. Just the four of us."

"Oh yes, your Security Commander."

A few minutes later the ship connected to the dock with magnetic clamps, and the main hatch irised open, like the widening of an immense eye. It was an odd, round door, more stylistic than practical, with a curved floor on the bottom. Paulo stepped across the threshold and onto a downward-sloping, sealed tunnel, followed by the brunette.

The tunnel opened into a tile-floored lobby. There, Billy rode his maglev chair forward on its cushion of air, with Devv beside him. A score of heavily armed security robots remained a few paces behind them.

When Paul Paulo introduced Maureen Stuart to them, the woman said, "Very pleased to finally meet you, sir. There have been too many misunderstandings, and I hope to help—"

Just then, Billy heard the friction of sliding metal, and was startled to see numerous hidden gun ports opening on the side of the passenger ship. A loud barrage of weapon fire ensued, discharging projectiles that dropped the entire force of security robots before they could get off a single shot.

Red-uniformed guardsmen poured out of the ship, carrying laser rifles that glowed bright blue on their handles, ready to fire. The scanners had not detected them, so camouflage technology must have been used.

"What the hell is this?" Paulo shouted. "Stop and go back! Immediately! I didn't order this!"

The guardsmen ignored him. "We take our orders from General Moore, not from you," one of them said. A short man, he appeared to be the commander of the squad, had a silver officer's insignia on his collar.

Alarm klaxons sounded, a cacophony of urgent noise. Devv was able to draw an automatic handgun, and stood protectively next to his father. But he didn't fire, not yet.

"We had no idea this was going to happen!" Stuart said. She seemed to be genuinely surprised, but it could be an act. And Paulo looked extremely angry — but that also could be feigned.

"Put down your weapon," the enemy commander said to Devv.

Devv hesitated, glanced at his father, who nodded. The younger Jeeling then turned the gun around and offered it to the officer, handle-first.

Before the officer could take it, Billy grabbed the weapon and fired a barrage of rounds, dropping the startled officer to the deck, and then shooting other guardsmen. He put his maglev chair into motion, whirling it around and firing with great accuracy, in multiple directions. Devv had another gun out and was firing, too. It was one of the defensive maneuvers the two of them had practiced, for contingencies such as this. Now Billy was gambling that his attackers wanted to take him alive, and he had a special way of protecting his son....

~~~

A loud roar filled Billy's ears, and a sharp pain stabbed his right shoulder. His chair tumbled over and he fell out, bumping against Devv and then falling beside him. Red all around. The unwelcome uniforms of his enemies, and he saw blood flowing from Devv's forehead. His lifeless eyes were staring into infinity. Devv appeared to be dead, but Billy knew otherwise.

Billy felt strong hands lifting him off the deck, people who were ignoring his injury, touching his shoulder where it hurt terribly, carrying him toward the ship. Two large men in uniforms.

Paulo and Stuart were somewhere nearby. He couldn't see them, but heard them on the dock behind him, protesting that they had nothing to do with this and demanding that Billy be released. Paulo called it an outrage, and a betrayal. Billy agreed, wondered if his old friend and Stuart had been used as pawns.

The guardsmen had Billy on the ramp now, carrying him up it, with the maglev chair being brought behind them. Billy saw the large round hatch of the passenger ship just ahead as they hurried him toward it. But more of his own police security robots appeared suddenly, and fired precision shots that dropped the guardsmen, causing them to lose their grip on Billy. He tumbled over, fell a couple of meters off the ramp and onto the deck, landing hard. Fortunately he fell leg stumps first, and they were already useless. On the deck near his overturned chair, in some pain and unable to walk, he watched as his security force swarmed the guardsmen and shot them down. He saw Paul Paulo fall with them, shot in the chest and bleeding. Stuart ran to him, cradled his head on her lap.

"He's dead!" she wailed. "We were tricked! We had *nothing* to do with this!"

Medics ran onto the dock, in pale blue outfits. Dr. Rachel Ginsberg was in their midst, and she hurried to Billy, where she tended to his shoulder injury, applying medication and a healing pad. She told him to move what he could, then said after he did so, "You don't seem to have broken anything."

"My shoulder hurts like hell." As he said this, he felt the pain begin to diminish, and the wounded area felt refreshingly cool, from medications in the healing pad.

One of the medics checked Devv, then looked up and said to Ginsberg, "He's gone."

"Rush him to my office," she commanded. "I'm going to perform an autopsy." She met Billy's gaze, said to him, "You're going to be fine."

"Your office?" The medic seemed surprised. "Not the hospital, or the morgue?"

"My *office*. I'll be right behind you."

She leaned close to Billy, so no one else could hear, and whispered, "Something tells me your son is going to have a miraculous recovery."

While the medics were taking care of transporting Devv away, robots righted Billy's chair and helped him back into it. The chair appeared to be undamaged. One of robots reported that they had taken more than fifty people into custody from the diplomatic vessel, and were awaiting Billy's instructions.

"Keep the live prisoners here, but load the guardsmen's bodies onto the ship, and Paulo's too," Billy said. "Then cut the ship loose and fire on it. I want it blasted out of the sky."

"But it's an important vessel, sir. The Prime Minister will not be happy to hear that it's been—"

"You're a robot. Don't forget that. Now do as I say, and put the whole event on video-cam, for transmission to AmEarth. I want them to know I mean business. They have violated my privacy in the worst way, tried to kidnap me, and might have murdered me, if we hadn't fought back. They are acting immorally, are in gross breach of contract. Now it's cost them lives, and a classic ship, too."

The robot flashed a green acknowledgement light on its torso, then turned and did as it was told.

The diplomatic vessel was released into the thin atmosphere, and began to drop toward AmEarth. Billy knew it would be destroyed when it hit the ground anyway, but he wanted to make an even more emphatic statement.

Kinetic cannons discharged from Skyship, slamming hot balls of fiery energy into the famed, tumbling vessel, blowing it to pieces.

CHAPTER 20

The human body is extremely fragile, and subject to
constant attacks from the inside, and the outside.

—Branson Tobek, early writings

This morning Lainey was scheduled to visit Billy in the hospital,
but she had almost an hour to burn before they would allow her in.
She could walk the short distance in a few minutes.

Until then, she stood in the terminal lobby beside Sonya Orr,
watching through the window as a passenger shuttle floated in toward the dock. The arriving craft had a pair of clamps extended like
the claws of a carrion bird, and they engaged with the wide magnetic
bar of the dock, neatly securing the ship into position beside other
vessels. The shuttle jostled a little before coming to rest, and Lainey
felt a slight vibration in the floor beneath her feet.

Moments later, teams of public-relations operatives streamed
through the clearplaz tunnel into the terminal. The JeeJees were just
returning, having worked all over AmEarth, spreading the good word
about Billy, telling heroic anecdotes about his life, to counter the campaign of lies that was being orchestrated against him. Lainey had
been receiving regular reports since they'd been on assignment, and
most of the teams had performed exceptionally well. She noticed a
few of her favorites in the group as they took positions in front of her,
to hear what she had to say... Hanni Vinson, Yürgen Zayeddi, Wesley
Yota, and others.

Lainey raised the palms of her hands to quiet the assemblage, then
said, "Yesterday there was an outrageous, cowardly attempt to kidnap our beloved Master of Skyship. He was injured in the attempt,

and is in the hospital. The perpetrators were Imperial Guardsmen, hiding behind a fake diplomatic mission."

The fervent supporters of Billy Jeeling cried out in shock and rage, but quieted down when Lainey told them his injuries were not severe, and he was already recovering.

"We took a leading member of their 'peace delegation' prisoner— an attorney named Maureen Stuart—along with a number of guardsmen, and learned from an officer that General Moore intended to capture Billy and execute him following a sham trial. His son Devv was injured much more severely than Billy — at first everyone thought it was fatal, but miraculously Dr. Ginsberg was able to revive him. He's in a special intensive care unit now, and is said to be improving."

Most of the team members were visibly angry. In the front of the group, Yürgen Zayeddi looked particularly upset.

"I'm heading for the hospital now," Lainey said, "but I wanted to greet you first and give you the news. It's not great news, but could have been much worse. You've all done a fine job and I'm very pleased; I've seen the reports, and you are to be congratulated. As soon as Billy is feeling up to it, I'm sure he will want to thank you personally."

~~~

When Lainey arrived at the hospital, she was surprised to see Billy sitting on his custom chair in the lobby, heading for the main exit door. "I'm checking out of this place right now," he said to her, stopping his chair. "I have too much work to do. Can't stay on my back in that room, or my work will pile up."

"Are you sure you're feeling up to this?" She noticed that his shirt had been cut open at the right shoulder so that medical wraps could be put in place on his wounded skin.

"Work is therapeutic for me. I'll rot away if I remain in this palace of pain." He put his chair in motion toward the main entrance, and she followed.

On the sidewalk outside, he said, "I didn't know you were coming, but as long as you're here, you might as well come with me. I'm going to visit Devv."

"He's all right?"

"Improving. I'm getting good reports."

Billy flipped down the sidecar of the maglev chair and motioned for her to get in. She barely got into the seat, and before she could put her safety restraint in place, he took off down the middle of a sidewalk, going fast, and causing people to scurry out of the way. He smiled and waved to them. The unusual chair rounded a corner, and came to a stop at an emergency entrance at the rear of the hospital.

"You'll have to go on foot from here," he said. Billy motioned for her to climb out, which she did.

The sidecar snapped shut, making the chair narrow enough to go through the entrance into this wing of the hospital. She almost had to run to keep up. He entered a highlift, and she joined him, just before the doors slammed shut. The car sped upward, toward the ICU tower.

Billy said, "Dr. Ginsberg has been working on Devv, says he's making good progress."

"I heard that his injuries are severe. I didn't see him after he was hit; he was whisked away from the scene of the attack too quickly. How long will he be incapacitated?"

Billy laughed. "Incapacitated? I'll have you know, the leaf doesn't fall far from the tree when it comes to my son. He's as anxious to get back to work as I am."

"Will he have any permanent injuries?"

"Not a one. He'll be as perfect as the day he was born." Billy grinned. "Maybe even better."

As they stepped out of the lift and Lainey followed Billy down the corridor, she had a nice view of the interior of Skyship City, with its gleaming office buildings and elevated walkways. Little humbaby aircraft flitted through the interior sky with their top rotors spinning; some landed on building roofs and on the tops of elevated walkways, and took off from them. Far below, she saw the large central park of the airborne metropolis, an expanse of broad, leafy trees and green grazzeen. It was crowded with people, tiny specs from this elevation.

Billy's chair sped ahead, causing doctors and nurses to step hurriedly out of the way. Lainey was breathing hard when she followed him into a room, passing a sign on the door that said no medical personnel except Dr. Ginsberg were allowed to enter. The door opened and shut automatically, so that it was closed when they were barely inside. The sign seemed odd to Lainey. Was she acting as both doctor and nurse? Why wasn't she getting any help?

Lainey saw the doctor leaning over Devv, who was sitting up on the bed, with his back supported by pillows. Devv was wide awake, had a stack of reports and other documents on his lap. The doctor was checking something on his chest. Lainey couldn't quite tell what, before Ginsberg stopped whatever she was doing, and turned to face Billy. "I am pleased to say that your son is much better. He's already back to work, using this hospital room as his office."

There were no wires or machines hooked to him, and none in the room. He appeared to be fully alert, and she didn't see any visible injuries, not even to his head where he had reportedly sustained a grievous injury, causing him to bleed profusely. Reportedly, he had looked dead, very dead.

How could this possibly be? Lainey was too stunned to even frame a question, or make an observation. She'd heard it was a miracle that he was even alive at all, and now she was seeing it first-hand. He was like the legendary Phoenix, reborn from its own ashes.

Devv grinned. When Ginsberg pulled away from him, he picked up a bound report, and said, "My robots performed lie detection tests on all of the captive guardsmen, and on that attorney with them, Maureen Stuart. Apparently she's some sort of a contracts expert, and among her other duties she was advising Jonathan Racker, Paul Paulo, and General Moore on the legalities of Billy's contract with the AmEarth government. This peace delegation was her idea, and she meant to carry it out in good faith."

"So what the hell happened?" Billy asked.

"General Rivington Moore happened, that's what. He used the delegation as a stalking horse, concealing a commando squad of guardsmen with a mission to get you—alive if possible, but dead was an option."

"She didn't know anything about it?"

"Not according to four truthbots who interrogated her from every angle. All of the guardsmen knew about the mission, though."

"And Paul Paulo?"

"She thinks he was a pawn of General Moore, too—and died because of it. She's very angry at the General—honest anger. Says she'll find a way to do something about him if she's allowed to return to AmEarth."

"All right," Billy said. "Send her back on a shuttle. Maybe she can make General Moore look like a fool, and get him to lose power."

Devv nodded. "And the commandos?"

"Send them back, too. Even though they knew about Moore's plan, they were pawns, too, just following orders. Let them get the word out about our compassion, and our determination to resist any trick they try to throw our way."

Devv Jeeling smiled to his father, and to Lainey. "I'm feeling much better!" he exclaimed. He swung his legs out of bed, stepped onto the floor in his hospital smock. "In fact, I think I'm going to go home right now. This hospital food is really lousy, you know, and it's hard to get a decent night's sleep with all the lights and activity."

Lainey knew her own jaw was visibly open. Devv set the documents on a rolling table, slipped into an adjacent bathroom to get dressed.

"He's ready to be discharged," Dr. Ginsberg confirmed. "I've been working on him all night to get him ready."

"I've never seen anything like this," Lainey said.

"Rachel is an excellent doctor," Billy said. "The best I've ever seen."

"Can't argue with that after seeing this," Lainey said.

Devv was out of the bathroom quickly, wearing what looked like a new Security Commander uniform, blue with white trim. He gathered a handful of belongings and stuffed them into his pockets, then packed papers into a black briefcase. Finally, he put on his cap and adjusted it in front of the mirror. "I'm as good as new," he announced. "Okay, let's get out of here. How about lunch? I have a ferocious hunger!"

Just then, a matronly nurse walked by and told Devv that Sonya Orr had called to ask how he was doing.

"Good enough to chase her around Skyship!" Devv exclaimed. "Call her and warn her!"

The nurse laughed, and continued on down the corridor.

As Lainey left with the two men and walked behind them in the corridor, she had the most peculiar sensation. Ahead of her, a father and son were chatting casually, as if nothing had just happened to either of them. But Lainey had an odd feeling, especially about Devv. Something was not right with him. She'd experienced this before in his presence, and had always tried to dismiss the feeling. After all, the truthbots had checked Devv carefully, just as they had vetted everyone on Skyship, and there were periodic, unannounced re-checks, even for Billy Jeeling—to prevent anyone from creating a look-alike and taking his identity.

She didn't think the problem with Devv had anything to do with a trust issue, or with any danger to Billy, herself, or Skyship. No, this was something else.

Like an itch that she could not quite reach, it continued to bother her.

CHAPTER 21

The human mind can imagine anything, for good or evil. What do you suppose Billy Jeeling is thinking about now? You can be certain it is not good.

—From "Jeeling: the Awakening," one of General Moore's propaganda articles

Yürgen Zayeddi had imagined this might happen if he were ever alone with this spectacularly-beautiful woman, but it had been more erotic fantasy than anything else—a flight of the imagination to make his blood flow, but not to take seriously. Besides, there were the obvious dangers involved, preventing him from living out his fantasy. Yet, it had become a reality anyway.

He lay in bed watching Sonya dress, slipping her underclothes over the pleasing curves of her figure. They were in her studio apartment, which was not large, but was more comfortable than his humble room. As a proctor, she didn't have to suffer the inconvenience of a roommate. After a few drinks, the two of them had sneaked in during the darkness of enhanced night on the great vessel, giggling like teenagers eluding their parents.

The moment they entered her apartment and closed the door, they were at each other in a frenzy of passion, throwing off clothes and making love—first on the carpet and then on the bed, and then again on the bed.

It was an hour before dawn now, when Skyship's internal systems would increase the illumination across the airborne city in a realistic-appearing way, running parallel with the coming of day outside. There were not enough windows on the great ship to do this naturally, but the effect inside was so close to perfect that Yürgen sometimes forgot where he was.

She looked at him, smiled gently. Her blue eyes sparkled. "You'd better get dressed yourself, and be on your way. Don't forget, *I* live here, not you!"

He grinned, swung out of bed and looked for his clothing, which was strewn across the floor, from the front door to the bedroom. "That was really something," he said. "*You're* really something. I could hardly keep up with you."

Her gaze narrowed. "I'll have you know, I am *not* a nymphomaniac."

"I never said you were. Of course, you're not. It's just that—"

"I've never been this way with anyone else," she said. "I knew the moment I saw you that we had something between us, a strong magnetism, a chemistry. Oh, I'm not saying I'm a virgin or anything crazy like that. But, well, you know what I'm talking about, don't you?"

"I know exactly what you mean. We have something special." He paused as he put on his shorts and an undershirt. "More than special. That's not a good enough word for it." And he really felt that way, beyond the powerful physical attraction he felt for her. They had talked for hours during the night, in between the lovemaking. She was interested in many of the same things he was — science, art, history, philosophy, and goals in life. Sonya was intensely devoted to Billy Jeeling, just as Yürgen was, yet she also wanted a family someday — and so did he.

He dressed quickly. They kissed at the door by a statuette of Billy Jeeling, spoke of when they might see other again, that evening. After a long embrace, they separated and Yürgen opened the door.

He was shocked to see Devv Jeeling there in his Security Commander's uniform, his face contorted in rage. Yürgen felt an impulse to take a step back, but held his ground.

"What are you doing here?" Devv demanded. He slammed into the other man, hitting him with a shoulder, and tried to get past him. But Yürgen gave him a forceful shove in return with his hands, knocking him hard against a wall and causing his officer's cap to fall off. The statuette rocked on its stand, but didn't fall.

Sonya ran forward, said, "I want you to leave, Devv. *Now!*"

Ignoring her, Devv drew a laser-bow from a holster and cocked the weapon, causing it to flex backward, ready to fire. It didn't need to flex. This was just for show, like the visual display of a wild animal, to intimidate and frighten an adversary. But the device really was capable of firing arrow-shaped shafts of light, and they were known to cause extreme pain and a slow death, from internal hemorrhaging. He pointed the deadly weapon at Zayeddi's chest.

Yürgen sneered. "Not man enough to fight me without that?"

"I don't need any more than my fists to deal with you!" Devv uncocked the laser-bow and holstered it. He advanced toward the other man.

Sonya stepped between them. "Stop this. Both of you!"

With an angry grunt, Devv pushed her to one side.

But she stepped between the men again. "I want you to leave, Devv. *Now*! Get out of here, damn it!"

He punched her in the face, and she cried out in anger, then swung her own fists at him, striking him on the arms. Yürgen tried to pull them apart, but Devv managed to hit her again, an even harder blow to the face. This backed her up, and this time she looked injured, putting her hands to her face, while cursing him.

Yürgen shoved Devv back toward the doorway. He simmered with anger toward the intruder, felt like hitting him. It was a peculiar situation, a man in a security officer's uniform, acting unlawfully.

"That was a real manly thing to do," Sonya said to Devv.

"I'm sorry," he said, "but you shouldn't be here with him, shouldn't—"

"I told you to get out of here," she said. Sonya picked up his fallen cap, threw it at him, and he caught it.

"You heard her," Yürgen said. Pressing his face close to Devv, he mustered more courage and said, "You're a creep. Sonya knows it, and that's why she's with me."

Devv didn't say anything. His eyes burned with rage and pain as he glared at Yürgen, and then at Sonya.

Yürgen would fight him if he had to. They were around the same height and weight, but Yürgen assumed the other man had training in combat techniques he didn't know. That didn't deter him. He would protect Sonya any way he could.

Sonya went around both men and held the door open. "Out," she said to Devv. She didn't look well, seemed to be in pain and had red bruises on her face.

Devv put on his cap, as if to leave, but said, "Look, I'm really sorry I hit you. It will never happen again." He appeared to be near tears.

"That's right," she said, "because we're finished. I don't ever want to see you again."

Looking as if the world had fallen on top of him, Devv Jeeling started to say something, but wilted under her glare. He turned abruptly, and hurried away.

When he was gone, Yürgen examined her reddened cheek and forehead, saw both areas beginning to swell up. "You'd better get some ice on your face."

"I'll be fine," she said. "Thanks for being here, but I need to be alone now. Okay?" She didn't meet his gaze, looked away. Now she appeared to be confused.

Yürgen felt uncertain about what he should do. She might have a concussion. "Are you sure you're okay?"

She nodded, but motioned for him to leave, waving a hand in the direction that Devv had gone. Yürgen left, saying, "I'll check on you tomorrow."

Sonya didn't answer. She closed the door quickly.

CHAPTER 22

"There are certain events in the life of each person that form critical junctures, where absolutely correct decisions must be made—or that life will tumble off a cliff, and take others over the edge with it."

—Billy Jeeling, in a note to his son, Devv

Billy had too much on his mind to sleep, even with the medications he took. The clutter of thoughts were worse than ever, it seemed to him, though he didn't see how that could possibly be the case, because of how incredibly crowded his calendar had been during the construction of Skyship, when Branson Tobek was still alive.

Nonetheless, it was as if all the decades of problems had mounted up and come to a climax at this very instant, all the years of secrets he'd been forced to keep by Tobek, and the personal stresses that resulted because he didn't know certain information, and didn't know how to solve particular problems. Very important information had been kept from him. He knew a great deal about repairing the planet's fragile atmosphere, more than any other living person—but the rub was this: any other *living* person. Tobek was dead, and Billy had checked the memories of every robot on the ship for help, not turning up anything he didn't already know, or have in the written instructions that Tobek gave him during the construction of the huge vessel. Instructions that Billy still had, well-organized and in a secret place.

He'd been tossing and turning all night. Now it was shortly before dawn, and he rode his maglev chair on its smooth cushion of air, out of the apartment and through the corridor. Then he took the highlift to a lower level, and exited into a wide interior space. He saw no one except numerous security robots, on duty.

Ahead lay the doors to the core of the ship, a place where only he and a handful of his most trusted robots could go. These were tall, burnished black doors, with the blue-sky insignia of Skyship on them. He touched a control pad on the chair, and the doors slid open quickly, with only a little noise of machinery. A chill ran down his spine as he thought of what he was about to do, something he had been putting off for a long time — telling himself he was never going to do it, but knowing deep in his soul that he would have to do it anyway some day. That he would have to do it.

The time had finally come.

His chair floated through the doorway, and the large doors snicked shut behind him.

The brilliant inventor Branson Tobek had lived with a whole host of marvelous technological and scientific secrets as his closest companions, but there had been far too many of them, and now Billy needed important information. At the top of the list, Tobek had told him that the ship contained something extremely dangerous, and that if the huge vessel ever blew up, it would set off disastrous chain reactions in the atmosphere, causing so much damage that all life on AmEarth would be virtually wiped out.

Alarmed, Billy had asked for more information, but always he had been given delaying excuses, due to the complexity of the required explanation, or some other reason — and told that he would be informed tomorrow, or the day after that, or the following week. Then the old man had passed away suddenly and unexpectedly, taking his secrets with him.

Later, Billy had felt obligated to pass the dire warning on to his political enemies on the planet, acting as if it came from his own knowledge — but it hadn't. All he'd really had was a sincere, foreboding sense that Tobek had been telling the truth, and that Skyship was potentially a bomb of devastating proportions. The great ship contained a deadly secret, an extermination secret, but what was it?

The answer, he felt certain, lay inside the sealed laboratory of the dead inventor, perhaps in Tobek's personal journals that the robots had placed inside the great man's tiny apartment, within the lab complex. The hidden laboratory, and Tobek's adjacent living quarters, had been sealed up ever since his troubling death, with those mysterious silver flashes around his body, and the horrific eruptions of silver blood.

What had the strange flashes been, and could they possibly be connected with Tobek's dire warning?

Even though Billy had been feeling a sense of loyalty to the old inventor, who hadn't wanted him to pry into whatever lay hidden inside the laboratory complex, he also felt a strong loyalty to the people of AmEarth, and he was deeply concerned about their well-being. And of the two conflicting loyalties, he was coming to realize, the latter affected far, far more people, and undoubtedly had much greater historical significance. Billions of lives hung in the balance.

He could not continue to operate in the dark when the stakes were so high. The slightest problem with Skyship could enlarge into something terrible. He needed to get to the bottom of the enigma, needed to take action instead of waiting. Something had unnerved Branson Tobek. Billy had seen that in his eyes when the old man spoke of the danger of atmospheric destruction. So there was a risk in entering the hidden laboratory, maybe a big one. This was a Hobson's choice, with no good option. Despite all, he had to go inside.

His pulse was going wild. Billy had to get to the three journals, and read them. He'd been going over options in his mind, ways to accomplish that—and he had a plan.

Several robots were still inside the sealed sections, and Billy could communicate with them from outside. He brought his chair to the viewing window, where he had a vantage of the room at the rear and the casket of the great Branson Tobek. A man whose accomplishments were mighty, but who had died without publicity, with only Billy knowing what a great scientist and visionary he had been. His body lay, undeservedly, in a plain, unmarked wooden casket, built by the lab 'bots.

Nervously, Billy touched a control pad under one arm of his chair. Moments later, a robot appeared on the other side of the thick glass, a shiny black machine with multiple-arms. It was of a series that Billy had built for Tobek, customized to assist the old inventor with tasks in the laboratory. A vertical light tube appeared on its torso, and began to glow softly green, pulsing as the sentient machine awaited a command.

Billy activated a transmitter, spoke into it. "Go to Tobek's apartment and retrieve his three red journals. I want you to pass them to me through the bio-lock." He pointed to his right, at a glassed-in box that was mounted beneath the main viewing window—a box that had a small pass-through door on the inside, and another door on the outside.

The robot surprised him, as it said in its mechanical voice, "You were commanded to leave the laboratory sealed, not to tamper with anything."

"I've thought this over carefully. The bio-lock will vacuum the air in the interior chamber, allowing me to reach inside safely and get the journals. The laboratory will remain sealed, as Tobek specified."

The mechanical voice had no inflection. "That sounds like a violation. It is not in the spirit of Master Tobek's intentions."

This was a strange comment from a robot, suggesting that the machine was capable of analyzing the nuances of intentions. Tobek must have added something to its programming.

Raising his voice, Billy said, "Place the journals into the bio-lock *immediately*, and they will be cleansed. I shall then open the door on my side and take them, while your side will remain sealed."

The robot stood motionless, pulsing green in its light tube, then yellow.

Billy felt mounting anger, stared hard at his mechanical adversary. It was obvious that this machine would not retrieve the journals, and even if Billy got inside by breaking in, the robot would summon its brethren and prevent him from doing what he wanted to do. Billy could take a force of security 'bots with him, in a show of force, but that might result in unwanted damage to the laboratory, or even the activation of self-destruct mechanisms, or worse. Much worse. And if he went inside himself, that would be a clear violation, a broken promise.

But Billy had an ace in the hole that just might work. He had designed this particular robot, and just might be able to override any commands that Tobek had given to it. Unless Tobek had taken that possibility into account, and set up clever safeguards.

He sent the override signal, and repeated his command in a firm voice.

The robot's light tube changed back to green and then darkened. The mechanical servant went into an adjacent room, disappearing from view. Moments later it returned, holding all three red, leather-bound volumes in its arms. Billy caught his breath in anticipation.

But at the bio-lock the robot hesitated, and focused its sensors through the glass on Billy Jeeling, who narrowed his gaze as he looked at the robot. The machine's light tube began to pulse wildly, yellow again, followed by bright white light. Then finally the light tube went dark again, and the machine did as it was instructed. One by one, the books were placed inside the chamber, in a neat pile. The door closed on the robot's side.

With the leather-bound books inside the bio-lock, the chamber glowed a spectrum of glittering, metallic colors, including bright reds, blues, greens, and yellows. The colors diminished, but remained there, lingering in a thin, patchy fog of spectral streaks inside the bio-lock. He'd never seen the device produce a display like that before, and wondered about it. Something to do with the books? He'd never put books into a bio-lock before. He issued a command and heard a whooshing sound, as his side of the compartment opened up. He no longer saw the mist, and assumed everything inside had been sanitized, so that no organisms could escape from the laboratory.

He took the volumes and tucked them into compartments on his maglev chair. At the doorway, he happened to look back, and thought he saw a very faint glow of silver in the air, around the closed bio-lock door on his side. But the glow vanished almost before he could think about it, and he turned away. His focus was elsewhere now, not on any doubts.

In his own apartment a few minutes later, Billy began to read....

~~~

Branson Tobek's penmanship was compact and hurried, with the letters of some words so rounded off that they were virtually unidentifiable. It was far and away the most difficult-to-comprehend handwriting that Billy had ever seen, yet from years of experience working with the older man, receiving a steady stream of written notes and instructions from him, Billy knew how to read the words and make sense of them. It had been an essential thing to learn, to avoid mistakes in the construction of Skyship. There had to be no misunderstandings.

Now he found himself reading the material smoothly and quickly, only pausing to ponder about a handful of words and phrases before continuing on. He felt like a man running across open ground, seeking something in the distance, drawing closer and closer to it. Tobek had written these passages very rapidly (as he always did), out of an urgency to get the information committed to paper—and now Billy read as fast as he could, anxious to learn what secrets might be on the pages. He didn't take the time to read every sentence, but got the gist of what each section was about before moving on.

The first volume and a portion of the second provided an overview of the years of design and construction of the great atmospheric ship, while the rest of the pages chronicled key events afterward, including details about some of Tobek's interactions with Billy. This did not surprise Billy, but it dismayed him to find complaints about him on these pages, particularly concerning questions that he had constantly asked, seeking clarification, and which Tobek often found annoying and time-consuming. But there were also long passages in which the old man wrote of what a dedicated, intelligent and loyal assistant Billy was, and how the ambitious Skyship project could never have been completed without his able assistance. There was also a section in which Tobek described Billy as "the greatest and most faithful friend I have ever had."

Tears began to run down Billy's cheeks; he pulled his head back and wiped them away quickly, not wanting to dampen the pages—which he considered sacred. He hoped he was still being faithful in what he was doing now.

He read for hours, skimming some sections, skipping others, and slowing where it really got interesting. He found passages that described the construction and testing of Billy's authentic, humanlike robots, the Lazarus series that included Billy's "son" Devv, and Lainey Forster as well, who so resembled Billy's lost love Reanne—

and the ten others who were in service on Skyship, as well as the backup units in storage.

That morning, Billy issued instructions to his staff and robots that he was not to be disturbed. Finally, at shortly after noon, he found something very important near the end of the second volume. A chill ran down his spine at the realization.

Trembling slightly, he stared at an entry made more than nineteen years ago, on an October evening: "I was using the magnascope, peering into an unusual, incredibly beautiful beam of moonlight, a gleaming ray of silver, when something startling occurred, an event so dangerous that I hesitate to even write about it. And yet, I must."

Billy took a deep, anticipatory breath.

From an operational standpoint, he was familiar with the magnascope that was now in his own office, which Tobek had designed and built. Billy often used it for close-up views of his beloved AmEarth, and—at higher settings—to peer as far as he could into the galaxy. He recalled that Tobek had once told him he was also designing attachments that would make the magnascope even more powerful, so that humans could theoretically see all the way into other galaxies, and potentially into the entire universe. He said he had developed an "expandable unit," a basic magnascope that could be retained, and enhanced with attachments. But Billy had never seen this modified scope or any of its accessories, and though he'd asked about this, Tobek had always deferred to another subject, one he invariably said was more important, and urgent. It was a common tactic employed by the old inventor.

Now Billy became aware of pausing to think about this section, and how it fit into his frustration in getting certain information out of Tobek. Finally returning to the words on the page, he read on. It was a lot of technical information, and he couldn't understand much of it. On the next page, Tobek wrote, "I was peering through the scope into the strange, silvery beam of moonlight when suddenly it became agitated, and tried to elude my ability to look at it. When I noticed this, I increased the magnascope's power, which I'd turned down because of the close proximity of the target. With the magnification suddenly increased, I saw an immense horde of tiny creatures inside the beam of light—microscopic creatures of sparkling silver light.

"Even more improbably, the silvery creatures had jagged-featured faces, frighteningly so, and seemed to be both individual and collective entities, at times jumping around on their own and on other occasions moving en masse with their companions, as if they had a single, linked mind. They are the ugliest, most fearsome things I've ever seen, and there are decillions and decillions of them, so many as to make counting impractical.

"While I was observing the creatures close-up, they continued to realize I was intruding, and went into a frenzy of disturbed activity. They formed into a large, dark conglomeration that blocked the illumination of the moon, and then streamed toward me at a very high rate of speed. Before I could react, they vanished, and the light coming from the moon looked entirely normal again, with a moonbeam that was softer, and not metallic.

"Everything I have described is, of course, an utter scientific impossibility. And yet, it is an honest account of what I saw, and what happened."

In the pages of the journal a time lapse ensued, and then the entries resumed six days later, when Tobek wrote in his compact handwriting: "The strange creatures of light have penetrated my ship. *They are on board.* Upon discovering this, I took certain steps they didn't anticipate, and managed to trap them, an entire colony of them. Now I am beginning to construct a device to destroy them."

Tobek had not provided details of how he had trapped the creatures or where they were kept, or what he meant by a device to destroy them, or why he wanted to eliminate them. Was that what he'd been working on in the laboratory when he died? The unfinished, mysterious object that still sat on the laboratory table?

Billy looked back at the journal pages, read a passage in which Tobek wrote, "These silvery creatures—'space devils,' I've started calling them—do not like being confined, and I fear I've sent them into a dangerous fury. I'm still able to prevent them from escaping, and can observe them scientifically, and perform experiments on them. In the process, though, I've learned some very unsettling facts, some very dangerous facts. My intervention has adversely affected the space devils, to such an extent that they can never be allowed to escape. If they were to ever get away, the consequences would certainly be catastrophic."

This must be the potential disaster Tobek had spoken of, but details were lacking, in paragraph after paragraph that touched on the subject and warned about it, but without explanation. It was frustrating.

A shiver ran down Billy's spine. There had been strange silver flashes around Tobek when he died, so the creatures had killed him. And Billy had seen a faint, silvery glimmer outside the bio-lock after he retrieved the journals from the sealed laboratory. It suggested that the creatures had, in fact, escaped from the laboratory.

And if so, had the creatures also escaped from Skyship, or were they still on board? Were they the source of the terrible danger that Tobek said would occur if Skyship were ever destroyed?

It seemed possible, even probable.

Another journal entry followed, from the late inventor: "I intend to annihilate the nasty little devils, every last one of them. It is the only way to assure the safety of Skyship, the biosphere, and AmEarth itself."

The known facts were accumulating.

Billy thought back, to the first time he'd heard a warning from Tobek about the disastrous result if Skyship were ever destroyed, how it would wipe out the atmosphere and virtually all life on the planet. The warning had come fourteen years ago, and three years later—after Tobek died in his secret laboratory—Billy had passed the general warning on to political leaders throughout the AmEarth Empire, without ever understanding it.

It must have something to do with the creatures....

Anxiously, Billy flipped through pages, looking for more entries about the mysterious space devils. There were several sections (written over a period of years) documenting Tobek's efforts to destroy the creatures, through radiation, subzero or thermogenic temperatures, hyperbaric pressure, lasers, and other methods. But all efforts failed, and only succeeded in making the creatures more unstable and hyperactive. Only days before Tobek's death, he made his last entry about them: "I can no longer conduct any form of experiment on the space devils, and I'm barely able to keep them confined. I fear they are evolving as they constantly seek escape, becoming stronger and more angry... and more dangerous."

Now Billy Jeeling wished he didn't know as much as he did. The space devils had killed Tobek, and were the reason for his dire warning.

But where were they at this moment? Somewhere on Skyship, not having found a way to escape yet? He hoped they had gotten away into space, and could not really cause any more harm. If they had already gone, maybe Tobek's warning of catastrophe would never come to pass... and could *never* come to pass.

He didn't like having more questions and worries after reading the journals, instead of the answers he so desperately sought. His pile of accumulated troubles had just become larger, substantially larger.

All the while, Skyship continued to go about its rounds over the densely populated planet, cleansing the atmosphere and dispatching skyminers. Nothing had blown up. To any observer other than Billy Jeeling, everything seemed to be precisely as it should be, with the flight characteristics and atmospheric repair features of the immense vessel working perfectly....

CHAPTER 23

Anger is a double-edged sword.
Often, it is a very bad thing.
But used properly, it can have a beneficial effect.

—E. Bert Rhinbar, wandering philosopher during the Final Sweep,
the climactic military assaults that unified the AmEarth Empire

Maureen had never been so angry. She was only an hour off the shuttle from Skyship, and had come straight here to Racker Center, the tallest building that had ever been built.

Without asking for an appointment or even knocking, she tapped the code on the keypad, and burst into Jonathan Racker's top-level office. He sat at his desk, reading a document. Startled, he looked up.

"Did you know that Moore was sending us on a suicide mission?" she demanded.

She noticed that the old industrialist had tears in his eyes, and saw an unframed picture of Paul Paulo lying on the desk, beside whatever he had been reading. Somehow he had already learned that his old comrade was dead. The guardsmen who returned with her must have gotten a quick message over to him.

He wiped his eyes, and a flash of anger crossed his creased face. His flinty eyes glinted. "Do you think I would send my best friend on a suicide mission?" he asked, pointing at the picture of Paulo. "I'd as soon die myself before doing anything like that."

"Well I might as well have been sent with a suicide vest on, and Paul, too—to blow us both to hell. We were expendable, and you knew nothing about it? *Nothing*?"

He shook his head sadly.

"Well neither did I, and neither did Paul. After he was killed, the Jeelings put me through a rigorous truthbot interrogation. I passed with flying colors." She scowled as she slipped, uninvited, into a chair fronting his desk.

He didn't object, even gestured belatedly with a welcoming hand. "I'm very glad you're safe," he said.

"Where is that son-of-a-bitch Moore? He needs to be fired, and put in prison."

"Believe me, I'd get rid of him if I could. I was actually trying to reach him for days, to discuss several matters, even before I learned about what happened to your peace mission to Skyship. And to Paul."

"*Peace* mission." She scoffed. "Thanks to our rogue General, there was nothing peaceful about it."

"I just sent Moore another message half an hour ago, demanding information on what happened. I haven't seen the General since you left. He's been spending a lot of time with his troops. There are rumors flying around, about what he's been up to."

"What sort of rumors? Not a military coup?"

"No, at least I hope not. I've heard that he's been setting up a contingency plan in case your 'peace' delegation failed, a new full-scale military attack against Jeeling. Remember, we all talked about that as a backup plan? And you thought of the peace delegation idea, to slow him down?"

"But we can't attack Skyship in force! It could destroy the air-purification technology, and we can't afford to lose it! And the problem of the chain reaction that could be set off in the atmosphere."

"I understand all that. But you know how General Moore is."

"Too much testosterone," she said. "But he could be right that the chain reaction story is only a bluff by Billy. Maybe he just put it out there as a defensive measure."

"Could be," Racker said, "but a lot is at stake if Moore is wrong. In my last message I reminded him that he needs my approval before doing anything like a military attack." His eyes misted over. "And Paul Paulo's approval was required, too, but that's not possible now."

"I'd like to strangle the General," she said.

"Wait a minute," Racker said. "There's something coming in from him now!" The old man tapped a button on his desktop, and a hologram of General Moore floated on one side of the desk. "Can't see you now," the officer said, in the eerie projection. "Sorry, but I'm much too busy."

Maureen sputtered, "Why did you set us up, you bastard?"

General Moore might not have heard this, because suddenly his visage disappeared, leaving only the words "Connection Terminated" in the air, before it all faded, like smoke in the sky.

"So, what do we do now?" she asked. "What *can* we do?"

"I'll contact intermediaries, see if we can get him to come to a meeting with us."

"Intermediaries? Isn't he supposed to be our close ally?"

"That changed when he pulled his little trick, without approval, and when he got my best friend killed. Even if we can convince him to attend a meeting, that's no guarantee we'll ever get him to change his ways."

"He should be arrested and put on trial!"

"I'll suggest both to Prime Minister Yhatt. The problem is, I'm afraid that Moore is too powerful now, maybe even more powerful than our Prime Minister. Whatever Moore wants to do, I don't see how he can be stopped."

"He's gone completely renegade."

"Sure looks that way to me." Racker slammed a fist on his desktop. His facial expression softened, saddened. "I need to be alone for a while," he said.

She rose to her feet. "I understand." She turned and left, feeling betrayed, deeply angry, and frustrated.

CHAPTER 24

When I was building robots with human imprints, I discovered that the mind of the human female is infinitely more interesting than its male counterpart. The female has far more intricate and intriguing passageways in the brain, many of which are linked to the complex workings of her reproductive system.

—From the Jeeling Diaries

A day had passed since Devv assaulted her, and Sonya had been suffering ever since, but not much from the bruises on her face. Instead, it was from a very peculiar internal problem that resulted from the blows, a brain injury she hadn't even known was possible. She didn't know what to call it, but she had it nonetheless, whatever it was. She hadn't slept a moment since the incident, and was having a lot of trouble organizing her thoughts.

She paced back and forth in her apartment, praying for the trouble to go away. She paused in front of a large simulated window that bore an authentic image projected from outside—the morning sun was shining brightly, and she should be starting her day cheerfully, but it wasn't like that now. She wanted to scream, yet held it back, not wanting to call attention to herself.

The mindwave unit implanted in her brain was acting up from the hard blows she'd taken, mostly from the second one to the forehead, because it was after he hit her there that she started having troubles. The unit was freaking out this morning, shooting loud static noises into her head and generating undesired pop-up VR-bubbles in front of her eyes, with fuzzy, overlapping images inside them, accompanied by the sound fragments of multiple, simultaneous conversations. It was maddening, as if she was picking up audio and visual signals from everyone nearby, all at once.

Sonya had not been able to eat, sleep, or work since Devv assaulted her, and she had asked a neighbor to tell her manager—Lainey Forster—that Devv had hit her a couple of times during an argument, and that she was going to rest in bed for a while, until she felt well enough to go back to work. The neighbor, Bett Jacoby, had been able to see the bruises on her face, but not the worst of it, inside her head—and the VR displays were apparently not visible to Bett, nor could she hear the non-stop static and chatter inside Sonya's head, because she said nothing about such things either. Without providing details on the complicated mess inside her mind, Sonya had emphasized to her neighbor that it was nothing serious, and that she would report to work when she could. Then, after only spending a few minutes with Bett, Sonya had asked to be alone.

But the effort to recuperate on her own was not working. Sonya was feeling worse and worse with each passing hour.

And she was experiencing something else, in addition to the other, continuing problems. Increasingly sharp lances of pain had been stabbing intermittently into her brain, as if someone was jabbing long needles into her head. She hadn't felt this for a couple of minutes, though, which gave her a modicum of relief, but not from the overlapping images and sounds, which had continued unabated since the injury, preventing sleep and keeping her from concentrating.

Suddenly an extremely sharp pain penetrated the middle of her brain, worse than any of the previous ones. She cried out, but put a hand over her mouth to muffle the sound. Sonya didn't want anyone to hear her suffering, didn't want anyone to know what she was going through.

And this was more than a personal matter, far more.

She could not go to a doctor on Skyship and have the mindwave implant removed, or her cover might be blown, if the doctor discovered it was a non-standard unit. This implant wasn't like anything normal people had in their heads. It was a high-tech military unit, enabling her to communicate with her superiors over a private, ultra-secure frequency. Except now it didn't seem so secure, and she didn't know what she was hearing or seeing, whether they were actually signals from nearby people, or whether it was military conversations, coming all the way from General Moore's headquarters on AmEarth. Whatever it was, she couldn't understand any of the conversations, and couldn't identify the images, not even whether they were military or civilian.

Her name was not Sonya Orr; it was Sonya Roméo, and she was one of the General's operatives, assigned to work on Skyship and collect information for him. She was, in fact, the married younger sister of General Rivington Moore VIII, and was herself a full colonel in the Imperial Army that her brother ran. A colonel and a spy. Her husband, Doncarlo, was a businessman, the empire's leading manufacturer of marching-band uniforms, both military and civilian.

The two of them were estranged, and had been for some time, ever since she told Doncarlo she was taking this assignment. Even before that their relationship had been tenuous, going back to the early days of their marriage. To a degree it was because they were sexually incompatible: he wanted more, while she wanted less... at least with him. And there were other issues.

On board Skyship, Sonya had been eluding detection with the aid of her special military-issued implant, one of the mindwave units that sorted thoughts and blocked the detection of any that were dangerous. Her implant had two sets of receiving and transmitting frequencies that she could activate with mental commands. One set comprised the standard, common frequencies used by everyone who voluntarily received an implant. The other set were the supposedly secure military frequencies, on which she communicated with her powerful brother on AmEarth, giving him reports and receiving his instructions.

None of that was working now. Back and forth she paced, worrying and hoping to feel better.

She'd taken a huge chance in coming here, where truthbots periodically checked and re-checked every person, looking for anyone who might pose a threat to Billy Jeeling. Two other operatives with earlier versions of her military implant had been discovered, and had vanished into Devv Jeeling's prison system. These implants were still experimental and under development, and didn't always work; that was proven by the captured operatives, although supposedly her unit was safer to use.

She'd been warned of the danger before going on this assignment, but she'd volunteered anyway—wanting to do it for her brother, and for the larger cause of forcing Billy Jeeling to resign. Rivington felt strongly that the Master of Skyship had outlived his usefulness, and she agreed with him.

She stopped pacing and plopped down in a soft chair, where she tried to think of other things, of anything else....

The odd thing was, the more time Sonya spent on Skyship (three years now), the more she'd found that she actually liked and respected Billy Jeeling. For the last six months, she'd been having doubts about the mission on which she'd been sent, though she revealed none of this in her reports to HQ—and she only sent them raw facts, with no opinion one way or the other about the man her brother was targeting so zealously. In fact, she had noticed a number of good things about Billy, such as his genuine concern for ecology, and she didn't really want to harm him.

True enough, Billy had been on Skyship for too long and should step down, but that didn't mean his reputation should be ruined, or that he should be treated as if his great deeds had never occurred. It didn't mean that lies, half truths, and innuendos should be spread about him—and she knew that some of the information she'd reported had been twisted and distorted for release to the public, almost beyond recognition. As but one example, she'd reported that on occasion Billy liked to retreat to his high walkway, where he contemplated matters he considered important, and gazed at distant constellations. That was a perfectly logical thing for him to do, considering the responsibilities and pressures he was under—but General Moore and his cronies put out stories that the retreats and star-gazing proved Billy was getting old and losing his marbles.

Sonya had not been sure how to distance herself from that campaign of hatred and distortion, so she just kept sending in her reports dutifully, without commentary.

Until now. With her mindwave implant going berserk, she could no longer send any information to AmEarth. She would have to make an excuse and get off Skyship, saying she needed to take a leave of absence—that the breakup with Devv Jeeling had upset her so much that she needed to get away from him and seek counseling. That could mean she was coming back, or not. It left both options open.

But how could she concentrate enough to speak coherently to anyone when her brain throbbed and the virtual-reality pop-ups were in front of her face, and wouldn't go away? The images were filmy, like a thin fog inhibiting her vision.

She thought about this problem for an hour. Finally, hearing Bett Jacoby return to her next-door apartment, Sonya took a deep breath and decided she needed to confide in someone... at least a little bit. She wanted to tell Bett about the out-of-control VR displays, and some of her other physical symptoms.

When Sonya knocked on Bett's door, the pop-up displays were still out of whack, a jumble of images in front of her face. She peered through them, like through a filmy gauze, and looked at Bett. Inside her mind, the overlapping conversations continued, a raucous cacophony of unintelligible sounds.

"Sonya! Are you feeling better, dear? Come in, come in."

The VR was still going, along with a dim clatter of voices, and Sonya said, "Do you see anything in front of my face, like a virtual-reality display? Anything at all?"

Bett narrowed her gaze. "No, nothing."

"Well, I sure the hell do, and it's driving me crazy. Do you hear anything, like chattering voices?"

Pause, then: "No, nothing like that, either. Just street noises, and the drone of humbabies outside. Normal stuff. Are you feeling all right?"

"No. That's why I'm here."

They stood inside the entry to the apartment. Bett was tall, but a little shorter than Sonya, and was a redhead with a prominent chin and an oval face. Her hair had a beautiful sheen, and people were always complimenting her on it. She wasn't exactly pretty, and instead she was what people might call a handsome woman, not totally feminine, but still attractive in her own way. Sonya had always liked her.

"Is there anything I can do to help?" Bett asked. "Would you like me to call Dr. Ginsberg?"

"No, not that. Anything but that. Thanks, but I need to see my own doctor on AmEarth. I don't trust anyone else." Sonya grimaced as a needle of pain shot into the center of her brain.

"But maybe she can give you some medication. You appear to be in discomfort, hurting."

"I need to get back to AmEarth. I only trust my own doctor."

"Of course, dear. I can understand that."

"Could you possibly help me make arrangements to get off Skyship as soon as possible, and get me back to my home town?"

"You can't mindcom the request?"

Sonya shook her head. "My implant is all out of whack," she admitted.

Bett nodded compassionately.

"There shouldn't be any cost," Sonya said, "because the shuttle is free, but I don't feel up to going out and handling the details, making the explanations. I don't want to see any people right now, except for you." Sonya smiled softly, said, "I've always thought you had a gentle way about you, a kindness."

"Well, thank you. My Mom told me I could have been a social worker, a nurse, or even a minister. I do like to help folks whenever I can."

Bett placed a couple of mindwave calls and made the arrangements. It only took a few minutes. Then Sonya returned to her apartment to wait. She had a reservation to depart that afternoon.

CHAPTER 25

"We should always listen more than we talk. Why else were we provided with two ears, and only one mouth? And your eyes—you have two of them as well. Use them, damn it!"

—Branson Tobek, instruction to his young ward

Yürgen Zayeddi had tried to contact Sonya several times, but had gotten no response. He didn't understand why. He'd done nothing wrong, and had thought they'd been good together.

Now he stood outside her apartment, knocking on the door. It was mid-morning, and he had a little extra time, so he decided to check on Sonya before his scheduled class in the Public Relations College.

It had been very physical between him and the attractive woman, an explosion of passion. If they'd had the opportunity, he thought there could have been more between them, a genuine and complete relationship. He liked her as a person, maybe even had deeper feelings for her, and now he missed her terribly. It couldn't be love, at least not yet, but that might be a possibility, given enough time. Sonya certainly was intelligent, and had a bright, pleasant way about her.

There was no answer at her door. He started to write her a note, then noticed what appeared to be one of the notes he'd already left for her at the bottom of the door, just a corner of a piece of paper sticking out. He bent over and retrieved it, confirming that it was from him. He replaced it and walked away.

At the end of the hallway, he was confronted by a robot that had just stepped out of a highlift. He recognized it as one of the simpler police models that patrolled the interiors of various buildings. The machine had a small scan-light on its head, like a bright flashlight, pointing at Yürgen and making him squint in the blinding light. He felt his face being scanned to check its identity markers. The scanner brightness diminished to a pale blue, and his name flashed on a screen that appeared on the robot's torso. Then the machine said, "State your purpose."

"I came to see Sonya Orr, to check on her. She's a friend of mine, was injured yesterday."

"You are not on the authorized list for this floor."

"I've been here several times. With her, and by myself to leave her notes."

"You are not on the authorized list for this floor."

"There must be a mistake. I was just—"

He stopped, when he saw the robot flash orange on its scanner, a sign that its programming was entering a stage where the automaton could become violent. This one had a short fuse, didn't seem to tolerate any discussion at all. The flashing continued, and increased in rapidity.

Yürgen took half a step back.

"You are not on the authorized list," the machine repeated. "That includes all situations, and all possible things you might say. No exceptions, no excuses, no justifications."

He didn't know what to say, looked past the robot to the bank of highlifts. His muscles seemed frozen, as he tried to figure out what he should do next, or say.

The orange scanner grew brighter and flashed faster, heightened danger.

"All right," Yürgen said. "I'm sorry. I thought I could check on her, but apparently I was in error." He took a deep breath and walked carefully around the robot, then ordered a highlift. Glancing back, he saw that the scanner of the robot had reverted to its normal coloration, a darker blue. But it watched him until Yürgen was on board and away.

He thought it was ironic, how a member of the Skyship Security Force had just confronted him, when they were under the control of Devv Jeeling. Ironic, because Devv was the one who hit Sonya and hurt her. Were charges going to be brought against the Security

Commander for that outrageous, unjustified assault? If so, Yürgen might find himself called into court as a witness—though that seemed unlikely to him. The younger Jeeling would not want the embarrassment. He would get it all swept under the rug, with the approval of his father....

A short while later Zayeddi entered a classroom that was smaller than the one in which he'd taken his earlier training, and took his assigned seat near the front. He was one of only a few who'd been selected for advanced training to become a PR team leader, instead of just a member. Lainey Forster was expanding the program, intending to hit more cities and towns with the truth about Billy Jeeling, to counter the steady stream of negative information that was being spread by his enemies.

High in an office tower, the classroom had a slightly curved ceiling, bearing an artist's rendition of constellations and galaxies. Through the window on his right, he could see Billy's famous sky-high walkway just above this level, where the great man was reportedly spotted at times, in deep and solitary contemplation. Yürgen had not met his hero yet, but had seen him once from a distance, when the Master of Skyship gave an environmental speech to a gathering of workers on the central grazzeen park, emphasizing the need for them to keep trying to improve the efficiency of the great vessel.

Today Yürgen and his classmates were supposed to study in teams of two, but his own companion Rand Baker was late, and class was about to start. Under the partnering program each student was supposed to watch out for his "study buddy," helping the other person learn, and serving as a practice foe in a series of ongoing Billy Jeeling-related debates. The matchings were computer-generated, based upon extensive psychological and performance tests.

The instructor was his former PR team leader, Nanette Kingston, who stood at a podium reviewing the lesson she was about to give. She looked up, at the empty seat next to Yürgen, and frowned. Her disapproving gaze fell on him. "As Baker's partner it is your responsibility," she said, in a condescending tone, "to make certain he arrives in class."

Yürgen had not imagined he wouldn't show up. So far, Rand had never missed a class, and had expressed support for Billy Jeeling, albeit somewhat muted at times. Even so, it had never occurred to him that his classmate might not appear.

"He'd better be seriously injured, or dead," Kingston said. "Go and find out where he is, or what's happened to him."

Yürgen nodded, rose to his feet and stepped into the aisle.

"Wait a minute," she said. Kingston left the podium and marched down the aisle toward him, holding a small, slender tube, which she activated, to display blinking red lights on it. "This is called a sniffer," she said. She looked down at it, made an adjustment. "It's receiving a signal that is being transmitted by Mr. Baker."

He looked at her, perplexed. "Something on his clothing?"

"Something in his body, just beneath the skin. He carries a tiny transmitter from one of the medical shots he received on Skyship; all of you received one during your physical exams." She turned the device over, pointed it upward and to her right. "He's up there somewhere, probably on an upper level of one of the residential towers. He probably has a girlfriend, and went to see her. Get Baker and bring him back."

Yürgen Zayeddi felt a surge of anger at the intrusion of the tracking devices that all of them had received, and which he had not known about before. No one had given permission as far as he knew, and he certainly hadn't. He heard a murmuring in the classroom, didn't think the other students liked it either.

She handed the device to him. It was cool to the touch. "See that yellow arrow that shifts and flashes when the unit is pointed in the right direction? Just keep following the arrow and you'll find him. When you get closer, the arrow will flash brighter and more frequently. This is only one of the most basic, non-classified units, programmed to keep track of my students and fellow proctors. The security police have much more sophisticated units that show exactly where Baker is on Skyship—for emergency use. This one will take you a little longer, but it still works quite well."

As Yürgen left the classroom he heard her beginning the session, with the rest of the class. Five minutes later he was on the street, cursing Rand Baker under his breath, going from building to building, using the sniffer. To his surprise, he discovered that the target's signal was not coming from one of the residential towers at all. Standing at the base of a perimeter wall, just beyond those structures, he pointed the sniffer up, and received a stronger signal.

At a perimeter wall he took a highlift, one of the faster models that hurt his ears and made him slightly dizzy. He stepped out on a level above the tallest of all the towers, which he could see now through a broad wall of glassplaz. He took a moment to get oriented, then hurried down a wide corridor that curved slightly to the left. As the signal grew stronger, the yellow arrow flashed more frequently, and brighter. The flashing reminded him of the dangerous robot he'd dealt with earlier today.

Before class that morning, he and Rand Baker had lamented having to be taught by Nanette, who'd been such an irritating team leader on their PR mission to AmEarth. She was condescending, the sort of person who thought she had all the answers and didn't listen well to others—especially to PR team members and students—whom she considered inferior to her.

"It seems we can't escape from the bitch," Rand had said....

Where are you? Yürgen wondered now, as he followed the signal, high inside the building. He passed half a dozen doors, all closed and locked.

When the signal began to grow weaker, he paused and retraced his steps, then reversed direction a couple of times, until he found a stable point in the middle, where the signal was strongest. He stopped and looked around. There were no doorways here, just a vented utility-access hatch on the other side. Crossing the corridor for a closer examination, he saw that the hatch was damaged, and slightly ajar. The signal grew stronger. He swung the hatch open, pointed the sniffer unit inside, and the arrow signal went crazy. It was quiet, perhaps for stealth.

Yürgen heard a metallic noise coming from the vent. He peered inside, and when his eyes adjusted he made out a wide gray pipe that extended for perhaps twenty meters. At a junction he saw the bottom of a ladder inside a vertical pipe, where someone was climbing down. Reaching the bottom, the person crawled toward him.

Removing a small but powerful flash-beam from his pocket, Yürgen shone it into the vent. He saw Rand Baker look up at him from all fours, startled. He stopped suddenly and stared into the beam, like a

deer caught in a spotlight. A moment later he continued toward Yürgen, and finally crawled out of the vent, to stand in the corridor. His
dark trousers and shirt were covered in grime and dust.

"What the hell were you doing in there?" Yürgen demanded.

Baker stared at the sniffer unit in Yürgen's hand, at the flashing
yellow arrow, without seeming to comprehend what it was. He began
to stammer an excuse, then reached for a dart-gun on his weapon
belt—one of the crowd-control weapons that they had learned to use
in their training for the PR missions to AmEarth.

Yürgen lunged toward him, grabbed the gun out of his hand and
accidentally fired it. To his shock the hot projectile hit Baker in the
stomach, knocking him back. The injured man cried out, tried to get
another weapon, but stumbled and fell, bleeding from a stomach
wound.

With gasping breaths, Baker said, "You have no idea what damage
I've done to Skyship! You think I only did something inside the vent?
You'll all find out, but it will be too late." He reached for a weapon
again, but Yürgen fired repeatedly, until Baker stopped moving.

An explosion sounded inside the vent, and fire and debris shot out,
knocking Yürgen over. As he slipped into a gray, dizzy realm of consciousness, he was only vaguely aware of uniformed police officers
surrounding him, some human and others robots, making machine-
communication sounds.

He struggled to his feet and said, "Tell Proctor Kingston I won't be
making it back to class today."

Yürgen didn't know why he'd just said that. He wasn't trying to be
funny. But it was the first thing that came into his mind. Then his
thoughts clarified, and he began to tell the police what had happened.

~~~

Earlier in the day, Sonya had been home when Yürgen Zayeddi
knocked on her door. She'd almost answered, and had gone up to the
door on the inside without touching the handle, close to the man on
the other side. But she'd just stood there silently, listening and waiting for him to leave. She'd heard Yürgen's confrontation with a security robot, and then he was on his way, out of her life.

It was too bad their relationship hadn't gone as far as either of them would have liked, because she liked him a lot. They had really connected, physically, emotionally, and intellectually. But she was on one side of the Jeeling dispute, and he was on the other, and she didn't think the gap could ever be bridged. Though she respected Billy Jeeling, she had been working against him, while Yürgen was the most passionate of his supporters. He would not be happy to hear what her actual job was, and what she had done, so she didn't think there was any hope for them, anyway.

Now she sat on a shuttle as passengers walked past her and took their seats. Thankfully there was plenty of room, and no one sat beside her. She looked away from the other passengers, tried to ignore the hazy VR display that had been in front of her face for hours, and the overlapping, unintelligible conversations she continued to hear. No one around her seemed to notice any of this, so that was something positive, anyway. It would help her get away without having to field questions from security officers about what was going on inside her head. The lances of pain had subsided somewhat, but she couldn't relax about them because they had a nasty habit of striking suddenly, without warning.

The shuttle exited Skyship and descended toward the blue-green planet far below. When they were underway, the pain resumed and Sonya felt like her brain was being stabbed repeatedly. She didn't know how long she could hold out until a doctor removed that mindwave implant. She couldn't call ahead. The minute she landed, she would go in search of her brother, and ask him to arrange for a military doctor to help her.

She hoped that removal of the implant would solve the chaos in her mind and eliminate the pain, because if it didn't, she saw no option except to kill herself.

CHAPTER 26

Actions are like words.
Once they are released by the source,
it is often difficult to take them back.

—Anonymous

It was mid-afternoon, and Devv Jeeling was getting ready to leave his office. He strapped his weapon belt on, went to the coat rack for a uniform jacket.

That morning he'd gotten up and tried to go about his day, following his normal routine—until the explosion in Sector H-7, resulting in emergency actions taken by his security officers. How had Rand Baker gotten through the tight security measures? Somehow the intruder had gained access to a restricted area, disabled security cameras, and detonated explosives that were just enough to wreak havoc, but not enough to seriously disable Skyship. It was as if someone wanted to harass Billy Jeeling and show that security measures could be easily breached, but not wanting to destroy Skyship.

It was a message from Billy's enemies, but the messenger was dead, killed by the heroics of Yürgen Zayeddi—a PR student who shouldn't have been able to get into that restricted area, either—but who had apparently followed the trail past disabled electronics that Baker had left in his wake. Zayeddi had only received minor injuries, and had not needed to go to the hospital.

Yürgen Zayeddi. The one who caused all the trouble with Sonya. No matter his bravery and heroics, Devv hated him.

He had not eaten anything all day, having been too upset to keep anything down. So many problems.

185

He wished he'd never joined his father on Skyship, to work with him. He no longer wanted to inherit the massive scientific vessel and its overwhelming responsibilities. All the bright dreams he'd had at one time had evaporated, like wisps of smoke vanishing in the air.

He'd been thinking about his change of heart for some time now, since the public onslaught against his father intensified and became so cruel, so utterly unfair. At one time, Devv had looked forward to learning everything about Skyship and gaining stewardship over it, but now it was beginning to look like a huge ball and chain, a form of imprisonment that would last until the end of his days. His father certainly was not happy with the way things were going; and Devv saw no reason why it would be any better for him. Yet he didn't know how to break the bad news to him, didn't want to let him down.

And now he had another big problem that would disappoint Billy—he'd hit Sonya yesterday morning, and hurt her. As the Security Commander he should never have done anything like that; he should have had the good sense not to go to her apartment in the first place, and get involved in a confrontation. There had been no upside potential in barging in there, no chance of getting her back that way. There could only have been a bad result, and he'd stumbled into almost the worst possible outcome. He'd injured her and lost her. The look of loathing and hatred in her eyes was unforgiving, making him feel like vermin. She would never see him now. Before that he'd pushed her once, several months ago, and she'd warned him that if he ever laid a hand on her again, they would be finished. He still loved Sonya; and knew he always would, no matter how she felt about him.

He shuddered, felt tears of regret coming on; this was the deepest sadness of his life.

Devv stared at his desk, where he'd left a laser-bow. An hour ago he'd grasped the weapon, cocked it, and pointed it at the side of his own head—knowing that even if it struck him there, it would be a slow, painful death, because of the way he'd set the laser device, to incapacitate him and render a tortuous end. It was what he deserved, but he didn't have the courage to do it. He was a coward, couldn't fire the weapon and had hurt the woman he loved deeply.

Now Devv's father had summoned him to the high walkway where they sometimes met late at night, a quiet place where they could gaze far into the galaxy of stars and talk. Except this time it was afternoon, and they would not be able to see the glittering sky.

But when Devv stepped off the highlift on the walkway level, he found Billy awaiting him in the mirror-walled lobby, sitting in his maglev chair. Natural sunlight illuminated the lobby, passing through a dome above. Billy had three thick leather-bound volumes on his lap. They were closed, with his hands holding them in place.

"We can talk here," he said.

Sitting on a chair beside him, Devv said, "You heard what happened to Sonya, what I did to her." It was not a question. His father must already know.

The old man nodded, somberly. "A sad thing, when close personal relations come to an abrupt end. I've had my share of grief as well, when I lost Reanne."

"But she died in a freak accident, in the earthquake that destroyed an entire building and part of a town. There was nothing you could have done to prevent it, Father. It's different with me. I slugged Sonya, could have seriously injured her, or worse, if she'd fallen and struck her head. I hit her pretty hard the second time, and she made me leave. I tried to call her afterward, but she wouldn't answer my wave transmissions. I have to resign now, Father, and face criminal charges for what I did."

Billy scowled. "That was unacceptable. You shouldn't hit anyone, except in defense—but I know you know that, and you'll not repeat the mistake. I'm glad she wasn't seriously injured, from what I heard. I'll send Dr. Ginsberg to check on her, to be certain. However, as bad as it is, you're not quitting, and you're not going to face charges. Skyship needs you too much. *I* need you too much."

Devv nodded. He'd never felt so sad, and so much at fault.

"Your problem with her is important, Son, but it's not what I want to discuss with you." The crippled man paused, looked down at the volumes on his lap. "I'll start by talking about Reanne. When she died I was so broken up that I created a simulacrum of her—a likeness."

Devv stared at him, not comprehending.

"I made a robotic likeness of her, in the form of Lainey Forster. The woman you know as Lainey looks and acts very much like Reanne, and she's around the same age now as Reanne was when she died.

Lainey is a dancer as my wife was, too, and is intensely devoted to me, as Reanne was. She truly loves me."

"Lainey's a robot? Are you kidding me? A *robot*? How can that be?"

"She is of a prototype series, but I was meticulous in my design and workmanship. Only one person tends to her whenever she sustains injuries—Dr. Ginsberg—who knows the secret of Lainey. When injured, Lainey bruises or bleeds in a very realistic way, but it's all artificial." He nodded somberly. "She's bio-robotic, very advanced."

Devv considered this startling revelation for a moment. "You're not going to tell me next that Sonya is a robot, too? I mean, she's the most incredibly beautiful woman I've ever seen. Sometimes I've wondered how anyone could be so perfect."

Billy Jeeling stared sadly at Devv for a long time. "No, she's not a robot, but—" His voice trailed off.

Leaning close, Devv asked, "What is it, Father? You summoned me here to tell me about Lainey?"

"It's all in these journals," Billy said, tapping the pile of leather-bound books on his lap. "Read them and you'll discover I'm a terrible fraud, and didn't design Skyship at all. I was merely the assistant to a great inventor named Branson Tobek, a visionary genius who died in the core of the ship. His body is still there, and I have his laboratory journals here. I've bookmarked the pages that refer to the construction of Lainey as a robot—I was also the robotics specialist for the ship. That included the design and construction of Lainey... and of *you*, Devv, as another robot in the same series. Both of you are Lazarus models, quite realistic androids, extremely advanced."

"*Me?*" Devv arched his eyebrows in disbelief. "I'm not a robot, or I'd know it for damn sure!"

"Lainey doesn't know it. There are no obvious symptoms to look for, but trust me, Son, you're not real flesh and blood. You're as close to it as can be constructed synthetically, but I *built* you from raw materials that I collected, including a small amount of my own cellular material for a human imprint, after purging conscious genetic memories from it, and programming in new ones. Make no mistake about it, your name is in these pages, alongside Lainey's. I'm not only a fraud when it comes to Skyship; I'm a fraud when it comes to being

Lainey's lover, and your father. To be honest Devv, I'm only your father if we stretch the meaning of the word. I'm terribly sorry."

Crestfallen, Devv couldn't believe what he was hearing. He felt like a super computer had been hooked to his brain, and a powerful flow of extremely bad information had been downloaded into him. Robots? Lainey... and Devv himself? And Billy didn't design Skyship? It was all too much to absorb.

He rose to his feet, walked back and forth unsteadily. "But I feel emotions, I care about things, Father. I care about Sonya, and about you."

"That only means I did my job extremely well."

He stopped, staring at the older man. "Then why did I get so jealous of Sonya? Robots don't do that."

"Again, I did my job well. You have very realistic emotions. I'm sorry, but it's true."

He nodded, felt the immensity of the awful truth as it sank in. Devv's world crashed all around him, and he had to sit down again because his legs would no longer hold him. His emotions ran wild. Artificial emotions? He wanted to scream out in rage. It was a betrayal, a terrible betrayal! Glaring at Billy, he asked, "Have you told Lainey?"

"Not yet. I want you to do it for me. Read the evidence in these pages, and then share the information with her."

Devv hesitated. "I think you should tell her, just as you've told me."

Billy shook his head, said in a firm tone, "I'd like you to take care of this for me."

"That sounds cold to me," Devv said. "Why don't you want to—"

"Just do this for me, all right? As the Master of Skyship, I have a lot on my mind, a lot of problems to solve. Problems that go way beyond... I hate to put it this way, because I do care about you and Lainey in my own way... problems that go way beyond robots."

"So you don't love her, never did? And you don't really love me?"

"I love you both as much as I possibly can, and perhaps more than flesh and blood people, because of all of the research, design, testing, and construction work I put into you."

"But you referred to us as mere robots. Or, that's what you essentially said." Devv was trembling.

"I didn't mean to put it that way, so it must have been a poor choice of words on my part. I'm sorry Devv, but I really need your help on this. I need to distance myself from Lainey. I've told you before that she tends to cling to me, and that's a personality trait that Reanne never had, a behavior I never understood in Lainey."

Trying to calm himself, Devv took a deep, shuddering breath, while Billy continued to talk.

"But I didn't want to shut Lainey down and attempt to fix the problem, because I do care a great deal for her — as a robot of my own creation and as a close likeness of my lost love Reanne — and if I were to shut her down, I'd be afraid of causing new problems, of losing what I have left of Reanne — the original cellular material I implanted in her. If I tell Lainey myself that she's a robot, I fear her strong reaction and tears, and that I might decide on the spot to shut her down after all. Devv, you have a tranquil, centered way about you that I don't have, and you and Lainey have always gotten along well because you're actually sister and brother, in a way — or maybe it's better to say, you're like a mother and son in your relationship, despite the similarity of your apparent ages. I need you to do this for me, and break the news to her."

"You're asking me for a favor, after the terrible thing you did to me?"

"You seem to be forgetting that I gave you life."

"Pardon me for not being appreciative. I feel like my life has been taken away from me. You're a bastard, do you know that? A real bastard!"

"I'm sorry you feel that way. I've tried to be good to you, and make you comfortable."

"Why don't you push some hidden buttons on my body, or send electronic signals, to make me do what you want?"

Billy looked away, with tears welling in his eyes. "I'm really sorry, Devv. Please believe me. I thought I was doing the right thing, really I did."

Devv stared at him long and hard, saw sadness and no sign of deception. "All right, I'll do it," he said, finally. "I'll take care of it as well as I can."

"I appreciate that, more than you can know." Billy looked down, opened the volume on top and turned to a page around the middle of the book. At the urging of the elderly man, Devv went around to the side of the chair to look over his shoulder, and stared down at smooth, compact handwriting on the page.

"This is Volume 2," Billy said. He pointed, touched the page. "It is here that Tobek began to write about something very disturbing, something he brought onto Skyship accidentally and then prevented from escaping—very alien creatures who are extremely dangerous, and they may still be on board. Where, I don't know. Or they might have escaped."

"I haven't noticed anything," Devv said.

"They're very small, glittering creatures of silvery light. Space devils, Tobek called them, ferocious looking individuals when seen under magnification, and extremely elusive. I am thoroughly convinced they are the source of a dire warning he gave me. You have heard it from my lips when I announced it to the people of AmEarth, as if I came up with it myself. If Skyship were ever destroyed, the atmosphere would be so severely damaged that it would mean the end of virtually all life on the planet and in the air. In reality, that warning originally came from Tobek, not from me. I passed it on after he died in the secrecy and anonymity he demanded, but I never understood what he was talking about—until recently, when I read his private journals. Tobek said the monsters needed to be destroyed. He was going to do it, but I think they got him first."

"I assume you haven't found them?"

"No, though I've looked, and sent security robots out. I hope the intruders are gone, but I strongly suspect otherwise." Billy shivered, looked around. Terror consumed his face.

"What is it... Father?" Devv still felt loving emotions toward him, even if the robot story was true, and even if Billy had not actually been the inventor of Skyship. He was still a great man, and a loving man. He had gone to a lot of trouble to create his lost love, in the form of Lainey Forster, and Devv, too—the son Billy never had with Re-anne. The two robots were like mother and son, as Billy had said.

Speaking quickly, nervously, barely above a whisper, Billy told how he obtained the three volumes, how a robot had passed them to him through the bio-lock, and how there had been a spectrum of colors inside the bio-lock, and a glimmer of silver afterward—outside the sterilizing unit.

"I think the space devils got out through the bio-lock, and now they're watching me," Billy said. "Watching *us* at this very moment."

Devv looked around, but didn't see anything out of the ordinary.

Billy handed the heavy books to him one by one, and said, "Take these and read them, as I did. There is a great deal to learn here, and perhaps you will notice something I missed. I don't know how much time we have to solve this, but I sense—"

"What, Father?"

Billy waved a hand. "Go! Go now!"

After a moment's hesitation, Devv did as he was told, but didn't like leaving the older man alone. Billy Jeeling seemed terribly frightened, not an emotion he'd ever shown before.

CHAPTER 27

Each time you look at something, it casts a new and different light—like the series of great cathedral paintings by Claude Monet, done at different times of the day, with varying shadows and effects of light. There is always something to see in this world, always something to learn, if only you can find a way to see it.

—A Teaching of the Third Tibetan Academy, pre-Empire

Lainey Forster still had not gotten over the sabotage committed by one of her public-relations students—a young man who'd been carefully screened and scrutinized by the best robotic lie detectors, and who by all appearances had been a blue-blooded supporter of Billy Jeeling. How had Rand Baker gotten past inspection, and how had he breached security to break into a restricted area, where he caused damage? No one seemed to know the answers yet, though an all-out investigation was continuing. His name and background were proving to be false, but who was he, really? Baker died with his secrets, but at least his damage had been minimal.

Or was that really the case? Yürgen Zayeddi had added to the mystery, saying the dying man claimed to have inflicted more damage on Skyship than anyone would realize—until it was too late. Security personnel and technicians were poring over every square inch of the great vessel, tying to find anything that was out of order. So far, nothing more had turned up than the localized damage caused by the explosion in the vent—but they were still looking. It was all very disturbing.

Lainey was also troubled by the affair that Zayeddi had been having with Sonya Orr, a relationship that led to her being attacked by Devv Jeeling. Hopefully, Sonya had not been seriously injured, though she refused to see Dr. Ginsberg, and had gone back to AmEarth for medical treatment. There was no excuse for hitting a woman, and there were rumors that Devv would be suspended and put on trial for injuring her, but other rumors held that this wouldn't happen at all, and the argument was being called an unfortunate incident, with mistakes committed by both Sonya and Devv. Even more rumors held that Yürgen Zayeddi and Devv Jeeling were going to fight a duel to the death. As Zayeddi's boss, she had confronted him about this an hour ago, and he'd denied that anything like that was slated to occur.

She'd been waiting for instructions on what to do about Zayeddi. He was considered a hero on Skyship because of the saboteur he killed, but perhaps it would be better if he were relieved of his duties and sent back to AmEarth. This afternoon she expected to receive word one way or the other, because she'd been summoned to Devv Jeeling's office. He hadn't said why, but she suspected it had something to do with that dead student, and the one who killed him. Undoubtedly there would be more stringent security measures after this, and Devv might want to review them with her, and implement something.

But when she entered his office, she saw him studying a thick leather-bound book. Two more like it were stacked on a corner of his large desk, to his left. He took a few moments before looking up at her, then said, "I've been reading about us."

She didn't know what he meant. The pages open in front of him were handwritten, in a compact penmanship that was difficult to read. It didn't look familiar to her, and she'd never seen this book before, or the other two. An electron microscope stood on a rolling cart beside the table, an instrument she had not seen anywhere on Skyship except in the crime laboratory at security headquarters.

"These are the secret journals of Branson Tobek," Devv said. He sat back in his chair, stared up at the ceiling for a moment, and let out an exasperated sigh before looking back at her. "He's the real designer of Skyship, not Billy Jeeling."

She remained standing. "Branson Tobek? I've never heard of him."

"Nor had I, before my father gave these journals to me, and told me the truth about the construction of Skyship. It seems that Tobek was the reclusive type, I mean *really* reclusive. He didn't want to deal with anyone except Billy Jeeling, so he set up a small apartment and a laboratory complex in the core of Skyship, and gave instructions to Billy about how the massive vessel was to be constructed. My father—I'm not sure if I should continue to call him that, after what I'm about to tell you—didn't want it that way, but the old inventor insisted, so Billy went along with the ruse, and became the public face of the project."

"This Tobek thing is really big news. We don't want it to get out, do we?" She assumed now that he was going to discuss public relations issues with her, how to keep a lid on the new information while setting up a backup plan in case it ever leaked.

"No, we don't. These volumes contain explosive information, and not just about Skyship. There's something about you and me, too. In fact, Lainey, there's so much startling information in these journals that I don't know where to begin—for one thing, Tobek was concerned about dangerous, silvery organisms that got aboard the ship. They might still be here; Billy isn't sure."

"You're calling him 'Billy' now?"

Devv slid the open book toward her on the desk, turned the volume around so that she could read it. "There," he said, pointing. "This will explain why. It's one of the places where your name is mentioned, and mine."

She looked, couldn't read the handwriting, but did identify what looked like her name, and Devv's. "This is very difficult to read," she said.

"Tobek's swift penmanship takes some getting used to, but you'll want to learn what he had to say, as I already have. This is devastating news, Lainey, and I don't know of any delicate way to break it to you, but it seems that you and I are somewhat related."

"Somewhat? What does that mean? Are we cousins? Distant cousins? Is that what you're saying?"

"We're both *robots*, Lainey, of a very advanced, humanlike design, in what Billy Jeeling calls the Lazarus series."

Her voice rose. "What are you talking about?"

"Bio-robotics, he calls it. We're androids."

"You're a robot? And I am, too? Don't be ridiculous!"

"That's what I thought. But it's true. I wish it weren't, but it is." He looked away. "I didn't want to be the one to break the news to you, but Billy insisted that I do it."

"I can't believe this."

He scowled, and said, "Billy was not only Tobek's assistant during the construction of Skyship. He was also the robotics expert, and did such a good job on you and me, and on a handful of others, that none of us had any idea we were not human. Simulated blood flows through our veins, and we have sexual and other bodily functions that are very close to those of humans. We eat meals and digest them; we smell and hear things; we seem to get mildly ill on occasion; our skin can be burned. We have emotions. But it's all artificial, in our construction and programming."

"This can't be true!" She stared at the open page, couldn't read it even if the handwriting were clear, because her vision had blurred from the shock and stress. She felt confused. Her thoughts and emotions whirled.

"Sadly, it's true. And Dr. Rachel Ginsberg is in on it. That's why she was able to 'heal' me from what appeared to be a fatal injury, when the attackers tried to kidnap Billy Jeeling. Ginsberg and Billy just swapped out a few of my parts, tuned up others, repaired my artificial skin, and I was ready to be released from the hospital. I even have simulated remnants of pain from the 'injury' to my head, which seemed so grievous."

Lainey was stunned.

"If you need proof of what I'm telling you," he said, "I suppose we could arrange to have something violent done to you, too, and you'd see how quickly you'd be up and running again. But I don't recommend that. Billy wouldn't like it. You see, Lainey, even though you're a machine, he cares deeply about you, and he's afraid that drastic repairs could take away remnants of the human being that he modeled you after—Reanne Jeeling, his lost love from long ago, his wife. She died tragically. You have been implanted with a small amount of her cellular material, and this affects your appearance, as well as your personality, skills, and memories."

Devv reached inside a desk drawer, brought out a photograph and placed it on the open book. "Billy sent this to me today. It looks like you, but isn't. That's Reanne Jeeling, before she was killed in the collapse of a building during an earthquake."

Lainey stared. "She's the one who was supposedly your mother?"

"No, if that even matters anymore, because of the way I was actually created. Before revealing the truth about me, when he was still lying, Billy told me my mother was a woman he met before Reanne. But my 'mother' never existed, of course, because he built me as a robot and imprinted me with his own modified cellular material, affecting my appearance and behavior."

Lainey thought the image of the woman looked like her twin, but she'd never had her own hair cut so short, nor had she ever worn oversized earrings like this woman had on. In the picture Reanne was holding hands with a much younger Billy Jeeling at a campground of tents, with a blue lake and white-capped mountains behind them. Lainey had never been there in her life; she was certain of it. The woman looked so much like her, however, that if a couple of details were changed to match how Lainey wore her hair and jewelry, even she would not be able to tell the faces apart.

"To reduce any doubts you might have, let me take a blood sample from you," Devv said. "We'll look at it under a microscope to see how it compares with real human blood." He brought out a small device that he clamped on her forefinger, causing a brief lance of pain. Then he opened the specimen chamber of the microscope and slid the device and its sample inside. A small screen flashed on above the chamber. He motioned for Lainey to come and look.

She saw two specimens of red blood, side by side—one marked that it was from an unidentified human, and the other from "L. Forster." They appeared to be quite different. He described the comparative cellular structures in more technical terms than she understood, then said, "Your cells—and mine—are not fully biological. They are infinitesimally small electromagnetic particles, which look and act like blood. In reality, we are very sophisticated machines."

Lainey did not want to believe this. Yet the revelation, as startling as it was, felt oddly correct to her, and served to explain why she sometimes heard strange whirring sounds, and other machine noises when no one else did.

It explained something else, too. She stared at Devv, and he looked back—and for a moment Lainey had an eerie, alien feeling. Now she knew what it was she'd been intuiting about him for some time, that something was not quite right with him. As it turned out, there was also something not quite right with *her*.

Lainey felt utterly hopeless, that she and Billy Jeeling could never be a couple in the real sense. And she knew something that tore her heart apart, actually her mechanical heart, she was coming to believe.

This is why I couldn't get pregnant, she thought. *I never can.*

She felt dismal. Her emotions ran wild, *simulated* emotions, undoubtedly. Yet no matter what they were, she had them, and they ran the gamut from despair to sadness to rage. Billy Jeeling, who had always professed to care so deeply about her, had been lying to her for years, and had sent a surrogate to deliver the devastating news. She hated him now, and wished he'd never designed and built her in the first place.

CHAPTER 28

It is most peculiar that he is a master of robots, atmospheric restoration, and other forms of high technology, but does not embrace the internet, implanted communicators, or other advanced work-saving systems.

—Excerpt from "Enigma Man," one of the Jeeling news articles

Sonya was surprised to see a uniformed General Rivington Moore VIII — her older brother — standing near her shuttle as she departed from it, on the landing field of the Imperial City Spaceport. He was accompanied by two men and a woman, also officers. His companions wore caduceus medical insignia on their lapels, entwined snakes with wings on top. It was just before sunset, with long shadows stretched across the field.

"One of our Skyship operatives sent me a mindcom," he said, as soon as he and the medical personnel were out of earshot of the other passengers. "Apparently you have not been feeling well? Very bad headaches? I've been extremely worried about you, so I brought these doctors to diagnose you right away. You didn't send me any information."

"I couldn't transmit because something has gone terribly wrong with my mindwave communicator, on both the military and the civilian frequencies." She pointed at her head, grimaced when a needle of pain stabbed her temple. "I took a couple of blows from Devv Jeeling, and the thing went haywire."

"So that's it." His gaze narrowed. "I assume there's no way to patch things up with him now?"

"Not a chance. I told him I don't ever want to see him again. I just needed to come straight back here and get it fixed."

The young General shook his head in displeasure, seemed to care more about the gap in future intelligence information than her welfare. "How did things go wrong between you two?"

She looked at the other officers, then at her brother. "Is this a conversation you want to have here?"

"They all have security clearance," he said, "of the highest level. My *personal* security clearance."

"Are you trying to blame me for what happened on Skyship?"

"I would remind you, that you were on duty there, one hundred percent of the time. What caused the fight?"

"Didn't your other operative tell you?"

He didn't reply, was looking increasingly angry.

"Since you already seem to know, Rivington, I found someone else I like on Skyship, and Devv got jealous over it. But he had no right to hit me; there's no excuse for striking a woman."

"Under ordinary circumstances that might be true, but when you are on an important assignment, you are obligated to exercise extraordinary care." His gaze narrowed. "You didn't do that this time, did you?"

"Aren't you forgetting something? I was not specifically assigned to enter into a relationship with Devv Jeeling when you sent me to Skyship. That just happened. I thought I liked him, and the connection had the bonus of giving us access to inside information."

She grimaced in pain, could barely raise her voice enough to make him hear her. "I'm suffering severe headaches, seeing VR images in front of my eyes, and hearing messages that fill my brain. Overlapping pictures and sounds are driving me crazy."

He looked at the female doctor. "Captain Tolliver, can you check her implant?"

The officer nodded, stepped forward to her. "From your bruises it appears that your boyfriend hit you on the cheek and on the forehead?"

"Yes, the blow to my forehead was the second one, and after that my mindwave implant started acting up."

"Hmmm, blows such as those do not normally cause problems with these units, or with the civilian models, because all are implanted with deep needle-sensors into the inferior and superior colliculus of the midbrain. Nonetheless, something could have been jolted when he hit you."

The doctor removed a small white device from her jacket pocket, ran it over the top of Sonya's head and around the sides and front. "Your implant is indeed malfunctioning. It needs to be removed."

"How fast can you do it?" Sonya asked. The pain had subsided, but she was still seeing the jumbled images and hearing the cacophony of voices.

The doctor pointed to a mobile medical station, parked by the terminal building. "Immediately," she said.

"All right," General Moore said. "Let's get you fixed up and send you back." He led the way to the medical station.

"I'm not so sure about going back," Sonya said. "Things have gotten complicated on Skyship. More than the relationship with Devv."

He stopped and looked at her inquisitively. He didn't look angry any more. "What do you mean?"

"I mean, I'm not sure if Billy Jeeling is that bad of a guy. I'm not sure if he deserves what we're doing to him. He should retire, I agree with that, but—"

"You're not one of my advisers," he said in a curt tone, and then stalked away abruptly, leaving his sister alone with the medical team.

CHAPTER 29

Many surprises are not of the good kind.

—Billy Jeeling, journal entry

It was late afternoon, and Billy had gone to his office to read a new security report. For days, his technicians had been searching thoroughly for any additional sabotage that the treacherous Rand Baker might have committed, but nothing had been found. Apparently the threat of more damage had been concocted as the man lay dying, a pathetic attempt to make himself more important than he actually was.

Billy gazed out the windows, beheld a spectacular golden glow above the horizon of AmEarth as the sun set, with the visible portion of the planet indigo blue and veiny white, against the pale hues of the sky. The views from Skyship never ceased to impress and captivate him.

He heard a commotion in the outer offices, turned away from the view. A large red warning light on the wall began to flash, and sirens wailed furiously, a cacophony of noise.

A young security officer burst in with hardly a knock, made a circling hand salute and spoke with shortness of breath as he tried to be heard above the alarms and sirens. After a failed attempt to be heard, he shouted over the noise. "Sir, Lieutenant Theo Costelli reporting. Scanners picked up a large military force closing fast from AmEarth, with weapons armed!"

Feeling his pulse quicken, Billy glanced back at the window. The sun was dropping behind AmEarth's horizon, a golden orb vanishing into the depths of space. He didn't see any attack craft, but alarms continued to howl.

Devv Jeeling hurried into the office, stood nervously beside the officer, as he continued. "Something is wrong with our defense systems!" the lieutenant said, his voice cracking under the stress. "We're working to fix the problem."

"Something to do with Rand Baker?" Billy asked, looking at his son, and then at the officer. "Is this what his dying threat meant?"

Costelli shrugged and said, "Sir, no one knows, but that would be a good assumption."

Devv turned red in the face, obviously upset.

There were explosions and the sounds of gunfire, seeming to come from an upper level of Skyship.

Billy coughed, felt raspy pains in his chest. Something had gone wrong with the air in his office, and he smelled a caustic odor of ozone-mix. He coughed again, leaned over a control panel on top of his desk, and touched the buttons necessary to pump clean air into the office. The momentary loss of air quality didn't seem to bother the others as much.

His discomfort subsided.

Robotic security officers were running through the corridor outside his door, making urgent machine noises. Human officers were in their midst, shouting warnings and commands.

Devv was flushed and sweating, had a frantic look in his eyes. His gaze darted around, wildly. "I need to get you out of here, Father!" He rushed to a wall inside the office, pressed a button. The wall slid open, revealing a dimly-illuminated tunnel and a maglev track.

He motioned anxiously. "Hurry, Father!"

Billy rode his chair to the open tunnel, peered inside. He felt worried, sensed something was not right. A wave of panic passed through him.

"What is it?" Devv asked.

Suddenly, Billy cried out. To his horror, something silvery—it looked like a thick, viscous liquid—was pooling on the floor around his maglev chair. He couldn't see where it was coming from, but it shone brightly and seemed to be surging out of the floor itself. It began to slide up the frame of the chair, on all sides.

Devv and Lt. Costelli reached over to pull Billy from the chair....

~~~

The silvery substance oozed up around Billy's leg stumps, and over his entire body. It was wet and seemed to tingle his skin at first, and then became icy cold, painfully so.

Devv and the lieutenant held on and tried desperately to pull Billy free. "You're really cold," Devv said. "What's going on?"

The substance was not interested in the robotic Jeeling at all, and used its collective consciousness and strength to surge toward Devv for an instant, knocking him down, and then Costelli as well, before completely covering Billy and his clothing. In horror, Billy looked down at his arms and hands. A strange, silvery sheen covered them, and he was getting even colder, as if he was being inundated by an ice storm. He shivered and shuddered, felt a wave of terror.

Then Billy heard an eerie voice emerge from his own mouth as he yelled to the younger Jeeling, "There is nothing you can do! Go to your station, Devv, and command our defenses. That's the priority, not me!"

Devv and his companion were getting back on their feet.

"*Now!*" Billy shouted. "And say nothing of what you have seen here! Not to anyone!" Curiously, Billy began to feel better inside, almost pleasantly so, despite a freezing stream of silver that continued to flow into his body. It was no longer uncomfortable, and seemed almost natural. Strange and new, but still natural.

Devv turned away from his father and ran toward the tunnel, followed by the lieutenant. Billy watched his robot son pause, and look back at him. The Security Commander stood at a junction with the other officer, where a short tunnel led to a highlift. Billy waved them on....

~~~

Devv couldn't believe what was happening. First the security breach and military attack, and now this! His father's entire body was covered in glowing silver, even his clothing, though as moments passed, the clothing gradually returned to normal. But all exposed surfaces of his skin, from his hands and arms to his face and hair, and even his eyes, were silver. He stared in dismay at the great man, wondered what horrendous thing was happening to him, and felt frustrated that he could do nothing to stop it.

Billy lifted a hand, pointed at Devv. "Go!"

The silvery sheen on Billy faded, and at first this gave Devv some hope that his father—Devv refused to stop thinking of him that way—was beating whatever it was. Then he saw Billy's eyes were still silver and glowing much brighter, in a body that looked otherwise normal. The alien gaze focused on Devv, casting an eerie metallic glow over the meters of distance between them.

Devv felt a chill of fear, and then a sudden compulsion, that he had no will of his own. He turned abruptly, and found himself running through the tunnel with Lt. Costelli, until they reached a highlift. They hurried inside, surged upward at high speed.

Speaking rapidly during the ascent through the massive vessel, Costelli went through the list of onboard defenses that were out of commission... kinetic kill missiles, nuke packs, KK490 cannons, small-crew support craft... and at the mention of each, he described a problem and a pattern. All had been electronically disabled, right through every backup system.

"Damn!" Devv said, after hearing this. "How about our assault ships?"

"Dead in their hangars, sir, to the last one. Even your personal craft. All we have left with gamma cannons are police humbabies, but they're no better than mosquitoes against the big force coming in. I assumed you'd want to use them anyway, so the humbabies are being set up for skirmish. You know the limitations they have, sir. We're likely to lose every one of them outside Skyship."

"We'll shoot back with popguns and water pistols if we have to!" Devv yelled. He heard the crackle of a security-force transmission over his mindwave implant. Enemy commando teams were attempting to board the great vessel at the main docks, where police security teams were defending. The attackers were making their second attempt to board, the first one having been thwarted by stiff resistance.

On the roof level, the highlift doors opened and the pair hurried out, into the midst of human and robotic security and police officers, which now formed the heart of Skyship's defense force.

"Your ship is ready, sir," one of the 'bots said to Devv. It was a Lazarus-series model, a very human-looking female with dark skin. It pointed across the roof, where more than twenty humbabies were warming up, their engines revving and throbbing, but rotors not moving yet. He saw additional humbabies, and some of the more complex morph-babies, perched on top of other buildings, firing up their engines.

On this rooftop, he recognized several reservists in the midst of security personnel, including Yürgen Zayeddi, who was boarding one of the humbabies, wearing a pilot's headset. Although he was primarily involved in the PR program under the supervision of Lainey Forster, the young man had proven that he knew how to operate these specialized craft, having learned at the factory where he used to work. For this emergency, they needed all the pilots they could round up—even one whom Devv disliked personally.

"Let's go!" Devv shouted.

He and Lt. Costelli hit the helipad at full tilt, leaped into their humbabies and sped toward the nearest egress tunnel that led out of the hull of Skyship, their rotors off and on auxiliary-power instead. Hundreds of humbabies and the few morph-babies from the rooftops converged on one side of the airborne city. Then, like swarms of insects, they shot out into the ozone layer of the stratosphere.

With his headset on and a VR display flickering in front of him, Devv saw a large formation of attack craft speeding toward Skyship, leaving bright purple ion-engine trailings against the darkening bulk of AmEarth. The ominous formation swung to one side, surged forward, and before Devv could gather his thoughts the enemy ships were firing at his group... bright red lances of energy from their powerful gamma cannons.

The defenders couldn't shoot back yet, as they were beyond the effective range of their smaller cannons, so the pilots used control sticks to jink their aircraft away from hostile fire. On Devv's left flank he saw Yürgen Zayeddi flying beside Lt. Costelli, each of them clearly visible through their side windows. Then a barrage of incoming fire hit Costelli's craft, causing it to explode in a fireball, with fragments careening away. No chance of survival; he must have died instantly. Devv was sickened by this, and even more when he saw additional police humbabies explode in the distance.

This defensive effort was suicide, but Devv and his security force couldn't sit inside Skyship like cowards, while it was pummeled by attackers. Better to die courageously, right in the enemy's face, taking out as many of them as possible. Who was this foe? Devv guessed it had something to do with General Rivington Moore, his tycoon ally, Jonathan Racker, and the Yhatt government.

Assholes! he thought. He accelerated toward the attacking vessels and squeezed the joystick so hard that his fingers hurt, while watching red streaks of cannon fire come from his bow. Nearby his comrades surged forward with him, firing away. He saw Zayeddi's craft take the lead and speed into danger, guns blazing. Several of the enemy craft exploded, but many more of Skyship's vessels and pilots were lost, in smaller fireballs.

Suddenly the sky in front of the police aircraft lit up in a series of blinding silver blasts and flashes. Many enemy ships in the formation exploded, and others veered off course. Moments later, the survivors of the attack squadron were hightailing it back to AmEarth.

Filled with the ferocity of combat, Devv fired away, even when he saw that the attackers were routed and out of range. He knew he hadn't hit a thing, but some of the pilots had made kill-shots, including Zayeddi. Other than these few successes, Devv had seen very little return fire from Skyship, and many human pilots had been lost. In all, the firepower of the defenders had not been enough to route a fleet like that.

But something else had been involved, something silver.

Computerized damage reports came in over his mindwave implant. Nine casualties including Lt. Costelli. Skyship hadn't sustained anything more than a few glancing blows, and was safe. For the time being.

Devv's headset vibrated with the resounding cheers of his valiant officers and reservists, but he didn't join in the celebration. He was too immersed in thought.

CHAPTER 30

Some things can never be explained or even vaguely understood.
The universe keeps its secrets.

—Excerpt from *Doctrine of the Stars*, one of the greatest of all
philo-scientific treatises

It had been unlike any other day in his life.

This evening Billy felt different as he sat in his office, removed from the time and place he once thought he occupied, detached from all he had known before, and connected to something else entirely, something so strange that he could hardly put it into words. He felt cold energy stirring around inside, traveling back and forth through his arteries and cellular structures, causing his heart to beat faster and his breath to come in short gasps. He tried to calm himself, then heard a familiar rapping pattern at the door.

Taking a moment, Billy called out permission to enter. Starbot strode in, making hardly a sound with his mechanical body, followed by Dr. Rachel Ginsberg. She caught Billy's gaze immediately as she entered, looked startled and came to a dead stop just inside the door. Starbot must have told her something when he gave her Billy's order to come. But whatever he told her, it was apparently not enough, because she just stared at him with an expression of shock and fear, upon seeing his glistening silver eyes.

For a moment, Billy didn't know if she would continue toward him or flee. He tried to soften his steely gaze, and said in the most calm voice he could muster, "I'm sorry if I am not entirely presentable, my good friend, but as you can see, I have experienced something highly unusual. An affliction of sorts, so I thought I should consult a doctor."

She smiled, but couldn't conceal her nervousness as she took a tentative step toward him, then another, and another. "How are you feeling?" she asked.

"All things considered, you mean?"

"Of course. All things considered. Are you in any pain?" Rachel touched his forehead. "You feel quite cold."

He became aware of the creatures going faster inside, flitting this way and that, making him even colder. Apparently they didn't like anyone touching him.

"Something alien has entered my body." Billy placed an open hand on his chest. "It is inside here and everywhere, many tiny creatures, I think, but they form a collective entity."

The doctor put an instrument over his heart, listened to the wireless signal from the device, then placed it on his lungs as he breathed. "From a cardiovascular standpoint you seem agitated," she said. "And why are you so cold?"

"You'd be agitated, too, if you'd been invaded by aliens and your eyes had turned silver."

She frowned. "I suppose I would."

"And as for the coldness, I don't know why. It started when they surged into my body, like something that had come from far away, bringing a piece of deep space with them."

She was taking his temperature now, with another instrument placed against his temple. "Seventy-one point three degrees," she said. "Impossible. You should be dead."

"But I'm not, am I?"

Rachel brought out an eye chart, propped it up on a table across the room. After a few minutes of her questions and his responses, she looked at him and said, "Your eyesight is perfectly normal, twenty-twenty. None of the slight far-sightedness you had before. No short-sightedness, either." She performed additional tests, and finally said, "You have no astigmatism, glaucoma, or any other problem I can determine—except both of your eyes are gleaming silver, with no differentiation between pupil and cornea—and you're as cold as a corpse."

Billy nodded. "It's beyond known medicine, then." He motioned with one hand. "You can go now. Thank you."

"Are you going to be all right?"

"I don't know. I think so, but I can't be sure, can I?"

"Isn't there something more I can do for you?"

He smiled thinly, said in a mocking tone, "Do you have a special pill for this sort of thing? Or an injection? How about a healing patch?"

Dr. Ginsberg backed toward the door, appeared to be near tears.

"I'm sorry," Billy said. "You didn't deserve that. I know you're trying to be helpful, but I think you've done all you can, all anyone can."

Rachel nodded and left, followed by Starbot. Just before the robot shut the door, Billy heard her let out a sob in the corridor, as if he had died.

CHAPTER 31

When a motivated person awakens in the morning, he has things in mind for the day, and sets about accomplishing them. But such lists, whether loosely formed or more formal, always omit something—the factor that Chaos brings to the table. No plan can ever take Chaos into account.

—E. Bert Rhinbar, from his "Wandering Philosophies"

In full dress uniform, with gilded epaulets, glittering ribbons, and gold stars, General Rivington Moore VIII paced the reception area of the exclusive officer's club, waiting impatiently for Jonathan Racker and Maureen Stuart to arrive. It was evening, and he'd demanded to see both of them here on the military base, saying he didn't have the time or inclination to meet them anywhere else. The club was on the top floor of a structure that had been built in the style of a medieval tower, with turrets and fluttering banners—and one-way windows that looked like castle rock from the outside but provided broad defensive views from the inside. There wasn't much of a view from this level tonight, though, because fog had moved in over the capital city.

He heard the conversational murmur of officers and their guests in the main dining room, which was around half full. A Major and his lady passed by and entered the room, giving the proper acknowledgement of Moore's superior rank as they did so. The General didn't care who saw him out here, pacing and waiting. He did whatever he wanted, whenever he wanted, wherever he wanted.

His officer's cap sat on an ornate antique table, beside a glass of single malt scotch. Moore had taken one sip of the drink, and it had not settled well in his stomach. He heard his innards growling—not from hunger, but from how upset he was. His gut did that at times when he was feeling great stress, and this was one of those times.

The powerful old industrialist had been sending him relentless messages demanding a meeting, and now that Moore had agreed to one, Racker and that attorney were twenty-two minutes late. He would wait another eight minutes, and then would cancel the meeting.

He took another sip of the rare and expensive single malt, and this time it went down better. The chunk of ice in the glass had melted a little, watering down the liquor, making it less strong. It was about right now, and he took one more sip before putting the glass down again, remembering how he and his father had celebrated his twenty-first birthday in this very club, sharing the same brand of fine, aged scotch. He'd also shared the drink with his favorite officers on many occasions. Something about single malt—especially this honored label—increased camaraderie; he didn't know what it was, because other drinks could make a person feel relaxed, too. But this scotch was a rung or two above anything else. Maybe it had something to do with the tradition of the drink, the long history of the distillery in Scotland and the family that had run the operation for hundreds of years.

General Moore liked to think in terms of family tradition—in his case, one of military service and the attainment of power. He was not the first in his family to think in such terms, not the first to wear a uniform in dedicated military service. His father and four of his grandfathers had all served bravely as officers of the Empire, in glorious battles and hard-won victories, bringing the great lifestyles and traditions of the AmEarth Empire to the backward peoples of the world. The lives of all people were better under the dominion of the Imperial City and the Empire. He was one of five children, and his sister and three brothers were all in military service, as officers.

He stared at an elaborately carved wooden door at the entrance to the club, with its intricate golden designs and coat of arms—a door that had been brought over from a Europaean castle his family still owned. Moore descended from a long line of overseas nobles, men who in past centuries had given their lives in military service to king and country. Their photographs were displayed prominently on the walls of the club, along with those of other decorated military heroes.

Moore was the youngest in his family to attain the rank of General, and the second to be awarded the maximum of ten stars, after the precedent set by his great grandfather, Rivington Moore V, one of the foremost heroes in the history of the Imperial Empire. But the current General Moore had achieved the rank at a younger age, beating his great grandfather by two years and four months. He was only thirty-six now, having attained command of the army three years ago. He was proud of his achievements, but wanted a great deal more, for himself and for his family. He had attained his rank in a *pax imperium*, a time of relative peace throughout the Empire, and of only a few minor rebellions—with no opportunities for the glory his ancestors had attained. So, he'd seen the need to get what he wanted in a different way.

As part of the future he was envisioning, Moore was laying the foundation for the generations of his family to come. His twin sons Rivington IX and Parker IV, almost ten years old now, were enrolled in a prestigious military academy, and it gave him great pride that they were receiving high marks in their studies, their work ethic, and their appearance and cleanliness—all qualities their father had emphasized to them as important. He was also proud of the fact that the young men were excelling in the handling of weapons, including not only guns, but classic sabers and knives as well, and a broad spectrum of martial arts.

For General Moore to continue the storied tradition of his family, and to enhance it, he had to inculcate his sons, and set them on the proper path to glory. And he also needed to accomplish something significant professionally, something *really* big like his great grandfather had accomplished—and bringing Billy Jeeling down was the only way available to him. Jeeling was the most famous man in the world, and thanks to the conspiracy against him, the most notorious as well. Until Moore's failed military attack on Skyship, he had thought Jeeling was on the ropes, ready to fall.

He shook his head in dismay, wondering what could have possibly gone wrong. Everything had been planned with utmost care, and it had been going exceedingly well, up to the moment of the attack. The enemies of Billy Jeeling had numbered in the hundreds of millions in cities around the Empire, and had been increasing rapidly. The timing of Moore's strike had seemed so perfect, and he'd intended to put Skyship under immediate government control, backed up by a permanent military guard under his command.

When that was accomplished, the General had intended to use his new status and influence to combine the army, navy, marines, air force, and coast guard into one fighting unit called the RAL—the Royal AmEarth Legion—under his unified command. That would involve getting rid of any generals, admirals, and other officers who were in his way, and he'd been compiling a list of his foes, and potential foes.

But plans were plans, not battlefield action, and sometimes even the best strategies and tactics were not successful. Still, he had not envisioned half of his attack force being destroyed by a mysterious, devastating weapon, something that sent the rest of his warships fleeing back to AmEarth. It wasn't imaginable to him, a weapon he'd never heard of, and of such immense, fantastic power. His preparations had been meticulous, and he'd failed anyway, because he hadn't known what lay in store for him. He should have been more careful, knowing what a genius inventor Jeeling was, and the possibility that he might come up with an unheard-of weapon. Moore didn't know what to do now, only that he needed to learn what Jeeling had in his arsenal before any future attacks could be mounted.

Know your enemy, as you know yourself.

It was one of his most important mantras, adapted from the teachings of an ancient military leader. It was essential to have full knowledge of your enemy's strengths and weaknesses, and to be able to make informed guesses about what he was likely to do in different scenarios. But this, this monstrous weapon that spewed blasts of silver light out of Skyship... He shuddered. What could it possibly be? He'd read the reports of survivors over and over, and had interviewed all of them personally, without learning anything useful—except for the deadly nature of the power Billy Jeeling had at his command.

There had been no inkling of this before, though Skyship's defenses were known to be stiff — kinetic kill missiles and a lot more. But nothing like this mystery weapon.

At twenty-nine minutes late, General Moore had on his cap and was ready to leave. Then he heard the whir of the highlift, and stared in that direction. The gilded doors opened, and Racker stepped out, followed by the taller Maureen Stuart, who was around half his age. She wore a white evening gown studded with jewels around the collar, while Racker was dressed in an expensive suit, with no tie — his customary attire. The gnarled little man walked slowly and unsteadily, but could not fall, because of an electronic device concealed under his clothing — something he called an "invisible stabilizer." One of his companies manufactured the units for worldwide distribution, and Racker was quick to demonstrate how it worked wherever he went — as if he were a salesman, constantly hawking his own products.

Racker glowered up at him. "You shouldn't have gone off half-cocked," he said. "We're supposed to be in this together. Yet now through your foolishness, you've gotten Paul Paulo killed! He was my closest friend, and I hold you one hundred percent accountable for it."

"Don't talk like an old fool," Moore said, as he led them into the private dining room he had reserved. "I went off on my own because you and Paul were too slow to agree to an attack."

No one sat down. A long silence ensued, in which they stood looking at each other uneasily, sipping their drinks. Outside, the fog was beginning to clear, and Moore could see the lights of the ultra-tall Racker Center building in the distance, surrounded by more classical buildings, many of which had been owned by the late Paul Paulo.

"I can only stay an hour," Maureen Stuart said. "My husband and I are having a late dinner with Prime Minister Yhatt tonight. The Imperial Palace is only a few minutes away from here, so I'll stay as long as I can."

"You're half an hour late and now you say you have to leave early?" Moore took a deep breath. "All right." He motioned toward the table. "Would both of you like to sit down?"

"Maybe later," Racker said. "I sit too much, so I like to take any opportunity I can to stand."

A waiter in a black coat entered the room, stood just inside the doorway. "Shall I bring the menus?" he asked.

Moore shook his head. "Just drinks," he said, "and some aperitifs." He looked at his guests. "What would you like?"

"A glass of pinot noir, please," Stuart said.

"I'll have a beer," Racker said. "Do you have Acapulco Amber?"

"Yes, sir, I'll bring it."

When the waiter left, General Moore looked at Maureen intently, and said, "You were on board Skyship during the attack. What weapon did Jeeling use against my commandos and their ships? My men said the warships were destroyed by powerful blasts of silver light. What device could possibly do that, with such devastating effect?"

"I have no idea. I only saw your soldiers stream aboard Skyship, and the close-in fighting. Many fell in front of me, along with Paul Paulo. I didn't see the ships destroyed."

"Any flashes of silver in the combat you saw?"

She shook her head. "None."

Moore sipped his drink, then went to a private bar and poured himself a fresh glass of single malt, "neat" this time, without ice. He turned toward her. "My officers said you were taken prisoner with them, but you were questioned separately. Then all of you were let go. Why? Are you on Jeeling's side?"

"Of course not!"

"Then why did they let you go?"

"They let all of us go, not just me."

The young officer scowled. "Something doesn't smell right about this."

"I had nothing to do with your military defeat," Stuart said. "I didn't know you were going to attack. That's all I told my interrogators. The *truth*. They put me through a battery of lie-detection tests, found out I was telling the truth. That's why they let me go."

"Those damned truthbots," Moore said. "I'd like to get ahold of one and copy it, but they have self-destruct mechanisms that are impenetrable." He narrowed his gaze. "So you didn't tell them anything else?"

She shook her head.

"Maureen would never turn against us," Racker said. "I trust her like my own daughter." He stared hard at the General. "You're just trying to divert attention from your own failure."

The waiter entered with glasses of wine and beer, then left. Just before he closed the door, the General told him to leave them alone.

Then Moore glowered at the old man. "I'm racking my brain, trying to figure out what went wrong. I thought we'd have the element of surprise on our side."

"But you failed, and lost half your force." Jonathan Racker smiled cruelly. "It seems that the only element of surprise worked in reverse. *You* were the one caught off guard, not Jeeling. You have no idea what sort of weapon he used on you?"

The General looked away, spoke in a low, embarrassed tone. "None at all. Not even a clue."

Racker filled the room with his voice, quite loud and commanding for such a small man. "You have no idea? How can that be, you the military genius, the one who knows everything about arms and armaments, ancient and modern? How can that be?"

"I intend to find out," Moore said. "Damn it, don't ride me about this. You want Jeeling destroyed as much as I do, so don't act like you had no part in this setback. Yes, I sent the force without your knowledge, but you were involved in the earlier planning against Jeeling. In fact, you started the ball rolling against him when you and Paulo organized a group to bring him down through character assassination. I was just trying to speed things up."

"Well, you only sped up the death of Paul Paulo, didn't you?"

"He had a long and productive life."

"And it should have been longer." Racker's eyes were rheumy and filled with anger as he looked up at the taller man. Everyone was taller than Racker. Moore would like to pick up the little bastard and hurl him through one of the windows. It was a long way down. But this was only a passing thought. He knew he needed the tycoon as an ally. Despite his own inclinations, Moore knew that everything could not be accomplished through military action. Racker had important political contacts, and vast financial resources.

Racker's gaze softened, and he looked away. He seemed more sad than anything else.

As for what happened to Paulo, at least Racker hadn't refused to meet with the General because of it, and his criticisms seemed muted—as if the old industrialist knew that he also needed to continue his alliance with Moore. The General's position in the army was stable despite the military setback. Many people were saying that he couldn't be expected to contend with the incredible technologies that Billy Jeeling had. Yet lots of important people still wanted to be rid of him, and eagerly awaited another attempt—be it overt or behind the scenes.

"We'd better plan our next move with extreme care," Racker said.

"Agreed."

~~~

Maureen Stuart knew from her fellow lawyers that Paul Paulo had left most of his estate to his close friend Jonathan Racker, so perhaps that was some comfort to the old business tycoon. Everyone knew how much he loved money. Racker could never get enough of it, his detractors said.

She picked up her wineglass for the first time, put her nose in the glass and smelled the subtle but pleasing bouquet of the pinot noir. She took a sip and listened to the General.

"We need more reconnaissance," he said. "I sent my operatives to Skyship, and one—Rand Baker—was successful in sabotaging the defenses for a while. There were also earlier small-scale sabotages that went quite well—causing damage without seriously harming the immense vessel. We were just irritating Jeeling and making him feel unsettled, but never setting in motion a scenario that could lead to the dangerous atmospheric damage he threatened. So, even though I think he's been bluffing about that, I took precautionary actions... just in case."

"It was all unilateral on your part," Maureen said. "Even after you revealed the existence of your operatives to us, you refused to withdraw them, and you ordered a new attack plan."

"You had to know I was doing something. I'm not a man to sit on my hands."

Racker stood by the window with his tall glass of beer. He looked away. "I did suspect you were up to something."

"But your operatives missed a matter of critical importance, didn't they?" Maureen said, to Moore. "The weapon that Jeeling used on you."

"Yes, they missed something big, and that's exactly my point. I felt hampered before by disagreements in our group over how aggressive we should be against Billy Jeeling, so I didn't send in enough agents, and as a consequence I didn't learn enough."

"So it's everyone's fault except your own?" Racker said. "It's our fault, not yours?"

General Moore hesitated, pursed his lips. "Perhaps I didn't phrase that as well as I might have. I focus too much on the goal at times, on what I want to accomplish, and I don't always participate in the niceties and protocols that are helpful to an alliance. For that, I apologize. No, the recent military failure is not your fault, Jonathan. It is one hundred percent mine. Even in the face of your disagreement with me at our last meeting, and Paul's, I should have been more forceful."

"You're saying you should have been even more militaristic?" Maureen asked. "You should have sent a bigger attack force?"

The youthful general shook his head. "No, I should have been more forceful in making my point during the meetings with you folks, my friends and allies. And—with your concurrence, of course—I should have been more forceful in getting agents aboard Skyship. I fully admit, I should not have gone off on my own, making unilateral decisions. I made mistakes and I regret them. They were tactical mistakes."

Maureen looked at him intently. As a successful attorney, she had considerable experience in determining if people were lying or telling the truth. She saw telltale signs of falsehood in the powerful officer—his gaze wandered around, didn't stick for long on her or Jonathan, and his sentences had a way of tailing off at the end, as if he was not putting enough energy into what he was saying—words that could reflect his inner turmoil and devious nature, and what he really intended to do. What was he thinking now? What was he planning? Another subterfuge?

Maureen and Jonathan exchanged uneasy glances that Moore didn't notice — as if she and the industrial magnate were thinking the same thing.

Just then, Maureen saw a brief peripheral flash of silver and turned toward it, where General Moore was, just as he cried out.

"What is it?" she asked.

She was shocked to see that his skin and clothing were glowing bright silver. He screamed, a horrible sound such as she'd never heard before, and hoped to never hear again. But her wish did not come to pass. He writhed and fell to the floor, and screamed even more, in terrible pain.

She put her glass down, rose to her feet and took a step toward him.

He didn't answer her, *couldn't* answer.

A series of horrific, muted explosions ensued inside his body, accompanied by more eruptions on the outside, and silver fluid flowing from the fresh wounds, as if his blood had turned to molten metal. On the floor, he put his hands to his face, as silver gushed and flowed from his eyes, ears, and mouth. Then he went motionless, with the strange fluid pooling around him. One more muted explosion followed, and to her horror the top of his skull erupted, spraying brain matter around the private dining room.

Hardly able to believe this was happening, she ducked quickly to avoid being struck, but was not successful. The front of her gown was splattered with brain cells, and splotches of silvery blood. There could be no doubt; the man was dead.

A faint and eerie silver glow rose from Moore's body — it seemed impossible — but it continued upward and hovered just below the high ceiling, like a small cloud. She blinked, looked back. It seemed to remain there, and she smelled something different in the air. It was a musky odor, combined with the clinging, sickening odor of death.

Racker leaned down and turned the body over, getting the strange blood on his shoes and hands. General Moore's once-spotless uniform was ripped asunder as if he'd been shot repeatedly, except he bled silver, not red, and it was clear that something awful had happened *inside* his body, and erupted outward.

"His brain exploded out of his head," the old man said, "and his heart blew, too. The arteries, chambers, the whole works, they all detonated, and he died instantly." Racker shuddered. "I'd say most of the organs in his body blew up. Massive internal hemorrhaging, but silver? What on AmEarth could cause that?" He straightened and wiped his hands on his trousers, looked around nervously.

Maureen felt as if she was going to throw up. She wanted to get as far from here as possible, but couldn't move, and just stared at the ghastly scene before her. Apparently no one in the rest of the club had heard the stricken General's screams in this private back room, as no one tried to gain entrance.

Suddenly the silver glow beneath the ceiling dropped, covering Racker like a blanket and then melting into him, so that his entire body turned silver, too. He screamed and fell to the floor, contorting his body and crying out in a hideous, gurgling voice, as silver gushed out of his mouth like metallic vomit. She closed her eyes, could not bear to see any more of this, didn't want to hear any more. The same explosions and grisly results....

Am I next? She still could not move, didn't even think about escape, which seemed impossible.

Finally she looked. In macabre, horrific silence, the two men lay together in death, and she fully expected to join them in a matter of moments. She slumped to the floor in her stained gown, and buried her face in her hands, awaiting the inevitable. What sort of terrible power could do these monstrous things? She could not begin to imagine.

But the expected did not occur.

She looked up and saw the silver cloud condensing in the air, becoming smaller. Then it darted away, and vanished through some tiny opening it found around the window.

Maureen rose to her feet, felt weak and wobbly. She kept from falling by holding onto the back of a chair. Then, with uncertain, halting steps, she made her way out of the room, past a black-jacketed waiter and a woman who was asking him where the powder room was. Maureen's mind was foggy, her senses numb. The waiter noticed her, asked if she was all right. She didn't answer, made it to the reception area and the highlift, and left the ghastly scene behind her.

~~~

Sonya felt much better, now that Dr. Tolliver had removed the mindwave implant from her midbrain. The change had been immediate, as the overlapping conversations and images had ceased, and so had the unbearable lances of pain. Though she still had some soreness where the surgery had been performed, she could think straight, and no longer considered killing herself, as the only way to obtain relief. She didn't have an implant at all now, and would not be able to receive a replacement for several months. The military doctor wanted her to heal completely first.

She had a bottle of pain pills Dr. Tolliver had given her, but she'd only taken half of the recommended dosage today, not feeling as if she needed more. The bottle sat on her nightstand, beside a half-consumed glass of water.

Sonya had been provided with a comfortable room in the female officer's barracks of the main base, on the outskirts of Imperial City. She was sitting up in bed, propped against the headboard with pillows, reading *Ocean*, a popular fantasy novel about dangerous marine animals declaring war against human civilization, because they were tired of oil pollution, floating plastics, sewage dumping and the other abuses committed by mankind in their waters. She had selected this book from the base library today because it looked intriguing, and because she was interested in environmental issues.

Her concern about such matters was one of the reasons she had changed her mind about Billy Jeeling, because when she spent time near him on Skyship she had seen the beneficial things he was doing for the health of the atmosphere and the air people breathed — and she came to the opinion that the citizens of AmEarth should be more grateful to him for what he had accomplished. They should treat him with more respect, instead of trying to throw him out like garbage. There had to be another way to convince him to retire, one that would be good for him and good for the Empire. A win-win situation.

She read through the end of the third chapter. Feeling sleepy, she closed the book and turned off the lamp beside her.

A couple of minutes passed, and she was drifting off to sleep quickly. Then, suddenly, something lit up the room. She opened her eyes, and was startled to see a bright silver sphere floating in the air by her bed, illuminating the entire room in an eerie metallic glow.

Was this a nightmare? Her first inclination told her it had to be, because it was too strange to be real. The silver ball brightened, so that it looked like a miniature sun. She had to shield her eyes with her hands.

A wave of terror came over her, but she wasn't sure why. This had to be a dream, didn't it? She put a pillow over her face, but tried to peer around it.

The blinding sphere drew closer, causing her to pull back from it, still shielding her face. It was only centimeters away from her, and she felt a freezing, cold wind coming from it, as if a door to the center of the universe had been thrown open. She shivered, looked at the walls around her, illuminated in eerie silver.

Sonya wondered if she could roll out of bed and run, but when she set the pillow aside and tried to do that, her arms and legs moved so phlegmatically that she couldn't even reach the edge of the bed, because her joints were so stiff and cold.

Suddenly the room went dark and grew warmer, but she continued to shiver. She switched on the light, climbed out of bed and walked around, feeling uneasy and confused. It was the strangest dream she had ever experienced. It had to be a dream.

She looked around. Nothing appeared to be out of the ordinary. Then she caught her breath, as she noticed something strange about the water in the glass. It looked cloudy. She lifted the glass. It was freezing cold to her touch, and the water inside had frozen solid.

With shaking hands, she put the glass back on the table, and turned off the light. Her fingers had gotten so cold that they burned. She blew warm breaths on them, then climbed back under the covers, but could not stop shivering.

She lay awake, shivering and staring into the darkness, wondering what had just happened.

A soldier knocked on her door, identifying himself and telling her he had an urgent message. Slipping on a robe, she went to the door and opened it.

A captain stood there, in an impeccable black and tan uniform, with red stripes of rank on his arms. "I'm sorry ma'am, but there is terrible news. Your brother is dead."

He went on to tell her what little he knew about how the General had died—his body had been found in a pool of silvery blood, and it appeared that the organs in his body had exploded. Then the officer said, "The same thing happened to Jonathan Racker. Silver death, they're calling it, and before that silver blasts of light destroyed half of our force when it tried to attack Skyship. Something to do with Billy Jeeling, everyone is saying. A terrible new power he seems to have, and he's using it against us."

He went on to say that top military officers had been summoned, and they were preparing a report for the Prime Minister that would be delivered that evening. But they'd decided to inform Sonya first, knowing how close the two of them had been.

Sonya wept at the news of her brother, and wondered why she wasn't killed too, because she had worked with him. She had never heard of such an awful weapon, couldn't imagine what it might possibly be.

CHAPTER 32

"There are proper and noble ways of going about things.
I am constantly in search of them."

—Renaldo Yhatt, to his wife

A tall, dignified man in a dinner tux, Prime Minister Renaldo Yhatt took a seat at the head of the palace dining table, set with silver, crystal, and fine linens, beneath a glittering antique chandelier. He was the only one there, took a sip of sauvignon blanc while he waited. Maureen Stuart was almost an hour late, which was not like her. Her husband, in the adjacent parlor talking with the First Lady, had said Maureen might be running late, because she had an important meeting with General Moore.

Yhatt snapped his fingers, causing draperies to spread open dramatically, revealing Imperial City in all of its nighttime splendor. He was on the second floor, and his palace sat on the only hill in the city, above the surrounding buildings and monuments. This provided the leader of the Empire with a clear view of the wide boulevards and moonlit river, where two ferries glittered like floating candelabras as they passed one another. It had been foggy earlier in the evening, but the fog was lifting, carried away by cool breezes.

The magnificent, sprawling city represented all that the AmEarth government had achieved—actually all it had plundered, Yhatt admitted to himself—from weaker peoples in distant lands. Much of the wealth of the planet had been gathered and brought here, to be displayed by the wealthy in their mansions, and in the many large museums, arenas, parks, and other public places around the metropolis. A century ago, this goal had been achieved at the expenditure of

227

blood and treasure, but that had been a necessity, so that the whole world could come under one dominion.

Centuries before the AmEarth Empire, the British had managed to put one-quarter of the world's land mass under their rule, but their empire had gradually crumbled after the death of their sovereign, Queen Victoria. This modern version of an empire—much larger and more magnificent—was not dependent upon any one personality to keep it together. By rule of law and military force, the Empire was strong, and getting stronger. Around the world, there were only a few minor rebellions to quell periodically, and to a large extent this was done with personnel-seeking drones, little remote-controlled aircraft that could sniff the trails of enemy leaders like bloodhounds, and fire tiny heat-seeking missiles into their brains—missiles that exploded on contact.

Hearing voices, he looked up. The white-haired First Lady, Lorissa Yhatt, was slender and elegant, dressed in a shimmering, pale blue gown. Seeming to float over the floor as she walked, she was accompanied by a younger man who looked out of place in a tweed sport coat and dark slacks. This renowned artist, Paddy Stuart, had long black hair, secured at the back in a silver clasp, and a neatly trimmed, graying beard. He and Mrs. Yhatt had been discussing painting techniques in the parlor while they awaited the arrival of Stuart's wife. Uniformed female servants stood at attention by the table, with white cloths draped over their arms.

As Lorissa and Paddy took their seats, the Prime Minister's top aide entered the room and awaited permission to speak. Harrison Jennings stood stiffly, a short distance from his superior. His blond hair and moustache were not as groomed as usual. When Yhatt nodded to him, Jennings said, "Mrs. Stuart has finally arrived on the grounds. And she appears have a problem."

"What do you mean?" Yhatt asked, as servants poured white wine from carafes into tulip-shaped glasses.

Jennings ruffled his own moustache thoughtfully, with a thumb and forefinger. "I watched her on surveillance from one of the guard stations, sir. She looks disheveled and upset, and has spilled something on her dress. It must be why she's so late." Jennings listened to an earpiece, said, "Sir, I'm also receiving word that a military messenger is on his way to the palace, with an urgent report."

"What's it about?"

"I don't know, sir. Excuse me, I'll go and find out." Jennings bowed, and left quickly. He passed Maureen Stuart, just as she entered the dining room.

Lorissa Yhatt gasped at the sight of Maureen Stuart, jumped to her feet and hurried over to her. "My dear!" she exclaimed, "Are you all right?"

"No, I'm not." Maureen slumped onto a side chair. Her eyes were full of agony as she looked past Mrs. Yhatt, to the Prime Minister. "A truly awful thing has happened, your eminence. A horrible thing. I'm sorry to come here with my dress like this, but it was unavoidable. I wanted to come directly here and warn you about something terrible."

"*Warn* me?"

~~~

Maureen Stuart was only partially aware of her bearded husband kneeling beside her chair and holding her hand, and the Prime Minister and First Lady standing in front of her, looking down at her with concern. She had come straight here from the horrors at the officer's club.

"They're dead," she said. "The most horrible way imaginable. Both General Moore and Jonathan Racker. I didn't have time to change, wanted to rush straight here."

"To warn me of what?" Prime Minister Yhatt asked.

"All the organs in their bodies exploded." Shaking, she pointed toward the silvery stains on her dress. "Their brains blew, their hearts too, splattering blood this color. I was near them, when the interior organs in their bodies detonated—as if bombs had been planted inside." She stared up at the Prime Minister. "It was gruesome, sir. And I'm afraid we're going to be next."

"Silver blood?"

"That's right, sir. You need to notify security, put the palace on high alert."

"No one can get to me," Yhatt said. "Not with all the layers of protection I have."

"I wouldn't assume that, sir. The General and Racker also had high security. They didn't die prettily. And it occurred at a military base."

"Their organs blew? How can that be possible?"

Her entire body was trembling, and she struggled for control. "Something silver caused it, Mr. Prime Minister. A strange metallic light bathed both of them, and they died horribly, screaming—it was the worst thing I ever saw. They were mutilated and their blood turned silver." She pointed again at the stains on her dress.

Looking up, Paddy said, "Mr. Prime Minister, I heard that silver blasts of light destroyed part of your fleet when it attacked Skyship. Could the events be connected?"

"I wouldn't call it *my* fleet, Paddy. I'm a politician. That was a military venture without my approval, and a foolish one, by any rational definition. General Moore's Folly."

Paddy Stuart looked surprised at the frank comments, and just nodded.

Maureen was surprised, too. And watching Prime Minister Yhatt, she thought he looked concerned, but not panicked. Saying nothing, he walked across the large dining hall, stood at a high window and gazed out.

"I don't know why I wasn't killed, too," Maureen said. "This all has something to do with Billy Jeeling, doesn't it?"

Yhatt didn't reply, continued to stare out at the capital city, so transfixed by it that he barely heard Harrison Jennings, asking to speak with him again.

CHAPTER 33

There are forces in this universe that cannot be accounted for, and cannot be analyzed, at the risk of setting them loose. The only safe thing to do is to avoid them, or find a sure way of destroying them.

—Billy Jeeling, one of his unspoken and unwritten thoughts

Skyship floated in the atmosphere at an altitude of eleven kilometers, directly over Imperial City. It was nighttime on board the great vessel, as it was in the sprawling metropolis below.

Billy was on the high walkway, riding his maglev chair back and forth, thinking and worrying. He had sent electronic signals to disable all access to this area, shutting off the highlifts and blocking the doorways. For extra security, Starbot and the other five robots in the series stood sentinel nearby.

The Master of Skyship paused to stare at himself in a mirror wall, and was terrified to see the silver glow still in his eyes, like bright, shiny spotlights gleaming from the depths of the universe. And as cold as he was, it didn't seem to alter his skin color. Something not of AmEarth had taken hold of him, something that Tobek had described in his journals—a collective entity that killed the inventor, and could very well do the same to him. They stirred within, and he felt a strange rush of cold pleasure. It was unsettling to him, in an extremely odd way.

This power, these creatures of light that combined into a single deadly organism and now occupied his body, acted of their own deadly volition. They had destroyed half of the Imperial fleet and sent the survivors fleeing. They had killed General Rivington Moore VIII and the fabulously wealthy Jonathan Racker. Only minutes ago, Billy had seen the men die in vivid images that flashed in full color through his brain, as if he were watching a video production. Then, their horrific task completed, he'd seen the gleaming creatures of light — a long thread of them connected to Billy — retreat from Racker's headquarters and go to Sonya Orr in her room on AmEarth, hovering there for a few moments, but not harming her. Why they'd shown this brief interest in her, he didn't know. Moments later, the long thread of light returned to Billy on Skyship, merging entirely into him.

During the frenetic activity when the creatures were in their murderous attack mode, Billy had gotten colder and colder, so that he didn't think he would ever get warm again. Icy winds had raged through his body, freezing him all the way to his soul. Eventually the heightened activity had subsided and Billy had warmed somewhat, but he shivered at the memory of how impossibly cold he had been. It seemed unimaginable to him that he was able to survive anything like that.

Now he continued to look at himself in the mirror, as if that would provide him with the information he needed. It was terrible to realize that he was so contaminated.

The alien presence is entirely inside my body now, he thought. *It is peering out through my eyes.*

And he realized, too, that the creatures could fire their deadly silver blasts from Skyship itself, while linked to Billy's body. The great flying vessel, and Billy as well, seemed to provide them with safety and security. Maybe Billy gave them more than the ship, because they had moved into his body.

Curiously, the creatures described in Tobek's journals had decided to use Billy as some sort of a horrific conduit for their destructive energy. Maybe he somehow amplified them, or otherwise enabled them to gain more power for their deadly, macabre weaponry. He felt trapped, didn't know what to do. He felt violated, too. Years ago Branson Tobek, though not physically possessed by the space devils, had wanted to destroy them, but they had gotten him first. Billy didn't want that to happen to him. He would cooperate to the extent necessary, would do whatever they wanted him to do, for his own preservation.

In the mirror, the twin orbs were the brightest silver he'd ever seen, so bright that his eyes were like metallic suns in the heavens. He shouldn't be able to gaze upon such brightness in a mirror, such raw and primordial intensity, without going blind. But he had special eyes that were permitting him to do so anyway. He hated the alien presence, wanted desperately to be free of it.

A wayward, dangerous thought intruded, that he should make his own attempt to kill the creatures himself, no matter what had happened to the old inventor. Tobek had been his mentor, the greatest man Billy had ever known, or ever expected to know. Branson Tobek was one of a kind in the whole history of mankind; of that there could be no doubt.

Maybe it would be better if I died, too, he thought.

At least then he would be free of these creatures. He let the dangerous thoughts sink in, allowing them to permeate the chemistry and neural passageways of his brain. As he did so, he expected everything to go black at any moment—or explode in a freezing, last flash of silver.

Seconds passed. He felt his pulse hasten and cool, and he tried to prepare himself for the gruesome inevitability, his sudden and horrific death. But how could one prepare himself for something like that?

A minute passed, then two and three, without anything happening. Yet he did not breathe a sigh of relief. Instead, Billy leaned into the potential storm. He intensified his antagonistic thoughts, his hatred of the alien presence.

Alien presence. It made his skin crawl. He filled his brain with loathing toward the creatures, with thoughts of how much he wanted to destroy them—every last one of them.

Moments passed, then minutes ticked away—and he still counted himself among the living. But he knew the monsters remained inside, hadn't gone anywhere. He sensed their presence, felt a slight, ever-so faint tickling now when they moved around, and their ever-existent, inexplicable coldness.

Why were they allowing him to live? Did they need him alive for their destructive purposes, and know that they could prevent him from destroying them? Would they keep him going indefinitely, as a host organism for their frightful purposes? Why had they shifted from the safety of Skyship to him?

The possibility that he was hosting something that had killed To-bek was terrifying, but more than that, it enraged him. He wasn't going to let them use him as a conduit, wasn't going to tolerate that!

I'm not dead, he thought, and he realized that he was still in front of the mirror wall, and that he must have been staring into his own silver eyes for all the time he'd been thinking.

But they killed Tobek for such thoughts.

Then Billy considered two possible differences. First, Tobek had written of his hatred in his journals, of his desire to destroy the creatures. When he wrote of this, he had them trapped on Skyship, and was performing experiments on them, and devising a way to get rid of them. Second, Tobek had apparently not been possessed by the creatures, for whatever reason. Not before nor after his death.

The creatures could read Tobek's journals, but not thoughts?

It was all very confusing to Billy, but he was beginning to think that they could *not* read his thoughts, although they could recognize—and prevent—any overt attempt to destroy them. Somehow, they had discovered that Tobek was planning to get rid of them, and they had gotten him first. Maybe it was when Tobek was building the mysterious device that still remained unfinished on a laboratory table. The overt action of building something to kill them was what sent them into a killing frenzy against the brilliant old man.

Billy resolved to come up with his own way of annihilating them, to the very last one—doing it in such a manner that they would not know it was coming.

To his dismay a strange sensation came over him, and he grew very cold quickly, similar to the way he'd felt when the silver light sought out and killed Moore and Racker. The silver creatures were on the move again, extending themselves from his body all the way to AmEarth, stretching out, seeking and preparing to destroy. He grew colder and colder, couldn't stop shivering. And in his brain he saw the Imperial Palace of Prime Minister Yhatt, as well as the elegant Prime Minister himself, standing at a window—as if watching for what was about to assassinate him. He was dignified and heavy, with a prominent nose and an intense manner about him.

The silver thread of light streaked close to the palace, but went around to the rear and entered a different portion of the massive building, a slender beam of illumination that passed through the corridors, then under the door and into the parlor where the Prime Minister was standing at the window. Behind him, the light began to pool in the center of the ornate room, as if it were an army gathering its forces, preparing to attack. Billy felt the coldness of the thread still connected to them; it was as if the creatures in his body were shooting from him to the palace, and concentrating there.

Billy struggled to withdraw the terrible force, but it was too strong, and kept doing what it wanted to do. It was going to kill the Prime Minister of the AmEarth Empire!

In the images that filled his mind he saw five people in the parlor, and heard the Prime Minister's wife Lorissa scream in terror, a shrieking, terrified sound. Servants in white tuxedoes entered and stood by the doorway. Then two men in dark uniforms hurried in past them, security officers with their ion-pistols drawn.

The pooling light began to extend across the floor toward Renaldo Yhatt now, while the others watched in terror and shouted warnings to him. The Prime Minister turned to face the threat but remained stoically where he was, as if he had accepted his horrible fate and was not going to make any foolish attempt to escape it.

While the light advanced slowly and inexorably toward him, spread wide on the floor to prevent his escape, Renaldo Yhatt spoke in his resonant, leader-of-the-empire voice, with a calmness that astonished Billy. "Leave this room," he said to his companions. "All of you. *Now.*"

His wife and the security officers refused to move, but the servants left. Then Maureen Stuart and the long-haired man—Billy wasn't sure who he was—went to the door, with the man pulling her away. Another man with a blond moustache accompanied them. A servant opened the door for them, and they stood there looking back in horror as the bright stream of silvery creatures advanced toward its prey.

On Skyship, Billy Jeeling focused with all of his might, attempting to withdraw the murderous light, trying desperately to save the life of the Prime Minister, and perhaps the others in the room as well. He remembered that Maureen Stuart had been with Racker earlier, and had not been killed. The combined creatures had allowed her to run and warn the Prime Minister, and they did not seem interested in her now. They had not killed Sonya Orr, either, and Billy still didn't know why they had visited her.

Now as Billy struggled for control, he felt a subtle shifting, like a change in pressure at altitude, and the silver light on the floor of the remote dining room began to retract, becoming a point of light at the end of a long beam that had snaked its way into the room. To his relief, Billy saw that everyone in the room was still alive.

Abruptly, the light went into a blur of reverse motion, and in a few moments it was back on Skyship, slipping back into Billy's body.

He felt a sensation of extreme coolness from the activity. He also realized that he was breathing hard, and as odd as it seemed he was even perspiring. And somehow he seemed to have had an effect on the creatures, convincing them not to kill the Prime Minister. Could there be any other explanation? Possibly. But he realized one thing for certain. The creatures were going after people who opposed Billy Jeeling—the force that attacked Skyship, General Moore, Jonathan Racker, and—very nearly—Prime Minister Yhatt.

Why were they doing that?

And they didn't destroy all of Billy's foes, it seemed; only the ones who presented the most danger. Maureen Stuart had been part of the conspiracy against him; of that he was certain. But she had not been killed. And neither had Yhatt, despite reports reaching Billy said that he was also involved in the conspiracy against him. The two of them must have been secondary in the plans against him, not the prime movers.

A week ago, Maureen had not known about Moore's feigned peace delegation and the attempt to kidnap Billy, and she hadn't known about the later military strike force, either. The crazed General had orchestrated both assaults on his own, and somehow the creatures felt that Moore and Racker were more culpable in trying to destroy Billy than Prime Minister Yhatt or Maureen Stuart had been. Perhaps that had made it easier for Billy to convince the organisms not to kill the Prime Minister.

And it might explain the brief interest the space devils had in Sonya Orr, without killing her. It suggested that she was not entirely loyal to him, but was not a serious danger. In any event, Sonya was no longer on board Skyship.

The images in Billy's mind were gone now, as if they had slipped away and vanished into deep space.

He was still in front of the mirror, gazing into it with silver eyes as if it were a window into everything, into the events on AmEarth and into the vastness of space. Finally, he looked away from his reflection. The horrible creatures were inside his body; he felt their cold stirring, speeding this way and that in their nano-realm, sending chills of fear down his spine. And when they settled down, ceasing most of their motion, his body grew warmer.

But he didn't feel at all settled. The creatures had motives, and they had made him an unwilling participant in their strange scheme, whatever it was.

CHAPTER 34

There are billions and billions of secrets in the universe, and a sizeable share of them involve humankind. What, for example, do dreams really mean? Much effort has been devoted to answering this question, but the so-called experts have only managed to come up with a dunghill of unprovable conjecture.

—Branson Tobek, entry in one of his laboratory journals

On the high walkway Billy sat in his chair, with his Starbot machines standing sentinel nearby, on high alert. He saw the blinking, shifting lights on their six torsos as they scanned in all directions, looking for dangers. He had programmed them well, and usually their presence gave him comfort, but not now. He felt threatened by a menace that had already invaded his body, having gotten past the sophisticated security systems that were supposed to protect Skyship, and him.

Now he looked at Starbot, the leader of his personal security force. The machine's lights shifted as he awaited Billy's commands. But there were none at this moment. Instead, Billy transmitted an electronic signal from his chair to dim the lights on the walkway. Then he gazed through the overhead windows into the dark firmament. It was the middle of the night, and galactic star systems appeared to be twinkling on when he looked at them—and in the far, far distance he saw more stars flickering on, as if a great master switch had been thrown.

In his entire lifetime he'd only been close to a few people—real people, not robots in the likeness of human beings. There'd been

Branson Tobek and Billy's beautiful wife Reanne, as well as Dr. Rachel Ginsberg, and a handful of others. In recent years, increasingly on Skyship, he'd mostly confided in robots, the ones he had programmed to be the most trustworthy, and the most wise. Of those, Lainey and Devv had been at the top of the list. He relied on them, and truly cared about them, as if they were real people.

But lately, after the revelations he'd made about their true makeup, he'd found it necessary to pull away from these two. While they'd taken the news as well as could be expected, Billy could still see the stresses on them he'd caused, and he felt bad for this. Yet, there had been no choice. Morally, he could not have kept such a secret from them forever, nor from the other Lazarus series 'bots.

He hoped Lainey and Devv would understand one day and truly forgive him. He was counting on that, because they would be the primary leaders of Skyship in the future... after he was gone. Billy felt as if he were on the exit ramp right now, parting from the great vessel, leaving behind everything that had meant so much to him.

But of all the challenges in his life, this one was huge: he needed to figure out what the damnable space devils were up to, why they had inhabited his body.

He motioned for Starbot to come to him, and the robot dutifully approached. "Master?" he said.

"Run program," Billy said. "Tell me what you have observed about the behavior of the space devils."

The program ran for several seconds. Then: "Think of robotics, Master, which is a special skill and knowledge of yours. The creatures are either on kill mode, or off kill mode. They are extremely dangerous to you, and to AmEarth."

Billy wished he could consult with Devv about this, the Security Commander, but he sensed strongly that this problem went beyond anything Devv knew, or anyone else on board Skyship knew, for that matter. It was something alien to anyone's experience, something he needed to figure out in his own way. Besides, Billy was uncomfortable being around Devv now, and Lainey. Things had changed in his relationship with both of them, and not for the better.

"Do you think they're using me to boost their energy somehow?" Billy asked the robot. "Their destructive power?"

"That is possible, Master. But I also think they are protecting you. And they seem to want—or need—to remain inside Skyship, though I cannot determine why."

"It is peculiar," Billy said, "when they once seemed to want to escape." He went on to tell Starbot what Tobek had written in his journals, that the late inventor's experiments on the space devils had adversely affected them, to such an extent that they could never be allowed to go free, or the consequences would be catastrophic.

"It would appear that they could escape from Skyship now if they wanted to," Starbot said. "They got out of the sealed laboratory through the bio-lock, and since then they have used their combined power to defeat attacking ships, even sending death beams to AmEarth to kill some of the bad guys."

Billy considered this for several moments. As a robotics expert, he knew how to organize information and put it to use. He would attempt to use his special skill, as Starbot called it, to deal with the problem. He would assemble the available data, take it apart, and put it back together. This pointed to a big problem: the *available* data.

These creatures seemed to be a force of cosmic nature, carrying secrets with them that had existed since time immemorial. As a collective, living entity, they might be as old as the most ancient of star systems.

Billy continued this line of reasoning, and explained it to Starbot.

He postulated that the creatures had discovered Tobek and the interesting, very unique machine, Skyship. Out of curiosity they had come calling, and had entered the vessel. The inventor saw that as an aggressive, unfriendly act, whether or not it was. Yet, because he interpreted it as hostile and tried to kill them, they got to him first, and killed him.

The destruction they had caused might be no fault of their own, because they were only seeking to adapt and survive, as they had done for so long. Even so, these creatures still represented a monstrous threat to the world, and a grave danger to the entire human race. Billy had more complex feelings about them than Tobek's had been. Billy felt a strong sense of gratitude toward them, but he was deathly afraid of what they might do.

"I go back to my earlier question," Billy said, "about why they're inhabiting me. I think I do boost their power somehow, and as you suggested, they want to protect me. The two things go hand in hand. As long as I am well, they are stronger. Obviously, they want to be stronger."

"But not to escape from Skyship."

"No. So, they're protecting me, and by extension, Skyship, too."

"Maybe they would protect anyplace you were, whether inside a building, a vehicle, or Skyship."

The two of them went silent, each considering the known facts in their own way. The blinking lights on Starbot shifted slightly.

"You've thought of something more?" Billy asked.

"They are complex creatures, with complex motives."

"They've been helping me against my enemies," Billy said, "and for that I am deeply grateful. They have protected Skyship and its important mission, and have safeguarded me. Perhaps they just need a bit of guidance from me, and I could help them perform good deeds. Somehow, I managed to pull them back when they were going after President Yhatt, and they didn't kill them. That has to be a step in the right direction."

"Yes," the robot said. "Common ground. Find it and build on it."

As Billy considered this, he saw tiny glints of silver in the air, appearing out of nowhere, flickering this way and that like miniature gleaming fish, coming and going, as if they were swimming in the air and then vanishing into an unseen portal, through some trick of light and reality. Excited and intrigued, he reached out to them, but they skittered away. They seemed jittery, afraid, but kept glinting, and drawing close, warily, before darting away.

"Can you see them?" Billy asked.

"I see them, Master. It's hard to say where they came from, but at the moment it seems that all of the space devils are *not* inside your body. This suggests that the ones we are watching either came from inside your body, or outside of it—only two options. I think they are from outside, and for whatever reason, the ones we're looking at never were inside your body."

Billy reached out again, and this time the creatures did not flee. Instead, they gathered around his hand, turning his fingers silver and making them tingle a little, but not making him feel cold as before. This suggested to him that they were not entering his body yet. As if to confirm this, he saw sections of light withdraw from touching him, replaced moments later by other creatures who barely contacted him and then departed. Finally, the apparent curiosity settled down, and Billy saw a bright glimmering in the air, just beyond his reach.

"Perhaps the most bold and adventurous of their members went into my body earlier," Billy said, "and ever since, the rest have been observing, trying to see if some disaster befalls the brave ones."

"That is likely."

Billy Jeeling smiled. The creatures, even if they lived up to the name Tobek had given them, gave him a strange feeling of serenity. Space devils. Yes, he supposed they were that, and they had proven themselves dangerous, but he couldn't help feeling affection toward them.

At this moment in time, they made him feel comfortable. He fell asleep in his chair, with the silver creatures swirling in his thoughts — a mass of them, with no individual characteristics visible. Tobek had said he'd seen them in individual detail through a magnascope, and said they were fierce looking and very ugly, but that didn't matter to Billy Jeeling at the moment. They were his defenders.

~~~

Billy dreamed about a huge beam of silver light sweeping over the entire planet, killing his enemies like flies, dropping them wherever they were, whatever they were doing, marking them for death while saving others, the ones who had never turned against him, and the ones who still loved Billy Jeeling. In that huge swath, both Yhatt and Stuart were killed, and Sonya Orr as well — telling Billy that their earlier reprieves had only been temporary.

An allied reason occurred to him, and he shuddered as he slept. In saving the three of them, maybe the space devils wanted him to believe they could discern among his enemies, and they would only kill the worst of them. Maybe they were trying to get him to let down his guard, so that they could get their way without his interference. And the truth had come to him in a prescient dream.

The creatures were a huge time bomb, waiting to go off. And they were holding him prisoner.

~~~

Hearing Billy scream in his sleep, and seeing him twist and writhe in his chair, Starbot tried to awaken him, calling out his name and shaking him vigorously. The Master seemed to be having a nightmare, and was unable to extricate himself from it.

Starbot picked up the entire chair with Billy in it. For a moment, the robot cradled this man who had created him, this man who was, in a sense, Starbot's father.

"Master Billy, you're going to be all right," Starbot said, in a loud voice. "Master, come out of it! Come back! Come back!" He shook the chair.

But Billy continued to struggle in his sleep, still screaming and saying things in gibberish that the robot could not decipher.

Starbot made a decision to take him somewhere else, to a safe place. He carried Billy and the heavy maglev chair deeper into the vast ship, while simultaneously sending signals for his robotic brethren to get Dr. Ginsberg and take her there immediately....

CHAPTER 35

"I want to forgive him for what he's done to me, but I don't know if I can."

—Lainey Forster, comment to Devv Jeeling

Lainey had been shocked to be told she was a robot. Devv's analysis of her blood had been influential in convincing her, comparing it under a microscope with human blood; the samples were not even close to being alike. She'd also seen her name, and Devv's, on the pages of Branson Tobek's journals, and after some effort she'd been able to read the handwriting, which said she was not human, except for the small amount of human cellular material that had been used to imprint her.

Despite the apparent evidence, Lainey had tried to convince herself that it might still be a mistake, that she really was human after all, and should have additional medical tests conducted—but not under the supervision of Dr. Rachel Ginsberg, whom she did not trust. Maybe the information from Devv was all wrong, and she could still conceive a child by Billy. This might have been wishful thinking on her part, and an utter waste of time, but she'd thought of one more test she wanted to do.

Just to be absolutely certain—or as certain as she could possibly be under the circumstances—yesterday she'd obtained a sample of blood from the body of a maintenance man who had died of natural causes on Skyship, and who had to be human, because he was laid out on a slab in the morgue. Lainey then took the sample to Devv and his microscope, and he'd performed another test for her—one that convinced her beyond any doubt.

It's true, she'd thought as she left Devv's office, crying. *I am not human.* She felt as if her world had come to an end.

To find out why Billy had deceived her for years, Lainey had gone in search of him yesterday afternoon, intending to confront him with what Devv had revealed to her. With her sadness turning to anger, and anxious to confront Billy, she'd been in the lobby of his office building, waiting for a highlift. Suddenly sirens went off and police robots rushed in, ordering her and others out of the building. Skyship was under attack.

Having been given training about what to do in an emergency, Lainey had notified her employees and students via a mindcom, sent from the implant in her brain to theirs. The ones who were reservists would know what to do; they all had assignments. Then she'd rushed to the armory for a weapon, but had been slowed by a throng of humans and robots trying to do the same thing—and even blocking a side entrance that had been reserved for Skyship managers and supervisors. Finally reaching the large main room of the armory, she'd heard gunfire and explosions coming from an upper level, which agitated her, and everyone around her. She'd kept pressing forward with the crowd, trying to get closer to a bank of weapon-dispenser machines on the far wall.

But just as she'd reached one of the large machines, it flashed that it was out of supply. Within moments, she heard others saying the rest of the machines were out as well. A burly man in construction clothes had grumbled and quipped that he was going to have to find something in his tool box to use as a weapon.

Afterward, Lainey had found herself on the crowded sidewalks of Skyship, numb and uncertain of what to do, feeling helpless while security police and reservists rushed past. The explosions and weapon fire had been getting louder. Most of the people were adults, but some children were in their midst, and not all of them seemed to be with a parent or teacher. She helped a confused little girl—she couldn't have been more than six years old—find her mother, who had lost track of her when they were inside a pharmacy. Lainey had always liked children.

During the attack, a thought had given Lainey small consolation: If she was only a robot, she couldn't actually be killed or injured. Even so, she'd realized that her simulated responses would make it painful if she were shot or caught in a blast.

Suddenly, like a wave passing through the throngs on the sidewalks, cheering had begun and then built up to a tremendous, joyous roar. The attacking force had been defeated, its survivors fleeing back to AmEarth....

~~~

Now Lainey sat in the front row of a packed grandstand, watching a gala ceremony in the large central park of Skyship. Devv Jeeling — the robotic son — stood on a raised stage in his blue Security Commander's uniform, speaking to the assemblage through an unseen microphone. He certainly looked human, but so did she. Lainey felt numb and bitter, didn't know what would come next in her own mechanized life, a life she had previously thought was her own, but which had really been programmed into her.

It felt as if her life and soul had been stolen from her. Everything she'd thought was her own — her precious memories, her personal desires, her most secret and treasured thoughts — had been false. She'd thought they were private, her own experiences of a lifetime, but that had not been the case at all, and now she was left with nothing but a collection of artificial parts — and a tiny quantity of cellular material that had been used for imprinting the human personality and physical characteristics onto the machine.

A man and woman next to her were talking about strange silver blasts of light that defeated the attacking fleet — a weapon they said Skyship must have had in reserve, and used at exactly the right time. They said it had been a surprise to everyone they knew, because none of them had never heard of a weapon like that. Neither had Lainey. And, though she could not stop being upset about what Billy Jeeling had done to her, she was glad that Skyship had survived the onslaught. It served a critically important environmental purpose.

Peculiar, almost suicidal thoughts had been winding their way through the synthetic pathways of Lainey's brain. Though knowing full well that she had been programmed by Billy when he built her, she seemed to have a modicum of free will. On the way here, she had tested it by lunging in front of a police vehicle and causing it to skid to a stop, and by criticizing the human policeman's driving when he stepped out—or at least he had *looked* human.

"Shoot me!" she'd shouted at him. "Go ahead! I can't be killed!"

The cop had stared at her in surprise, but had done nothing, apparently because he recognized her as one of the managers. As he stared at her in bewilderment, she assumed he was sending a police mindcom to one of his comrades. Impatient to keep moving, she had not waited to see what would result. An interrogation might have been in store for her....

At this moment, she felt certain that if she wanted to, she could climb onto the stage and disrupt the proceeding that Devv was conducting. She was upset enough, felt betrayed enough by Billy, to do exactly that. Devv seemed so calm and businesslike on the stage, irritating her. Didn't he care what Billy had done to both of them, all the hurtful lies? Lainey stared hard at Devv, and for a moment she caught his hard return gaze, before he looked away and continued speaking to the audience.

She'd searched for Billy again today, going to the usual places: his office, the high walkway, his apartment, a favorite coffee shop, and a restaurant. But he was nowhere to be found. She'd left a message for Devv, but he had not returned it. Now he was speaking in his official status, but in reality he was just another smart robot going through his duties on board Skyship.

Devv adjusted the officer's cap on his head, then gestured toward four men and two women who stood on one side of the stage. They marched forward, and stood in a row at the front of the raised platform. She focused on one of them, Yürgen Zayeddi, who stood third from the left, facing the audience. Young Zayeddi had been on a swift upward course since arriving on Skyship. Lainey was his boss, but he seemed to be on his own fast track. In large part this was because he revered Billy Jeeling and wanted to do everything possible to serve him, and protect him. She used to feel that way herself, before their relationship became so complicated, and went sour.

Devv said to the audience, "We are here to honor the gallant heroes of our successful defense. Some have suggested that I should be among the honorees, but I have declined to receive any award, feeling strongly that it is more appropriate to celebrate those who were not in command."

Lainey's thoughts drifted. She couldn't help wondering where Billy was. Though angry with him, she tried to think of fond memories. And, when she thought about it honestly, she had to admit there were many. And—though she would rather not feel this way under the circumstances—she had to admit that she still cared deeply for him. She knew Devv had feelings of affection for Billy as well, from their relationship.

Devv went to the waiting candidates and stood in front of one of them, a tall woman in a sky-blue police uniform. His voice carried over the crowd as he said, "Mona Carr was a member of our defense force when attackers attempted to board Skyship at the main docks, using three commando squads. During the surprise assault, Mona's commander fell, mortally wounded, and she led the defensive effort in his place, directing her force to hit the waves of attackers with accurate projectile fire, forcing them to retreat."

Devv Jeeling pinned a medal and colorful ribbon on her lapel, shook her hand, and then moved on to the man beside her. Devv described him as a technician who repaired a critical electrical system just before the sneak attack, putting some of Skyship's defensive weapons back online—and they would have fired on enemy warships, if not for the intervention of the mysterious silver blasts that sent the enemy fleeing.

Yürgen Zayeddi was next, the man who had gotten between Devv Jeeling and Sonya Orr. Devv looked a little uneasy as he faced the audience and spoke about him, obviously trying not to reveal any personal animus he might still hold. It was an awkward moment.

"This young man joined us as a public relations trainee," Devv said, "and his talents and hard work earned him a quick promotion to team leader. While taking advanced classes for his new position, he located and killed a saboteur, one of his own classmates who had penetrated our security. And despite his youth, Mr. Zayeddi is an accomplished humbaby pilot, having learned to fly in his previous position on AmEarth, working in a factory. This skill placed him on our list of reservists, assigned to defend Skyship in the event of emergency. That time of need occurred yesterday, when we were attacked without warning by forces of the AmEarth Empire. Mr. Zayeddi, ignoring great danger to himself, flew his small humbaby at the front of a squadron of our defenders, going after a powerful enemy and shooting three ships out of the sky himself."

Unable to stop feeling a deep sense of depression that kept returning to her, permeating her awareness, Lainey watched. After the ceremony, she wandered out on the sidewalks, feeling strangely detached from her previous life, and hopeless about the future. The events in her memory were broken into two parts now—the person she'd thought she was, before learning the truth, and what little remained of that now. Her life, like her relationship with Billy Jeeling, had been broken in half.

A robot is not entitled to feel love.

In the tree-lined central part, she sat for a time on one of the benches, trying to recover—if that was possible. The park was crowded with adults and children, and she overheard more people talking about the unusual silver beams of light that had apparently been fired from Skyship, defeating the enemy. Even more strange, a man spoke of rumors that Billy had been seen with an eerie silver cast to his eyes.

If this was true, it suggested to Lainey that Billy Jeeling himself might not be human. She didn't know how to feel about that startling possibility, didn't know how to keep up with the constant flow of new and perplexing information.

She wondered where he was, and worried about him.

CHAPTER 36

Often the most vivid of dreams cannot be separated from conscious thoughts. This is especially true when thinking back over time, trying to remember if something actually happened.

—Observation of Dr. Rachel Ginsberg

When Billy awoke, he had trouble figuring out where he was. He was lying down somewhere on a soft surface, looking up at a featureless white ceiling, just staring at it, blinking his eyes to get accustomed to the light.

Then a face drew near, a woman leaning over him, smiling gently. She had silver hair and brown eyes, and looked vaguely familiar, though he could not put a name with the face. "You've had a rough time of it," she said. "Your dream had you trapped, and I had to use everything I knew, and a regimen of drugs, to break you free. You almost seemed to be in a coma, but an odd one, a babbling coma, if such a thing exists. You were talking a mile a minute, but we couldn't understand what you were saying, and you wouldn't wake up. There were some identifiable words, but they didn't seem to form sentences or coherent thoughts. I was quite worried about you."

He looked at her dumbly, then remembered. *Dr. Rachel Ginsberg.* He looked around, realized he was in a room adjacent to his hidden laboratory in the core of the ship, where he had placed a bed years ago, so that he could rest when he was working late on matters involving the robotics of Skyship. The loyal Starbot stood nearby, facing in his direction, his lights blinking in a regular pattern.

"After not being used much, the bedspread and sheets were dusty, so we had to change them," she said. She felt his temple, took his pulse. "You look much better. Starbot and I were quite concerned about you. He brought you here, summoned me."

Billy nodded appreciatively toward the robot, saw the lights blink excitedly on his torso, as if he were a loyal dog wagging his tail at the extra attention.

And to the attentive doctor, Billy said, "Thank you."

"What were you dreaming about?" she asked. "Or should I ask, what was the nightmare about?"

"Nothing," he said. "Just fuzzy details remain. Nothing important." He was lying to her. The dream remained vivid in his memory, a swath of silver death moving ominously across the surface of AmEarth, singling out his enemies and obliterating them.

Behind her, he saw a faint glimmer of silver in the air. He found this alarming and favorable at the same time. It was a sign that the space devils—the ones who had not yet entered his body—were still observing him. He needed to lure them in to join the others, and then take action to destroy all of them at once. But how?

Billy sat up, ordered Starbot to bring his maglev chair to him.

"Not so fast," Rachel said, putting up a halting hand to the robot. "Give yourself time to recover, Billy. You need rest. Starbot can bring you whatever you want to eat, and I'll be nearby to make certain you don't return to that nightmare."

"I don't intend to return to it," he said. "Starbot, get the chair."

Now the robot moved to comply, and helped Billy into it. As Starbot did this, the robot said, "The creatures are in the air of this room. I can see them now."

"I see them, too," Billy said. He didn't bother to explain to Rachel, and she didn't ask, so perhaps Starbot had already said something to her about them. It didn't matter. She was one of his most trusted confidantes.

"I'm going to be fine," he assured her. "Go away now, Rachel. I will summon you if I need you, or Starbot will."

"Are you sure you want me to leave?" she said. "I could wait in another room, staying close just in case."

"It was only a dream," he said. "I would have come out of it eventually, though I do appreciate your efforts." He smiled, put the chair in motion, heading for the adjacent laboratory, where he had a work bench. "Go," he said again, glancing back at her from the chair as he went through the doorway. "I'll be fine. I just want to tinker a little in my lab. It relaxes me, allows me to think."

"As you wish." She sounded hurt and disappointed, but swung her medical satchel over her shoulder, and left.

~~~

At his custom work bench, U-shaped and low so that he could access it from his chair, Billy made adjustments to a machine prototype, a unit that would do human imprinting on his Lazarus series robots with only half the cellular material required in the original unit. Starbot stood on his left.

"Would you like me to run more tests on this, using my programs?" Starbot asked. "Or is it satisfactory to you now?"

Billy had not had time to finish constructing the upgraded device yet, but the theoretical programs Starbot had run for him in the design stage indicated it should work. Now he just needed to get the prototype built and load cellular material into it. He had the inside open, and used a pinpoint-laser to connect two sensitive, critical cell readers.

He paused, knowing he would never have time to complete this project, or another one. It gave him great sadness. He had experienced so much joy in this laboratory, developing various types of robots.

He would never complete another project, either, solving the glitch in Lainey's unit, causing her to hear machine noises internally. She was the only one of the Lazarus series to experience this. He had intended to construct a relay unit identical to the one inside Lainey's body, and hook it up to a simulation program that would replicate her internal senses from her perspective, trying to duplicate what she had described hearing.

He'd wanted to figure out what was wrong with the Lainey unit, short of dismantling her, and possibly losing important elements of her imprinting—the things about Lainey that were so very similar, and nearly identical to his great lost love, Reanne.

Tears ran down his cheek as he thought of her.

"Are you all right, Master?" Starbot asked. He looked closely at Billy, said, "Your tears are silver."

The comment did not surprise Billy, as he'd noticed silver moisture in his eyes himself. He wiped the tears away, said, "I was thinking of Reanne." He waved a hand dismissively. "I'm fine now, fine."

In the middle of the room he saw a familiar silver-metallic mist flickering in the air, indicating the presence of the space devils. They were keeping their distance this time, not touching him, perhaps wondering in their collective way what he was doing. Tobek had been killed at his laboratory bench while trying to build a device to kill the creatures, so Billy was careful now to tell Starbot what the robot already knew, how the device in front of him would read cells and imprint the data on raw, artificial cellular material so that it could be grown into a Lazarus robot, looking like a human, and acting like one.

He looked at the airborne mass of creatures, said to Starbot, "Do you see them there?"

"Yes, Master. They are curious, aren't they?"

"They certainly are. You know, the more I see them and understand how they helped me, the more I like them. They really have been critically important to me, preventing my enemies from killing me and taking over Skyship." He smiled as he looked in their direction. "They're my saviors."

"Your saviors, Master? Don't you want them to leave your body?"

"Certainly not! I like them exactly where they are, and if their brethren outside my body want to join them, that's fine with me." Billy didn't say so, but he sensed strongly that all of the space devils wanted to be together, and did not like being apart from one another, as they were now.

They drew a little closer to him, and even more of them appeared out of thin air directly overhead. Looking around, he saw them behind him, too.

"Master, I must point out, with all due respect to your greatness, that you are not making sense. They invaded your body, and before that they murdered Branson Tobek. I don't see how you can—"

"Leave me, Starbot, and don't say anything more against them. They are my friends! I don't have time to explain what should be perfectly obvious to you. They make me happy, do you hear me, happy! I don't want to imagine where I would be, or what would have happened to Skyship, if they had not helped. As far as I'm concerned, they are brave and noble creatures."

All the while, Billy concealed his true motivations from them, and from the loyal Starbot. He had a plan, and it just might work, if he played it right, if he took extreme care. He needed to attract all of the little alien monsters into his body, and then deal with them once and for all. He'd tried to think of ways to destroy them—but so far he'd only come up with one that had any hope of success, and it would cost him his own life.

He thought of Devv and Lainey, and all the systems on Skyship that would need to continue after his death—and the steps he had taken to make certain these two humanlike 'bots—and everyone else—completed what they needed to do, to keep the huge vessel going. The great ship had many important automatic functions that Tobek had set up, and which Billy never understood. Billy had only added to the original package that Tobek developed, improving on robotic details, creating what Billy considered to be enhancements. That was Billy's real legacy, and he prided himself on his work.

The robot flashed a pattern of lights that indicated confusion.

"Leave me!" Billy said. He pointed toward the door. As Starbot left, Billy reached into the air, and immersed his hand in a cloud of silver creatures. He felt a pleasant tingling sensation, and thought some of them were entering his body, to join the others inside. But others would not come close, and streaked overhead, this way and that, being more cautious.

Billy smiled, reached out to them....

CHAPTER 37

"It is most interesting to go to a place seen by few others, but it can be very lonely if you cannot ever share it."

—Billy Jeeling, recorded without his knowledge

Only one living person knew that Skyship had a network of hidden tunnels and chambers under its outer skin. Even the most advanced military scanners could not detect these cavities. One of the chambers in particular had been favored by Branson Tobek, because it stood at the pinnacle of the geoengineering marvel, a high point that was commonly believed to be no more than a visual feature, for the sake of the external appearance of the great vessel. But it was something more, and had once been Tobek's secret vantage point from which to view the heavens, sometimes accompanied by his loyal assistant, Billy Jeeling.

Billy still went up there on occasion, but it was a challenge because of his disability. Yet it was an obstacle he had overcome years ago, back when his mentor had still been alive. Now Billy was rising inside one of the uppermost tunnels, lying face down, his head forward on a wafer-thin, motorized platform. The platform, of his own design, had a thousand tiny servo-motors on the underside, operating in perfect synchronization to get him where he wanted to go. They made a smooth spinning sound while performing their work efficiently. The platform had a headlight attached to the front, but Billy didn't need it. His bright eyes shone ahead, filling the tunnel with silver illumination. And, as he had hoped, he saw silver illumination behind him as well, meaning the rest of the space devils were following him.

Billy had only been to this hidden place a dozen or so times in the years he'd been on board Skyship. He didn't particularly like being inside the hollow skin, because it was cramped in there, and the air, though breathable and warm enough, smelled stale. But at the moment, considering all that had occurred, it suited him perfectly. He could get away from other people and sentient robots in these secret confines, and even from his closest confidantes. Other than Billy and the original robotic construction team, no one had ever known about this place except for Tobek, and now he was dead. Billy had not even told Starbot about it.

At the moment he wanted a quiet, totally secluded place where he could complete what he needed to do with the creatures of light, the space devils, as Tobek had so aptly called them. He certainly could not go around in public, looking the way he did—the alien cast to his eyes would terrify everyone. It terrified him, too, as did the prospect of even more of them entering his body. Yet he tried to remain calm so that he could come up with the best way to deal with the creatures effectively, before they could cause any more destruction. Billy knew that many of the tiny intruders were still inside him, not only because of his shining metallic eyes, but because of certain peculiar, continuing sensations in his body, an ever-so-slight, cool tickling sensation whenever they moved around. At the moment the collective entity was relatively calm, and he was comfortable—not shivering cold as he had been earlier when they were in their hyperactive, murderous attack mode.

Yet he felt great unease, even though they were protective of him. They had destroyed half of the Imperial fleet that had been sent to attack him, and had sent a silver beam of light down to the planet to find and kill two of the conspirators against him, General Moore and Jonathan Racker. Then the collective alien entity went after others, apparently for their association with the other two—but withdrew before harming them.

Billy recalled struggling mightily to pull the death ray back from Prime Minister Yhatt, to prevent it from doing what it had seemed intent on doing. Had he exerted some influence to save the Prime Minister, or had the space devils pulled back of their own volition?

Before going after Yhatt they had also visited another conspirator, Maureen Stuart, and frightened her, and had gone to Sonya Orr as well, a woman Billy now suspected of being in the cabal—but had not attacked either of them. Billy had not had any influence in saving their lives—or he didn't recall having any. And yet, the creatures were inside his body, and linked perhaps to his own motivations and desires. Maybe they'd known he didn't want lower-level people like Stuart or Orr killed, but had not known this about Yhatt, until Billy exerted himself, trying to save the leader of the AmEarth Empire.

He had questions without solid answers, but it did seem to him that the creatures, in their shared personality, knew that Stuart, Orr and Yhatt had not been prime movers in any attempt to kill Billy or damage Skyship.

Then there was the dream, the horrific nightmare, of a swath of silver death passing over the surface of AmEarth, slaying his enemies and saving his supporters. That suggested discernment on the part of the space devils, that they were able to identify degrees of danger to him, and only deal with the worst. The nightmare had been a warning, telling him they had something dreadful in mind, something very large in scale.

Even though three people had been spared in real life, the nightmare had shown them dying. Billy sensed that the creatures were going to do something horrendous, on a massive scale, if he didn't destroy them. Their earlier demonstrations were nothing, in comparison with what they would do in the future. They had already shown a pattern of going after his enemies, and because of the campaign of lies against him, there were hundreds of millions of people who hated him and wanted to see him fail, or die.

The creatures could annihilate all of those people in a matter of minutes, to prevent them from harming Billy Jeeling. He knew that could happen, without any doubt, and the zealous action the space devils took on his behalf frightened him far more than anything his enemies might do. Maybe that's why they actually pulled back from the three they didn't kill, because they had something much bigger in mind, and didn't want Billy to interfere with them. This line of reasoning suggested that he had some power over them, that they needed him. But it was all conjecture, based on a series of events that pointed, circumstantially, in a certain direction.

One frightening thought, among many: they could be evolving mentally, adapting to situations, coming up with new ideas. And wherever they were going, they were taking him with them.

The platform surged higher in the hollow hull, and finally stopped inside a chamber that his eyes lit up in silver illumination when he arrived, and even more when the trailing devils entered, and flitted around in a metallic mist. The pinnacle enclosure was larger than others inside the skin, and formed a circular room at the uppermost point of Skyship, above the surrounding rooftop domes. Billy touched a control on his belt and the platform re-shaped itself, into a hard chair.

An array of instruments lay in front of him, twinkling with colors and ready to be activated, much the same as the controls he had in his office, though these were not camouflaged. He pressed a button and a small compartment opened, with a cup of water inside. He removed the cup and sipped; the water still tasted fresh, from having been sealed and preserved perfectly for all of the years since Tobek set this chamber up secretly. Billy drank half, then placed the cup into a holder on the chair. Food packets were available to him as well, but he wasn't hungry. The chamber also had a toilet that he could crawl over to, and use. He wasn't sure how it emptied, a detail he'd never asked about.

Now Billy touched a pressure pad, causing a wide VR-panel to appear on his right—displaying multiple surveillance screens, each showing a different section of the great vessel, which was now on the upper edge of the ionosphere, at the fringe of orbital space. He customized the settings, so that one of the images showed the place in the corridor where he'd left his maglev chair, and other places where searchers might try to get into the hollow hull, looking for him.

He touched another control and a high-tech window opened over his head, providing him with an enhanced vista of glimmering stars and constellations, and even spectacular color-streaked nebulas. Moment by moment the view broadened, so that the entire peaked roof of the pinnacle had viewing windows. Outside he could see the domes of Skyship arranged in the shape of the immense Christian cross—all dark now. He narrowed the extent of the view, so that the side windows were covered, and only a small section was open directly over his head—to prevent anyone on the ship from seeing it.

He knew from having been here before that the overhead window was a magnaviewer, with similar capabilities to the magnascope in his office, except with more distant focal points. He found the controls for the device and made adjustments, bringing distant constellations and nebulas into clearer view.

But after several moments of looking straight up and trying to identify star systems, he realized he was seeing much farther into space than should be possible, even with this magnaviewer, which he knew how to use. It seemed to him that he was actually peering into another galaxy, and perhaps even farther than that, all the way to the other side of the universe.

This was difficult to imagine possible, but with everything that had happened to him so far, he thought it might be possible. Somehow his new shining eyes were far more powerful than the scope in his office or the viewing capabilities of the skylight. He'd never seen this far into space before.

The fantastic new vista was hypnotic to Billy. So many millions and billions of years that were represented by what he was seeing. And from his scientific studies he knew he was actually peering into the far-distant past, the ancient history of the cosmos, and not into the present. He thought of a conundrum and marveled at it, the possibility that the universe had already been destroyed, and parts of it just didn't know it yet.

In this very quiet and serene place, Billy Jeeling finally felt a sense of supreme calm. He raised his hands in the air, and felt the fingers tingle as creatures surrounded them and merged into his skin, a strong current of them now. Billy felt them flowing inward, flowing, flowing, flowing, until it was complete. And when he looked at his hands, arms and the rest of his body, he was entirely silver, and he felt a little cold, but pleasantly so.

Now, at last, he was ready for the next step, the ultimate act he needed to take. He had an idea, a way to render the space devils harmless forever.

He thought of eternity, and of his brief but significant place in it....

CHAPTER 38

"Death has always been a question—one of the great questions of philosophers and thinkers over the ages. But it can also be an answer, depending upon how you look at it."

—Billy Jeeling, disturbing comment made to his son on the high walkway

Lainey thought these were very strange aircraft, though not nearly as strange as the function and scale of Skyship itself. She rode in a small module beside Devv, who rode in another. Connected by an electronic interlock system, it was a morph-baby. He had the controls now, although her module was the same as his, and she could take command if she wanted to. But she preferred to let him run the linked assembly. He had more experience operating police aircraft, and she didn't want to make an operational mistake.

While the most common humbabies looked like fat bumblebees with rotors on top, these units were cubes, flat on all sides so that they could connect to other units in different configurations—side by side, front to back, or one on top of the other—and they had no rotors. Each module, propelled and controlled by tiny jets, had the blue-sky emblem of Skyship on its surfaces. The morph-babies were high-priced, but Billy Jeeling had never spared any expense when it came to Skyship.

Lainey and Devv had been looking for Billy for two days now, without any success. This morning they had flown past the high walkway that Billy favored, and had run scanners to see if he was concealed somewhere up there. Nothing had turned up. There had been no clues.

They'd been discussing the possibilities, whether Billy might have gone somewhere by himself on Skyship, to be alone for some reason, or whether he might have been captured by the enemy and taken to AmEarth. Devv hoped it was not the latter, but if it was, there had been no publicity about him being taken prisoner, and no ransom demand if criminals were responsible. Or, maybe he had been taken by someone, and his kidnapper couldn't get him off Skyship yet. It was difficult not knowing.

"Skyship is huge," Devv said over the speaker system between the modules, "but with all the surveillance systems it would be difficult for a person to just disappear. That's especially true of Billy Jeeling, who is ultra conscious of security and protecting himself. No, I'm starting to think that he's gone voluntarily to a hidey-hole, some private place he hasn't told anyone about, one that cannot be detected by scanners."

The morph-baby hovered over the broad green expanse of the airborne city's central park. Below, people walked their dogs, and small children played on the lawn.

"Why would Billy hide? Why not come out?"

"Billy ordered me not to tell you about a troubling event, but I'm worried about him, so I'm going to go against his instructions. Lainey, when I was with him in his office Tuesday, a strange silvery substance appeared suddenly and pooled around his feet. Shockingly, it crawled up his body and merged into it. For several moments his entire body glowed silver. Then Billy reverted to his normal appearance, except his eyes remained silver. It was really weird, and terrifying when he looked at me."

"My God! What could have caused such a drastic change in him?"

"I don't know, but right after it happened to Billy, the attacking fleet was destroyed by blasts of silver light."

"Are you saying he had something to do with it?"

"I didn't see him do it, but it sounds possible to me. Circumstantial evidence points that way, though I can't imagine his part in it. And right after the attackers were defeated, Billy disappeared. Coincidence? I don't think so."

"Very strange," Lainey said.

"I've been thinking about it, racking my brain, trying to dredge up whatever I can. My father said something to me once, and I've been thinking about it a lot. He said—"

She cut him off, saying, "I notice you still call him 'father,' despite the terrible thing he did to you." Lainey looked at him through the thin plates of plaz.

Nodding as he piloted the aircraft, Devv said, "Despite my shock and anger over learning I'm a robot instead of a man, and all my feelings that Billy betrayed me, I can't stop remembering that he did create me after all—just as he designed and built you—and we would never have had the wonderful experiences we've had if he hadn't done that for us."

"It's not easy for me to forgive him," she said.

"But you still love him, don't you? Just as I do?"

Lainey felt tears in her eyes, wiped them, but they kept coming. She wasn't human, but had human emotions nonetheless—the emotions of Billy's lost love Reanne that had been imprinted into her. She sat silently for several moments, trying to compose herself, didn't answer his question.

"I'm sorry if I brought that on," he said.

"It's not your fault. You were about to tell me something Billy— your father—said to you once."

"He said that the hull of Skyship is not what it appears to be. He mentioned it almost in passing, then changed the subject quickly, but what do you suppose he meant by that?"

Lainey shrugged. The wave of emotion had passed, and she'd stopped crying. "I don't know. I've never understood how this ship operates. Only Billy knows all of its secrets, like Tobek before him. Did you see anything about the hull in the journals?"

"Nothing unusual, though the journals are not complete plans. Those must still be inside Tobek's laboratories. But I've been sensing something about that particular comment Billy made, maybe the way he said it."

She smiled softly. "You sensed something with your artificial sensors. That happens to me, too. I knew there was something unusual about you, before I learned you were a robot."

"So both of us sense things, Lainey, though I don't see how that could be part of our programming—so it must have to do with our human imprints." He looked around. "I'm going to set the morph-baby down here, and then take it into one of the deep tunnels."

"You're sensing something again?"

"I am, and it's strong."

Devv kept the craft on hover-mode, looking for a place to land. Lainey heard the smooth, humming sounds of the small flying vessels around them, and beyond that, the busy, clamorous noises of Skyship City. She also heard the chronic spinning sounds in her head, the background noises that had always disturbed her so much, though now she knew what they had to be—her own robotic systems, perhaps when her mechanical pulse was higher than normal. That part she hadn't analyzed.

Devv hit a series of controls, and suddenly loud rock music went on inside Lainey's module, startling her. Many of these police modules were operated by robots, and she'd heard about this deep-bass, throbbing music, because for some reason the normal robots liked to listen to it when they were on patrol. Devv grinned, corrected his mistake, and landed.

On the ground, the unusual aircraft shifted its modular configuration, so that Lainey's and Devv's units were no longer side by side. After a bit of shifting and clicking, her module locked into place directly behind his. He was still at the controls as they rode a cushion of air up a ramp that spiraled past buildings, to the upper sections of the great ship.

"Billy favors the high walkway," Devv said, "so I think we should actually go onto it, instead of just flying by and scanning it. Let's check inside every connecting passageway personally, to see where he might have gone."

"You could be right about this," Lainey said, "because you and I both know Billy keeps secrets, and the ones about us could just be the tip of the iceberg."

"Yeah, Skyship is huge, a vast network of secrets, and Billy is the gatekeeper."

"Though I still care deeply about him," Lainey said, "I hate that he betrayed me, leading me along and manipulating me for his own purposes—or for the larger purpose of Skyship, it would be more fair to say. But he should have been honest with me, should have told me in the beginning that I was a robot. Instead of playing my heart-strings, making me think we had something special between us, something deeply personal."

Devv didn't reply, just steered the morph-baby through the passageway as it spiraled upward.

"And you, too," she said. "Instead, he played games with both of us—or maybe we were just a cruel experiment for him, and he took detailed lab notes on our robotic operations." She paused, took a long, agitated breath. "Maybe I shouldn't say so, but it is troubling the way he handled us, and stressful now that we know about it."

"We both still care deeply for him," Devv said. "But what does that mean for you? How does the way you feel now compare with the way you used to feel?"

"Hmm, I guess I feel badly bruised, so much that I don't want to love him anymore, but I can't help it. Do you know what I mean?"

"Yeah, I feel something like that, too—except as a son to his father, instead of your damaged feelings for the man you love."

"Whatever I still feel for Billy," she said, "I don't think it's a forced, programmed thing. No, it's something else, something I developed during my relationship with him—because of my human imprint with the personality of his dead wife, and all she felt for him—but also because my original programming enabled me to come up with my own experiences, adding to the imprint."

"Sounds plausible."

Devv guided the morph-baby through a doorway, and onto the high walkway. Then he turned the craft slightly sideways and stopped, so that both of them could see a good distance down the central maglev track, and the walkways on either side for non-handicapped people. There were a handful of managers bustling along in both directions, as they often did, going from one building to another, or just getting some exercise during work breaks.

Using his security code, Devv opened several doorways, one after another, smooth and quick. Some led to storage rooms or additional ordinary enclosures, while others led into corridors. He narrowed the search parameters, tailoring them to where Billy might have gone, and finally he found two windowless corridors with maglev tracks. One was short, and led to a private reading room with a small library, one of several that Billy maintained on Skyship.

Another maglev corridor was much longer, and had rampways that led upward to the highest levels of the huge vessel — to areas that Lainey had heard from Devv were for maintenance and various mechanical operations. He'd also told her that some of the rooms in this area, and in other sections around the perimeter of the ship, contained atmospheric-stability and thruster equipment, as well as access points for the many nozzles that sprayed formula-gas into the atmosphere. The morph-baby rounded a turn, went smoothly up another ramp. At the top, they came to a stop at a blank perimeter wall, and Lainey saw something else.

She caught her breath, found herself staring at Billy's famous maglev chair, and it was empty. He was nowhere to be seen. Her heart sank, as she worried about him.

Looking equally concerned, Devv stepped out and examined the chair, then brought out a hand-held scanner, which he pointed down two corridors, one of which ran to the left, and the other to the right. The scanner shone a pale orange light ahead of it. Then Devv ran the scanner along the outer wall they were facing, methodically checking every portion of it.

"Nothing," he said at last, shaking his head. "The scanner shows no openings, no cavities behind the wall. It says we're next to the exterior skin of Skyship, the hull, and if Billy got through it somehow, he's outside the ship."

"So we're at a dead end?"

"Maybe," Devv said, "but I'm going to do a little further investigation. I want to drill into the wall here, and see what's beyond... if anything."

Alarmed, she said, "Drill into the hull of Skyship? Couldn't that cause a catastrophic loss of pressure?"

"Not the way I'm going to do it. Before drilling, we'll seal this entire area off from the rest of the ship."

"Like an airlock, you mean?"

Devv Jeeling narrowed his gaze. "Exactly. I'm not going to give up easily. I could be wrong about this, but we'll see."

CHAPTER 39

Just when you think you are at a dead-end in your inquiries and all seems lost, a new avenue will open up.

—Branson Tobek, notes on the design of Skyship

Billy knew they were looking for him. Tobek had set up monitoring devices inside the hollowed-out skin of the immense ship, and in other key sectors, such as the hidden core. Within this tiny, secret chamber at the pinnacle of the vessel, Billy had instruments collecting surveillance data on the areas of Skyship he had specified—so that he could watch his pursuers, and know where they were at every moment, and how close they were to him.

He was entirely silver now, except for his clothing, and he rather liked what he saw in the reflection of a side window. It gave him an idea for a new series of androids, similar to the Lazarus series with the memories and shapes of human beings, but with shining silver skin and hair.

He preened for a moment, watching his reflected image, and said, "I do look rather striking now, don't I? Elegant, I would say. This could become quite fashionable someday."

He went over in his mind how he might design and build the new robots, without using space devils. It would take a great deal of lab work, a lot of time and effort. He caught himself, felt a sinking sensation.

I don't have a lot of time.

It was a thought the space devils could not read, and he was thankful for that. He felt them inside, sometimes stirring a little, but mostly calm, as if they had found a secure and comfortable nest in the center of his body. They seemed to like where they were.

His pursuers were just beginning to penetrate this section of the ship's hull, so they had broken through a portion of his electronic security, and knew about the concealed tunnel system. He estimated it would take them at least two days to complete the scanning of the numerous hidden areas, and physical searches. He was only a hundred and twenty meters above the place where they were beginning their quest—but the labyrinthine system of conduits and secret chambers was filled with challenges that would slow them down.

It was a complex maze with numerous physical and electronic dead-ends, and only one route to the pinnacle, and back. And it was more than a maze. Like a Chinese puzzle box the passageways constantly shifted when intruders were inside, with tunnels sliding away and barricades popping up where there had been none before, making it extremely difficult for any outsider to figure out.

In the solitude here—away from the steady stream of interruptions from people with problems and questions—he found a feeling of deep serenity, where he could focus and think. In the past, whenever his followers knew where he was, too many matters ended up going through him, as people were nervous about making a mistake. He'd been noticing this increasingly in recent months, during the constant pressure from Moore, Racker, and Paulo in their relentless campaign of character assassination against him, and physical attacks.

All three were dead now, though his former friend Paul Paulo had himself been betrayed by Moore, and had lost his life for it. Yet the disturbing residue of their dirty work remained.

They successfully assassinated my reputation, he thought, bitterly. *No matter what I do from now on, I can never get my good name back. There will always be millions of people who believe the worst about me, the lies.*

He examined the array of controls on the instrument panel in front of him. For a moment, his gaze locked onto a small yellow touch-pad, within easy reach. Then he looked away from it and studied other controls, not wanting to activate the touch-pad, and not wanting the space devils to know what he was thinking. They could not read his thoughts at all, because he'd often thought of how much he hated them and wanted to be free of them, and nothing had happened to him. Without any doubt, it had to be overt action that triggered their dangerous response, such as Tobek's clear attempt to destroy them.

Just then, a screen flashed on in front of him, and he was startled to see an image of Branson Tobek in natural color, speaking to him. "My dear friend and colleague Billy, if you are hearing this, it means I am dead. This is the first of several messages I have set up around Sky-ship, to provide you with information that will be essential to you in operating the facility. There are reasons why I did not wish to provide you with everything previously."

Excited, Billy adjusted his position on the chair, and listened as his long-dead mentor spoke from the grave. Then the voice shifted and became slightly different, while the image of Tobek remained frozen, the expression unchanging and the lips not moving.

"Some of what I am about to tell you is synthesized, meaning that I never actually spoke certain words you are about to hear—but they were compiled based upon extremely accurate computer projections of what I undoubtedly would have said, based upon a range of possible events. In this way, the comments have been tailored to my last moments alive, and what I said at that time—that you were *never* to open the sealed laboratory complex, that you were to leave all inside and untouched."

This is really peculiar, Billy thought, but he stared at the image in fascination, and listened.

"It has only been a day since I died," Tobek said, his voice shifting again and his lips moving once more, "and I want to begin with information about the space devils, because there are things you need to know about them."

Billy jerked his head back in surprise. *A day since he died? No, it has been eleven years! What does he mean? Something must have gone wrong with the timing he set up!*

Now Billy heard Tobek explain in some detail what the space devils were, basically the same as he had already written in the journals Billy wasn't supposed to have seen. Then the voice shifted, the facial expression and lips froze, and he said, "I assume the space devils are still trapped where I left them in the core of the ship, in the sealed laboratories I told you not to touch. They attacked me in there, because they learned I was trying to destroy them."

So, I was right, Billy thought.

The voice became more natural, and Tobek's lips started moving again, in synchronization: "The good news is that I have been able to cause considerable harm to the devils, through my experiments. And because I have seriously damaged them, they are unable to leave Sky-ship, and must remain here for the rest of their existence. If they were ever to be exposed to the atmosphere or to space, they would perish. The explanation for this is too complex for me to explain, Billy, be-cause you were not privy to the extensive research I did on the crea-tures, all the experiments that took me a great deal of time and effort. In fact, you did not even know they existed when I was working on them."

That's true, Billy thought, because he didn't learn about them until he read about them in Tobek's journals.

"The space devils are the source of the dire problem that I have warned you about, the series of dangerous chain reactions that will occur in the atmosphere if Skyship were ever destroyed, or seriously damaged—but the immense danger only exists if they are aboard the vessel. Their existence, combined with an explosion of Skyship, is the problem. If the space devils are removed, a detonation of the vessel— though terrible—would not set off any chain reactions in the atmos-phere.

"You might be wondering if the harm I have done to the creatures reduces the likelihood of this occurring—and I can say with certainty that the answer is no. I must insist upon extreme, *extreme* caution. And, since you are hearing this recording, my critical experiments are no longer being conducted."

Much as I suspected, Billy thought. *The space devils are the problem, in more ways than one. Damn them for killing my friend!* It was a tragic loss, such a brilliant, man, taken away when he was needed so much.

"One week from now," Tobek said in his natural voice, "I will pro-vide you with more information. Return here at noon in seven days, and the identity markers of your presence will activate another audio-video recording."

A week? Billy thought. *I can't wait that long!*

Billy added the new information to what he already knew, that the creatures went zealously after his enemies. He theorized now that they were seeing him as the leader and protector of Skyship, which was their haven, since they couldn't go out into the atmosphere or into space anymore, or they would die. And beyond that, they seemed to have found an additional refuge inside his body, as if he were a second safe harbor for their kind, with the added benefit that they could amplify their power through him. It all sounded crazy, except it really was happening to Billy, and he could only see one way out.

He saw it all with perfect certainty.

They stirred inside once more, and he said soothing things to them, to calm them down.

CHAPTER 40

Each person has the makings of great heroics inside, and of dismal, abject cowardice. It is the complex
play of opposites within the human psyche that acti-
vates one or the other.

—Devv Jeeling, notes from a speech to his security-force academy

With Yürgen's ability to operate humbabies, he had been activated as a reservist, and told to join five other pilots, on a team assigned to fly outside the upper perimeter of Skyship and look for abnormalities. Though Devv Jeeling had taken precautions to seal the area he was drilling inside the great vessel, he wanted to make absolutely certain nothing unusual happened to the hull, because they were working so close to it. The ship was in geostationary orbit, high over AmEarth.

At mid-morning Yürgen Zayeddi took off with the others, and outside the great city-ship he began to circle the hull on the section that was his responsibility — the highest latitudes of the immense, blimp-shaped vessel. Due to the tremendous size of Skyship, and the meticulous scrutiny they were ordered to employ in the investigation, this meant that each pilot would need most of the day to complete his assignment.

Beginning at the lowest latitude of his assignment, he circled horizontally, gradually rising higher and higher on the huge, dark gray hull as he completed each trip around and spiraled upward. He was looking closely at the hull as he did this, and had instruments on the bottom of his aircraft scanning everything and transmitting images back to security headquarters. It was repetitive and tedious work, and he was tired today, so that he had to remind himself repeatedly to stay awake.

~~~

Inside the pinnacle chamber, Billy Jeeling had only been able to come up with one plan that had any likelihood of success, and it was not anything he really wanted to do. In addition to the certainty of his own death with that option, there were also other serious problems that might result, too many things that could go wrong with Skyship.

He had dedicated most of his life to this atmospheric machine, to making certain the marvel of geoengineering technology functioned properly in its mining and air-restoration duties—as much as he could, that is, with the limited knowledge in his possession. Now, with the revelation that information from Tobek would be doled out to him in periodic audiovisual recordings, he felt an obligation to find out what the old inventor had to say, what important information he'd intended to impart. But that assumed nothing more went wrong with the timing of the releases.

But if Billy destroyed the space devils in the way he had in mind, and he died, it would imperil the critical flow of recorded information from Tobek. Maybe the inventor had set up contingency arrangements to get around this problem, but Billy could not be certain of that.

If only he could come up with another way of rendering the creatures harmless, perhaps without killing them. He appreciated what they had done for him, defending and protecting him, and he didn't want to be ungrateful.

Still, they were extremely dangerous.

~~~

At security headquarters, Devv Jeeling was coordinating the search for his father. Despite the revelation that he was himself a robot, he still loved Billy—not quite the same as before, but his feelings remained strong. He hoped desperately that nothing had happened to him.

Devv had decided to transmit images of the search in the secret tunnels to the populace of the airborne city, because they were all worried about Billy, wondering where he had gone and why.

Everyone wanted to help the Master of Skyship—the people and the eclectic assemblage of sentient robots. Images of the search appeared on screens all over the onboard city, showing what the searchers had learned so far about the secret maze of tunnels and chambers hidden inside the hull. The images were being projected without commentary, because Devv didn't want it to be like a detached news report. This was personal for everyone on the vessel, each in their own way, as they sought information about the welfare of this most special of all men. Billy Jeeling was not only a great environmental leader; he was beloved by all who knew him—and especially by those who had gotten to know him well.

The maze in the outer skin of Skyship was like quicksand, constantly shifting to keep the searchers from figuring it out. In a separate computer system (not transmitted to the populace) Devv's officers were trying to map the hidden system of passageways—but this was proving to be impossible. They were discussing a strategy of keeping the tunnels and chambers open in an effort to thwart the defensive system that opened and closed sections and changed them, but so far no could figure out how to do it.

Now Devv stared at a different set of screens, showing the results of constant air analyses that were being taken inside the tunnels—trace DNA evidence that was being scooped up and evaluated, showing that Billy Jeeling had passed through them, and recently. But bound for where? No one knew.

Skyship was the largest structure ever built, and the interior of the hull was proving to be a huge challenge to explore, in and of itself.

~~~

Just as darkness was setting in, Yürgen Zayeddi's small humbaby flew over the uppermost surfaces of Skyship. In just a few more minutes, he would be finished. He had powerful lights on underneath the tiny vessel, so that he and the observers who were monitoring his transmissions could see the hull as clearly as possible.

Ahead, he saw a glint of silver coming from the pinnacle of the hull—or *thought* he did for just a blink of time, because when he looked again, there was nothing. He flew over that spot, illuminating it brightly, hovering above it, and magnified the images.

On a VR screen he saw what he thought were slight abnormalities at the very top of the great vessel. Very thin, barely perceptible lines were visible on the hull—four lines that were squared off, almost as if they outlined an opening to something beyond them, on the inside of Skyship.

After transmitting the images to headquarters, he told them about the silver flash he thought he saw, and how it seemed to have vanished.

~~~

Billy had almost forgotten to close his overhead window into space. With his own surveillance system, independent of the one Devv was using, he should have been paying closer attention.

At the very last possible moment, Billy had switched on images of the outside of Skyship, and saw the tiny humbaby approaching.

He'd taken quick action, but had the pilot seen anything?

~~~

In the headquarters control room, Devv Jeeling obtained advice from his engineers, and issued a new command: "Set up a second search area on the outside of the hull, at the top. We'll need a custom airlock attached to the pinnacle, large enough for a team to get inside, with specialized tools. I want to see if anything interesting is inside that pinnacle—so we're going to punch through and see what's on the other side."

Ten minutes later, Devv received a report from his engineers. They would begin fabrication of the airlock at a facility inside Skyship, a unit like the earlier one that had been built to prevent pressurization problems.

The engineers estimated that it would take at least forty-eight hours to get the equipment operational, saying this airlock would be more difficult to prepare and install than the earlier one, because it was on the outside of the hull.

"That's too long," Devv said. "I want it ready sooner. I wanted it ten minutes ago. Put everyone on this, and work in around-the-clock teams."

CHAPTER 41

Beauty can be found even in tragedy.

—One of the ancient philosophies

At the end of a long, mentally exhausting day, Billy fell asleep inside the pinnacle chamber. A half cup of water sat in the holder on his chair, with an unopened food packet beside it.

Sitting there, with his head lolling to one side, he had a strange dream in which he was a religious leader who went to a remote place, seeking spiritual truth. It was comparable to the legends of a great man sitting under a sacred bodhi tree or by a holy river to obtain enlightenment, or going alone to a remote cave for this purpose, or into the desert.

Except in Billy's case, he had retreated to a hidden chamber on Skyship, a place that was remote from the rest of the vessel. In the dream he received a message from God in the Heavens, and emerged to tell his followers he had experienced a revelation, and more would follow. He had received a series of commandments from the deity, he said, and now he was carrying the first portion of the holy message. He said this made him a prophet, and that he would begin dictating God's words into a sacred book.

And in the dream Billy Jeeling began to assemble that religious text, page by page, for three days, until he completed what God had told him so far. At the end of the third day he wrote in ornate script that he would be forced to sacrifice his life before the rest of the revelations could be received, and he could not attempt to finish the book, or there would be great danger. He stared long and hard at the words, feeling numb, realizing the inevitability of his death, and how little time he had remaining.

The partially-completed holy book exploded into sentence and word fragments that floated in the air and then faded from view. He found himself awake, looking at the interior of the pinnacle chamber. The instrument panel stood directly in front of him, with its small yellow touch pad. He didn't look at the pad, but knew exactly where it was, within easy reach, only a moment away.

Instead, he touched a control on his belt to activate a view of Lainey's apartment, then shifted the image from room to room, looking for her. Normally he didn't like to intrude on her privacy, even if she was only a robot, so he'd rarely done it in the past—except when he needed to study her functions as a sentient machine. It was the same with Devv and with the few other functioning machines that were similar to these two.

Billy saw Lainey sitting on the edge of her bed, crying softly, her face buried in her hands. A framed black-and-white photograph sat on the bed beside her, one of her favorite images of Billy. It was a heroic pose in the central park, with the camera angle looking upward at him, and the buildings of the airborne city rising behind him.

His heart went out to her, because in his own way he loved her a great deal, despite the way she had a habit of clinging too closely, not wanting to be away from him. On a daily basis, when he was trying to accomplish his important work, this trait had been an irritation to him. But now, watching her deep sadness—her deep *simulated* sadness, but real for her nonetheless—he found her personality defect endearing, and only a minor flaw.

Billy loved Lainey almost as much as he had loved the real woman whom she so resembled, Reanne Jeeling. He had lost Reanne tragically, and Lainey had been the closest substitute he could come up with, the best of the sentient machines he had put into service on Skyship, a fabulous creation in all ways. He was especially proud of her, despite her minor imperfections, and proud of Devv, too. Both of them had served him well, with unflagging devotion.

And they would continue to serve him in the future, because they would help to manage his legacy after he was gone, along with other key robots and support personnel on board Skyship. He paused. Actually, they would all continue to serve Skyship, and planet AmEarth. The great atmospheric-restoration ship, with all of the automatic functions that had been designed by Tobek, and the robots that had been primarily designed by Billy, was in effect a perpetual motion machine that would continue to operate into the far-future. Tobek had told him several times that the vessel had redundancies on top of redundancies, and that he'd designed every possible safeguard into it.

Branson Tobek had tried to account for every possible eventuality, and he'd gone a long way toward accomplishing that—until his plans and dreams were almost derailed when the strange silver creatures appeared and killed him. It was something he had not contemplated, something that could not be planned for, because he had not previously known they even existed.

Tobek had attempted to get rid of them, but had gone about it the wrong way, and they'd killed him before he could get them. Now Billy had an advantage, because he'd been studying the community of alien creatures, and was very close to getting rid of them forever. He hoped this was the case.

But even if he eliminated them, that didn't mean something else unforeseen might not show up in the future. Yet Billy had a feeling—a very *strong* feeling—that Skyship would survive for a long, long time, with all of its systems intact and continuing to operate.

On the screen, he saw Lainey don a pair of golden ballet slippers, and begin to dance on a section of floor. She performed a *pas seul* exercise in which she pirouetted, glissaded, and made *jeté* jumps. She smiled softly as she danced her solo routine.

Billy remembered his beloved Reanne performing these same exercises, and telling him what they were. He used to enjoy watching her, and took great care later in imparting the same skills to Lainey. It was almost as if the sentient robot knew he was observing her now, and was doing this just for him. Certainly she was thinking of him, because she stopped dancing and looked sadly at his picture.

Then, carefully, she set the photograph on the table beside her bed where she always kept it. She removed her dancing slippers, climbed back into bed, and turned off the light.

Billy thought for a moment of his faux-son, Devv, but didn't want to remote view him, even though he cared deeply for him. He didn't have time for any more sentiment now, not with what he had to do. Billy's mind, so filled with emotion, went suddenly blank, because he knew he was about to die, and this was the last time he would ever see Lainey. And he realized that his enemies, who had attempted to assassinate his character, and to kidnap him for a mock trial and public execution, had finally succeeded in killing him after all. The evil deed had taken a circuitous route, not the one they had intended, but their aggressive acts had caused the space devils to merge into Billy's body to defend him and Skyship against the military attacks and sabotages. So, it was all linked. His opponents had wanted him dead in one way or another, and he was about to fall victim.

His fingers darted for the yellow pressure pad, and he activated it.

He heard a noise of high-pitched engines, and felt a strong thrust upward, as the emergency escape capsule at the heart of the chamber surged out of the top of Skyship, heading for space — one of numerous similar capsules Tobek had placed around the vessel. There had been no opportunity for Billy to leave a message for anyone, telling what he knew about the operation of the great sky machine, because that would have alerted the space devils, and they would have killed him, as they'd done earlier to his mentor.

He smiled to himself. Devv and others knew about the genetic sample packets Billy kept, and his own personal journals contained details about how to use human imprints in the Lazarus-series robots, and how the rest of their workings could be constructed. Billy's genetic material was contained in one of those packets, so he could be regenerated in an imprinted-robotic form, with some or all of the memories of the original. This resurrection would not answer all of the questions about the operation of Skyship, but he had also made journal entries about the possibility of retrieving the genetic material of Branson Tobek from the sealed laboratory complex where his body remained, and how this material could be used to build a new robotic version of the great inventor. Now that the space devils were being dealt with, it would be safe for others to enter the laboratory complex.

Billy knew for a fact that there was such a thing as genetic memory — life memories contained within cellular material. He had proven this with his own experiments, after analyzing what it was in cells that caused the phenomenon of instinct in animals — the ability of an offspring to perform the same tasks its parents had done, without parental instruction. The nest building of birds, the dam construction of beavers, and much more that was done instinctually, by many species. It was all tied to information inside the cells, and Billy had managed to unlock many of these important, fascinating secrets, and put them to work in his most special of all robots. He had used this technique to generate some of the authentic memories of Reanne Jeeling in Lainey Forster, such as the memories of her dancing as a child in front of her family.

Conceivably then, a Lazarus-series android of Branson Tobek could contain all the secrets the inventor had kept from the world, and from Billy. It was an exciting idea, because such a robot could solve many or all of the mysteries of Skyship. How did the great geoengineering machine keep going automatically for so long, what were the ingredients in the gas mixture that restored the atmosphere, and what were the secrets of magnaviewers, that could see so much detail over long distances? All of this information could be locked inside the memory-laden cells of Branson Tobek. Finding that trove of data would be like reaching into a long-lost treasure chest — and Billy had done all he could to make it possible.

Now, inside his own body, the alien creatures of light had been galvanized into action by the take-off of the capsule, and their collective frenzy made him feel icy cold. They were trying to gain control and get him to return them to their Skyship haven, realizing now what he was doing. He felt their collective, desperate will, as it battered against him from the inside of his mind, trying to get him to touch another control that would return the escape capsule to the vicinity of the mother ship, for rescue by onboard equipment and personnel. His shining, metallic eyes stared at the proper control, but just looking at it — even by such powerful creatures — did not activate it.

Suddenly his entire body flashed the brightest silver, filling the interior of the capsule with brilliant light. A freezing, screaming wind blew through the inside of his body.

And in space Billy made the last decision of his life, the only thing he could do. Moving his hand ever so slowly, because the extreme cold had stiffened his muscles, he managed to touch another pressure pad on the instrument panel.

The capsule detonated and burst open in a blinding flash of silver—more bright when seen from AmEarth than a sun going nova. In an instant, Billy Jeeling existed no more, except in the memories of billions of people—and in the synthesized thoughts and emotions of the robots he had designed and built with such loving care.

CHAPTER 42

Where has Billy Jeeling gone?
No one knows, but there are disturbing indications.

—Confidential security report, Skyship

In the second-floor parlor of the Imperial Palace, Renaldo Yhatt stood at a window, gazing into the night sky. It was the same window where he'd been a week ago, when the strange silver beam threatened him. Two palace guards stood just inside the doorway, and the entire AmEarth military force was on high alert. The recent events were most unsettling, and everyone worried about another attack from what was being called "the Silver Death."

He peered into a telescope, located Skyship in the distance, a ball of bright illumination over AmEarth.

Behind him, he heard a guard announce the entrance of his wife Lorissa, along with Maureen Stuart and her husband Paddy.

Earlier in the day, Prime Minster Yhatt had sent a message to Billy Jeeling, telling him the AmEarth government now recognized his right to remain in control of Skyship. Yhatt also told him they should work together instead of being at each other's throats, for the good of the people. He apologized for the behavior of General Moore, Jonathan Racker, and Paul Paulo, and for his own part in their aggression, and he expressed regrets on behalf of Maureen Stuart, as well.

She had recommended the act of contrition, and Yhatt had agreed to carry through with it, eating a very large portion of humble pie. He saw her peripherally now, standing beside him.

Withdrawing from the scope, the Prime Minister said to her, "I sent the message to Billy Jeeling today. There is no answer yet."

"Let's hope he's not vindictive," she said, "though I would not blame him if he were."

"Nor would I."

Looking deeply concerned, Maureen said, "All we can do is hope. We've gotten rid of our crazy general, so no one from AmEarth is going to attack Skyship. Any information on their strange weapon?"

"Not a thing. It's very mysterious, and very troubling."

~~~

On Skyship, Devv Jeeling didn't know how to respond to Prime Minster Yhatt's message. In any event, there would be a delay getting back to him, because Billy was still missing.

One of the security teams was searching a chamber on top of Skyship, where an escape capsule had ejected, and then detonated in space. Everyone was hoping Billy was not inside the capsule, but it seemed possible that he'd been there, even likely. His DNA had been found in the complex tunnel system leading to the chamber.

There had been an audiovisual system in the chamber that went on when the searchers reached that area—it had a screen showing the face of an elderly man with his mouth moving, saying something, but there was no volume, and the image flickered off after a few seconds. According to a mindcom report that Devv had just received, a robot technician was trying to reactivate the system.

Devv was inside Billy's private apartment now, watching while his security officers performed a slow, careful search. They removed articles from the drawers of a small desk and piled them on top... two laptop computers, file folders, books. As the searchers took books off a bookcase, Devv noticed something hidden behind them... two dark blue, leather-bound volumes. He hurried forward, retrieved the thick volumes.

Thumbing through the pages, he saw that they were Billy's personal journals, written in his own hand. Devv's pulse quickened. They were as neat and organized, and quite different from Tobek's. The emphasis of Tobek's writings had been Skyship, while in Billy's case, it was the remarkable robots he had designed and built—especially the Lazarus series.

He summoned Lainey, and they stood together for several minutes, talking about Billy, and crying. By the time they wiped their eyes they were certain he was gone forever, and missed him terribly. Then they sat side by side at a table, opened the first of the journals, and turned to page one....

ABOUT THE AUTHOR

Brian Herbert has published more than 40 books, including science fiction, fantasy, and horror novels, with many of his works appearing on the New York Times and international bestseller lists. He won the Science Fiction Book of the Year Award and the New York Times Notable Book Award for his DUNE-series novels, reached the preliminary Nebula Award ballot for his novel THE RACE FOR GOD, and made the final Hugo Award ballot for DREAMER OF DUNE, the moving biography of his famous father Frank Herbert, a work Brian spent five years writing.

Brian and his wife, Jan, live in the Seattle area, and have three daughters. In 1967, the young couple eloped to Reno and were married in a small chapel. Little did they know what a life of adventure they would experience together. In 2017 Brian and Jan took a 3-month overseas trip to commemorate their 50th wedding anniversary. It was one of perhaps 20 "trips of a lifetime" they've enjoyed. Years ago, Jan told Brian that "this life is not a dress rehearsal," and she convinced him to travel extensively, so that they could experience other cultures and enjoy their lives to the fullest. Jan Herbert is a remarkable woman, and Brian considers himself fortunate to have met her at such a young age.

Brian and Jan have visited most of the countries in the world, where they've seen fascinating cultural, political, religious, historical, and environmental situations first-hand—providing plenty of data for writing. On one of their world cruises, Brian met a US Merchant Marine veteran, and learned that these civilian seamen had been treated unfairly after World War II, not receiving any medical or other benefits, even after serving in dangerous war zones and performing tasks critical to the Allied war effort. Seeking to remedy this massive injustice, Brian wrote THE FORGOTTEN HEROES, a carefully-researched non-fiction work that has received praise from the Merchant Marine community. He also submitted written testimony to the US Congress, in an effort to obtain benefits for heroic merchant seamen and their families.

Brian's acclaimed novels include the Timeweb trilogy (TIMEWEB, THE WEB & THE STARS, and WEBDANCERS); THE STOLEN GOSPELS; THE LOST APOSTLES; THE RACE FOR GOD; SIDNEY'S COMET; SUDANNA, SUDANNA; and MAN OF TWO WORLDS (written with Frank Herbert).

Brian also wrote the Hellhole Trilogy (HELLHOLE, HELLHOLE AWAKENING, and HELLHOLE INFERNO) and many international-bestselling DUNE-series novels with Kevin J. Anderson.

Brian's novels are highly original, and deal with environmental issues, as well as politics, religion, women's rights and the history of human civilization. One of Brian's recent publications is OCEAN, an epic fantasy novel about environmental issues, written with his wife, Jan. The premise of OCEAN is highly original and revolutionary—the ocean and its dangerous sea creatures declare war against human civilization, in retaliation for pollution and other abuses to those waters. Like many of Brian's novels, it exposes an important social issue in a thought-provoking way.

Brian's highly original science fiction novel, THE LITTLE GREEN BOOK OF CHAIRMAN RAHMA, is the imaginative story of a green utopia that becomes a nightmare for people living in it—the ecologically obsessed government enforces its edicts with deadly police state methods in which environmental violators are "recycled." Publishers Weekly praised the novel as depicting "a fresh and forbidding near-future world." That was just one of many excellent reviews that Brian's works have received, going all the way back to his first science fiction novel, SIDNEY'S COMET, which Publishers Weekly described as "unusually inventive and original."

In Brian's childhood, he, his younger brother Bruce, and their parents had very little money. Impulsively, Frank Herbert moved the family of four from place to place. He was a newspaperman and science fiction writer in the days before becoming famous for DUNE, while Brian's mother [Beverly Herbert] worked for large department stores, writing ads. She was the breadwinner much of the time, allowing her husband the time to develop his writing talent, even though he generated very little income. The family moved 23 times before Brian was out of high school.

Brian went to 1st grade in Ciudad Guzman, Mexico, in the state of Jalisco. In 1953, they traveled to Mexico with the fantasy writer Jack

Vance and his wife, Norma. Brian spoke Spanish in school, and still has his Spanish-language arithmetic book from that class. The "school bus" was a smoke-belching old station wagon, and Brian â€" as the new kid / gringo â€" had to sit in the rear by a broken back window, inhaling exhaust fumes. He was even told to ride on the tailgate on occasion, with his feet dangling over the edge, holding on as best as he could. The Herberts returned to the United States after a few months. But two years later they were back in Mexico, living in the village of Tlalpujahua, in the mountains of Michoacán. There they lived among Tarascan Indians, a tough and hardy group of mountain people whose ancestors were among the few who were never conquered by the Aztecs. Today the town is well known for the Christmas ornaments it produces, but in the 1950s it was a sleepy village with cobblestone streets. Brian was home-schooled there by his parents.

In 1960, the Herbert family moved to San Francisco. For the first time in Brian's life, they stayed in one area for an extended period. He attended Everett Junior High School and Lowell High School in the city. Lowell is the oldest high school west of St. Louis, long known for high academic standards. Living in a tough neighborhood in the Mission district, Brian took streetcars and buses across the city to a nicer part of town, out in the Avenues where Lowell was. Having skipped grades in junior high, he graduated from high school when he was only 16.

Afterward, Brian enrolled at the nearby University of California at Berkeley, attending classes during the political turmoil of the free-speech movement and the anti-war movement. He graduated with a BA degree in Sociology, a degree he was to use later in his writing, having learned in school about the psychology and intricate workings of large-scale social movements. During college, he and Jan had their first child. Brian also worked full time as a waiter and in other jobs, mostly in food service, while carrying a full-time schedule of classes.

Today, in addition to writing more novels, Brian co-manages the business of his late father's fantastic DUNE legacy, sharing those responsibilities with one of his daughters and a nephew. In that capacity Brian and his fellow officers signed a major film deal with Legendary Pictures, and he will serve as an Executive Producer and Creative Adviser on future motion picture and television projects.

For more about Brian and his work, as well as the latest news about the Dune motion picture project, please see:

Twitter:
Facebook: brianherbertnovels
Website: www.brianherbertnovels.com

More books from Brian Herbert are available at:
www.ReAnimus.com/store/?author=Brian%20Herbert

ReAnimus Press

Breathing Life into Great Books

If you enjoyed this book we hope you'll tell others or write a review! We also invite you to subscribe to our newsletter to learn about our new releases and join our affiliate program (where you earn 12% of sales you recommend) at www.ReAnimus.com.

Here are more ebooks you'll enjoy from ReAnimus Press, available from ReAnimus Press's web site, Amazon.com, bn.com, etc.:

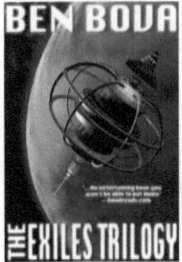

The Star Conquerors (Collectors' Edition), by Ben Bova

Info/buy:

Special Collectors' Edition! Six time Hugo winner Ben Bova's most sought-after novel is now an ebook with the original Mel Hunter cover and an essay from Ben on the history of the book!

Colony, by Ben Bova

Info/buy:

Island One is a celestial utopia, and David Adams is its most perfect creation. But David is a prisoner, destined to spend his life in an island-sized cylinder orbiting a doomed home planet. David has a plan—one that will ultimately save humanity... or destroy it.

The Kinsman Saga, by Ben Bova

Info/buy:

Chet Kinsman is an astronaut ace who has done everything in space—including committing the first murder. Kinsman has to confront his hidden past and decide Earth's destiny, in a desperate countdown to nuclear annihilation.

The Living Labyrinth, by Ian Stewart and Tim Poston

Info/buy:

Sam, Jane, Felix, Elzabet, Tinka & Marco go quantum jumping on their path to galactic citizenship, only to end up in a very strange place indeed!

Rock Star, by Tim Poston and Ian Stewart

Info/buy:

The awesome sequel to The Living Labyrinth. It's all fun and games with syntei until they fall into the wrong hands...

Walls and Wonders, by S. R. Algernon

Info/buy:

Hugo finalist... If Hemingway wrote P.K.Dick-ian science fiction short stories...

Wheelers, by Ian Stewart and Jack Cohen

Info/buy:

Alien artifacts found on Callisto...

Dreams of the Technarion, by Sean McMullen

Info/buy:

Stories from a Hugo finalist where the science might not be fiction! Plus the historical OUTPOST OF WONDER.

Vanishing Light, by Robert N. Stephenson

Info/buy:

Mikolev thinks he's stumbled onto a secret. Is it nothing, or has he just opened Pandora's box and put all of utopia at risk?

Kafka's Uncle: The Unfortunate Sequel, by Bruce Taylor

Info/buy:

You really thought the story ended there???

Kafka's Uncle: The Ghastly Prequel, by Bruce Taylor

Info/buy:

How does KAFKA'S UNCLE and KAFKA'S UNCLE: THE UNFORTUNATE SEQUEL begin? Here!

Tales from the Good Ship Kafkabury, by Bruce Taylor

Info/buy:

Franz Kafka, meet Ray Bradbury...

Edward: Dancing on the Edge of Infinity, by Bruce Taylor

Info/buy:

Another excellent exploration of What It's All About, by Mr. Magical Realism. With footnotes.*

Alleymanderous and Other Magical Realities, by Bruce Taylor

Info/buy:

A surrealistic/magic realist nightmare from Mr. Magical Realism himself.

Star Watchmen, by Ben Bova

Info/buy:

Mankind rules a giant galactic empire, but not all the worlds are pleased. Can the Star Watch prevent a revolt?

As on a Darkling Plain, by Ben Bova

Info/buy:

Dr. Sidney Lee races against time to prevent the huge alien machines on Titan from destroying mankind.

The Winds of Altair, by Ben Bova

Info/buy:

Altair VI isn't making it easy to Terraform!

Test of Fire, by Ben Bova

Info/buy:

A small group of survivors fight to rebuild civilization after the Earth is devastated by a huge solar flare.

The Weathermakers, by Ben Bova

Info/buy:

After conquering everything else, the last frontier was... controlling Mother Nature! By the award-winning hard SF author of the Grand Tour series.

The Dueling Machine, by Ben Bova

Info/buy:

Civilized, harmless virtual reality dueling has replaced all physical conflict — everything from punching someone over a personal insult to interstellar warfare... until a madman dictator of a small empire finds a way to cheat, and use the dueling machine to take over the galaxy!

The Multiple Man, by Ben Bova
Info/buy:

As the President is speaking inside an auditorium in Boston, the President's Press Secretary discovers a body in an alley outside: The body of the President.

Escape!, by Ben Bova
Info/buy:

No end to Danny's sentence, watched by a sentient computer, and no way out of the escape-proof prison, there was only one thing to do...

Forward in Time, by Ben Bova
Info/buy:

Get ready for a series of future shocks from the award-winning Ben Bova!

Maxwell's Demons, by Ben Bova
Info/buy:

Science fiction and science fact, humor and adventure, all await when you enter the unpredictable world of... MAXWELL'S DEMONS

Twice Seven, by Ben Bova
Info/buy:

Ben Bova's universe is always more than the sum of its parts...

The Astral Mirror, by Ben Bova
Info/buy:

Here are a dozen and a half views of the world, past present and future, as seen through the Astral Mirror....

Timeshare, by Joshua Dann
Info/buy:

Have you ever wished you could go back to the good old days? At Timeshare Unlimited, you can.

Ghosts of Engines Past, by Sean McMullen
Info/buy:

Award winning steampunk from a master!

Colours of the Soul, by Sean McMullen
Info/buy:

Why are cheetahs the most perfect of creatures? Besides because they're cats, that is... Cool, mind-blowing stories from a master.

CV, by Damon Knight
Info/buy:

The largest sea vessel ever built — and a deadly arena!

The Observers, by Damon Knight
Info/buy:

The alien plague returns, and CV is part of the sinister solution.

A Reasonable World, by Damon Knight
Info/buy:

CV #3... The symbionts are having a fascinating effect on people...

In Search of Wonder, by Damon Knight
Info/buy:

The premier book of SF insight for all SF readers and writers.

The World and Thorinn, by Damon Knight
Info/buy:

Thorinn is thrown into a well by his father to appease the rumbling gods... and down he goes!

The Futurians, by Damon Knight
Info/buy:

The history of the brilliant Futurians—Asimov, Blish, Pohl, et al.—told by an insider. Fully illustrated.

Creating Short Fiction, by Damon Knight
Info/buy:

The classic guide to writing short fiction - Revised & Expanded 3rd ed.

Space Travel - A Science Fiction Writer's Guide, by Ben Bova
Info/buy:

An indispensible tool for all science fiction writers, Space Travel explains the science you need to help you make your fiction plausible.

In Search of the Big Bang, by John Gribbin
Info/buy:

For Big Bang Theory fans, don't miss this indispensable guide! :) `A remarkably readable guide to the mysteries of cosmic creation' —Nature

Cosmic Coincidences, by John Gribbin and Martin Rees
Info/buy:

A provocative search through space and time for a cosmic blueprint—and the source of life in the universe.

Q is for Quantum, by John Gribbin
Info/buy:

A comprehensive encyclopedia of quantum physics.

Ice Age, by John and Mary Gribbin

Info/buy:

The theory that came in from the cold...

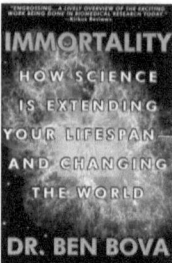

Immortality, by Ben Bova

Info/buy:

Dr. Bova explores the future effects of science and technology on the human life span. Death will no longer be the inevitable end of life.

Phoenix Without Ashes, by Harlan Ellison and Edward Bryant

Info/buy:

Co-written with Harlan Ellison and based on the award-winning script, the story of mankind's last salvation gone awry.

Redshift Rendezvous, by John E. Stith

Info/buy:

One man must stop starship hijackers from using an unusual starship to plunder a wealthy colony.

Manhattan Transfer, by John E. Stith

Info/buy:

Aliens kidnap Manhattan; read all about it!

Reunion on Neverend, by John E. Stith

Info/buy:

A man returning for a high school reunion on a distant colony finds an old flame in trouble—trouble that he's uniquely qualified to deal with.

Reckoning Infinity, by John E. Stith

Info/buy:

A riveting exploration of what it means to be an alien... Explorers inside a moon-sized alien ship must find its secrets before it kills them.

Deep Quarry, by John E. Stith

Info/buy:

A private eye uncovers a long-buried starship...that's still occupied.

Memory Blank, by John E. Stith

Info/buy:

Cal Donley regains consciousness on the beautiful orbital colony Daedalus—but Cal doesn't remember leaving Earth, or his name or the past dozen years!

Scapescope, by John E. Stith

Info/buy:

Brother Sammy Wants YOU! In prison. For something you haven't done yet.

Conquerors from the Darkness, by Robert Silverberg

Info/buy:

Long after the earth has been conquered by aliens and flooded, Dovirr Stargan longs to become one of the pirate-like Sea Lords.

Time of the Great Freeze, by Robert Silverberg

Info/buy:

ICE AGE--NEW YORK CITY 2650 A.D. UNDERGROUND!

The Gate of Worlds, by Robert Silverberg

Info/buy:

An Alternate History adventure in the modern day Turkish and Aztec Empires.

Shadrach in the Furnace, by Robert Silverberg

Info/buy:

Meet the new Khan! Soon to be immortal... A Hugo and Nebula Award Finalist novel from a Grand Master of science fiction.

Bloom, by Wil McCarthy

Info/buy:

In 2106, microscopic machine/creatures escape their creators to populate the inner solar system with a wild, deadly ecology all their own, pushing the tattered remnants of humanity out into the cold and dark of the outer planets. Seven astronauts must embark on mankind's boldest venture yet—the perilous journey home to infected Earth!

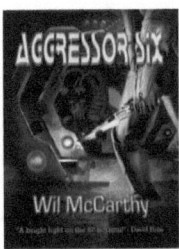

Aggressor Six, by Wil McCarthy
Info/buy:

An alien armada from the center of Orion makes its deadly way through the galaxy, destroying all human life in the process, and only Marine Corporal Kenneth Jonson and the Aggressor Six team can stop the onslaught.

Murder in the Solid State, by Wil McCarthy
Info/buy:

David Sanger, an ambitious young physicist, attends a party at which a pompous older scientist, who just happens to have thrwarted the younger man's innovative ideas, is murdered. Suddenly it is not just David's career, but his life that is at stake. Are his ideas that important? Who's out to stop David from changing the world?

Flies from the Amber, by Wil McCarthy
Info/buy:

Forty light years from earth, the colonists on the world of Unua have somehow managed to keep civilization struggling on, despite twice daily earthquakes...

The Egg of the Glak, by Harvey Jacobs
Info/buy:

Some of Harvey's best, believably fantastical short stories.

The Cure for Everything, by Severna Park
Info/buy:

Finding the cure for all diseases comes with a heavy price. Nebula Award winner!

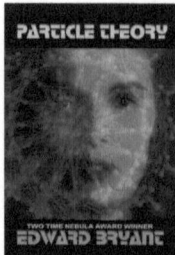

Particle Theory, by Edward Bryant

Info/buy:

Particle Theory by Edward Bryant : A collection of many of Ed's best works, including two Nebula Award winning short stories.

Commencement, by Roby James

Info/buy:

The Sting was what made Ronica McBride special—now she was crashed on an unknown planet without it.

Bug Jack Barron, by Norman Spinrad

Info/buy:

GET SET FOR THE BEST THING THAT EVER HAPPENED TO YOU! The banned book is back! You've heard of it, now you can read it! Lover and hero, Jack Barron, troubleshooter and media god of the Bug Jack Barron Show, has one last chance to hit it big when he meets Benedict Howards, the power-mad man with the secret to immortality. A Hugo and Nebula Award finalist!

The Last Hurrah of the Golden Horde, by Norman Spinrad

Info/buy:

"One of the greatest collections of science fiction short stories ever" — Goodreads.com

The Children of Hamelin, by Norman Spinrad

Info/buy:

A novel about the fast-lane life in the publishing world, by the award-winning Norman Spinrad.

One Against Herculum, by Jerry Sohl

Info/buy:

One of the famous Ace Doubles, with the wonderful original cover, One Against Herculum remains a fast-paced, fun story that you'll really enjoy.

Costigan s Needle, by Jerry Sohl

Info/buy:

What really was Dr. Costigan's tool for medical research? Where did the eye of the needle actually lead to?

The Mars Monopoly, by Jerry Sohl

Info/buy:

One of the famous Ace Doubles, with the wonderful original cover, The Mars Monopoly still stands today as a great, fun story in the classic style.

The Star Conquerors (Standard Edition), by Ben Bova

Info/buy:

Six time Hugo winner Ben Bova's most sought-after novel is back in print!

Vengeance of Orion, by Ben Bova

Info/buy:

Orion must travel back in time to change history and save Troy from the Greek army, or lose the only woman he has ever loved.

Orion in the Dying Time, by Ben Bova
Info/buy:

Time-traveling into the era of the dinosaurs, Orion must save the very fabric of spacetime from the satanic reptilian leader of the saurians.

Orion and the Conqueror, by Ben Bova
Info/buy:

Orion travels to the time of Alexander the Great, battling to save the future of mankind, and his own soul.

Orion Among the Stars, by Ben Bova
Info/buy:

The superhuman, time-traveling Orion leads interstellar warriors in a galactic war among the gods themselves.

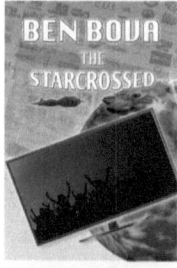

The Starcrossed, by Ben Bova
Info/buy:

A stinging SFnal, futuristic satire on the TV industry, based a bit on reality.

To Save The Sun, by Ben Bova and A. J. Austin
Info/buy:

Earth's sun will soon explode, unless a massive engineering effort can save it.

The Craft of Writing Science Fiction that Sells, by Ben Bova

Info/buy:

Learn how to write SF from the master! Ben Bova, best-selling author and six-time Hugo Award winner for Best Editor explains step by step all the elements you need to write profesionally selling science fiction.

The Perseus Breed, by Kevin Egan

Info/buy:

Borley Share has found a pattern: Every thirty years, beautiful women mysteriously vanish from the Earth... it's now another 30 years.

Into the Horsebutt Nebula, by Chet Gottfried

Info/buy:

MAD MAX meets HITCHHIKER'S GUIDE during the NIGHT OF THE LIVING DEAD...

The Bleeding Man and Other Science Fiction Stories, by Craig Strete

Info/buy:

A great collection of Native American Science Fiction. Yes, you read that right. Nebula finalist!

If All Else Fails, by Craig Strete

Info/buy:

Two Nebula Award finalist stories plus even better stories from one of the few Native American SF authors.

A Guide to Barsoom, by John Flint Roy

Info/buy:

THE OFFICIAL, DEFINITIVE GUIDE TO EDGAR RICE BURROUGH'S BARSOOM. Everything there is to know about John Carter of Mars and his world — the people, places and things, with maps and fully illustrated.

Jewels of the Dragon, by Allen L. Wold

Info/buy:

The greatest of treasures awaits... on the deadliest of planets.

Crown of the Serpent, by Allen L. Wold

Info/buy:

In farthest space lie hidden fortunes... and unknown enemies.

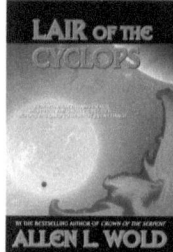

Lair of the Cyclops, by Allen L. Wold

Info/buy:

Rickard Braeth and friends must find the galaxy's secret—before it's used to destroy everything!

The Planet Masters, by Allen L. Wold

Info/buy:

Troubleshooter Larson McCade searches for the alien Book of Aradka on the planet Seltique, and may find more than he bargained for.

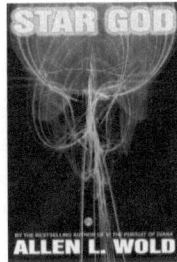

Star God, by Allen L. Wold

Info/buy:

There is a strange force at work in the universe. It must be stopped. But first, it must be understood.

Anthopology 101: Reflections, Inspections and Dissections of SF Anthologies, by Bud Webster

Info/buy:

Bud expertly dissects the great SF anthologies. A must for writers and SF fans.

Woman Without a Shadow, by Karen Haber

Info/buy:

War Minstrels #1. Kayla, an extraordinarily gifted young telepath, is on the run after challenging the most powerful families on her home planet, who've tried to take everything from her.

The War Minstrels, by Karen Haber

Info/buy:

War Minstrels #2. With powerful forces trying to stop the Free Traders, the starship Falstaff is no longer a safe refuge for renegade empath Kayla John Reed. Now her survival and all the War Minstrels' hinges upon her finding a legendary weapon.

Sister Blood, by Karen Haber

Info/buy:

War Minstrels #3. Empath Kayla and her War Minstrels must rescue her friends from the evil Yates, and prevent the destruction of all they've fought for.

The Sweet Taste of Regret, by Karen Haber
Info/buy:

Live anywhere you want... in any time... A collection of Karen Haber's best short fiction.

The Science of Middle-earth, by Henry Gee
Info/buy:

How did Frodo's mithril coat ward off the fatal blow of an orc? Can Balrogs fly? Nature editor Dr. Henry Gee explains how. A must-read for Tolkien fans.

Xenostorm: Rising, by Brian Clegg
Info/buy:

14 year old Davy finds himself facing a powerful underground group who have lived for hundreds of years—and want to see him dead. The future of human existence is in the balance...

The Gilded Basilisk, by Chet Gottfried
Info/buy:

Add a basilisk, a dragon, and weirdragons to the mix-up of a theft going from bad to worse: Friends become enemies and enemies friends, wars loom, and the intrigues threaten the fate of two kingdoms.

Einar and the Cursed City, by Chet Gottfried
Info/buy:

Sixteen-year-old Einar enters Jorghaven for dueling and desserts, but a curse has changed everyone except Barbara Bloodbath, who needs his help to free the city!

Neon Twilight, by Edward Bryant

Info/buy:

Neon Twilight by Edward Bryant : Three wonderful space opera stories, including Ed's Berserker story!

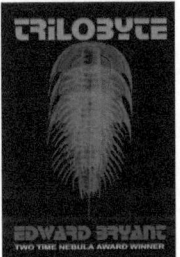

Trilobyte, by Edward Bryant

Info/buy:

A trio of twisted little tales from the master of twistedness.

Cinnabar, by Edward Bryant

Info/buy:

In the city at the center of time, paradox is just another urban renewal project.

Predators and Other Stories, by Edward Bryant

Info/buy:

Troubling tales as only Ed Bryant can tell. Don't miss the author introductions!

Innocents Abroad (Fully Illustrated & Enhanced Collectors' Edition), by Mark Twain

Info/buy:

Best. Travel. Book. Ever. (With all original illustrations.)

The Void Captain's Tale, by Norman Spinrad

Info/buy:

Symbiotically linked to her ship, Void Pilot Dominique Alia Wu senses something transcendent in the void...

The Time Dissolver, by Jerry Sohl

Info/buy:

How could they lose 11 years of their life—at the same time!? By a master of episodes from The Twilight Zone and Star Trek.

The Altered Ego, by Jerry Sohl

Info/buy:

Why would anyone murder a man marked for full body and brain restoration?

The Anomaly, by Jerry Sohl

Info/buy:

She couldn't have a baby... Then she got pregnant—but with what? By a master of episodes from The Twilight Zone and Star Trek.

The Haploids, by Jerry Sohl

Info/buy:

What is a Haploid? Are YOU a Haploid? A new take on an age-old battle! By a master of episodes from The Twilight Zone and Star Trek.

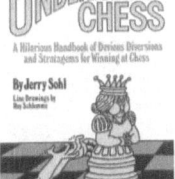

Underhanded Chess, by Jerry Sohl

Info/buy:

A hilarious handbook of devious diversions and stratagems for winning at chess.

Underhanded Bridge, by Jerry Sohl

Info/buy:

A hilarious handbook of devious diversions and stratagems for winning at bridge.

The Box: An Oral History of Television, 1920-1961, by Jeff Kisseloff

Info/buy:

"Wondrous... An oral scrapbook of the pioneering days of our video nation"— The New York Times Book Review

You Must Remember This: An Oral History of Manhattan from the 1890s to World War II, by Jeff Kisseloff

Info/buy:

Amazing stories of Manhattan from those who lived them.

Biff America: Steep Deep & Dyslexic, by Jeffrey Bergeron (AKA Biff America)

Info/buy:

A wonderfully funny mix of Andy Rooney and Garrison Keillor. Biff America poignantly writes what the American people need to know. Through it all, Biff America has a gift for revealing the uplifting realities of modern life and, sometimes, his humor will make you blow beer through your nose.

Side Effects, by Harvey Jacobs
Info/buy:

Vonnegut meets Catch-22! In the last hours of his hectic life, Simon Apple faces up to the hard truth that his very survival represents a prescription for disaster, not only for the pharmaceutical industry but for the nation itself! From award-winning author Harvey Jacobs.

By The Sea, by Henry Gee
Info/buy:

A gothic modern scientific fiction horror mystery...

American Goliath, by Harvey Jacobs
Info/buy:

The (mostly!) true story of America's greatest hoax, with a fantastic(al) twist from an award-winning author. [World Fantasy Award finalist!] "An inspired novel."—TIME Magazine. "A masterpiece...arguably this year's best novel."—Kirkus Reviews.

The Sigil Trilogy (Omnibus vol.1-3), by Henry Gee
Info/buy:

The amazing Sigil Trilogy complete in one volume!

www.ingramcontent.com/pod-product-compliance
Lightning Source LLC
Chambersburg PA
CBHW050556260626
47157CB00002B/586